A MAN OVER FORTY

A MAN
OVER FORTY

A Novel
by
ERIC LINKLATER

LONDON
MACMILLAN & CO LTD
NEW YORK · ST MARTIN'S PRESS
1963

MACMILLAN AND COMPANY LIMITED
St Martin's Street London WC2
also Bombay Calcutta Madras Melbourne

THE MACMILLAN COMPANY OF CANADA LIMITED
Toronto

ST MARTIN'S PRESS INC
New York

PRINTED IN GREAT BRITAIN

To

Rupert Hart-Davis

with old affection

Every man over forty is a scoundrel

GEORGE BERNARD SHAW

One

THE face grew larger until it filled, and over-filled, the luminous panel of the television-box ; for to magnify its mobile parts, and show the emotion they might record, the top of his head was sliced off, and all that remained visible — the head was in profile — was the area between eyebrows and Adam's apple.

It was a clean-shaven face, oddly young for his known years ; his hair still curled, though not with the golden efflorescence of his nonage. His detractors had sometimes called him an overgrown schoolboy : a lanky, tall, indignant schoolboy who had been overtaken by rich living. Now in his middle forties, the luminous eyes retained a semblance of innocence, and the mouth betrayed his intemperance. The animation of his features defied a positive analysis, however, for they could be at home to innocence and wrath and arrogance, and were not quite exempt from silliness.

Perhaps his voice was more important. It was musical and deep, it could thunder or woo at will ; and with practice he had made it a magnificent instrument for the person he had become. That is to say, for a man of forthright and determined character — notorious, indeed, for intransigent, often unpopular opinions, and vigorous expression of them — and when, after the interrogation had been going on for several minutes, he was startled by an inadvertent noise and turned full-face to the nearer camera, most of the several million people who were watching him thought the pin-points of light reflected in his eyes were a premonitory flash of the sudden temper for which he was admired. Only to a very few did it look like a sign of alarm.

'You have just been acclaimed as Television Personality of the Year,' said the smooth voice of the Interrogator. 'You have been recognised, that is, as a leader, a person of great importance, in a new profession. But your profession has been called a profession without form or purpose——'

'That may be so, but it isn't new. Or rather, it's new in scale, but not in sort. In every village, when villages were centres of life, there was someone to whom people got into the habit of listening. Sometimes he was a clown, sometimes a home-grown philosopher ; often enough a mixture of both.'

'Is that how you see yourself?'

'It's how a lot of people see me. And it's their vision that matters, not mine.'

'The image in their minds is that of a village philosopher who, on occasion, isn't above a bit of clowning? Would you accept that?'

'If you'll accept the fact that when they think I'm clowning I'm usually more serious than when they fancy I'm philosophising.'

'Is that true?'

'I always speak the truth. And the world to-day — the life of the world — is more like a habitation of clowns than a well-swept promenade of philosophers. You can't deny that.'

'The world of to-day hasn't treated you badly, Mr. Balintore. It has made you a rich man.'

'I might be, if I could keep what I earn. But the Government takes most of it.'

'Do you resent having to pay taxes ?'

'I resent having to subsidise inefficiency ! I resent having to pay for an educational system that doesn't educate — for fighting services that couldn't defend us — for workers who don't work, for prisons that only breed criminals, and for roads I can't drive on. I resent having to give my money to fat farmers who spend it on noxious chemicals to poison their fields. They're poisoning the whole countryside, and doing it with my money !'

'But in spite of taxation you manage to live fairly comfortably ?'

'I do.'

'You haven't always been rich, have you ? I want you to tell me something about your early life.'

'For a while, when I was young, I lived pretty thinly. But that was my own choice.'

'You ran away from home, didn't you ?'

'I have always done what I wanted to.'

'Was that your only reason ?'

'There was no compulsion on me to go.'

'Boys don't run away unless they're unhappy ; or so I've always thought. Were you unhappy ?'

'Who isn't, at fifteen or sixteen ?'

'What made you unhappy ?'

'Initially, I suppose, my father's death. When I was twelve.'

'You were very fond of him ?'

'I was devoted to him.'

'You were an only child ?'

'An only child. And I deserted my widowed mother — who, incidentally, had married again — and ran away to sea. At sixteen I signed aboard a sailing-ship in the proper romantic style.'

'Thirty years ago ? I thought sailing-ships had disappeared by then.'

'There weren't many left. But a man called Erikson, a Finn, had found it was possible to make money out of them when everyone else thought they were obsolete. He economised on food, and economised on his crews ; which were small and young.'

'Where did you sail to ?'

'Australia for grain, and back round the Horn. I made the trip three times.'

'And that was the prelude to your Spanish adventure ?'

'If you like to call it an adventure——'

'You fought in the Civil War ?'

'I did.'

'And a few years later you were a commissioned officer in our army, when we were at war with Germany and Japan ?'

'I was in the Intelligence Corps. That wasn't uncomfortable.'

'Perhaps not, by your standards. But it all adds up — everything you've told me — to a romantic story. And then, as if to cap it, you write a novel called *Scorpio my Star*, and your first novel — your first and only novel — becomes a best-seller.'

'Everyone writes a novel nowadays.'

'But not many write as well as you did, or sell 40,000 copies. Why did you never write another ?'

'I didn't want to.'

'It was that novel which made you famous, and gave you an introduction, at first to journalism, and then to this curious profession to which we both belong. And I still find it difficult to understand how you, after so varied a life — a life that we stay-at-homes all regard as romantic — how you find contentment, or satisfaction, in a career that certainly offers no physical adventure.'

'I don't. But I like my comfort.'

'But for a good many years — for quite a long time — you seem to have gone out of your way to avoid comfort. And I still don't know why. I don't know what was the impulse that made you leave home, or the mainspring that kept you going. Was it only the normal unhappiness of a growing, imaginative boy ?'

'That may be the reason. It's as good as any other.'

'Was it a persistent unhappiness ?'

'Call it recurrent.'

'You said you were devoted to your father ?'

'And the corollary to that is that I didn't get on with my mother.'

'Was there any special reason for that ?'

'I may shock a lot of people — I may shock you — by saying that, as far back as I can remember, I never liked her. And her second marriage, after my father's death, did nothing to make me like her better.'

Several million of the people who were watching him — most of them in their own homes, many united by family affection — heard this admission through a murmur of disapproval ; and saw, with a rising interest, that Balintore himself appeared to share their disquiet. Little beads of sweat, glistening in the light, showed on his upper lip, then on his forehead, and a narrow rivulet ran down his nearer cheek. He mopped his face with a coloured handkerchief, and the Interrogator asked him : 'So, then, when you went to war in Spain, there was anger in your heart — an anger that had nothing to do with politics — but you hoped to get rid of it by political action ?'

'That's a shallow explanation. And glib. Far too glib.'

'Well, it may be. It's never easy to analyse a motive——'

'I didn't want to go home: that was my motive. And the Civil War gave me an excuse for going to Spain.'

'Did you enjoy it?'

'No.'

'But when another war began, in 1939, you joined the army again. A different army——'

'And don't ask me why I did that.'

'I wasn't going to. No one has ever doubted your patriotism, Mr. Balintore. But in your second war you did find some opportunity for enjoyment?'

'I didn't join the infantry. I got a commission — as I've told you already — in the Intelligence Corps.'

'And in India, where you spent a year or so——'

'Longer than that.'

'In India you found time to get married?'

Leaning forward in his chair, Balintore shook a menacing finger at the Interrogator. Anger tautened the contours of his face, and the beating of a pulse in his temple — perhaps by some accident of lighting — became suddenly conspicuous. 'If you want to make a parade or raree-show of married life — my married life! — just tell me, and I'll save you a lot of trouble,' he said. 'I'll give you the whole story, if that's what you're after.'

His domestic audience of several million viewers now watched and listened with a rising expectancy. Now, they thought, he's going to cut loose! Now there'll be an explosion! — For the enormous popularity that Balintore enjoyed, throughout the whole country, was due, in part, to his irascible temper and the freedom with which he gave vent to it. Again and again his audience had seen the eruption of his anger, and heard with delight his intemperate denunciation of egregious folly — or, as often, of some harmless opinion with which he happened to disagree. He had no fear of rank, he was no respecter of persons, and many of the victims of his anger had been men eminent in their profession or elevated above the common mean by wealth or a noble name. It was widely known that he and the Interrogator disliked each other — each, on more than one occasion, had spoken of the other with memorable acerbity — and many viewers in quiet sitting-rooms had been waiting eagerly, as if for fireworks, for a discharge of squibs and verbal rockets, for the match that would touch to flame a set-piece of splendid fury. And now, they thought, now we're going to have it.

But the Interrogator was skilled in his trade, and expert in controlling a difficult subject. He had no wish to excite or anger Balintore, and mildly — with a note of laughing apology in his voice — he said, 'I wasn't going to ask embarrassing questions : please believe that. All I had in mind was to ask you about a story that was current after you and your wife had separated. Your defence — according to the story — was that you had never been able to buy her pearls and caviare.'

Balintore refused to be mollified. He paid no attention to the Interrogator's effort to keep debate on civil ground, but with defiance in his mien and provocation in his voice, said harshly, 'My first marriage went on the rocks, my second landed me in quicksands, and my third blew up in a nuclear explosion ! There's no secret about that, and no need to varnish my failures with politeness or equivocation.'

'Well, that's an example of the frankness for which you're so well known——'

'All my marriages have ended in divorce, and the reason is that I'm not a domestic animal. Women want a man who'll sit and listen to them talking, and that I can't do. Not for very long. But I've no cause for self-reproach ! All my wives have done extremely well for themselves, and the improvement in their condition they owe to me and what I taught them.'

'You've never been handicapped by modesty, Mr. Balintore ?'

'Why should I be ? I was well brought up, as a child, and taught to read the Bible. And if you had the same advantage, you'll know that it's a grave mistake, if not actually a sin, to hide your light under a bushel.'

'You have never done that ? You have never concealed anything ?'

Balintore was slow to answer. He was sweating again, and again he mopped his face with a large handkerchief. Then grudgingly he answered, 'That's too much to ask, and too hard to answer. No one can afford — and no one should be asked — to tell everything.'

'I'll try to be more specific,' said the Interrogator, 'and I want to go back to a previous question — to a topic that you galloped away from before I had finished with it. I mean the matter of the Spanish war.'

'I told you why I went to Spain, and what else is relevant ?'

'You didn't tell me which side you joined.'

'Did you ask me ?'

'I'm asking you now.'

'People talked a lot of nonsense about that war. A great deal of nonsense ! And a vast amount of nonsense was written about it. Many people still think that all the intervention, by foreign powers, was Fascist intervention. That Germans and Italians were the only foreign troops who fought there. But the truth is that the earliest intervention was Russian.'

'There was confused thinking: no one denies that. We didn't know enough, either about the causes of the war or what was happening, to be realistic or objective. We were misled by clever propaganda: I admit all that, and I still want to know which side you fought on.'

Balintore's ill temper had become a fretful uneasiness. He made an attempt, which the Interrogator ignored, to interrupt; and then, clumsily, felt in his pocket for a cigarette-case. He let it fall, and the image on the lighted screen was blurred as he stooped to pick it up.

He lit a cigarette, and a multitude of viewers saw that his fingers trembled. Many grew uneasy on his behalf, for it was known that he had lately been ill — he had left a nursing home only a few days before — and now his strained and anxious look, his shaking fingers, showed clearly enough his remnant weakness.

He blew a puff of smoke that clouded the screen, and through its haze said, 'On Franco's side.'

'Was that wise?'

'No. It's never wise to take an active part in someone else's war.'

'I want to know——'

'There were atrocities on both sides, but I did nothing to be ashamed of — if that's what you're suggesting.'

'I would never suggest such a thing. I was going to ask if you saw much fighting.'

Balintore muffled a fit of coughing in his handkerchief, and threw his cigarette into a glass ash-tray. 'As much as most people, I suppose. I was in several battles. There was a long one, a sort of suburban battle, for Madrid. I was wounded there.'

'Are you a brave man? I mean naturally brave?'

'Far from it.'

'Well, if that's so, I'm more in the dark than ever about why you went to Spain, and enlisted on Franco's side. Unless you saw Franco as the symbol of authority — the authority of church and state — and so identified him with your father: your father to whom, as you said, you were devoted.'

'That's far-fetched. I think — oh, it doesn't matter. But it's too far-fetched.'

'Are you feeling ill? There's water on the table beside you. Would you like a drink?'

'I'm all right.'

'Are you sure?'

'Quite sure.'

'Well, then, if this doesn't embarrass you — did your mother know what you were doing? Did you write and tell her?'

'My mother,' said Balintore harshly, 'was dead.'

'I'm sorry! I apologise for a stupid question. I didn't know—'

The Interrogator waited while Balintore drank a glass of water. Then, in a light and conversational tone of voice — a tone to put Balintore at his ease — he said, 'You have told us that you're not a naturally brave man, and though I find that hard to believe, I'll accept what you say — or pretend to accept it — and turn to the other side of the picture. If you're not brave, tell me what you're afraid of: what sort of things. Tell me what you're most afraid of.'

'Afraid?'

'Of what? What are you most afraid of?'

There was a long pause before Balintore replied, 'I suppose — I suppose — of being found out.'

Then, with consternation in their hearts and minds, several

million viewers saw him grasp the arms of his chair and try to rise. He stood for a moment, a bowed figure, and in sudden collapse fell heavily to the floor. A voice was heard — the voice of someone unseen in the studio — that said loudly, 'He's fainted !' And a million screens were darkened.

Half a minute passed before they were lighted again to show a young woman who, with a smile that exposed her teeth in an expression of untimely gaiety — but it was meant to be reassuring — said, 'We are very sorry that the interview with Mr. Balintore had to be curtailed because of his sudden illness. You will be glad to hear that he is already feeling a little better, and a doctor who was fortunately in the studio has assured us that there's no need for anxiety. You will be given a further report of Mr. Balintore's progress in the late news, and now, to fill the gap before the next programme, we are going to show you a film taken on the Dalmatian coast. Some of you may have seen it before, but it's a very beautiful film, and I think you'll be glad of the chance to see it again.'

Two

On the following day the newspapers made much of the story, and showed a general sympathy with Edward Balintore in his misfortune. He had, in the past, often given them good copy, and his mysterious collapse, in all the publicity afforded by television, was a windfall that compelled respect.

The *Daily Mail*, in a leading article, said: 'Broadcasting and television are among the most notable innovations of our century, and like all innovations they claim their victims. Subject to strains that few of us could endure, Edward Balintore is paying the price of fabulous success in a new profession. . . .'

The *Daily Express* opened comment more dramatically: '£30,000 a year! A lot of money, but not enough to buy happiness, as Edward Balintore had discovered. Three times he has been married, and three times come to grief in the divorce courts. Now he himself has succumbed to the pressure of a life as artificial as that of a goldfish in its bowl. . . .'

There was a third leader in *The Times* which began: 'Nowadays we ask too much of our entertainers. In an earlier age the clowns and comedians of Drury Lane or a suburban Empire were not expected to maintain their popularity with timely philosophy or learned opinion. In recent years, however, a certain form of entertainment, borrowing heavily from the lecture-room, seems to have usurped an authority which, in the Victorian era, was enjoyed only by leading politicians, outstanding clerics, and a few popular scientists.

'But the authority of the television studio is founded on no institution, neither on church nor parliament. It rests only on the suspect strength of personality. In the last few years the outstanding example of this new form of leadership has been that remarkable and gifted man, Mr. Edward Balintore. To many of his innumerable admirers he is hardly less than a contemporary Socrates, impelled to question the truth of many accepted ideas. But Socrates, though he lived in the open, was not subjected to the intolerable stare of modern publicity. . . .'

The *Guardian* hoped 'that his malaise may be of short duration, and that he will soon return to stir our minds with outrageous conjecture and disturb our thoughts with the simple question, "But is it true?"' At the week-end the *Observer*'s diarist wrote: 'He has a large and excellent vocabulary, and that has been enough to set him apart from many of those who nowadays claim our attention. Even more impressive is his ability to keep his command of language intact when he loses his temper: he has made anger seem an enviable gift, and turned its expression into a fine art.'

Comment in the *Sunday Times* was brusque and salutary: 'No one believes that Edward Balintore has any guilty secrets, or that there is any truth in his hysterical confession that he is a fraud. The fact is that he has been living for several years under heavy pressure, and when he succumbed to it, the nature of his trade made it almost inevitable that he should succumb in circumstances of the utmost publicity. Many of us who can remember serious illness have reason to be thankful that television cameras never came to our bedside.'

The *Sunday Telegraph* drew attention again to his large earnings. On its third page its diarist wrote: 'How much has

Edward Balintore been earning? Some people say as much as £30,000. That, I think, is an exaggeration. But £20,000 a year is a reasonable estimate, and when tax is subtracted from that, the residue is not an excessive reward for all he did. And he probably needed every penny of it. He lives extravagantly, and there are three wives in the offing whom he has to support.'

The newspapers were generous, as English papers usually are to those in trouble, and none made scandalous copy of his collapse. But Balintore needed more help than columnists or reporters could give, and he who carried him through disaster was a young man of whom the vast majority of newspaper-readers had never heard, and whose name remained generally unknown till some two years later.

Guy Palladis was a lapsed scholar who for nearly four years had been Balintore's secretary: his secretary, his business manager, the manager in some degree of his private life, and his faithful friend. He was a young man with enviable connexions: his father, a gallant and distinguished soldier — but passed over for promotion because of wilful independence — had been for some years before his death a member of the Honourable Corps of Gentlemen-at-Arms; while his mother, the grand-daughter of an Irish peer, was the younger daughter of an eccentric but rich and learned Egyptologist.

Palladis had gone to Eton as an Oppidan Scholar, and left it without further distinction of any academic sort. He went up to Magdalen College, Oxford, with pleasant memories of a hard-won victory over Winchester in the rackets finals, with the coloured waistcoat he had worn as a member of the Eton Society, and with his tutor's outspoken regret for his failure to make use of an exceptionally gifted mind. He excused himself by saying that he had inherited from his father a useful indifference to success; that he remembered his maternal grandfather as a very tiresome example of what uninhibited scholarship can do to a man; and that several generations of absentee Irish landlords had bequeathed to him — in lieu of lost acres — a habit of indolence and irresponsibility. But as if to assure his disappointed tutors that their assessment of his ability had been sound and judicious, he wrote, while still an undergraduate, an essay on the Merovingian kings Chlotar II and Dagobert I which was published in the *Historical Review*, and excited some very learned controversy.

He read History, but, as he insisted, only for amusement; and was humiliated when he took Second Class Honours. He had tried for a minimal Fourth, to show disapproval of his teachers, but like a natural swimmer had failed to drown.

An uncle who was an amateur physicist tried to interest him in science, but Palladis said, 'It's too late for that! Even in my lifetime you've changed your ground so often — you're always shifting your postulates and upsetting poor Lavoisier's table of elements — that science seems to me an ephemeral thing; and scientists are so portentous about it that they alienate all sympathy. Philosophy, of course, is in much the same state.'

His mother thought he should go in for politics, but Palladis told her, 'That's out of the question. I read *Coriolanus* when I was very young — perhaps children shouldn't be allowed to read Shakespeare? — and it shocked me profoundly. And politics haven't changed much, have they? They're far more stable than science.

'I want to involve myself in contemporary life,' he said, 'but science and politics are barred: they're too exacting, and to someone of my temperament without reward. I'm still interested in the Merovingians, but they're not contemporary, and while I'm very good at shooting snipe, I recognise that snipe aren't really significant in a social context. So what shall I do ? I wish you would give me good advice.'

Though reluctant and manifestly suspicious, he was persuaded to take a job in the City — another uncle was a merchant banker — and to the surprise of everyone who knew him, held it for rather more than two years. His mother was delighted. He had never, in any ordinary way, been a difficult child, for his temper was easy and his mind equable. But his brilliance — in which she believed even more firmly than his tutors at Eton — had teased her with thoughts, some of them extravagant, about what he might do if he applied himself; and his refusal to do anything at all had naturally worried her. There was, moreover, the physical disability he had incurred in infancy. He seemed unaffected by it, but it was a grave and incurable injury, and without the fortitude to endure it — or ignore it — it could have warped and distained his whole life. But the interests of a merchant banker — or so she imagined — were numerous and compulsive, and a career of ever-growing power and prosperity in the City might do much to reconcile him, or even reconcile him wholly, to the loss of a vital function.

When, after two years, he seemed to have become a happy and diligent young banker, his mother almost forgot her need to worry, and she felt no premonition when, early one afternoon in the third month of his third year in the City, he arrived at her house in Mount Street. She was inexpressibly dismayed when he told her that he had just written to his uncle a letter of resignation, and she could see no sense in the reason he gave her.

'Within ten years,' he said, 'I feel sure I could make a

lot of money: there's little doubt of that. It's not too difficult if you have some capital to start with, and reliable information to help you. But suppose I made £100,000, or £200,000 — what could I do with it? If I bought an estate my tenants would take the profit and I would pay the taxes. If I bought a yacht, the skipper would make a pass at one of my guests and have to be locked in his cabin, the engineer would get drunk, and I should be left tied-up in that boring harbour at Cannes. If I bought a football team the players would all go to Italy, and if I bought a symphony orchestra the Musicians' Union would drive me into a lunatic asylum. — No, my dear mother, the only thing you can do with money is to acquire property of some sort, and nowadays property of all sorts is a burden and a nuisance. I want none of it.'

'Then what are you going to do?'

'I should like to govern a colony, but now, of course, we have no colonies to speak of, so I shall have to think of something else. And there's no hurry, is there? I'm still quite young.'

A few weeks later he met Balintore at a party in Chelsea and, as he himself was soon to proclaim, found his *métier*. It was a party that began very respectably, but those whose presence made it respectable left early, and gradually it became rather noisy. Balintore arrived late, and not quite sober. He had been lecturing in Hove for a fee of forty guineas and expenses, paid in cash, of £100; and he was in a mood, to begin with, of expansive geniality. Before long, however, his temper was darkened by too much attention. A group of young people, loudly welcoming his appearance, made it evident that they expected him to entertain them. They penned him in a corner, where for a little while a very pretty girl and a large whisky and soda kept him quiet; but then some remark upset him — a remark, perhaps, of no more than ordinary stupidity, but whose stupidity seemed to him offensive — and his voice grew louder.

'Any fool can make money!' he declared. 'All he needs is something he can sell to bigger fools than himself, and there's no scarcity of them. Look what I've made to-day!'

From an inner pocket he pulled an untidy sheaf of £5 notes, and held them up. This evoked more noise, more attention, and Balintore said angrily, 'There's no lack of money in the country, but there's a lack of poverty, and we need poverty — poverty in the proper places — as well as riches. Poverty makes petty thieves, I know that, but money makes major crooks. It's money, too much money, that turns schoolboys into young thugs. Poverty could make them honest apprentices, and let them learn a useful trade; but give them £10 a week, and at best they grow up into white coolies. White coolies to be duped by some rascally Simon Legree who calls himself a shop-steward!'

The argument became confused, but Balintore stubbornly maintained that youth should exercise its muscles in poverty, and honest youth was too often corrupted by high wages. Trade Unions, he said, had become as mischievous as bygone rotten boroughs, and to emphasise all he said he continued to flourish a fistful of £5 notes.

Then, in a momentary lull, a young man said, 'You're suffering from a guilty conscience, that's what's wrong with you!'

'Aren't we all?' said Balintore, and was answered by a chorused 'No!'

'Do you know what conscience is?' he asked the very pretty girl who was still beside him.

'It's what used to handicap the middle classes.'

'God help you,' he said, and pushed his way rudely to the other side of the room, where there was a bar. There, drinking another whisky and soda, he fell into conversation with Guy Palladis who said, 'That girl you were talking to is a distant cousin of mine. I once told her it would be waste of time for her to see an analyst, she ought to consult an anthropologist.'

They remained in conversation for half an hour or more, and a week later Palladis walked from his mother's house in Mount Street to Balintore's chambers in Albany, and began his new life as secretary to a person of contemporary significance.

In several ways he was admirably adapted to such a life. Though Balintore was no longer living with his wife — his second wife, at that time — and Palladis often occupied his spare room in Albany, there was never any hint or suspicion that their relations were improper. Palladis in his childhood, at the age of six or seven, had fallen seriously ill with mumps, and in consequence had never developed a masculine ability. Nothing in his nature, however, had inclined him to a feminine attitude : the strength of his intelligence was such that he had felt no need for the possible compensations of a submissive emotion, and he had grown up, very happily, in a state of untroubled and benign neutrality. His voice was a pleasing mezzo-soprano.

His experience in the City was immediately useful in reducing the disorder of Balintore's finances. In addition to a handsome salary Balintore made a very large income by occasional lectures, by attending public luncheons, by judging beauty competitions, and by opening new dog-racing tracks, dance halls, bowling alleys, and bingo parlours ; and much of what he earned by these public services was often disguised as expenses, and paid in cash. Palladis handled these sums with a discretion that Balintore had seldom shown, and did what he could to curb his extravagance.

This became advisable when Balintore, having with unnecessary chivalry given his second wife evidence for divorce, married for the third time. Palladis strongly opposed the folly of this alliance, which no one expected to last, but Balintore insisted that he saw in it his last remaining chance of happiness ; and had to admit his mistake in rather less than eighteen months.

Again he insisted that he was the guilty party — whether moved by pride or chivalry, none could tell — and regretted his generosity when he counted the cost of paying alimony to three women. Thanks to Palladis' good management he was better off than ever before — Palladis had persuaded him to make some shrewd investments — but he fell into a panic at the thought of his burdens, and complained of nervous exhaustion.

A doctor suggested three weeks in a nursing home, and this restored him to favour with those whose sympathy had been strained by his third divorce. When, almost immediately after his release from a sick-room, he had insisted on keeping the engagement that led to his collapse, his courage and public spirit were warmly approved.

Fortunately for him, Palladis had insisted on going with him to the television studio, and it was Palladis who, at the first hint of Balintore's discomfort, had suggested that a doctor should be called. Within an hour Balintore had been put to bed in the London Clinic, and a bulletin issued to the press which announced that he had had a nervous breakdown, the result of overwork, and his doctors advised a prolonged rest.

A few days later he was removed to the nursing home in Brighton, where he had lately occupied a room, and a final bulletin gave his public the reassuring news that he was suffering only from serious exhaustion, and his complete recovery could be confidently predicted. But he had cancelled all engagements for the next six months.

Guy Palladis took a room at the Royal Albion, and every day spent a couple of hours with his exhausted friend. To begin with — while under the influence of sedatives, and for a day or two longer — Balintore had been quiet and withdrawn, unwilling to speak and apparently unable to tolerate the strain of listening. He slept long and heavily, and to Palladis it seemed that he must have suffered some physical injury, a shock at least as real as concussion ; but the doctors told him not to worry, and one afternoon he went in to find Balintore sitting up in bed reading a green paper-backed novel.

This he hurriedly put under his pillow, as if being caught with a detective story might injure his status as an invalid, and said firmly, 'I'm better, much better, and I want to have a serious talk with you. Tell me, for a start, what went wrong with me. What's your diagnosis ?'

'The doctors——'

'I know what they say, it's your opinion I want.'

'Well, I was worried, and though I know nothing about these things — I mean, about the physiology of them — I thought you might have had a mild thrombosis.'

'That,' said Balintore, 'is precisely my own belief ! The doctors say no. They say my blood pressure's low, and my arteries are like elastic. But I don't trust them. Not nowadays! Nowadays the doctors have become a pack of civil servants, and civil servants never tell you anything, do they ? They may quote a White Paper, but that's as far as they'll go. Well, let me tell you something — something for your own information, I don't want it to go farther — and that is that for some years now I've had a lurking fear of a thrombosis. And that, you'll agree, is a rational explanation of what I meant when I made that otherwise absurd statement.'

'About being found out ?'

'What I meant, you see, was that I was afraid of suffering or incurring a thrombosis ; or, if you like, of my tendency to it being discovered.'

'Oh,' said Palladis.

'Doesn't that seem reasonable ?'

'You remember what you said, do you ?'

'No,' said Balintore sharply. 'I remember nothing — nothing at all — of what I said or what I heard for perhaps five minutes before I collapsed. But one of the nurses — the night nurse, in fact — was watching the performance, and she told me. You can imagine what I felt ! Bewilderment to begin with, and I'm still bewildered when I think of it. But worse than that, there's the appalling embarrassment of it ! The embarrassment of knowing that eight million people——'

'Not as many as that.'

'I have a very large audience. A very large audience indeed ! And when seven million people — at least seven million — heard me say I was afraid of being found out — well, what do you suppose they thought ?'

'Most of them, I imagine, were deeply sympathetic. They felt the same as you did.'

'But I didn't ! I have nothing to conceal——'

'Oh, come !'

'I have no fear of that kind. None at all. I haven't always lived according to the rules — you know that — but when my time comes I'll face judgment without fear. A judge who's qualified to judge all mankind won't be much perturbed by anything I've done.'

He sat upright in his bed, looking frail and fevered in yellow silk pyjamas, and his voice trembled with the intensity of his conviction.

'Very well, then,' said Palladis. 'What you said was only a meaningless aberration——'

'The consequence of a slight coronary thrombosis.'

'Which fortunately has left no ill effects — except, perhaps a false impression in the minds of a lot of people who were watching you.'

'It has left me weak and exhausted,' said Balintore indignantly. 'I'm a sick man, and I'll need care and attention for a considerable time to come.'

'I've been thinking about that,' said Palladis, 'and a long rest will do you good in more ways than one. No one has any memory nowadays, and by the time you come back——'

'Come back from where?'

'Have you ever been to Jamaica?'

'No, by God, and I've no intention of going! I don't want to look at American tourists in tartan shorts, and international tax-dodgers, and twittering perverts cooing over their cocktails in Montego Bay. They're the sort of people who go to Jamaica, and they're welcome to it.'

'You have been reading novels written by discontented young men,' said Palladis, 'and you ought to know enough to disbelieve them. You must get out of England — away from an English February — and Jamaica, as well as being very beautiful, has a perfect winter climate: everyone admits that. The tourists spend all their time on the beaches, and if you don't want to see them, you can stay away from the beaches.'

'Where?'

'I have a remote cousin who lives there, and his house is

about fifteen hundred feet up in the hills. He's a very remote cousin — his great-great-very-great grandfather was a Regicide, and went to Jamaica after the Restoration of Charles II, when England wasn't healthy for him. He changed his name — my cousin's called Scroope : Weatherby Scroope — and that branch of the family has lived there ever since. But we've kept in touch, and the other day I sent him a long and expensive cable, to which he replied at once, to say we could come as soon as we liked and stay as long as we wanted. And from what I know of my cousin I'm pretty sure that he doesn't associate with tourists in tartan shorts or rich tax-dodgers, but I hope he won't exclude people with curious voices. I'm sensitive to criticism of voices, because my own is rather unusual.'

'What does he do ?'

'His father owns a lot of land, and they make rum.'

'How old is he ?'

'Weatherby, I think, is in his early fifties. He was the youngest of the family, so his father — well, his father's quite a lot older. I don't know his father, but Weatherby has been over here.'

For a thoughtful half-minute Balintore lay down on his pillow and looked silently at the ceiling. Then, with a profound sigh, he said, 'It may be the sensible thing to do. The truth of the matter is that I made a bloody fool of myself the other night, and the only cure for that is to go away and forget it : to go away, and hope that other people have bad memories too. And since your cousin has been so kind as to invite us to — what's the name of the place ?'

'Fort Appin. But it's more accurate to say that I invited us, and Weatherby, who's a kindly soul, offered no objection.'

Three

ABOUT three weeks later Balintore stood looking through a tall glass wall at an artificial landscape of winter-bleached grass and pallid concrete. It was a Sunday morning, they had arrived too early, and London Airport had a yawning, half-awakened air. There was a distant noise of engines warming up, and a murmuration in the large and scantly tenanted hall of official voices asking small, stereotyped questions. At a long counter Palladis was paying a surcharge on their luggage.

Balintore, though now in good health — his complexion clear and rather pale after a month in a nursing home — was in a mood of nervous gloom, and in the loneliness he felt, the loneliness that seemed to enclose him, he spoke his thoughts aloud.

'I feel a strange presentiment,' he said, and his deep voice reverberated from the transparent wall in front. 'I have a dark foreboding!'

A small movement startled him, and turning abruptly he saw, looking at him in manifest surprise, two young negresses in smart hats and tightly fitting skirts. They exchanged a confidential glance, and with a giggle, politely restrained, walked away from him ; their thin legs in transparent stockings precariously balancing plump haunches on stiletto heels.

Fellow passengers, he thought. Immigrants two or three years ago, and England has treated them so well that they can afford to go home again. That's true hospitality !

Palladis came towards him, smiling. He wore no hat, and his smoothly brushed hair above pink cheeks — above grey eyes, straight nose, white teeth and square-cut chin — gave him a look of youthful innocence intent on holiday. He was twenty-nine, but kept without self-consciousness the taut, expectant look of a happily extroverted undergraduate.

'That wasn't so bad,' he said. 'They haven't charged nearly as much as I expected.'

'We came too early,' said Balintore.

'Just what I told you! But you were suffering from plane fever — skin hot and dry, very irritable——'

'We've still time to cancel our tickets. I don't think I want to go. I've got a foreboding——'

'Oh, not again! You can't change your mind now.'

'I'm not superstitious, and in the ordinary way the thought of flying — even the Atlantic — doesn't make me nervous. But this morning I feel a strange presentiment, I feel we're running into trouble, and it may be very wrong — shallow and stupid and wrong — to ignore a warning of that sort. Look at that girl over there! You can't pretend that she's feeling happy, can you? If I know anything she's as full of foreboding, of dark foreboding, as I am.'

Not far from them stood a girl of nineteen or twenty. Obviously unused to far travelling, she was heavily encumbered by two overcoats — one of which she carried on her arm — and a large, shabby brown leather bag that ponderously depended from her other hand. She was a very pretty girl, and she looked about her, in a simple, naïve bewilderment, through eyes that were blinking to dispel unwanted tears.

'There's nothing to show she's coming with us,' said Palladis. 'She may be going anywhere: Amsterdam, Tokyo, Nairobi, Buenos Aires.'

'I hope she isn't going to Buenos Aires.'

'Now don't pretend to feel sorry for her. If she wasn't so pretty you wouldn't give her a second thought. — Come and have a cup of coffee.'

An hour later Balintore seemed resigned to fate. Nursing but not reading a sheaf of Sunday papers, he sat on a leather-hided bench surrounded now by a fairly large, variously coloured, and polyglot crowd of expectant travellers who looked lethargically into vacancy from a miscellaneous accumulation of handbags, parcels, brief-cases, and children's toys. From the concrete wilderness beyond the glass walls there sounded occasionally the fierce, high-mounting scream of jet engines gathering strength for their leap into the bright invisibility above a sullen roof of February cloud ; and presently there came a summons to travellers bound for New York, Nassau, and Jamaica. In the untidy queue ahead of them, beside two young negresses in smart hats, Balintore and Palladis saw the pretty girl who had been crying — or trying not to cry — and who now looked round, with a long, sad glance, to take farewell of home : of this strange forecourt to what had been her home.

'I told you so,' said Balintore. 'I knew she was coming with us.'

They climbed a steep ladder into the foreward part of a long aeroplane, and a well-laundered stewardess — trim and attentive, brushed and manicured — said, 'Good morning, Mr. Balintore. We're very pleased to have you with us, and I hope you'll enjoy your flight.'

'You heard that ?' said Balintore, as they settled in their seats. 'I can't go anywhere without being recognised.'

'You would be very disappointed if you weren't,' said Palladis.

'What nonsense ! What absolute nonsense. You promised me immunity from that sort of thing. Absolute privacy, you said.'

'That's what you'll get in Jamaica, if you want it. But we're not there yet.'

'Not by a long chalk,' said Balintore glumly. 'Not by the breadth of the Atlantic.'

He shivered slightly, and looked with manifest distaste at his fellow passengers. From the length of the queue that had formed for the rear entrance, it had been evident that the tourist cabin would be well filled, but a third of the first-class seats were empty. 'I've often thought,' he said, 'that if I could choose the circumstances of my death, I would ask, first of all, for good company. But there's no one here I want to die with.'

Presently he tightened his seat-belt, and listened to the shrill, increasing howl of the engines. The walls of the long tunnel in which they sat trembled with impatience — or so it seemed — and then, with a swiftly gathering speed, they were leaping down the runway with a sense of ever lighter contact with the earth ; till suddenly a smoothness proclaimed their freedom, the land receded, houses diminished, they were climbing fast and turning with a tilt to find, through murky cloud, their allotted lane.

A few minutes later the sun assailed their windows and filled the cabin with a daffodil light. A stewardess, smiling, walked slowly down the aisle, offering cigarettes ; and returned, before long, with a tray of champagne cocktails.

Balintore grew more cheerful, his expression more animated. His demeanour became confident, there was assurance in his voice when he said, 'There's a natural distrust of any sudden or violent transition from one element to another.

Little boys show it, standing on the edge of a swimming-pool, mustering their courage to dive ; and many of our fellow passengers felt much the same before we took off — though they did their best to hide it, of course.'

Palladis, who was reading the correspondence columns of the *Observer*, said, 'Here is someone writing about the violent feelings created by conscious transition from one generation to another ; and he suggests they will become easier in the future, when girls will mature earlier and start having babies at the age of eleven, thus diminishing the difference.'

'Is he writing seriously ?'

'He appears to be.'

'Well, infantilism is on the way : I've said that for a long time. Infantilism on the one hand, senility on the other : that's the prospect for our world,' said Balintore, and holding out his glass, let the stewardess refill it. 'Adolescents will fill the maternity wards, and suburbs will be erased to make room for Old People's Homes. Doctors will either be paediatricians or geriatricians, and a diminishing middle of adult workers will need a corps of hypnotists to persuade them that work's worth while.'

With pleasure and relief Palladis recognised his friend's return to a normal habit ; and happily resumed his humane study of Letters to the Editor while Balintore admired the umbrellas of pale-grey cloud over the wet fields of Ireland, and the brilliance of the sky that stood thirty thousand feet above its little hills. But presently both took a closer interest in the trolley from which a steward offered them, as a solace against the fatigues of altitude, caviare and smoked salmon.

The clouds below grew loose and detached. The blue pallor of the Atlantic showed beneath and between them, but their cabin was lighted by the much darker blue of the upper sky. Luncheon was served, and they ate with relish turtle soup, breast of pheasant, a bombe glacée under burnt almonds, a cut of Brie, and a few strawberries flown from Florida. From the other side of the menu-card they took their choice of a Rhine wine of '59, a claret of '55, and a champagne brut.

'A tolerable meal,' said Balintore, belching slightly. 'Very praiseworthy for the Atlantic sky.'

He had just accepted a glass of brandy when there was a small disturbance beside them. From the longer cabin behind came two stewardesses who supported the figure of a girl with sagging knees — chalk-white of face, with tremulous pale lips and fluttering eye-lids — and carefully settled her in the vacant window-seat of two unoccupied chairs on the starboard side of the aisle.

One of the stewardesses — she who had spoken to him before — said to Balintore, 'I hope you don't mind? She fainted, poor girl, and as they're rather crowded in the Tourist cabin, I thought it better to bring her here.'

'Of course,' said Balintore. 'And what she needs now is a glass of brandy. I'll give her mine — and bring two more.'

'Let me get past,' he said to Palladis, who sat on his outer side. 'I thought we'd see something more of her.'

He moved across the aisle, and putting an arm round the shoulders of the chalk-faced girl, held his glass to her lips. 'Now drink this, drink slowly,' he said, 'and in just two minutes you'll feel as good as new. There's nothing wrong with you that brandy can't put right.'

Ten minutes later her cheeks were pink and healthy, though her eyes were tear-stained, and she was sipping her second glass of brandy. 'Now tell me,' said Balintore, 'what upset you.'

'I was frightened,' she said.

His voice, when he answered, was large and comfortable, a great arm-chair of a voice that promised comfort and invited repose. 'Well, now,' he said, 'there's nothing surprising in that. Many, many people, even experienced travellers, are still secretly afraid of flying — though, as a matter of fact, aeroplanes in the sky are much safer than motor-cars on a road, especially at the week-end — but there it is: a native, instinctive distrust of the flying-machine. Even I — though I've flown a hundred thousand miles or more — even I sometimes feel a little sense of disquiet, the brief coldness of a passing shadow — the shadow of a bird, no bigger than that——'

'But I'm not frightened of aeroplanes,' said the girl. 'I like flying.'

'Then what——'

'Horses, for one thing. But it wasn't horses to-day.'

'I saw none at London Airport,' said Balintore gravely. 'But I saw you, and I saw that you were looking unhappy.'

'I saw you too,' said the girl. 'You're Edward Balintore, aren't you?'

'Do you know,' he said, 'I am still surprised when I meet people who recognise me? And usually I don't enjoy the experience: it's tiresome, it's a bore, it's an intrusion into one's privacy. But there are times — and this is one of them — when it's gratifying: very gratifying. You must tell me your name.'

'Polly Newton.'

'A charming name! I like euphony in a name, and yours has the melody of folk-song. — And now, Miss Newton, tell me what you're frightened of.'

'America,' she said.

On the other side of the aisle Palladis listened attentively to their conversation, and in a short-hand of his own invention recorded some of it in a note-book concealed in a copy of the Goncourt *Journal*, that he pretended to be reading.

He heard Polly Newton say she was going to New York as private secretary to a man she had met when he came to do business with her previous employer in Bucklersbury. A rich man, she said : a corporation lawyer. Not young, happily married, she had met his wife — Balintore nodded approvingly — and as well as offering her a handsome salary, he had told her that he went often to Europe, if not always to England, and never travelled without his secretary.

'But sometimes without his wife?' said Balintore suspiciously.

'Oh, no ! He collects Old Master drawings and engravings — have you ever heard of Piranesi ? I hadn't — and he buys nothing without his wife's approval.'

'In that case,' said Balintore, 'I don't see that you have any possible cause for alarm.'

'America,' she said. 'It's so big. And I've never been away from home before.'

'You're a very lucky girl.'

'That's what everyone told me——'

'To be frightened, in the way you're frightened, requires imagination — and imagination is the greatest of all gifts. Without it mankind is hardly worth a second thought — animals without much physical attraction, without strength to protect ourselves : that's what we'd be without imagination. But with it, a man becomes a poet, a maker of music — or, if not that, the sort of listener, receptive and sympathetic, without whom poets and composers can't live. Imagination, though I don't want to seem pompous about it, is the truly charismatic grace, and I say again that you're a very lucky girl.'

He took her left hand in his and patted it lightly, whimsically, as if half-envious of her. Polly Newton, though impressed by what he had said — apart from the fact that she did not know the meaning of charismatic — began to look a little anxious as his grasp grew warmer; while across the aisle, in the shelter of the Goncourt *Journal*, Palladis wrote busily and wondered what Balintore's next gambit was going to be.

For a minute or two there was silence. Then Balintore sat up — returned Miss Newton's hand to her lap — and in a brisk and genial voice said, 'In some of us, you know — and you're one, I can see that — there's a sort of universality that makes nonsense of the idea that only some parts of the world are familiar to us, while all the rest is strange and foreign. Don't believe that! Trust in yourself, and then you won't be frightened by the thought of America. You won't be frightened of anything. Because you'll realise that you're part of everything, and everything is part of you. Like Rilke's dead poet, you know —

diese Tiefen, diese Wiesen
Und diese Wasser waren sein Gesicht—

these depths (valleys, I suppose he means) and meadows and streams were his own face. And even New York, if you look at it like that, isn't so large and terrifying, but might almost be something that you yourself have helped to make.'

Palladis put away his note-book. He knew the gambit. Balintore believed in flattering, not a girl's face or figure, but her intelligence. He was surprised, however, by Balintore's show of enterprise. He seemed to be recovering from the gloom and *défaitisme* of his nervous collapse with unexpected speed. Palladis was a little worried, as well as surprised.

The attentive stewardess came slowly down the aisle, and Balintore said, 'I would like a whisky and soda, and for Miss Newton — what would you like?'

'No, nothing.'

'If Miss Newton has quite recovered,' said the stewardess, 'perhaps she would prefer to go back to her own seat.'

Her recovery could hardly be disputed, and at the stewardess's suggestion she made a move to get up and said, 'Yes, I must go. I'm feeling quite well now. And thank you — thank you both.'

'But you must have a drink before you leave us! Sit down again, I implore you.'

'It's irregular,' said the stewardess.

'Most pleasure is, from adultery to a Devonshire lane. Now be a good girl, and don't argue! I want a whisky and soda, and for Miss Newton — well, at this time of the day I'd suggest a cherry brandy.'

'Well, for you, Mr. Balintore. I wouldn't do it for anyone else.'

Polly Newton sat back in her seat, but with a look on her face of disapproval, of prim reluctance; and Balintore said, 'Your address in New York: I must have that before you go. And in case — just in case you feel lonely, and want to write to someone — I'll give you my address in Jamaica.'

Five minutes later she insisted on returning to the Tourist cabin, and Balintore showed a tetchy disappointment. Like a bout of indigestion his ill temper returned, and he looked at his fellow passengers with sour disfavour. At thirty thousand feet, above cloud that shimmered like pack-ice, the sky was still a luminous dark blue, and its light derided the colours of women with tinted hair, cheeks unnaturally pink, and arbitrary black eye-lashes. Misanthropy came in upon the heels of disappointment, and humanity offended him by its ungainly forms and recurrent weaknesses.

That well-fed man, stooping to pick up a book : how gross his hinderlands ! That over-dressed, lank ladder of a woman, going yet again to the lavatory : how ignoble her incontinence! And that girl, returning from the other lavatory — dark glasses, a painted pout, and hair a rook's nest of carefully ordered untidiness — what idiocy to parade such affectations ! He said to Palladis, 'In nothing is God more god-like than in his patience.'

The air grew ruffled, and invisible turbulence rocked the aeroplane. The stewardess, unwearied in benevolence, distributed button-holes of red roses, and looking through the window Balintore saw, far beneath, a land grey and white — the wrinkled grey of an elephant's hide, patched with snow — and a sharp-edged island that seemed to have fallen by hazard into a cold bright sea. They were crossing the coast-line of America.

Five hours were subtracted from their watches, and presently a long descent took them down to Idlewild a hundred and twenty minutes after they had left London.

Four

In London the air had been cold. At Idlewild it was 27° below freezing point on the Fahrenheit scale, and a fresh breeze blew upon them with an arctic draught as they walked towards the airport building. But Balintore would not hurry. Indifferent to the gelid wind, he stood, bare-headed, to look this way and that at the stooped and ruffled figures who made what haste they could — impeded by parcels and handbags, by lifting skirts and whipping scarves — to the shelter of the nearest door.

'Where is she ? Where has she gone ?' he asked. 'I can't see her anywhere.'

'For God's sake,' said Palladis through chattering teeth, 'come inside,' and dragged him, still protesting, into a waiting-room as hot as the Persian Gulf and odorous as a boxers' gymnasium.

Separated from passengers who were disembarking in New York, they were subject only to mild questioning and minor indignities ; but for Balintore separation was a pain indeed. With Palladis beside him — Palladis afraid of his getting into trouble — he pushed and threaded his way through groups of people who now were all taking off their coats, unwinding mufflers, wiping their brows ; and presently found a door into a larger hall where luggage was being assembled on long counters. At the far end they saw Polly Newton, but the door was guarded by an official of ponderous build and unsympathetic appearance who told them, 'Passengers in transit not allowed beyond this door.'

'Isn't this a free country?' demanded Balintore.

'Only to those who pay taxes.'

'There's a girl over there whom I want to speak to.'

'If she wouldn't listen to you over the Atlantic ocean, she won't listen here.'

'I want to tell her——'

'No dice,' said the official, and gently but persistently pushed him away. Palladis told him there was a bar on the floor above, and Balintore, still grumbling, followed reluctantly. Palladis ordered two Bourbon Old Fashioneds.

Palladis looked at the pictures in a copy of *Life*, and Balintore nursed his unhappiness. 'I'm worried,' he said. 'Worried about that girl. I should have told her — one thinks of these things too late — that if she found life in New York intolerable, or even unpleasant, she could come to us in Jamaica. I should have offered to pay her fare——'

'You're supporting three women already. You can't afford any more.'

'One should think of others, not of oneself.'

'You're still an invalid, or little better.'

'You don't need robust health to be capable of sympathy,' said Balintore; and sitting back in his chair looked through mournful eyes at some private vision of the world, and its misery that would not let him rest. Several people, passing their table, paused or turned to stare at him again, but he seemed unaware of their interest.

A mechanical voice summoned passengers on Flight 504, and they went out again to face the frozen wind and re-embark. Balintore fell asleep and woke three hours later to see through the dusk beneath them the sprawling shape of an island that lay flat as a rusty tray on the lapsing sea. They landed at Nassau, and were gratified by the dark warmth of the Bahamas.

Balintore, snuffing the kindly air, forgot his glimpse of the world's unkindness and declared, 'There's no artificial comfort to compare with the luxury of nature — if you go to the right place, that is. I suppose Jamaica will be warmer than this?'

'Not much, I think. Not up in the hills, where we're going.'

'I may decide to stay there. If, that is, I can find a suitable house. Not a big house, but comfortable. With a view, of course, and not too far from a good beach. In a climate like this I could settle down to contemplation. Serious contemplation, for three or four years at least. The great vacancy, the vast and terrifying emptiness in modern life, is our failure to find time for contemplation. But in Jamaica — well, I don't know, of course, but I'm beginning to feel that this notion of yours was a good one. Perhaps I shall live, my dear Guy, to feel everlastingly grateful to you.'

'I've given you occasion for gratitude before now,' said Palladis.

'Yes, yes, I know that. But this journey — though I started unwillingly — may be the beginning of the most formative chapter of my life.'

The remainder of their flight was brief. In the darkness they bisected Cuba, they passed over unseen little scraps of island in the warmth of Caribbean waves, and came down with a grating jar on the airfield near Montego Bay.

There was some confusion in the customs hall — a noisy woman who had lost her handbag was loudly blaming her husband for his carelessness — but within half an hour they had escaped the ritual of arrival, and a large, genial negro, cap in hand, was telling them that a motor-car waited at the door.

'You're Mr. Scroope's driver ?' asked Palladis.

'Yes, sir, that's right. And I've come here, at Mr. Weatherby Scroope's own express command, to bring you to his house.'

'Is it a long drive ?' asked Balintore.

'No, sir, not long. About three hours, no more'n that.'

It was a large American car that waited for them : not smartly new, but well used and beginning to look a little shabby. Their luggage filled the boot and the front seat beside their black driver. Solicitously he helped them in, and despite the warmth of the air put on a pair of leather gloves. He drove them swiftly to the main road, and turned eastward.

To their left an ebony sea glimmered fitfully under a young moon. The country was open marshland with a strong salt smell. They threaded a long village where dogs barked shrilly, and to the right saw mountains rising in a dark and ragged mass against the starlit sky. They skirted a broad bay with a selvage of white sand, and then their headlights opened a tunnel through the darkness beneath great trees. Another village, with lighted shops or bazaars.

Balintore fell asleep again, and was wakened by the car's rougher movement. They were now climbing a road with a loose and broken surface. The headlights showed tall forest on the one side, and on the other pierced the tops of trees that grew on a precipitous slope beneath them. The car went down on its springs with a bang, and a moment later they were bounced up to its roof. They swung round a corner on the edge of a deep and tangled gulf of darkness.

'Weatherby told me the last few miles would be rather rough,' said Palladis. His voice was apologetic.

'I hate jokes based on understatement,' said Balintore.

'The humour of meiosis — it's an English humour — is cowardly escapism, and nothing else. Oh, damn this road! How much longer have we got to suffer?'

'Not long now, sir,' said the driver, and stopped where the steep slope beneath was bare of trees and a vast landscape loomed of mountains rising black and tall against the thinner obscurity of the star-pricked sky. On the foreland of a long ridge, that seemed far above them, were the yellowish lights of a house.

'That's it,' said the driver. 'That's where we going.'

He set off again, jolting and bumping on the rain-channelled road, and Balintore said angrily, 'Is this what you expected? Did you know your cousin lived in a house on an inaccessible mountain in impenetrable jungle?'

'I only knew what Weatherby told me when I met him at home a few years ago. It's one of the old plantation houses — they still call it the Great House — and from the way he was living in London, I gathered he was used to living well.'

'In a hermitage! He and his father: a couple of hermits hiding behind long white beards in a shack in the woods, and living on yams and rain-water — that's what we're going to find!'

Palladis said nothing. Even his equanimity was a little shaken by the roughness of the approach, and faint qualms assailed him when he wondered if their reception was to be as gracious as he had expected.

But a few minutes later they both grew more cheerful when a negro servant opened white gates for them, and they drove slowly between flowering trees to a long, low house on whose brightly lighted veranda stood a tall, white-haired man in a white suit, and behind him a quartet of trimly-dressed, brown or black maids.

'I saw you coming,' said their host. 'If we're on the lookout we get about twenty minutes' warning when a car turns uphill. Sometimes it's very useful. Well, come on in. Don't worry about your luggage. The women will look after that.'

He led them through a long room, furnished with casual comfort and some display of haphazard luxury, to another and larger veranda that faced north. There a table was prepared for their comfort with whisky, both American and Scotch, with rum of various sorts and colours, with an ice-bucket and mineral waters. Presently one of the maids came in with a plate of sandwiches and a great basket of fruit. When Scroope spoke to her she said, 'Yes, sir!' in a deep, contralto acquiescence, and showed the brilliance of her teeth in a smile that seemed to expose a private, inexpugnable happiness.

Weatherby Scroope and Palladis were gossiping — talking of people whom Balintore didn't know — and Scroope apologised for his inattention to a distinguished guest.

'Give us ten minutes,' he said, 'and we'll have said all we have to say. We claim cousinhood, and though that's little better than a fiction after all these years, we like to keep in touch as far as we can. It's a harmless sentiment.'

Balintore, ill at ease in strange surroundings, had been looking at Scroope's eyebrows. They were mobile and luxuriant, and appeared to fan his red cheeks while he talked. His bright colour, thought Balintore — irritated by neglect — might well be the consequence of high blood-pressure rather than exposure to the sun.

He gave Balintore another whisky and soda, and Palladis said to him, 'I'm looking forward to meeting your father. How is he?'

'The old scamp!' said Scroope, and walking to the edge

of the veranda looked into the darkness. The overflow of light made luminous the huge white trumpet-blooms on a datura tree, and in the distance a faint light glimmered on the sea. The shrill sound of cicadas fretted the stillness of the air.

'He's gone to Palm Beach,' he said. 'Jamaica's too dull for him. Before Christmas he was complaining bitterly that there's nothing for a man to do here, and a month ago he went to Miami. And now Palm Beach.'

'How old is he?'

'Eighty-one.'

'The terrible frivolity of old men!' said Balintore.

'I apologise for boring you with family affairs. My father's behaviour is of no interest to you——'

'Indeed it is,' said Balintore. 'I remember how bitterly my mother resented my father's attitude to life. He was twenty years her senior, and much less serious.'

'Addicted to sudden journeys?'

'No, he died before he was old enough to be really irresponsible. But he used to laugh at things my mother thought important.'

'If the young were less solemn and the old more sensible,' said Palladis — but stopped when he saw Scroope beginning to yawn.

'I only talk like that when I'm tired out,' he added. 'Do you think we might go to bed now?'

Five

In the morning, an hour after sunrise, Balintore and Palladis stood on the veranda that looked northward, and before them, five or six miles away, saw a great arc of the sea whose colours were sharply divided. The shoreward water was apple-green, of lucent brightness, but the oceanic sea appeared to shine with a profound assertion of intrinsical dark blue.

Beneath them — between them and the sea — the land lay like a bowl broken by a shallow, meandering river. It was all green, but the various green of sugar-cane and the great drooping leaves of banana trees, of orange groves, and wind-tossed coconut palms ; and on either side it rose to the darker green of rain-forest on steeply climbing hills.

Immediately in front of them, on the one flank, was a giant-tall hedge of daturas, from which depended white flowers like trumpets ; and on the other side an enormous cotton tree on whose gnarled and ancient branches grew little orchid gardens. Three or four turkey-vultures dropped from the tall sky and came so near that their red scaly heads were clearly visible.

'I am favourably impressed,' said Balintore. 'We are to live in an eyrie from which, when we feel disposed, we can descend to the shore and watch the vulgarities of life from a suitable distance.'

'This isn't the sort of hermitage you feared.'

'That road, in the darkness, couldn't fail to excite fear of the worst. But I underrated your cousin when I expected his table to be furnished only with yams and rain-water.'

They went down a short flight of steps to a rough lawn, and turned the corner of the house towards the veranda by which they had come in the night before. Bougainvillaea and hibiscus grew on the one side ; poinsettias, trumpet vines, and poincianas on the other. The drive, as far as the white entrance-gates, was flanked by cassias and a scarlet bougainvillaea. Beyond the bright trees a precipitous mountain rose three or four thousand feet towards immaculate azure, and from a vast green distance a taller, more irregular crest came down to meet it and enclose, as if it were a deep inlet of the sea, a profound green valley.

'It would be vulgar if it were anywhere else,' said Palladis. 'Too much colour and too many colours ; or there would be, against a smaller background.'

'Or under a sky not quite so refulgent. But the sky——'

'Exonerates them.'

They stopped to watch a humming-bird hovering on the beat of its invisible wings before a flower, whose name they did not know, in which its orange bill was deeply engaged. It was a bird with a black head, a breast of coruscating green, and a tail divided into two long black tapes. Another of the same sort came to a neighbouring flower.

'I wonder what prices are like ?' said Balintore. 'The price of land, I mean. Of a small house with a big view. I said yesterday — in Nassau, wasn't it ? — that I might think of buying a property here, if I could find something suitable.'

'If you settle down to a life of contemplation, you won't need me.'

'But I couldn't live alone !'

'I daresay you could find a couple of well disposed and nicely shaped black girls to look after you.'

'No, no ! There are going to be no more women in my life. Unless, of course, I hear from Polly Newton. If I hear she needs me. — You know, I distrust that employer of hers. I admit I know nothing about him except that he buys pictures — or drawings : Old Master drawings — and when he goes to look for them he takes his wife with him. His wife ! You take my word for it, she's nothing but an old procuress !'

They returned to the north veranda, where Weatherby Scroope was already at the breakfast table. A black girl — she who had brought sandwiches the night before — welcomed them with a broad, shy smile of gleaming friendliness, and gave them grape-fruit of a pinkish hue.

Her long bare arms were as smooth as chocolate, her carriage stately, and she walked with an undulation like the unbroken swell of the deep sea. The grape-fruit were flagons of sweetness.

'Her name's Mary,' said Scroope when she had gone, 'and she's a very good girl. But don't give her any money. She's religious, in her own way, and a month ago she joined the Seventh Day Adventists. That's an American sect, and they take a lot of money from here. She'll take yours, unless you're careful. Because now she's collecting for a fund to send under-privileged American children — that's white children — to the seaside. I told her she'd be better employed collecting for Jamaican pickneys, and she said, "They got the seaside already." But I don't give her anything, and I advise you not to.'

'Are most of them religious ?' asked Balintore.

'Nearly all of them, in one way or another. Our slaves were Ashantis by origin — the majority of them — and the

Ashantis were a warlike people. Since fighting's been discouraged, they've taken to religion like retired colonels.'

'I'm not a practising Christian,' said Balintore. 'That's to say, I don't go to church, and much of what the church teaches seems to me a fabulous recital of improbable events. But fundamentally — yes, fundamentally — I'm a deeply religious man. Though not, of course, in a conventional way.'

'I've never thought religion a suitable topic for the breakfast table,' said Scroope, and helped himself to bacon and eggs. 'It was my fault for introducing it when I should have been talking about more practical things. I don't know what you want to do while you're here, but you mustn't feel under any obligation to me. There's a car you can use, and plenty to see. I do very little entertaining, but I know a lot of people, and if you want introductions I can probably supply them. Otherwise you'll have to look after yourselves.'

'Do you work?' asked Balintore. 'Daily work, I mean? It seems an unnatural activity in Paradise.'

'Some evening,' said Scroope, 'I'll tell you about the economics of Paradise. And now I must go to the factory.'

'This,' said Palladis, after Scroope had left them, 'is precisely what you asked for: total privacy, and solitude impaired only by me.'

'Yes,' said Balintore, 'this is all I had hoped for. More indeed — I hadn't expected vultures.'

He looked with a dubious eye at the large bird sailing insolently across the lawn. Its wings were motionless, but as it passed it turned its scarlet head as if to inspect him.

'He'll know you again,' said Palladis cheerfully.

The vultures came every morning, patrolled the valley, and presently rose to upper winds and sailed off. The big, long-tailed humming-birds were also morning visitors, but little vervains flashed and hovered about the veranda all day. When the afternoon sun had drained its colour from the landscape it was time to sleep for an hour or two, and at six o'clock Mary brought out the ice-bucket and put white rum and gin on the sideboard. After dinner Weatherby Scroope fell easily into conversation till about ten o'clock, when he grew sleepy.

The Great House, perched on its high, protruding rib of the mountains, seemed to command a silence of its own. Hardly a sound came to it — till the cicadas woke at night — except when a rising wind carried the bourdon of the sea or the murmur of moving leaves on a hillside. The servants and their several children lived quietly beyond a courtyard, and made no noise but an occasional chorus of laughter. For several days Balintore and Palladis felt no desire to leave their bird-bright isolation, but walked idly on rough hill-paths, and enjoyed indolence without reproach of conscience or the nagging of desire. Palladis had never seen Balintore so relaxed, so easy of mind. He seemed to have forgotten entirely the shame of his collapse, and even after dinner did not grow angrily rhetorical or argue loudly with Weatherby Scroope. He and Scroope got on well together, and Balintore persuaded their host to tell them something of the history of his family since the departure from England of his remote ancestor the Regicide.

It was Scroope who expelled them from their indolence and isolation. He said one night, 'I've been talking about the past, and you really must go and look at the present. There's a good car you can have — as I told you before — and the roads aren't bad. Go to Port Antonio, go to Ocho Rios, and see something of the country that's been ours for three hundred years. It's not going to be ours much longer — it isn't ours now — but we've had a long tenancy, and when you've seen it you'll understand why we took some trouble to keep it.'

'I'm fascinated,' said Balintore, 'by your knowledge of your ancestry. You've suffered all sorts of reverses — as a family, I mean — you've lost the lands you used to occupy——'

'Two hundred years ago we were grandees in a society of grandees. We had a couple of thousand acres of land — land that grew sugar-cane when sugar fetched forty-two shillings a hundredweight — and more than a thousand slaves. By 1830 we were broke. Sugar had fallen to twenty-eight shillings, and the slaves, anticipating the event, were in revolt because they thought slavery had been abolished. Then my great-grandfather — no, my great-great-grandfather — did a sensible thing. He married a mustee : a girl whose mother was a quadroon. But her father was rich and left most of his money to his illegitimate daughter. And their eldest son, my great-grandfather, married the daughter of a Portuguese Jew who had a lot of money too. So we began to recoup, and buy back some of the land we had lost.'

'The weakness of a family tree,' said Palladis, 'is that the cuckoos are so seldom recognised.'

'We established respectability against heavy odds,' said Scroope. 'There was a shortage of women in the early days — white women, I mean — and the Regicide's only son married a girl who'd been brought from a House of Correction in Bristol. But she was a good wife and a prolific mother.'

'To-morrow,' said Palladis, 'we'll begin a more active life. We'll go to St. Ann's Bay and try to imagine what the simple Arawaks thought when they saw Columbus's doom-laden caravels on the horizon.'

'They were naked, polygamous, and free from disease,'

said Scroope. 'They had no defences at all, and within fifty years were extinct.'

'But the Spaniards, with all their advantages, didn't last much longer,' said Balintore. 'Your Regicide and the young woman from Bristol had more staying-power. I wonder what her ancestry was ?'

They began to explore the north coast from Port Antonio to Falmouth. Balintore would not go as far as Montego Bay for fear of meeting tourists, but consented to visit an hotel near Ocho Rios that protected itself against overcrowding by the simple expedient of charging ten guineas a day.

In return for this sum the Morgan Arms offered easy luxury in a setting of extravagant beauty. Within a reef on which the ocean-sea broke like white chrysanthemums, a placid bay shoaled to leaf-green water and a sandy beach where coconut palms threw wind-tossed shadows, and parti-coloured umbrellas drew more firmly their circles of sophisticated shade. The hotel buildings stood discreetly within deep verandas and a circumference of palms and bright flower-beds ; while beyond them the mountains rose in the verdure of dense forest to a sky that was cornflower-blue, cloud-dappled, or deep ocean-blue. The tralucent sea was warm and buoyant : pink toes and round stomachs protruded slightly from it where elderly swimmers floated half-asleep, and small boats under large striped sails went to and fro like dragon-flies. Black waiters, bare-footed on the sand, brought rum punches to bathers who sat idly under the umbrellas, and luncheon was served on terraces that overhung the sea.

'I miss one thing only,' said Balintore when, on their third or fourth visit, a black boy had brought them their first rum-punch.

'Young figures,' said Palladis. 'But the young can't afford to come here.'

'This morning I can see four female figures under the age of thirty. Those two children, who are with their grandparents; the young woman who is obviously on her honeymoon; and the contoured blonde who, I imagine, is persuading her employer to forget her faults as a secretary. Except for them——'

'The company is mature.'

'Too mature for the scenery.'

'You ought to be grateful. There's no one here to excite your fancy, fret your mind, and hinder your convalescence.'

'I'm feeling very well.'

'You're looking very well.'

'I've made a complete recovery.'

'But the doctors said you had to have a long rest.'

'And I intend to! Make no mistake about that. I'm enjoying myself here, and I shall probably stay for a long, long time. And now I'm going to swim again.'

He waded into the warm, clear water, and as if to advertise his returning strength set off to seaward with flailing arms. But after twenty yards he turned on his back and floated with his face to the sun.

When Palladis joined him he said, 'I'm worried about prices. I don't want to pay too much.'

'For what?'

'A house. A house and an acre or two of land.'

'Can you really afford to retire?'

'Can I afford to wait till I'm too old to get any advantage from retiring? I want to retire with an active mind.'

'Would it remain active in Jamaica?'

'You've got a streak of Puritanism in you, Guy. You distrust pleasure. You think I couldn't devote myself to serious contemplation——'

'While floating in a leaf-green sea with a couple of ounces of rum punch washing the walls of your stomach.'

'And that's where you're wrong. I'm serious now, and to-night I'm going to ask Weatherby about the possibility of buying, quite cheaply, a little house and a patch of land. — Let's go and drink to that.'

Half an hour later, dressed like many of their fellow tourists in gaily patterned shirts and linen trousers, they sat on a vine-shaded terrace, eating rice and shrimps, and discussing their host, Weatherby Scroope.

'You'll find him sceptical,' said Palladis. 'He doesn't think much of rich people who come here to idle their lives away. He was telling me——'

'But I'm not rich, and I wouldn't be idle.'

'You would, in his opinion. There's a broad streak of Puritanism in him.'

'He seems to work hard.'

'He has to. His father's an idle, self-indulgent old man, and both his brothers had a remarkable faculty for enjoying themselves. They were killed in the war — one in the Desert, the other in Normandy — but they left wives and families whom the estate has to support.'

'Did Weatherby never marry ?'

'Yes, a long time ago. But it didn't work. She went off with an American trumpeter. A man who led a jazz-band.'

'And he didn't try again ?'

'He once told me that white women weren't worth the trouble and expense of maintenance.'

'So, for him, that was the end of it ?'

'You don't keep your eyes open, Ned. And you don't really listen to people, do you ?'

'What have I missed ?'

'That girl, Mary. Don't you think she's attractive ?'

'But she's black.'

'Oh, don't be so snobbish !'

'Well, I am surprised !'

'They've been used to black girls for three hundred years. And as they've kept going, as a family, for three hundred years, it doesn't seem to have done them any harm.'

'But the family tree ! There's no indication there of any mixture of black blood, except the girl he called a mustee. I found the family tree impressive ; really impressive. I was fascinated by it.'

'In the eighteenth century,' said Palladis, 'the Irish side of my family was seriously threatened — its continuity was threatened — when the succession passed to an only son who, though married, was known to be impotent. The heir presumptive was a cousin whom everyone detested — and to everyone's relief he was disappointed of his expectations.'

'How was that managed ?'

'Footmen. There were always plenty of burly young footmen in a big house at that time. So the succession was maintained within the house, if not precisely within the family.'

'Do you think Weatherby owes anything to unsanctified assistance ?'

'Not that I know of, though in three hundred years there's room for accident. But I don't suppose he finds sleeping with a black girl unnatural, or thinks of it as an innovation.'

'I'm going to ask him to help me. I shall tell him I'm serious — he knows I'm not idly rich——'

'Well, don't expect too much.'

To Palladis' surprise, however, Scroope took a warm interest in Balintore's proposal, but warned him it might be difficult to find what he wanted.

'If you're prepared to spend £50,000——'

'Good God, no!'

'I thought not. But anyone with £50,000 to spend can pick up a decent property any time. If, at the other extreme, you're looking for a couple of acres in a good situation—enough to build a cottage on, and ensure a little privacy—you may find a place you would like, and then be told it's in a part of the country set aside for development, for small holdings probably; or else it's on an estate whose owner, naturally enough, doesn't want to sell any part of it.'

'Haven't you a couple of acres you could sell?'

Shaking his head with apparent regret, Scroope said, 'No, I'm afraid not.'

'Down by the river, for example——'

'I'm putting in a new orange-grove there.'

'But on the other side?'

'There's no road.'

'Well, nearer the shore?'

'That would cut into the cane-fields, and you can't cut two acres out of a good cane-field.'

'Why not?'

'It would reduce the yield,' said Scroope, 'and I need to cut all I can to keep the factory going.'

'I suppose,' said Balintore, 'that every proprietor will give me the same sort of answers.'

'Not necessarily. You may find someone who isn't making use of all his land, and you may come across a speculator who's bought land in the hope of selling it again to people like you or people from Kingston who want a little holiday place on the north shore.—Do help yourself: that's rum, and that's gin.—Well, give me a few days, and I'll make some enquiries. And I'll tell you what I'll do as well:

I'll take you down to the factory and introduce you to my manager. He's our local politician, which makes him much more important than the salary I pay him ; and he knows a great deal more about what's going on than I do. His name's Hector McGregor.'

Two days later they met Mr. McGregor, who was a tall and handsome negro. He was plump and stately, with white hair cut *en brosse* and a remarkable resemblance to the late André Gide ; though his hue was much darker. He wore a flower in his button-hole, and drove with them to a large but derelict estate near Falmouth which was in the market for £42,000. He was a little hurt, as well as surprised, when Balintore told him that he had no intention of spending as much as that.

The following day he took them to Port Antonio, and showed them round a much smaller but more carefully maintained property that could be acquired for £28,000.

Balintore said to him, 'Now look here ! This isn't at all the sort of place I want. I am not a millionaire. I am a hard-working man, and by living carefully, even frugally, I have saved a little money——'

'I understand,' said Mr. McGregor. 'Yes, I understand. I myself have made a little money, and if I had my due I would be in a position, at this very moment, to be making a great deal more. Yes, man. Right now, I ought to be a rich man.'

He looked pensively at the sea — they stood on a wooded promontory that pushed a fist of land towards blue water, and from the fist a finger of reef curled about a pale-green bay — and said, 'When this new government was elected, I should have been made Minister of State for Internal Communications. That I fully expected, and I was looking forward to a prospect of hard work and handsome rewards. This government's going to spend millions of pounds on roads! Yes, man. I could have given Jamaica what Jamaica needs, and become a very rich man. But I was betrayed.'

'How did that happen?'

Mr. McGregor sighed and looked sad, but did not answer until, driving westward again half an hour later, he told a stirring tale of his narrow escape from death on the dangerous hill they were descending, and added: 'I went down on my knees and thanked God for His great mercy. Yes, sir. I'm a religious man, and always have been. I believe in our Lord Jesus Christ, and that's why I feel sick at heart when I think how I was betrayed, and my character blackened by unscrupulous enemies.'

'What did they say?'

'As a leading elder in the New Methodist chapel in Fort Appin, I'm a man of some influence in my community, and I use my influence for the general good. But I've got enemies, and my enemies spread a slanderous tale that I was telling members of my congregation that in future no one would be eligible to partake of the Blessed Sacrament who didn't vote for me at the forthcoming election. And that story spoiled my chances and ruined my career. Yes, man.'

'Though there was, of course, no truth in it?'

'What I had said,' replied Mr. McGregor with simple dignity, 'was that if the people of Fort Appin wanted to enjoy all the benefits, grace, and appurtenances of a full life, including better roads and the Blessed Sacrament, they would do well to vote for me and my party. But I was misrepresented, I was scandalised and betrayed. So I'm still a poor man working for a weekly wage.'

He had, by now, lost interest in Balintore's quest; but Balintore persisted in his search, and with Palladis to drive him, ventured on abominable side-roads and up forested hills to sudden views over enormous distances, or down to the warmth of enclosed and unexpected glens, where he would talk for an hour or more to the black and bewildered proprietor of a wooden shack and an acre of yams. He was determined, he now said, to live in Jamaica ; and sooner or later, he declared, they were bound to find a place of the sort he wanted.

At night, after dinner, he would tell Weatherby Scroope where they had been, and describe the people with whom he had talked. He was a good mimic, and could reproduce the tune of a conversation as well as its matter. He began to believe, and even to assert, that he understood the peasantry ; and the better he understood them, the more he liked them. The old and the gnarled, the lively and young — burly labourers in a cane-field with their dangerous cutlasses, and buxom women with their regal carriage and flaunting colours — the immaculate floral finery of children dressed for church : they all delighted him, and were, beyond a doubt, the people among whom he wanted to spend his remaining years.

'Yes,' he would say, 'you have everything here to cure the sickness of our times. A perfect climate, enchanting scenery — nature at the very height of opulence, at the top of benevolence — and a simple people with musical voices and an imperturbable piety.'

'They have their faults,' said Scroope.

'They are human beings,' said Balintore, 'and their laughter's as deep as Beethoven.'

Three days of cold and drenching rain did nothing to subdue his enthusiasm, nor did another meeting with Mr. McGregor, whose mood was as dark as the sky. His eldest son, who worked in Kingston, had been so pestered and plagued by a girl — who said he ought to marry her — that he had sought relief in drink, and being drunk had stolen a motor-bicycle which he had driven into the harbour. Then he had assaulted the policeman who, very bravely, jumped in to rescue him.

'It makes me feel despairing and humiliated,' said Mr. McGregor, 'it makes me sick at heart when I think of all the advantages that boy has had, and how he's made nothing of them. All his life he's had advantages that were denied to me. He's legitimate, for one thing — his mother and I are legally married — and I sent him to school : a good school. If I had had his advantages I could have become a scholar, I could have travelled abroad — with my abilities I could have done that — but I was handicapped from the start.'

Balintore, to comfort him, said the boy had been guilty only of youth's intemperance, of youth's exuberance and inexperience, and should not be blamed too harshly. He had, he said, been much impressed by the charming warmth of the Jamaican temperament ; and a little excess of warmth — if it did not occur too often — could surely be forgiven.

'There's no vice in the boy, that's true enough,' said Mr. McGregor. 'He's maybe too simple in his mind to ever make a great success in life, but he's kind to his mother, he's got a good heart like all our simple people. Yes, man. There's three kinds of people here in Jamaica, and two of them's good. All our country folk, they're good, and people right at the top, like Mr. Weatherby Scroope and his father, they're good too ; though there's not many of them. It's people of my sort, the middle classes, that I don't trust.'

Gloomily he shook his handsome silver head, and repeated, 'No, I don't trust them. But if you come here to live, Mr. Balintore, there'll be no hard feeling against you. Not as far as I'm concerned. I don't support any colour bar, and I've got no hard feelings against white people as such. So long as they don't belong to the middle classes. Yes, man.'

Their search had now continued for nearly a month, without Balintore having found anything to suit him. Palladis had shown exemplary patience, but insisted that every second day, at least, they should spend in the comfort of the Morgan Arms or one of the other hotels that offered good food and a bathing beach.

'You may regard yourself as a prospective resident,' he told Balintore, 'but I am a tourist, and I'm not going to be so silly as to deny myself the pleasures designed for tourists.'

After another day of heavy rain he proposed that they go boating on the Rio Grande. 'An exercise,' he said, 'that no self-respecting tourist will lightly miss.'

'You had better go to-morrow,' said Scroope. 'You need plenty of water and a good current, and the river will be high enough after to-day's rain. But it goes down quickly.'

Balintore protested. 'I'll do no such thing! Rafting on the Rio Grande, indeed! I don't know what it entails, or what it implies, but I suppose it's some sort of Caribbean fun-fair, a milling-crowd of trippers queuing-up in sweaty anticipation of factitious thrills——'

'Let me give you some more rum,' said Palladis.

'I'm sure it isn't as bad as that,' said Scroope. 'I've never done it myself, but I'm told it gives you a good view of some remarkable country. And on Friday — this is Tuesday, isn't it? — I'm going to take you to the other end of the island, to a cattle show.'

'Will there be tourists there?'

'A few, I expect. But essentially it's local entertainment, for neighbouring farmers and their friends. And a man I know there — a man I've known all my life — has a small house, with two or three acres, that he's willing to sell. It may be what you want. I've written to half a dozen people — more, I think — and told them the sort of place you're looking for, but till now I've heard of nothing that seemed to me worth going to see. Well, you may be disappointed, but I think it's a chance for you.'

'My dear Weatherby, what splendid news! I'm immensely grateful to you!'

Balintore stood up, with the manifest intention of shaking his kind host's hand; but thinking better of so ostentatious a gesture, chose instead to drink his rum-punch at a gulp, and refill his glass.

'I have always felt,' he said, 'that my search would be successful in the end. And now—'

'Don't be too confident.'

'No, no. Confidence is man-made, but I — well, I trust myself to Fate.'

In this good mood he was easily persuaded to risk vulgar association on the Rio Grande, and the following morning he and Palladis drove again to Port Antonio. There, from a score of men who competed genially for their favour, they chose one of honest appearance and burly stature, and with him in the back seat drove inland for another few miles till they came to the bank of the river. There Balintore again showed signs of uneasiness, for they were not alone.

At this point the river was fairly broad, and on the shingle beach were rather more than a dozen people about to begin their voyage. Most of them were of middle age and manifestly respectable, but a little man in short trousers of a bright red tartan, and a tall, blonde, bony-chested woman in a bikini, who complained loudly in a mid-American voice about the hard discomfort of her bench on the raft — these excited

Balintore's displeasure, and he frowned uneasily till they had disappeared downstream.

The rafts were simply but ingeniously constructed of long bamboos. Thirteen or fourteen stout trunks, bound together, made a loose, pliable floor, and a bench for two, like a garden seat, was built on its after third. Behind this stood the boatman with a long pole.

They pushed off, and a few minutes later were caught in a swift-running channel between a bar of shingle on the one side, and formidable rocks on the other. Their boatman, with agile movement and strenuous thrusting of his pole, kept their raft in mid-stream, and they slid down a bright green aqueous slope, edged with a dancing chatter of broken water, to a calm and placid reach under a rampart of tall trees. The sun shone hotly on the cool pellucid river, and ahead of them lay more rapids.

'I was wrong,' said Balintore half an hour later. 'Quite wrong. This is very pleasant indeed.'

They were being poled slowly down a long stretch beneath a hillside, thickly wooded, that rose abruptly to a tall green arc against the brilliant sky. Small birds flitted among the trees and little blue herons stood, contemplative, in the shallows.

'And not over-crowded,' he added.

The river quickened, and they approached more brawling water that turned a sudden corner beneath a low cliff. Dexterously their boatman navigated the awkward channel, but just beyond the cliff they saw another raft whose passengers had been less fortunate.

They were elderly people of massive build, whose bulk overflowed the garden-bench on which they sat, and their weight had anchored their raft to a narrow shoal. Its bow floated free — swung to and fro — but the river chattered mockingly and over-ran the stern, while their boatman thrust unavailingly, now on this side and now on that, to push her free. His passengers, in their gay holiday clothes, made no move to help him, but sat in a ponderous and placid immobility like Buddhas in a temple in the jungle.

The two boatmen exchanged some rapid conversation. What they said was incomprehensible, but Balintore and Palladis' man clearly regarded his colleague's mishap as a good joke, and made no move to go to his help. They swam down stream, rocking slightly on lilting water, and the shipwrecked Buddhas were soon out of sight.

'It could become a little crowded,' said Palladis, and asked their boatman where they should stop to swim and eat their lunch.

'Good place coming,' he said, and presently steered them to a green bank where the river was broad as a small lake, and divided, as if by its protruding backbone, by a long white shoal. On the far side several rafts had been beached, and some ten or a dozen people were swimming in smooth water.

Balintore looked doubtfully at them, but Palladis said brusquely, 'They're too far away to prick your privacy. Come and swim.'

But twenty minutes later, when they were sitting on the bank eating their sandwiches, Balintore said, 'There's a woman looking at us through field-glasses.'

A little apart from the other bathers on the far bank, she stood, with legs apart to give her stability, and stared fixedly at them. She was a woman of mature and generous figure in a pink and white swimming suit, and suddenly, to their surprise, she raised a sunburnt arm and called, not to them, but to one of her near-by companions.

A man walked slowly towards her — a man of middle age,

his belly plump above a red bathing-slip — and took the glasses from her. He too stared intently — put down the glasses and spoke to the woman — and stared again. Then both, with waving arms, called loudly across the river.

'Come on,' said Balintore, 'we're going. I don't know who they are, and I'm not going to wait and see. Oh, for God's sake hurry !'

'They may be friends of mine, or people we both know,' said Palladis.

'I don't care, I don't want to meet them. Old friends can be worse than total strangers, and the odds are — oh, the odds are always against you !'

He gathered his clothes together, shouted to the boatman, and began to push off the raft. Palladis, puzzled but not alarmed by his nervousness, shrugged his shoulders and stepped aboard.

'Go as fast as you can,' said Balintore to the boatman, and looking anxiously over his shoulder exclaimed, 'My God, she's coming after us !'

One of the rafts on the far bank had been pushed out, and while her companions looked on — or stared across at Balintore and Palladis — the woman in the pink and white bathing suit went hurriedly aboard — almost lost her balance — and a moment later, through the smooth water on that side, was being poled towards them. The plump man continued to wave excitedly, and shout ; but his words could not be distinguished.

'I'll give you a pound to get clear away from her,' said Balintore to the boatman ; who, as if it were the most natural sentiment in the world, said cheerfully, 'Yes, sir ! Now we go like steam-boat !' And thrusting with all his strength, drew gradually away from their pursuers till a quickening of the current pulled them swiftly into a hundred yards of dancing rapids ; where, to Balintore's loudly expressed pleasure and relief, the following raft fell out of control, slewed sideways, and went aground — but into no danger — on the rocks round which the river pranced in white plumes.

'And serve her right !' he exclaimed. 'Damn all who threaten privacy — that's what I say !'

Palladis looked at him curiously. He had thought Balintore's recovery almost complete. For more than a month he had been living in a calm and reasonable way — drinking very little, taking exercise — with nothing to worry him and the sun to colour his skin till he looked five years younger and ten years fitter than the shaken invalid who, so reluctantly, had boarded an aeroplane in early February. That Balintore had always shown an explosive, ill-regulated temper was true enough — it had helped to make him famous — and no psychologist had ever resisted the temptation to explain his outbursts by the postulate of a deeply hidden traumatic memory. Palladis himself, however, tended to accept the simpler hypothesis that some people were more irritable than others — had, as it were, tempers with a lower boiling point — and on innumerable occasions he had seen how easily Balintore recovered from, or threw off, an apparently devasting rage. Two minutes after an eruption of terrifying force he could summon from a well-furnished cupboard of his mind a quotation from Burke or Macaulay — from the Bible or a French poet — to quash the arrogance or ill-founded opinion of some rash opponent.

That his collapse in the television studio had been a symptom of illness or exhaustion — physical illness or mental exhaustion — was beyond doubt ; but Palladis had expected his power of recuperation from petty annoyance to show itself in recovery from graver injury ; and in the last few weeks he had seen, as he thought, the improvement he had looked for.

Balintore's persistent search for a cottage, and his reiterated intention to settle down in Jamaica, Palladis did not take quite seriously. What was apparently an obsession would, he thought, be quickly cured if he did buy a cottage : of which he would soon grow tired. But his sudden nervousness before the hail and summons of a distant stranger — a stranger on the other side of the river — and his obvious fear of pursuit, could not easily be accounted for ; and Palladis began to wonder if Balintore did in fact see Jamaica as a possible refuge from unknown enemies, whether real or imagined.

When they returned to the Great House, however, this discomforting thought was dispelled by a nearer and more urgent discomfort ; for Weatherby Scroope was in a state of perturbation that even his long habit of equanimity could not conceal.

He apologised to Balintore for boring him again with family affairs, but said, 'I must talk about this, for I have to leave you here, and I can't very well leave you without an explanation.'

'Leave us ?' said Balintore. 'But where are you going ?'

'Look at these,' said Scroope, and gave them a sheaf of photographs that showed a tall, lean old man of distinguished appearance — he was not unlike Weatherby — and a handsome woman, with resolute features, who seemed to be in her early forties. Several of the photographs had been taken beside a swimming pool, and clearly showed the disparity in age of the two figures.

'That,' said Scroope bitterly, 'is my father — my damned old rascal of a father — and *that* is the woman who, he says, he is going to marry.'

'At eighty-one ?'

'Eighty-two next month.'

'My dear Weatherby,' said Palladis, 'how I sympathise with you !'

'I had a letter from him to-day — a letter enclosing these ludicrous photographs — and he asks me to wish him joy !'

'Is he still at Palm Beach ?'

'Yes, but not for much longer. His *fiancée* — so he calls her ! — comes from a town called Peoria, which I think is in Illinois, and he proposes to go there with her to meet her family.'

'But in Illinois, at this time of year, he'll get pneumonia.'

'It might be kinder if he did. But no, she'll look after him. She's a widow with a married daughter and another at the University of Chicago — and if he marries her I'll have to look after them all, as I've had to work for him and my dead brothers' wives — their wives and children — all of whom I loathe and abominate.'

'What are you going to do ?' asked Palladis.

'Go to Palm Beach, of course, and break it up if I can.'

'But can you ?'

'I know more about my father than she does ; and she may listen to me.'

Weatherby Scroope, a temperate man, walked heavily across the veranda and filled a full tumbler from the dark red jug that held rum-punch.

'So I'll have to leave you,' he said, 'but you mustn't let that upset you. Treat the house as your own, and Mary will look after you. You know your way about now, and on Friday you must go to the Rochester Cattle Show and meet old Quigley Bone who's got a house to sell. Everybody knows him, and any of the stewards will tell you where to find him.'

'If I can do anything to help,' said Palladis—

'No,' said Scroope, 'I shall have to do it alone—and, if I can, cut him out from under her guns.'

Balintore, still looking at the photographs, said softly, 'The terrible frivolity of old men!'

Six

EARLY on Friday morning — a grey, beclouded morning — they set out for the Rochester Cattle Show in a mood of straitened or diminished enjoyment. It was twenty-four hours since they had said good-bye to Weatherby Scroope, whose departure had left them with a feeling, curious and unexpected, of loneliness and disorientation. He had driven to Montego Bay, to board an aeroplane for Miami, and the grimness of his expression had not been mollified by Palladis' suggestion that he might make the best of a bad business by marrying the woman himself.

They had spent an idle day on the veranda, disinclined for movement, only half-inclined to reading, and a little tired of intrusive humming-birds and redundant fireflies when darkness fell. They missed the triangular pattern of conversation to which they had grown accustomed, and Balintore had bored, not only Palladis but himself, with a prolix and unilluminating monologue on the uneasy relationship between tragedy and farce.

They felt hopeful, but not assured, of entertainment at the cattle show, and when, half-way to Rochester — it was a long drive — the sky cleared and the sun shone warmly, Balintore began to speak, with increasing happiness, of the cottage he was about to inspect. He spent the next hour in pleasant anticipation while Palladis gave his attention to the road in front and the map beside him.

They came by a minor road into a long open valley of

cultivated fields, and presently joined a dusty procession of buses, motor-cars, and many bicycles. Policemen at a cross-roads were directing traffic with well-drilled gestures, and at the entrance to the show yard stewards with red rosettes and soft voices took their half-crowns and car-fees. Busy young men controlled the car park, and girls with large yellow rosettes sold programmes. Through a loud-speaker an amplified voice issued incomprehensible instructions, and in a roped-off ring a dozen small, neatly fashioned, dark red cattle were inspected by two slow, deliberate judges and a circumference of intent and silent observers. Elderly ladies sat on wooden chairs in front of a marquee, and at another marquee cases of beer were being opened. Picketed in long lines were animals of different sorts and breeds, and in a long open tent were displayed potted plants, jars of jam, home-baked cakes and needle-work. Children ran noisily to and fro ; voices louder than the majority betrayed persons of more importance than the majority ; and the amplified voice from the loud-speaker made crackling noises which no one could understand.

'It is exactly like a cattle show at home ; a small county show,' said Palladis.

'But everyone is black.'

'Well, nearly everyone.'

'And I prefer their voices.'

'Their use of colour is less inhibited.'

'The weather is better.'

'The cattle are smaller.'

'The children are prettier.'

'Beware of chauvinism,' said Palladis.

'These people,' said Balintore proudly, 'may soon be my neighbours. — I wonder where Quigley Bone is ? We must try to find him.'

'There's no hurry. Let's have a glass of beer and walk round for a little while.'

For half an hour, or more, they admired the lively variety of the show — the cattle and their exhibitors, the gaily dressed children and a stall of fantastic vegetables, the self-possession of the English minority in their dowdy dresses and casual old suits — and then their attention was taken by the arrival of two bus-loads of tourists, who appeared to be American.

'Their choice of colour is also uninhibited,' said Palladis.

'But tartan shorts ! They shouldn't be allowed to wear shorts and pantaloons — look at that tiny man and that enormous woman — shorts and pantaloons of Stuart tartan !'

'They may be Royalists,' said Palladis. 'Fidelity to the Throne is not restricted to people with an athletic figure.'

Their attention was distracted by the voice behind the loud-speaker which, suddenly loud and clear, announced, 'Mr. Quigley Bone is anxious to meet Mr. Edward Balintore. If Mr. Balintore is here, will he kindly proceed to the Members' Tent, where Mr. Quigley Bone is waiting for him.'

'Come along,' said Balintore, 'come along. We mustn't keep him waiting.'

They found the Members' Tent, and standing in front of it saw the tall and slightly stooping figure of a man who wore an old-fashioned double terai hat, khaki slacks, and a bush-shirt. He had a lean and humorous face, bright blue eyes, and a meagre, drooping moustache. He came towards them and said, 'Balintore ? You're Balintore, are you ? Well, I'm in a hell of a pickle.'

'I'm sorry to hear that. Do you know Guy Palladis ?'

'A cousin of Weatherby's, aren't you ? Why isn't he here ?'

'He's in a pickle too.'

'His old father, I suppose ? Damned old scoundrel he is. Well, don't tell me about him. I'll hear the story in God's good time, and that's when it's all over, one way or the other. You want to talk about that cottage of mine, I suppose ?'

'I do.'

'I wish you had come a couple of days ago ! I was ready to sell, and sell dirt cheap to a friend of Weatherby's. But now — well, the fact is I've had an offer, or a tentative offer, from some damned fellow who says he's going to come and live here — made a packet of money, wants to retire, and thinks well of our climate — and his offer, or his tentative offer, is half as much again as I was going to ask you, and I've been afflicted by greed. Sheer, bloody, shameful greed.'

'How much has he offered ?'

'That's the cottage,' said Bone, and gave Balintore several photographs. 'Nicely situated, down by the river, but no use to me. My sister built it, after she got her divorce. Fool of a woman she is, can't learn her lesson. Married again now, and living in Vancouver Island, God help her. It's been standing empty for a year.'

'How much ?' said Balintore.

'Two acres of land with it, and some nice fruit trees——'

He was interrupted by a woman's voice that cried loudly, 'Ned, oh, Ned ! You got away from me two days ago, and I thought I was never going to see you again. And then we heard your name on the loud-speaker — we were away across on the other side of the field — and we came right over, and oh, Ned, how well you're looking ! You haven't changed a bit.'

His astonishment at seeing her was tinged with consternation — a vague, uncharted dismay — but because her intrusion angered as well as surprised him, he could dissemble his unease, and he responded to her exuberant manner with a tolerable imitation — an English imitation — of social greeting.

'Betty !' he said. 'What a long time——'

'Don't tell him how long,' she said. 'I've lied about my age. — You remember Chris, don't you ? Well, I'm Mrs. Bulfin now, and I bet that's a surprise. We're on our honeymoon.'

She was a handsome woman, but dressed too obviously in assertion of her remnant youth — a white dress with a pink sash, a broad-brimmed white hat with a pink ribbon — and the husband she introduced had the over-confident look of a man who knew what money could buy, and a face painfully reddened by sunshine hotter than he was used to. 'Yes,' he said, 'we've met.'

'Yes,' said Balintore, 'of course I remember. But to think you're married — well, I hope you're both very happy.'

'We've made a good beginning,' she said complacently ; and her husband offered his cigar-case to Balintore and Quigley Bone.

Balintore introduced Palladis : 'My friend Guy Palladis, Mrs. Bulfin.'

'Betty,' she said.

'And Chris Bulfin.'

'Have a cigar,' said Bulfin. 'Havana, not Jamaica.'

'Disgracefully but unrepentant,' said Palladis, 'I smoke only cigarettes. They're my link with suburban housewives and the sturdy proletariat.'

'I didn't realise you knew each other,' said Quigley Bone. 'Now I'm deeper in the pickle than ever !'

'How come ?' said Bulfin.

'He wants to buy the cottage too.'

'Do *you* want to buy it ?' said Balintore.

'I'm interested,' said Bulfin.

'Good God !'

'And you ?'

'I came here to see it.'

'I haven't made up my mind yet,' said Bulfin. 'I've been looking at another house a couple of miles away : a bigger house with a lot more land.'

'Well,' said Quigley Bone, 'as you know each other, you'd better talk it out between you. I want to offend no one. Never have ! I'm nobody's enemy except my own — and my own faults are simple indolence and from time to time a little plain, ordinary, inoffensive greed. See you later, I hope.'

'Oh, Ned !' said Mrs. Bulfin, 'we must have a talk. A proper talk ! Do you ever see anybody from the old days in Ceylon ?'

'Not often,' said Balintore.

'How well I remember them !'

Bulfin, walking with Palladis, asked, 'Have you known him long'?

'About four years.'

'Has he ever told you about my brother ?' asked Bulfin.

Seven

BALINTORE and Palladis shared a picnic lunch with the Bulfins, and left the show ground an hour later. They did not see Quigley Bone again.

For some while they drove in silence, and then Palladis said, 'It's often embarrassing to meet old friends.'

'Between them,' said Balintore, 'they are going to ruin everything.'

'As bad as that ?'

'The cottage,' said Balintore, 'is exactly what I wanted, and the original price — he told what he's prepared to give me for it — the original price I could well afford. But he can out-bid me, and I can't afford to out-bid him.'

'But if he buys the other place he spoke of——'

'They would be my neighbours — neighbours within two or three miles of me ! — and how could I live with those people on my doorstep ?'

'Why not ?'

'It's an old story. Too old to start now. Wait till we get home — home, by God ! I wish I'd a home to go to — but wait till we're on top of that hill again, and I've had a drink or two — wait till then. And you may have to help me.'

'It's what I'm paid for,' said Palladis.

The absence of Weatherby Scroope still left a sense of vacancy, of a partial vacuum, in the Great House ; but Mary and the other servants looked after them with undiminished attention, and the table on the veranda was furnished ready for their return.

Darkness came, and fireflies to decorate it, but after three drinks Balintore was still reticent.

'Your friend Bulfin told me quite a lot about himself,' said Palladis. 'He is one of our new rich — on a foundation of chemical manure.'

'A poisoner of the fields,' said Balintore.

'And now, having sold his firm or factory to a much larger firm, for a handsome price, he proposes to enjoy his leisure.'

'Why can't he enjoy it somewhere else?'

'His wife — she says I must call her Betty — has always wanted to live in Jamaica; and as they have been married for only six weeks, he still listens to her. She was engaged to his brother——'

'I know.'

'Then he lost sight of her for many years, and met her again in romantic circumstances.'

'In Paignton.'

'She told you, did she?'

'At great length.'

'It's a charming story. — He, newly enriched but lonely, a widower for two years, goes to spend Christmas at Torquay. He knows no one there, and makes no friends. He goes for a walk, and it starts to rain. It rains heavily. But he walks on, because he has nothing else to do. He walks all the way to Paignton, and there——'

'He sneezes.'

'He feels a cold coming on. He suddenly realises that he's wet and miserable, and across the road he sees a little tea-shop, warmly lighted, decorated for Christmas. In he goes, and takes off his coat. He sneezes again, and a sympathetic voice says, "Oh, you poor thing! What a day to be out!" He turns and recognises her——'

'A most damnable mischance that was.'

'And three weeks later they are married.'

Balintore got up to give himself another drink, and Palladis asked, 'How did you happen to know her brother?'

'He was with me in India. In Arakan when the Japs made their counter-attack and were beaten.'

'Was he in Intelligence?'

'Not precisely. He was an officer observer.'

'But you were in Intelligence?'

'I was doing a temporary job at that time. With the Fourteenth Army. They needed publicity. Badly needed it. It used to be called the Forgotten Army. So its Public Relations were reorganised, and I went down to Arakan. From Delhi. The new job wasn't altogether divorced from Intelligence. I had to censor the stories that correspondents brought in.'

'And later on, when you went to Ceylon——'

'Tom Bulfin was dead by then. After the Arakan affair was over, there was the Chindit fly-in. Tom went as an observer, and didn't come back.'

'In Ceylon, where you met Betty——'

'She had been engaged to him.'

'Yes, I know. But were you in Intelligence there, or Public Relations?'

'Public Relations. I had been asked to stay on. Mountbatten thought it was important. And he was right, of course.'

Mary came in to tell them in her deep voice — her teeth a gleam in the lamp-light — that dinner was served; and they ate their soup in silence.

'Your friend Bulfin——'

'You mean Chris ?'

'Yes.'

'I went to see him after I came home,' said Balintore. 'I think now it was a mistake. I went to tell him what I could about his brother's death. He was talented and very brave : wounded and decorated in Norway, right at the beginning, then wounded again in Burma. That's how he came to me. Well, I wanted to say how much we all thought of him — the usual thing — but Chris didn't take it in the usual way.'

'He said something to me about missing papers, or a lost manuscript. He was rather incoherent, but he seems to have a grudge against you.'

'For which there is no substance or foundation whatsoever ! The man's a fool. A fool with a mind of darkness where phantoms breed. — And jealous ! Jealous of success because he thinks success can't occur in nature or be won with honesty. There was a time when he tried — but no, he didn't go as far as blackmail. Blackmail was in his mind, but I showed him I wasn't to be frightened, and he thought better of it. But now he turns up again, to spoil a good day, and spoil, perhaps, my hope of living in the sun. To hell with him ! But they're light-weights, both of them — creatures of no account — and a week from now they may have gone, gone forever, with some new notion to steer their addle minds.'

They finished dinner, walked on the rough lawn and counted fireflies, and returned to the veranda. 'Where's the whisky ?' said Balintore. 'I'm going to take a long, stiff peg, a couple of sleeping pills, and forget them.'

He was not allowed to forget them for long, however. They arrived on the following afternoon, and for several minutes Balintore and Palladis listened, without comment, to Betty Bulfin while she spoke, in terms of extreme disparagement, of the rough approach to the Great House ; and then, with extravagant admiration, of the views it commanded. At some little distance from them her husband stared silently, and with what appeared to be a brooding dislike, at the far-off sea. Burnt scarlet by the sun, the back of his neck looked sore.

As if to embrace the whole scene, Betty extended her arms to their full length and exclaimed, 'Isn't it wonderful ? I don't know how many times I've said to Chris, "Why, it's just like Ceylon, only better ! Far better." — All these flowering trees, I mean. And coming up here, why, it's like going up to Kandy, isn't it, Ned ? Well, it would be if the Hotel Suisse was round the corner, and the Temple of the Tooth, and an Officers' Club, like the one at Peradeniya. Oh, those were the days ! I was in the Wrens,' she told Palladis. 'An officer, of course. And Ned was a major then. The first time I saw him he was bright yellow with mepacrine, except where he had nettle rash. You saw a lot of funny sights in the war.'

Then, suddenly, her temper changed — subdued by memory of another sort — and soberly she said, 'You'd been in Burma, of course — well, Arakan or Bengal or somewhere — that's why he was yellow : they all had to take mepacrine every day — and you came to see me, and told me how Tom had been killed.'

There was a little pause before she added, 'That's really why we've come here : to talk about Tom. Well, we wanted to see where you were living — Mr. Bone told us how to get here — but really it was because Chris and I — oh, I don't know how to put it ! He'll have to tell you himself. — Chris ! Come and explain what we want to talk about.'

Bulfin walked slowly towards them and said, 'I'm not a man who likes making trouble — either for myself or anyone else — but I believe in justice, and justice should be done even if it does cause a little trouble.'

'Is this going to be the old cock-and-bull tale all over again ?' asked Balintore. 'I told you, a long time ago, that your suspicions — all your libellous and malignant suspicions — reminded me of nothing so much as the description of Earth in the first verse of the first chapter of Genesis : when Earth was without form, and void. But if you want to repeat your story — so far as you have a story — and hear it refuted, yet again, we had better sit down and make ourselves comfortable.'

'Would you prefer me to leave you with your friends ?' asked Palladis.

'No, of course not. Stay and listen. It's a story that ought to amuse you.'

They left the lawn and found chairs in the shade of the veranda ; where Betty was momentarily diverted by a small humming-bird that flew closely round her head, attracted by the expensive scent she used.

'That might make a good advertisement,' she said. 'There may be money in it, Chris ! "Even a humming-bird's deceived" — how's that for a caption ?'

No one responded to her pleasantry, and her husband, still looking out to sea, said heavily, 'Last night Betty and I had a long conversation, and in consequence of adding up what she told me, and what I told her, we both decided it was necessary to have another talk with you.'

'Whatever your addition comes to, the sum can't alter the facts.'

'There may be two opinions about that. Now in the first place, my brother had told me — in his letters, that is — that he was writing a book.'

'Who wasn't, in those days ?'

'When you published a book, you called it *Scorpio my Star*. Well, Tom was born under Scorpio.'

'He wasn't the only one. Scorpio's the symbol of darkness. Scorpio in its claws holds Libra the Balance over waste land. Read Virgil, first book of the Georgics, if you don't believe me.'

'I don't know anything about Virgil, but I've read your book — or what you called your book — and a lot of things that happen in it are things that happened to Tom.'

'Things that happened between 1939 and 1945 happened to a great number of people.'

'But the girl in Chapter Nineteen,' said Betty, 'is me. You see, when I went out to Ceylon, Tom got a week's leave, and he was there to meet me. And that — well, that's how he got something else to write about.'

'This is what she told me last night,' said Bulfin, 'and I can tell you this : it didn't make me feel any the happier to hear her say so. But it was all a long time ago — I had to own that — and I respected her honesty for admitting it.'

He nodded his head, slowly, as if in solemn recognition of her fault and his broad tolerance ; and Betty, looking lovingly towards him, murmured, 'Oh, Chris, how good you are !'

'Do you suppose that in the whole course of the war your wife was the only girl to be seduced in the Galle Face Hotel ?' asked Balintore.

'Now you be careful what you say !'

'I think it's you who should be careful. You came here with the evident intention of blackmailing me——'

'Oh, no, I didn't ! I don't want your money. I've enough for my needs, and a bit to spare. All I'm looking for is justice.

If my brother Tom wrote that book, he ought to get the credit for it.'

'And he did write it !' exclaimed Betty. 'Because no one else could have said what he said about me — and that's true, Chris !'

'Are you really sure that you can identify yourself with the girl in Chapter Nineteen ?'

'Well, I knew he was writing a book, because he told me so, and it isn't likely that he'd leave out what happened — well, what happened in that chapter.'

'There was another girl, earlier in the novel.'

'She was a brunette.'

'Do they react differently ?'

'Well, he did !'

'What I want to know,' said Bulfin, 'is what happened to the manuscript that Tom left behind him when he flew in to join the Chindits. His effects — a few effects — were sent home to me ; but there was no manuscript.'

'When an officer is killed, or dies on active service,' said Balintore, 'every effort is made to send home, to his nearest relative, such small personal effects as a signet ring, a cigarette case, photographs, a pocket-book, and so forth. In the circumstances of active service it's usually impossible to send more than that, and his other possessions may be sold or given away, or — if they're of no value — destroyed.'

'Do you know if a substantial manuscript, belonging to Tom, was destroyed ?'

'I have no knowledge of that having happened, and it could hardly have been done without my knowledge.'

'Then somebody stole it,' said Bulfin, 'and the curious thing is that a novel which might have been written by Tom, was published under your name.'

'That's slander. Do you realise that?'

'Sometimes the only way to establish the truth is to publish a slander.'

'Why have you been so dilatory? It's fifteen years since *Scorpio my Star* began to shine.'

'I didn't know then what I know now,' said Bulfin. 'I wasn't married to Betty then.'

'I'm ever so sorry, Ned,' said Betty. 'You were kind to me in Kandy, and I'm still grateful, I really am. But it couldn't have been anyone except Tom who wrote about that night in the Galle Face Hotel.'

'You're flattering yourself. You think you're unique, but in those circumstances no one is. And your husband——'

'He's a good husband to me, and I'm not going to hear anything said against him!'

'He's deluding himself, and misleading you. You've come here on a fool's errand.'

'Come on, love,' said Bulfin, 'we're wasting our time here.' He turned to Balintore and spoke with muted fury: 'But you'll hear from me!'

Eight

THE morning broke in opalescent beauty, and expanded into a dome of green and cerulean tranquillity. Balintore and Palladis forgot the sullenness and ill-humour that their visitor of the day before had left behind ; and after breakfast drove to the Morgan Arms at Ocho Rios — a longish drive — ordered their luncheon, and swam in the leaf-green water of the guarded bay.

Within a little while — as if the systole and diastole of the gently rising sea had reassured their minds — they were enjoying a borrowed share of the equanimity that ocean gives to swimming things. — 'It's their reward for resisting the temptations of evolution,' said Palladis — and could look with some detachment at the embarrassment of life ashore.

'I discount all human motives,' said Balintore on his back, splashing the calm water with his large, pink-tipped feet.

'They have to be assessed,' said Palladis. 'I am an *aficionado* of the human struggle, but I like to watch it from a sheltered seat.'

'That man,' said Balintore, 'pretends that he wants justice done to his dead brother. But what he's looking for is a reflected fame for himself.'

'I rather like them,' said Palladis. 'Both of them. I think he's relatively honest — well pleased with his success in life — and she is simple, kind, and uncritical. Not wholly admirable people, but likeable.'

'Vegetables and the sea are all that's uncorrupted,' said Balintore, 'and salt water needs a vegetable corrective.'

They swam ashore, and a tall, very thin waiter, his bare black feet squeezing the sand between his toes, brought them rum-punches ; and two more. Then they took air-filled, buoyant mattresses from the beach, went back to sea, and floated on the ocean pulse.

'How much truth was there in their story ?' asked Palladis.

'A little, only a little,' said Balintore.

'Had Tom Bulfin written a novel ?'

'You couldn't call it a novel.'

'But he left a manuscript ?'

'A miscellany in a cardboard box. A chaos of impressionism, description, interminable dialogue, autobiography, and characters who couldn't remember their own names.'

'The rough material for *Scorpio my Star* ?'

'He said to me, the last time I saw him, "I may not have a chance to finish this. It needs a lot of revision. Take a look at it, and if you think it's worth anything — and if I don't come back — give it to Betty. But if it's no good, then burn it or keep it as a souvenir." — We were very friendly, and more than once I'd kept him out of trouble. He was talented, in a loose, off-handed way ; very brave, and quite undisciplined. I saved him from court martial, I paid his debts, I gave him an extra ten days' leave — on medical grounds — when he had overstayed his leave ; and to show his gratitude he made me his residuary legatee if I decided that his estate — his manuscript — had no value.'

'And your decision gave you the material for a very successful novel.'

'It had no value as he left it. I had to put it into shape : cut it, and pull it about, and rewrite. He had no sense of style, he didn't know how to organise a story. He would interrupt the story of a battle to write an essay on strategy——'

'Like Tolstoy.'

'He was no Tolstoy. But Chris Bulfin wouldn't have appreciated that. Chris Bulfin wouldn't know the difference between a novel and a hotch-potch of happy notions——'

'Sometimes it isn't easy.'

'— so there was no point in trying to tell him. Explanation's wasted where there is no understanding.'

'So you took your legacy——'

'And said nothing. — Do you feel ready for lunch ?'

They swam again in the afternoon, and fell into conversation with a visitor newly arrived from Kansas City, who introduced them to his wife, her mother, and an old schoolfriend of his wife who was travelling with them. Balintore, in his most genial and ebullient mood, gave them a great deal of useful information about Jamaica, and corrected some curious misapprehensions they had about the constitutional structure of the British Commonwealth. Dark was falling when they returned to the Great House, and found among their letters two of particular interest.

Balintore's came from Polly Newton in New York, and he read it twice with an expression of deepening concern. He had written to her several times, and received brief, punctual, and dull replies in a very attractive, highly mannered script. She was quite happy, and found her work interesting ; but said no more about it. Her employer — his name was Evershrub — was kind and considerate, and his wife had taken her to the theatre. The weather was very cold, and her room, though nicely furnished, was terribly over-heated. . . .

This display of emotional incapacity, as it seemed, had gone far to alienate Balintore's sympathy, and almost relieved him of anxiety about Miss Newton's safety. For why should anyone worry himself about a girl of such indifferent sensibility that New York — her first sight and sensation of New York — had failed to elicit rhapsody and awe in letters of passionate exclamation? She was, he decided — or had nearly decided — of poorer quality than he had supposed. But now he had cause to worry again, and be anxious too; for here in this letter was abundance of emotion, a high pitch of excitement that loosened the fine structure of her Italianate writing.

It was, however, not New York that excited her — she said nothing of New York — but the prospect of going home. Mr. Evershrub was going to London, then to Paris and northern Italy, and he would take her with him. 'He says he is pleased with my work, and he feels that I understand him better than any secretary he has ever employed! In London, he says, he couldn't get on without me. And so, after what seems an age since I left — though really it's only seven weeks to-morrow — I'm going home again, and no one will ever know, because I haven't the words to explain it, how thrilled and delighted I am. Mrs. Evershrub, too, is being very kind, and says she is so glad that Herbert (who is Mr. Evershrub) will have someone with him who knows her way about in London. She will be joining us some time later, in three or four weeks perhaps.'

'Look at that!' exclaimed Balintore, and gave the letter to Palladis. 'It's what I feared from the beginning! From my very first sight of her, I knew the poor girl was walking into danger. And here's the proof of it. That woman, his alleged or so-called wife — and this I told you before — is nothing more than his procuress. As for his Old Masters, you can be pretty sure why he collects them, and what they're used for: "Come up and see my Tiepolo!"'

'A friend of mine who collected French inlaid furniture used to say "Come up and see my Buhl."'

'This is not a time for joking. Unless someone intervenes, Polly Newton is going straight to her ruin.'

'Even before the Relief of Mafeking, that's a remark which might have raised some doubtful eyebrows.'

'We live in dissolute times, I know that, but virtue hasn't vanished from the world, and a girl who's naturally virtuous——'

'Are they ?'

'You're trying to be cynical, but cynicism doesn't suit you——'

'I'm trying to consider a problem of my own. You're not the only man who has female correspondents, and if my cousin Honoria is telling the truth——'

'Who is she ?'

'Her name's Honoria O'Turk. She's a widow. Her husband was The Turk of Mayo——'

'He was *what* ?'

'It's one of those old Irish family titles, like The Knight of Glyn, or The MacGillicuddy of the Reeks. He died three or four years ago, and now Honoria, trying to keep a small impoverished estate alive till the boy's grown up — he's an only son — finds herself in real danger. Not of seduction, that doesn't happen in Ireland — or if it does, the girl goes to England, and the National Health Service looks after her. No, danger in Ireland is more dramatic, and Honoria's afraid of being blown up.'

'I thought the I.R.A. had been disbanded ?'

'It isn't the I.R.A., it's a geologist. She says the house is being undermined by a neighbour who's a geologist, and she wants me to go and give her advice.'

'You can't leave me!'

'No, I realise that. I'm under contract.'

'And in any case, her danger doesn't appear to be very real. Neither real nor immediate.'

'An Irish geologist seems to me a lot more dangerous than an American collector of Old Master drawings — and nothing is more immediate than explosion.'

Their conversation was interrupted by Mary, who came in with sinuous, apologetic movements of her tall and dignified body to say, 'I sorry, sir! I forgot to bring you this letter, which those people left.'

'What people?'

'Those people in that red motor-car. They come yesterday, they come to-day, and you wasn't in. But he sat down and wrote a letter, and said I was to give it to you. And I wasn't thinking about nothing at all, sir, and I clean forgot all about it. But here it is, sir, and now dinner is served.'

Shrimps, sea-cold and firm, with a well-made mayonnaise, were their first course, but Balintore hardly tasted it. 'Listen to this,' he said, and read aloud the hurriedly written letter he had taken from a half-sealed envelope. '"We're sorry to have missed you this afternoon, because we'll have to have another talk, and the sooner the better. We're driving on to Port Antonio, and to-night we'll stay there, and perhaps go down the Rio Grande to-morrow. Could you put us up to-morrow night? We'll look in about five o'clock, and if you find it inconvenient to have us for the night, don't hesitate to say so. But we want to be sure of an opportunity to have another long talk with you. Betty is now even more determined than I am that justice should be done to my brother Tom, and if that's to come about, the memorial of his own work must be inscribed with his own name. Looking forward to seeing you again, and thrashing out how this can be done. Yours etc., Chris Bulfin."'

'Dinner for four to-morrow,' said Palladis. 'Do you want me to order it, or shall we leave it to Mary ?'

'They are not going to dine here, and most certainly they're not going to sleep here ! I shan't be here when they come.'

'Why not ? Sooner or later you'll have to face them, and if your conscience is clear——'

'It's more difficult than that. It's easy enough to clear one's conscience, but to clear someone else's understanding is a very different thing.'

After some ill-joined argument they failed to reach agreement — an admirable chicken risotto that Mary brought them was unappreciated — and having drunk a cup of coffee and a glass of brandy — having walked on the lawn for ten minutes to smoke a cigarette and look at the luminous white trumpet-blooms of the datura tree — Palladis went to his bed, and left Balintore on the veranda, drinking whisky and soda in sullen silence.

It was not very late — it was barely midnight — when Balintore beat heavily on Palladis' bedroom door, and came in to find, to his surprise, Palladis sitting at a table on which, still busily writing, he had filled some eight or ten closely written sheets.

'I thought you'd be in bed. You ought to be asleep,' he said.

'I've been doing a little historical research,' said Palladis, 'and I'm writing up my notes.'

'On Jamaica ?'

'On Jamaica and its visitors, from Columbus and Henry Morgan to the present time.'

'We're leaving,' said Balintore.

'When ?'

'Now. To-morrow — or to-day if it's after twelve — because I'm not going to stay here and play Saint Sebastian to a couple of malignant Bulfins who want to sit about, drinking our rum, and throwing poisoned darts at me.'

'Are you frightened of them ?'

'No ! But I'm not going to subject myself to vain, unnecessary torment. I'm going to get out, clear out, bug out ! We're leaving to-morrow.'

'Where shall we go ?'

'I don't know. I'll decide that in the morning. But I want to be packed, and ready to leave, at seven o'clock.'

'This is an island : you remember that ?'

'An island with several different air services. And I have written a letter that Mary will give to Bulfin when he calls. Would you like to read it ?'

Palladis took the sheet of paper and read : 'Dear Chris, You will be, alas, too late. We leave, early to-morrow morning, on a lecture tour that will take me to Caracas, Maracaibo, Bogota, and Quito — and possibly down the coast as far as Valparaiso. I have always wanted to see Chile. But if not there — which, I admit, doesn't seem probable — perhaps we shall meet elsewhere.'

'You are,' said Palladis, 'a Calvinist among liars.'

'You mean predestined ?'

'I mean that you lie with the conviction of predestination.'

Nine

ALL the servants stood waving good-bye to them — Mary in tears — and the solidly respectable chauffeur who, seven weeks before, had met them at Montego Bay, drove them to Kingston.

At the foot of the rough hill Balintore exclaimed, 'Stop, stop ! We must go back, I forgot to tip them.'

'I did that,' said Palladis.

'But I too——'

'I tipped them lavishly. With your money.'

They drove on, and soon were uncomfortably warm. They were wearing heavy clothes, because Balintore had decided to stay in New York for a few days.

'To see Polly Newton ?' Palladis had asked.

'It would be absurd to go there, and make no effort to see her,' Balintore answered coldly.

They booked seats in an aeroplane which would take off in the early evening, and spent the day in an hotel poised high above Kingston on a hillside carved into terraces and excavated to make a long and artificially azure swimming-pool. One end, to exaggerate its hue, was overhung by a rampart of crimson bougainvillea and a flaming poinciana that daunted, and seemed to thrust away, the brilliance of the sky. Elsewhere in gardened copses were frangipane and violet jacaranda, trumpet vines, yellow hibiscus, and the curiously imagined shrimp plant. Among the scintillant reflexions of many coloured petals Balintore and Palladis swam in the long, warm pool, and were acutely conscious of the luxury they were forsaking.

'Was it Mantegna,' said Balintore, 'who painted a damned lugubrious picture of the Expulsion from Paradise?'

'Masaccio,' said Palladis.

'Well, whoever it was, I feel like Adam.'

'He had no choice — but you had.'

'No,' said Balintore sombrely. 'I couldn't live with those vulgar inquisitioners round the corner: their questions pattering, day after day, like water-drops in a Chinese torture scene. I couldn't endure it, so I had to go — we had to go — but I feel as glum as Adam in that picture by — who did you say?'

'Masaccio,' said Palladis.

In the aeroplane Balintore fell fast asleep, and Palladis, pulling a note-book from his pocket, began to write. 'Once again,' he wrote, 'he has shown his almost indecent power of recuperation. Seven weeks ago he left London as if the Furies were at his heels: Furies released from their lair by his invitation. He was afraid of flying, afraid to think of the Atlantic thirty thousand feet below us, and only the greater fear of pursuit by phantom detectives, with serpents in their hair and tears of blood in their eyes, persuaded him to risk his life in a machine which, to a simple, pragmatical person like myself, seemed eminently safe.

'But that sort of nervousness was only a symptom of whatever disease or lesion — mental or physical — he was suffering from; and now he's cured of it. He makes up his mind, coldly and with a semblance of reason, to leave Jamaica in order to escape from two people whose joint knowledge menaces his security: or the security of his reputation.

'It's obvious, I think, that their suspicions come as close

to the truth as his own account of the genesis of *Scorpio my Star*. Much of it was written, and most of it imagined or invented, by Tom Bulfin, who conveniently flew into Burma to be killed. It's possible that Bulfin's manuscript has survived, and I shall try to find it. But now I must think of the future rather than the past. He has recovered physical health and self-assurance — Jamaica has done that for him — and out of a Balintore-full-of-confidence anything may hatch'. — I had better cable to my mother and ask her to send me some money, in case I am left behind, he thought.

Balintore woke as a stewardess paused beside them with a tray of drinks ; and Palladis put away his note-book.

'The Henry James,' said Balintore, 'is a very comfortable hotel in a good situation. I've stayed there before, and at this time of year it isn't likely to be overcrowded. I'm looking forward to a few days in New York — though I'm extremely sorry to have left Jamaica.'

'How long do you think of staying ?'

'It all depends. It all depends on — no, not so much on circumstances as events.'

From the darkness above it, New York was a galaxy more brilliant than the Milky Way, and from Idlewild to Manhattan a prolonged dazzlement of light and contrary movement on the many-laned highway — a ceaseless interchange of swift, bright shuttles on a loom of inscrutable purpose — till a toll bridge and a black river led them to the vast and multitudinously tenanted ramparts of the city ; where a brisk welcome at the Hotel Henry James conducted them to the suite reserved for Mr. Balintore high above East 54th Street.

Balintore, at the telephone, asked for a bottle of Old Grand-dad. It was brought, with a bucket of ice, and presently, when the impact of New York's enormity had been cushioned, they went to bed in rooms extravagantly heated in mockery, as it seemed, of the angry snow-flakes that spat against their windows.

In the morning the sun shone in sub-arctic brilliance, and after breakfast Balintore said, 'Let us go and look at the city.'

'Have you spoken to Polly Newton yet?'

'No,' said Balintore, 'not yet. New York demands attention first — and it might be a mistake, a tactical error, to ring her immediately after arrival. I want to see her, of course, but I don't want to show what she, or any girl, might misread as undue eagerness. Youthful impulsiveness gets you nowhere. Juvenile impatience shuts the door. I'm not going to make that mistake. No, no. We'll wait a day or two, and this morning we'll look up and let the roof-tops take our breath away. We might see what's new — whether monstrous or agreeable — at the Guggenheim Museum.'

They went out, and a boreal wind took their breath away. They put up their collars, and Balintore said, 'New York has this advantage, that anyone can find his way about in it.' They turned right, to reach Fifth Avenue, and found themselves on Lexington.

They retraced their steps, and came to a bright, enormous channel that divided with fearful precision a populous and mountainous honeycomb, man-made of steel and glass and stone. Dallying on Fifth Avenue in despite of a cold and searching wind, they admired the vast cliffs that towered in rectilinear grandeur above the pavements where passers-by were insufferably tempted by the shops' display of improbable costumes for ladies, jewellery of fabulous price, and extraordinary facilities for sailing to every other quarter of the globe.

'It is the most abstract of cities,' said Balintore. 'It caters for the ideal, and its architecture is designed for two purposes : to make the common run of humanity insignificant, but to exalt the status of the express-elevator pilot. I like it immensely! It bears no relation to common needs, but creates from uncommon skill an architecture of magnificent perversity. How beautiful it is — and how ponderous an impermanence ! In ten years' time it will look quite different, but still have no stability ; only a much larger rental value.'

'It is very, very cold,' said Palladis with a shiver.

'The United States has a climate far superior to ours,' said Balintore. 'Every American knows that.'

'One of my ears is frost-bitten.'

'We British have become decadent weaklings,' said Balintore. 'We have no resistence to the extremities of weather. In July New York can be an absolute inferno of damp and sullen heat. Not as bad as Washington, of course, but too much for us. We should die of it.'

'Are we going the right way ?'

'I think we must be. The Guggenheim Museum is opposite Central Park.'

'But surely Central Park is in the other direction ?'

'Perhaps it is. Oh, you can't lose yourself in New York.'

Again they retraced their steps, and at the intersection of 59th Street staggered slightly as they met the gale of icy wind that swept across the barren spaces of the Park.

'It is like a view of Lapland,' said Palladis.

Ten minutes later, at 86th Street, he stopped and looked at the concentric levels and apparent imbalance of the Museum. 'And that,' he said, 'is like a nest of flower-pots.'

'Sometimes,' said Balintore, 'you are quite offensively insular.'

'But this is fantasy. Fantasy realised in concrete. Suitable, perhaps, for a Californian juxtaposition, but not for the Lappish tundra of Central Park in winter.'

'It's a most ingeniously efficient design for the exhibition of pictures. Come inside, and you'll be convinced of that. — But wait a moment.'

A placard on the outer wall of the Museum announced an exhibition of 40 NEW WORKS BY THE ACTION PAINTER INGO POMADOR.

'What a nuisance,' said Balintore.

'They usually are, these action paintings. A public nuisance — not so much painted as committed.'

'I don't mean that. I mean that I don't, and I can't, look at pictures by Ingo Pomador.'

'Why not ?'

'A certain delicacy — an inhibition of delicacy — prevents me. But don't ask me to explain.'

He turned and walked rapidly away. Palladis followed, and was warned by his expression not to question him : he wore taciturnity like a placard saying No Admittance. But when, after a sombre march the length of sixteen blocks — an unimpeded march, for in that area, on so bitter a morning, no native pedestrians were abroad — they came to a building, a little way retired from the Avenue, of conventional elegance, Balintore said, 'Let us go in here and look at some of *our* pictures.'

They entered a warm mansion, and beyond a hall where fountains played in an atmosphere like that of Florida, saw many of the masterpieces assembled by the millionaire Henry Clay Frick. Constable, Gainsborough, and Reynolds ; Lawrence and Turner and Hogarth — perhaps, thought Palladis, Balintore was right in describing pictures by them as 'ours ;' but there were also Piero della Francesca and Vermeer, Rembrandt and Bellini and El Greco. 'Do you claim them too ?' he asked.

'I've no patience with narrow nationalism, I speak as a European,' said Balintore magnificently, and stood with the air of a proprietor before Velasquez' portrait of Philip IV.

'And in the old age of Europe,' said Palladis, 'it's pleasant to be shown proof — proof beyond all doubt — that there's no such thing as progress except in a price-list.'

'Change and decay, that's all,' said Balintore ; and looked with gloomy satisfaction at Holbein's grim portrait of Sir Thomas More.

They spent a couple of hours in the Frick mansion, but even the Fragonards could not dispel the cloud of dark discomfort which had settled on Balintore. When they left, he looked carefully behind him — northward into the chill vacancy of Fifth Avenue — as if to make sure that no one was following them.

In the evening they went to see a play-with-music for which Palladis had managed to get tickets by paying three times the official price. It was called *Natty Bumppo !*, and for rather more than a year had been running to unfailing applause. It included a dozen songs, sung with stentorian simplicity to tunes of elemental vigour, and a *corps de ballet* of lightly clad and handsome Mohicans who danced some intricate measures with great dexterity. When the performance was over, Balintore and Palladis walked back to the Hotel Henry James and finished the bottle of Old Grand-dad that Balintore had bought the night before.

In the morning Palladis questioned him about the many friends in New York of whom he had spoken : was he not going to see them, or ask them to come and see him ?

'It would introduce complications,' said Balintore. '*Tous nos malheurs viennent de ne pouvoir être seul.*'

'What are you frightened of now?'

'I'm frightened of nothing! But having recovered something like peace of mind, I want to preserve it.'

'Then why did you come to New York? It isn't usually recommended for a rest-cure.'

'I must see Polly Newton.'

'Why don't you?'

'So much depends on it. Her future — her future may be in my hands, and that's a responsibility one can't take lightly. I may be wrong — I don't think I am, but one can't exclude the chance — I may be wrong when I suspect that man's — what's his name? Her employer.'

'Evershrub.'

'When I suspect him of taking her to London on a *voyage de noces*.'

'She might enjoy it too.'

'Don't you remember our first sight of her? A frightened creature, all alone at the cross-roads: afraid of leaving home, afraid of the unknown. She's not the sort of girl to enjoy a vulgar romp.'

'And a vulgar romp may not be Evershrub's intention. You've admitted that. He may, quite simply, need a good secretary. More and more people do. Among men over a certain age, or with an income above a certain level, there's an incapacity for life which only a good secretary can repair. A secretary is much more likely to be a substitute-nanny than a disguised mistress.'

'It's possible.'

'What else is worrying you?'

'It's seven weeks since I saw her.'

'And you may be disappointed?'

'One's memory does play tricks.'

'Then forget her. Avoid disappointment and don't make a fool of yourself by saving her from non-existent danger. — That's good advice, if ever you heard it.'

'Admirable advice,' said Balintore, 'and only a coward would listen to it.'

He went into his own room, and shut the door hard behind him; but opened it again, a moment later, to say, 'I've lost her telephone number.'

'Your little book's on the table.'

Five minutes later he returned to their sitting-room to say complacently, 'She's coming here this evening.'

'Here?'

'I asked her to meet me in the tavern, as they call it. The Golden Bowl Tavern.'

Ten

In the course of his disastrous interview in the television studio, Balintore had boasted that all his wives had been able to better themselves in consequence of marriage to him, and the experience they had gained by it.

He had indeed treated them generously, and though their conduct had never been faultless, he had always refused to take advantage of casual misdemeanour and insisted, in an old-fashioned way, on naming himself as the guilty party. But many people, while admitting that Louise, his second wife, had shared all the benefits accorded to the first and third, would have hesitated to say she had finally — or in her present circumstances — 'bettered' herself.

She had been a student at the Slade School of Fine Art when he first met her ; she was older than most of her fellow students, and much disheartened because an early exuberant talent was not maturing but receding. She had a lively spirit, a strident voice, and a figure of exceptional beauty. Her face had a snub, faintly negroid prettiness of a sort that would not have attracted much attention in the early years of the century, but was generally admired by her contemporaries. She said her father had been a Colonel in the Gunners — or sometimes in the Royal Armoured Corps — but now, alas, was dead ; though in fact he had been a farrier-sergeant in a Lancer regiment and still lived snugly in Northamptonshire, much respected by his neighbours. It was several years since Louise had seen him. She had much on her mind, for as well as her work at the Slade, she was writing a novel.

Balintore had wooed her impetuously, and allowed himself to be divorced after four and half years of marriage. For a little while Louise had enjoyed the fame of being his wife, and acquired a brief notoriety of her own when a gossip-writer announced the sale of her novel to a film company for £25,000. But the novel was never finished, and all she got was £40 for an option on it ; which was not renewed.

Immediately after her divorce she left London, and for a valediction was photographed at the airport. 'I have always wanted to be a painter,' she said, 'and now I am going to make a fresh start. I have heard of a teacher in Mexico who has been successful, on many occasions, in releasing a dormant talent, and I am going to work under him.'

Her talent resisted all conventional efforts to awaken it, but in Mexico City she met the action painter Ingo Pomador, and presently became his mistress and collaborator. She wrote to Balintore : 'You once told me, contemptuously, that I had no temperament, but before very long you will see — yes, see ! — how mistaken you were. Art has no boundaries, and Ingo and I have won possession of an aesthetic province that no one before us had dreamt of exploring. The old ways were not for me, I had to wait for Genius to direct me. But when I found my Genius, I found myself.

'To my old friends my new name will mean nothing, but I want you to know it. Henceforth I shall be known only as *Nova*. This is Ingo's wish and mine.'

Balintore had never shown this letter to Palladis, nor told him that Louise was associated with a man called Pomador. At that time the name of Ingo Pomador meant nothing to Balintore, nothing to Palladis, and nothing to the vast majority of ordinary people on both sides of the Atlantic. Only to a very few, to the foremost of the *avant-garde*, was it familiar and significant. They spoke it with reverence and prophesied his fame. Already he had done more than any other of the action painters to expose the faded insufficiencies of orthodox art, and the shallowness of mind that had characterised the so-called masters from Cimabue to Chagall. He had bicycled over furlongs of wet paint, and thrown small furry animals into pools of crimson lake and Chinese white. He had flung vegetable refuse at ochre screens, and pushed wheel-barrows across canvases splashed with Prussian blue to spill upon them loads of mica and dried blood. With boxing-gloves soaked in cadmium red he had punched the incontestable image of his vigour on to shivered panels smeared with Naples yellow ; and daubed a tight-stretched pair of *pantalon de toile* with the varnished entrails of bats, young pike, and hamsters.

In a hundred ways he had demonstrated the new revelation of mind and matter, of impact and resistance, that action painting had made possible. But except to a few of the *avant-garde* he was still unknown. He had to wait, for general acclaim, until he was expelled from Mexico and found refuge in New York.

He made no claim to have invented a new mode of painting, but merely announced, in a manifesto which became famous, his discovery that new values could be created by the willing co-operation of artist and model. Participation, he declared, was the essence of all modern activity — gone were the bad old days of loneliness and individualism — and to achieve the impress of a conjoint emotion he covered the backward parts of his model with carefully selected pigments — he used, to begin with, only pastel hues — and embraced her on a prepared canvas. To the subsequent prints he gave the striking name of AUTOPORNOGRAPHS.

His early experiments were interesting, but, as he himself confessed, of no permanent value. It was not until he met the former Mrs. Balintore — whom he re-christened Nova — that he achieved a synthesis of dramatic effect and aesthetic composition which no art critic in the world dared deny. But with success came, as so often happens, disaster : he was expelled from the country where he had lived happily for many years.

Fortunately for him, and for Nova, the action of the Mexican Government was immediately denounced, by all the most enlightened people in New York, as an example of hide-bound, intransigent authoritarianism — as tyrannous and impermissible obscurantism — and they were received, at Idlewild, as honoured visitors for whom every comfort and facility, including a disused studio on Long Island, would immediately be provided.

This generous welcome was characteristic of the temper which had dominated the eastern states of America for many years. The last vestiges of New England's Puritanism had long since been discarded, and often, when some obscure relic of the past — perhaps domiciled in Boston — had protested against the importation of depraved writings from Europe, judges of the upper courts had vied with each other to proclaim the Four Freedoms of the Arts : Freedom of Expression, Freedom from Suppression ; Freedom to Shock, and Freedom to be Shocked.

In this great quadrilateral of freedom — for which the New World had been discovered — the art of Ingo Pomador and his collaborator, Nova, soon became famous, and was accorded official recognition when the magazine *Time* was published with portraits of Ingo and Nova on its front cover, and a large and magnificent Autopornograph, in sultry colours, was bought by the Chase Manhattan Bank for one of the dominating rooms which topped its imperial new building above the Atlantic waterways that washed and fed Manhattan Island.

Then came the exhibition, of forty new works, at the Guggenheim Museum; and a few days after its opening, Balintore and Palladis had walked to it along the cold pavement beside the frozen tundra of Central Park — and Balintore had been shocked by the sight of Nova's name on the placard which advertised it.

Was Nova in New York? It was more than probable, it was almost certain. Perhaps she stood with Ingo Pomador to welcome visitors to the exhibition! How horrible a thought. — And how fortunate that Palladis had never heard of Nova, and so knew nothing of the emotion which had compelled Balintore to turn his back on Guggenheim and, at all speed, to seek sanctuary with Frick. . . .

Now, when he was going smoothly down in an elevator through the spinal parts of the Hotel Henry James to meet Polly Newton in the Golden Bowl Tavern — now he remembered with a sudden shudder that shock to his precariously regained composure, and with renewed dismay faced the possibility — the probability — that at this very moment Nova was one of the several million people who, within half a mile of him, breathed the re-breathed and re-heated exhausted air of Manhattan. She might, even now, be in a taxi slowly moving down 54th Street!

The elevator stopped on the ground floor, and with a shiver he rebuked his nonsensical fear. The odds against his meeting her were a million to one, two million to one, and therefore he had nothing to fear. But he was glad when, looking at his watch, he saw that it was only five o'clock.

Not for half an hour — half an hour at least — could he expect to see Polly, and he had time to drink one or two of those dry Martinis that only American bartenders shook to such cold potency. One or two of them would drown the last remnant of his ridiculous fear of meeting Nova — and give him the assurance to take part in what might well be an emotional argument with Polly. 'Better Dutch courage than native diffidence,' he thought.

Except for a brightly lit Golden Bowl on one wall — a capacious chalice like a secular interpretation of the Holy Grail — the tavern was almost as dark as a Norwegian barn in late November ; but more comfortably furnished. Two elderly plump barmen — acolytes before a heavily furnished altar — presided over a gleaming hoard of internationally distilled liquors, and silently replenished the glasses of the paired customers who, almost unseen in the general shadow, sat at small tables to discuss their urgent problems. A pianist in a far corner played gently such old and sentimental tunes as *Valencia*, *Lily of Laguna*, and the *Destiny* waltz.

Balintore drank with appreciation his first Martini, and going to the bar asked, in a clear Britannic voice, for another. A wish to ingratiate himself with the barman — which barmen inspire as readily as traffic policemen, first officers of ocean liners, and the examining doctors of life-insurance companies — impelled him to say, 'I'm second to none in my admiration of shad roe, American poetry, and the late Mrs. Roosevelt, but I doubt if your national genius has ever been so agreeably refined as in a good dry Martini.'

'That's what I certainly like to hear,' said the barman — but was interrupted by the sudden emergence, out of darkness, of a voice with a far-carrying tone that exclaimed, 'Ned ! Oh, Ned, what are you doing here ?'

Balintore, more startled than the barman — for he recognised the voice — looked round and saw a pale familiar face rising out of shadow, and with it, like the branches of an olive tree shaken by an unexpected wind, two wavering pale arms that reached towards him.

'Louise !' he said. 'Good God, Louise !'

On reluctant feet, with a sensation of unreal movement, he went to her table, and was fondly embraced. 'This is a miracle,' she said, and pushed him away to look searchingly at him, as if to reassure herself that it was indeed her sometime husband whom she held in her feverish thin hands. The snub and slightly negroid prettiness of her face had been subtly changed — perhaps by cosmetic operation — and now she had something of the impersonal, even abstract look of the professional model advertising beach-wear or a new skin-food ; but there was a sad bewilderment in her eyes. 'It's a miracle,' she repeated. 'You have come at the very moment when I was praying for help.'

'Not so loudly,' said Balintore. 'Your voice — it's even louder than it used to be, Louise.'

'Call me Nova.'

The barman brought Balintore's Martini, and Nova said to him, 'Another for me.'

They sat down, and Balintore said, 'I'm sorry — I'm very sorry — to meet you like this, and find you unhappy. But what's making you unhappy ? I thought you were enjoying a great success.'

'That's it,' she said, and looked at him in sore perplexity. Tears welled into her wide eyes, but were not shed.

'Success ? Has success made you miserable ?'

'When did you come to New York ?' she asked.

'A day or two ago. The day before yesterday, I think.'

'Have you seen the new pictures?'

'No.'

'I'm glad,' she said. 'Oh, I'm thankful and glad.'

'You don't like them?'

'They cast a shadow on my immortal soul. Or so I've been told.'

'Who told you?'

'Maybe God. I don't know.'

Balintore moved uneasily, and asked, 'How long have you been here? I mean here in the Golden Bowl?'

'Most of the afternoon.'

'Drinking?'

'What else is there to do?'

It had become evident that Nova had not only had a little too much to drink, but through her association with Ingo Pomador and action painting had acquired a slight American accent. There was a touch of severity in Balintore's voice when he spoke again.

'If I'm going to help you — and I must warn you I haven't much time — you'll have to tell me what's troubling you. What sort of trouble you're in.'

'I've got a friend——'

'Ingo Pomador?'

'No, not him. Not a man. She's a woman.'

Nova blew her nose and said, 'I think it's a great mistake to make friends with people. They try to influence you. What's wrong with people is they're always trying to influence other people.'

'In what way are you being influenced?'

'You did it too,' said Nova. 'When we were married, I mean. You tried, not only to make me do things I didn't want to do, but to think thoughts I'd never have had, so that

I'd do what you wanted as if I wanted it too. I don't mean anything wrong, but like remembering to write letters to say thank you, and pretending to have read Proust, and using olive-oil in the kitchen.'

'I don't see what that has to do with your present unhappiness.'

'You don't, but I do. You made me listen to you, and I got into the habit of listening to other people. This friend of mine, for instance.'

'What has she told you?'

'She's very intellectual, and religious too. She lectures on Comparative Religion at Columbia — *comparative* religion, though she's a Catholic. A Roman Catholic. Well, that just means, of course, that other religions don't even begin to compare with hers.'

'How does that affect you.'

Nova's unshed tears rolled slowly down her cheeks, and mournfully she said, 'I shouldn't ever have got mixed up with a religious friend. It's just asking for trouble! She's got friends too, and one of them is a priest called Father Dominic. She took him to see those pictures at the Guggenheim Museum.'

'What did he think of them?'

'I went and had tea with them — with my friend and Father Dominic — and he said I shouldn't have lent myself to that sort of thing. Not even in the name of art. He said it was wrong. He said it was morally wrong.'

'And that upset you?'

'Well, naturally.'

'But why?'

'Well, it simply bewildered me! So the next time I went to see my analyst, I asked him.'

'Your analyst?'

'I go to him three times a week.'

'What for?'

'Well, everybody does. You want to understand things, don't you? Why you aren't happy, and what sort of motivations you ought to acquire. All that sort of thing. So I said to my analyst — there was I, lying on the couch, and he was sitting up at his desk, taking notes — I said to him, "Now you've got to help me. I want to know the difference between right and wrong."'

'Did he tell you?'

'He blew his top! He got up and stomped across the room, and said he'd no interest in the old, outworn negatives of an obsolete society, and if I thought a conditioned reflex had any conceptual validity I ought to go back to Grade One.'

'I don't think I know what that means.'

'I tried to make him explain, but he just got more and more angry, and said I ought to know that if science hadn't got rid of everything which couldn't be explained, it wouldn't be scientific. Well, that wasn't much help, so I went and told my friend, and she said I ought to have another talk with Father Dominic.'

'Did you?'

'Give me your handkerchief,' she said, and mopped her freely flowing tears.

Balintore waved a commanding hand to the barman, and ordered two more dry Martinis.

'What did he tell you?'

'He says I ought to go into a convent! It seems there's a convent in Connecticut that gives instruction to girls who want to become Roman Catholics, and know the difference between right and wrong. And that's where I ought to go, he says!'

'Do you want to go there?'

'No !' she said. 'But if it's wrong to be doing what I do with Ingo, I don't want to do that either. I don't want to do wrong — but how do I know the difference? Even my analyst doesn't know.'

'It's a question,' said Balintore, 'that requires close and scrupulous attention.'

'But is there a difference ?'

'Oh, certainly. Of course there is.'

'Well, what is it ?'

'There are different ways of looking at the question — I'd like more time to consider it — and don't you feel too hot in here ?'

'I've got cold shivers running over me.'

'Perhaps another drink would help ?'

'That'll make seven.'

Again Balintore summoned a barman, and told Nova, 'Perhaps you ought to do what Father Dominic suggests.'

'Go into a convent ?'

He knew a moment's hesitation — he was aware that a latent jealousy of Ingo Pomador was in part responsible for what he was about to say — but he accepted the fact that jealousy had always had a share in the giving of advice, and said firmly, 'Yes, go into a convent and receive instruction.'

'But I don't want to !'

'If, after a few months,' he said, 'you feel you can't accept all you've been told — but if, in consequence of what you've learnt, you aren't inclined to go back to Ingo Pomador and resume your partnership with him — well, you won't be entirely without means to support yourself. Your allowance, your alimony as it's called, has been paid regularly into your bank in London, and if you haven't been drawing on it, there must be a substantial sum to your credit.'

'You've been very good to me. Oh, too good!' she said, and sipped a cocktail heavily diluted with her tears.

'I remember — but no!' said Balintore. 'There's no point in recalling a felicity that's dead.'

'But you do remember it?'

'As something trodden underfoot.'

'Yes,' she said, 'I blame myself for a lot — a lot of misunderstanding. I'm more realistic now. But I would like you to meet Ingo.'

'I have no wish to meet him.'

'He's wonderful,' she said. 'Oh, but wonderful! Though I don't suppose you'd like him.'

'No.'

'And Father Dominic——'

'I might not like him either, but the advice he has given you is good advice.'

'To go into a convent! Oh, Ned!'

She flung her arms round his neck, and pressed her face to his cheek. He felt her tears move slowly, moistly, down his neck; and patted her shoulder in a vain attempt to stiffen a muscular resistance to sorrow. Attached to him like a leech, she cried convulsively, and the pianist in a far corner of the room played softly an old-fashioned suite called *Indian Love Lyrics*.

One of the plump, soft-footed barmen came to them and said, 'Mr. Balintore? There's a lady here wants to speak to you.'

He looked up, across Nova's quivering shoulder, and saw, with a look of cold enquiry on her face, the slim figure of Polly Newton.

'Polly!' he exclaimed. 'My dear girl, I'll be with you in a moment——'

'Oh, no,' she said. 'Oh, dear me, no! Not if you're engaged. Perhaps I should apologise for intruding——'

'No, no!' he said. 'I can explain everything in two minutes——'

'There's no need to explain what's self-evident.'

'But there is! You don't understand — oh, do be sensible, Louise! I mean, Nova! I've told you what to do — do what Father Dominic tells you to do — and now here's enough to pay the bill, and remember there's a lot of money to your credit at your bank in London——'

'Money isn't everything!' she cried.

'No, but it's a damned great help,' he said, and pushing off her restraining hands he put down two ten-dollar bills on the table, and shouted through the darkness of the tavern — against the dulcet accidents of the *Indian Love Lyrics* — 'Polly! Wait for me, Polly!'

But Polly Newton had gone, and Balintore, stumbling against unseen tables, followed her through revolving doors on to the bitterness of 54th Street, battered now by a new fall of fiercely blown snow.

He could see her, a hundred yards ahead, and followed unhesitating, though without hat or overcoat. She was walking fast among a host of people that thickened and grew larger when she turned right on Fifth Avenue. From shops and offices a countless horde of clerks and accountants, stenographers, and assistant managers and junior executives, were hurrying in their homeward quest of cabs and buses and subway trains: muffled and rubber booted, heads down against the snow. The white storm whirled and eddied out of darkness into light, and swiftly glimmered in a curtained brightness before it settled as a cold mantle on narrow shoulders and broad backs. This way and that, the quick crowd divided —

held now by scarlet lights at a corner, now released in a great wave by green — but Balintore still kept Polly in view, and pursued her recklessly, undeterred by jolting elbows or the menace of snow-shrouded taxi-cabs, the sleek rush of a dark Cadillac.

Polly fled like a startled doe, and as a running doe in autumn woods avoided contact, met no obstacles, but made her unerring way to her secret harbour. Her harbour, indeed, was a secret even from herself. She had no thought of where she was going, or where she wanted to go. Twice, looking back, she had seen that Balintore was following her, and indignation was enough to sustain her flight.

He had invited her to meet him — pleaded with her to come to the Golden Bowl — and how revolting was the scene she had witnessed ! Balintore in the arms of a drunken woman, a woman with drunken tears channelling the artificial pallor of a mask-like face, and above her shoulder Balintore a caricature of consternation and vulgar appeal ! Oh, it was insufferable, and as she hurried on — on towards Central Park, across 56th Street and 57th Street — she hardly felt the stinging slap of the snow-flakes that fell upon her, but was moved only by desire to put behind her even the memory of so disgusting an encounter.

At Central Park, however, she staggered and was halted by a blast of wind and a blinding squall ; and Balintore nearly caught her. She crossed to the west side of the Avenue, and still hurried north, beside the railings of the Park. Here there was no crowd, there was no one except herself, and her sudden loneliness unnerved her. She hesitated, stopped, and turned — and Balintore came towards her, hands held out, beseeching.

Her flight had tired her, and most of the anger which

started it had evaporated as she spent her strength. What was left of it now vanished when she saw the ludicrous figure he showed.

His bare head was thatched with snow, and snow had crested his eyebrows. There were ridges of snow above the lapels of his double-breasted jacket, and a white clot at their intersection. His suit — of dark blue with a pin stripe — was spattered with clinging flakes, and darker than it had been. He was wet through and through, and though his breath came short, his expense of energy had engendered no heat. He was already beginning to shiver, and she started to laugh.

'I owe you an explanation,' he said.

'You certainly do.'

'And when you've heard it, you'll realise that I wasn't to blame for that absurd situation in which you found me. The poor woman who was crying — I wanted to help her——'

'Why?'

'She's in distress, she's in need of help.'

'Why did she ask you for help, if that's what she was doing?'

'She used to be my wife,' said Balintore, and sneezed with great violence.

'Is that true?'

'This isn't a suitable time, or a proper place, for fiction,' he said; and sneezed again.

'How often do you meet ex-wives and let them cry on your shoulder?'

He ignored her question, and said, with a slight stammer in his voice, 'It isn't the cold that's making me sneeze, it's a curious smell. Do you smell anything?'

'Now that you mention it — yes.'

'Wolves,' he said. 'A feral smell. But no, not wolves, not carnivores. Elk or buffalo, or something wilder. —

Waterbuck. Kudu, perhaps ? But why should I smell kudu ?'

'It could be yaks,' she said.

'*Yaks* ?'

'This is Central Park,' she said. 'There's a zoo here.'

'O God !' he cried, 'life's insufferable ! Why should I be strung on a rack of pain between action painters and Tibetan cows ? Help me, Polly. Take me somewhere and let me talk to you. I must talk to you before I get pneumonia.'

By now he was shivering convulsively, and Polly Newton, moved as much by a trained secretary's efficiency as by a woman's pity for male weakness, went to the edge of the pavement and waved commandingly to a passing taxi-cab.

The driver looked suspiciously at the drenched and shuddering figure of her companion, but was reassured by her explanation of his plight. 'He's a visitor here. He's English.'

'Did he swim ?' he asked. 'Well, get in, but it's another dollar for drying out the cab. Where to, lady ?'

'The Hotel Henry James.'

'A b-b-bath,' said Balintore. 'A hot b-b-bath, and then I can tell you what I want to tell you. Oh, I'm glad to see you again, P-P-Polly.'

'Don't try to talk, just relax,' she said, and sat as far from him as she could, while he shook and shivered in his corner.

At the hotel she paid the cabman, and they were received with some bewilderment. In the elevator Balintore took a sodden dollar bill from his pocket and said to the goggle-eyed attendant, 'Tell someone to bring up a bottle of Old Grand-dad as quick as he can.'

Palladis opened the door of their suite, and Balintore said, 'Don't ask questions. Give Polly a drink, and bring me the bottle as soon as it comes.'

A few minutes later he lay in a white porcelain tub of

water so hot that steam rose from it, and on the ledge of the bath nursed a tall glass of Bourbon, ice cubes, and water. Palladis came in again and said, 'I've given her a drink, and now what am I to do?'

'Keep her happy for a quarter of an hour, fill my glass again in five minutes, and I'll take over.'

Palladis found no difficulty in entertaining Polly Newton. He had helped her to take off her wet coat and hood, she had discarded her galoshes, and gone into his bedroom to brush her hair and repair her make-up. She had said yes to a Bloody Mary, and now, when he returned from Balintore's bathroom, she accepted another as if from childhood she had been accustomed to drinking vodka. She told him, with admiration and circumstantial detail, of the good qualities of her employer and the many kindnesses she had received from Mrs. Evershrub. And now, she said, she was about to go back to London — and then to France and Italy — with Mr. Evershrub.

'When?' asked Palladis.

'To-morrow,' she said; and Balintore, flushed and hale from a hot bath and Old Grand-dad, came into the sitting-room.

'What happens to-morrow?'

'I'm, going to London,' she said.

He had dressed, as if for a cocktail party in Jamaica, in trousers of yellow linen, a beach-shirt of tawny silk patterned with small red chrysanthemums, and a pink-spotted white scarf. The excessive warmth of the room did much to justify his costume, and it made him look conspicuously younger, healthier, and more attractive than the shivering, snow-patched pursuer who had been disconcerted by the smell of a yak. Polly Newton regarded him with a respectful interest when he said, 'Well, that's a coincidence. So are we.'

He anticipated Palladis' question, and gave him no chance to speak, by laughing in a confident, low key and saying, 'I owe both of you an apology for some very odd behaviour, and if you'll give me time — but you'll have to be patient — I can explain everything that happened between the moment I went down to the Golden Bowl and my bedraggled reappearance here half an hour ago. You may find it an amusing story, and perhaps you won't be wrong; but to me — no, it was far from amusing. I've been involved in tragedy, and I've behaved like a clown: that's the pattern of the story. And if you want to hear it — well, we'd better have another drink before I start.'

He told it with considerable skill. He compelled sympathy for Louise — or Nova — and portrayed Ingo Pomador as a sinister mountebank who had played Svengali to an innocent girl whose misfortune it was to have a good figure and no faculty of judgment. As for his own part in the drama, he regretted the loss of sympathy which had ruined his marriage — he spoke as if he had been married only once — and frankly admitted his contributory faults.

'I was selfish,' he said, 'and insensitive. That I can't deny. And when I met her again in the Golden Bowl, quite unexpectedly, I was overwhelmed by remorse. That, Polly, is why you found me ludicrously embraced — hating what I submitted to, but submitting because I couldn't deny my own guilt — and when you turned and ran, revolted by what you saw, I followed you, driven by a new compulsion. I had to explain. I had to clear myself in your eyes. Because, in the vision of your eyes, I want to stand well. I want you to think well of me, and fondly of me.'

Both Palladis and Polly Newton appeared to find it difficult to comment on his final statement, but Balintore was unaffected by their silence and said cheerfully, 'Now let's order dinner, just a simple meal, and we'll have it up here. A friendly, homely little party *à trois*, and Polly will tell us all about her adventures in New York. — Call the restaurant, Guy, and no matter what we're going to eat, I think we ought to drink champagne.'

A waiter came with a yard-long menu-card, and Balintore insisted on prefacing their meal with oysters : oysters from Chesapeake Bay, a dozen each. He and Palladis chose shad roe and bacon, but Polly Newton asked for a tournedos steak ; and when it came, showed an appetite that surprised them. Her steak, which was thick, was surrounded by french-fried potatoes, string beans, spinach, and braised celery, and accompanied by a green salad : she cleared her plate, and afterwards ate a substantial wedge of strawberry short-cake. Nor did her generous meal prevent her from talking freely about her admirable employer and his wife.

Balintore looked at her with doting eyes — listened to everything she said with enchanted ears — but in the lassitude induced by several glasses of Old Grand-dad and a generous share of two bottles of indifferent champagne, made no offer to go home with her.

'Guy will take you home,' he said, 'but we'll meet in London. Give me your address and telephone number——'

'Brown's Hotel,' she said. 'Mr. Evershrub always goes there.'

'Turn left when you come to Piccadilly,' he said, 'and past Burlington House you'll find the entrance to Albany. That's where I'll be waiting for you.'

'But I may not have time,' she said.

'At your age,' he said, 'there's time for everything.'

Eleven

THEY were able to get two lately cancelled seats in a Boeing 707 due to leave Idlewild the following evening, and Palladis insisted on devoting the day to sightseeing. 'I am not too proud for simple pleasure,' he said, 'nor so affected as to deny natural curiosity. I am going to see Rockefeller Center, the Empire State building, Greenwich Village, and the home of the United Nations.'

Balintore said he wanted a restful day, and went no farther than a bookshop on Fifth Avenue. His intention was to buy two or three novels, perhaps a new biography or book of travel, and possibly a volume of poetry.

The outer part of the shop, which was large and splendid, displayed nothing but expensive folios devoted to the arts of Umbria and the Etruscans, of Breughel and Kandinsky, of Vuillard and El Greco — opulent picture-books that illustrated the works of Dali, Botticelli, Picasso, Grandma Moses, Giotto, da Vinci, George Bellows and a hundred others — or portrayed the art and artefacts of ancient worlds from the Lascaux caves to Yucatán, from Knossos to Peking. All this tended to induce in customers the uneasy belief that man from his earliest beginnings in the valleys of the Tigris and Euphrates, in Thessaly and Honan, had been dominated by respect for the visual arts and found the ultimate expression of his genius in the quarries of Paros, the great cathedrals of Italy and Spain, and the ateliers — so clearly complementary — of the Renaissance and the Post-Impressionists.

For a few minutes Balintore himself succumbed to such a fancy, but shrugged it off as too extravagant, and was saved from any lingering suspicion that it might be true by what he found in the inner part of the shop.

There he saw shelf upon shelf — tall stacks of shelves — all filled with books entitled *Sex on the Campus*, *The Mating Habits of the American Male*, *Oestrus in the Suburbs*, *Sex in the Deep South*, *Sex in Latin America*, *How to Enjoy your Aberration*, and *Sex at Seventy*.

Against a ten-foot high picture of the Kremlin a new book entitled *Sex in Soviet Russia* was ostentatiously displayed, with the rubric in flaming red, 'It's in its Infancy, say Anthropologists'. Shelves elsewhere held learned volumes on the orgiastic amusements of ancient Greeks and Romans, of Persians, Arabians, and Chinese ; and picture-books reappeared to illustrate the erotic motif in Hindu sculpture. But the major emphasis was on modern America's triumphant discovery and enthusiastic exploitation of the primal facts of life ; and regional reports — *Anomalies in Arkansas*, *Fetishism in Fort Knox*, *The Sexual Symbol on Madison Avenue* — all contributed to a ringing declaration that sexual activity was recognised, not only as the paramount interest of the American people, but as the foundation of new and richly rewarding industries.

Balintore spent an hour or more among these fascinating books — sampling each chapter, reading a couple of pages — but as if perplexed or embarrassed by such richness, bought none of them. Instead, in a remote corner where older volumes filled the shelves, he found a cheap edition of Bagehot's *English Constitution*. Returning to his hotel, he read till lunch time, and then wrote a long letter ; after which he took off his shoes and fell comfortably asleep.

Palladis returned with a vivid account of his adventures

at Rockefeller Center, the Empire State building, Greenwich Village — 'But it's nocturnal, it was aestivating' — and the United Nations. He had found the last-named the most interesting.

'It was full,' he said, 'of coloured people. And when I say 'coloured' I mean, of course, what we call black, though few of them were absolutely black, any more than we're absolutely white. — How horrible we should look if we were! — But there they were, a teeming great excursion of black Americans from Detroit; though pilgrimage might be a better word. They took possession of the whole building, and I got the idea it had really been built for them, as a sort of temple where we paid the priests, and the priests were distributing the kingdoms of the earth among the people of the dispossessed and darker half of the world. And like a really good old-fashioned temple it had a bazaar attached to it. Down in the basement. And all those happy people from Detroit were buying souvenirs like mad, just as we used to do, many years ago, at Port Said. It's Simon Arzt on the East River, and chocolate heaven's the view from its top windows.'

They dined early, but not at the Hotel Henry James. After packing, Balintore grew restless and seemed nervously intent on leaving as soon as possible.

'I thought you might want to see Louise again,' said Palladis.

'You mean Nova. — But no, that's the last thing I want. I've done all I can for her: I've written, at great length, and repeated what I told her yesterday. She's not a particularly clever girl, but she was well brought up — both of her parents staunch Wesleyans — and now, when she's in trouble of a spiritual sort——'

'I should call it ethical.'

'Spiritual or ethical, what the hell does it matter? Do you think she knows the difference? Of course she doesn't. But with her background she's more likely to believe a parson than some damned head-shrinker who doesn't know the difference between right and wrong. Who doesn't even know there is a difference! But that's what she wants to be told, and any parson who's worth his salt will take a positive relish in telling her.'

'If she listens to him——'

'She will.'

'Though presumably she'll have to break up her partnership with Ingo Pomador — and she won't like the idea of living alone.'

'It has occured to me, since writing to her,' said Balintore, 'that she may already have looked as far ahead as that; and if so, she may contemplate coming here for another talk. That's why I want to go now! So come along. We'll dine at Voisin's and come back here to pick up our luggage.'

Driving again through the dazzle of light on the many-laned highway to Idlewild, Balintore looked back again and again to see if they were being followed; and could not restrain some little exhibition of nervousness when he saw that several thousand motor-cars were pursuing them with what seemed a furious intensity. 'They *may* all be occupied by total strangers,' he said. 'They *may* all be going about their legitimate business, but it seems unlikely. No, I shan't be happy till we're in the air.'

At the airport, in the apparently witless concourse of incoming and out-going passengers, he continued to look on either side for those who might be dogging him — Nova, Pomador, or their emissaries — but when hatches were shut in the long aeroplane, and the menace of its engines shook its fragile sides, he leaned back in his seat, relaxed and easy of mind. Perhaps, thought Palladis, too easy. He appeared to be in a friendly mood, and Balintore's friendship was sometimes almost as embarrassing, to strangers, as his ill will.

The aeroplane was full, and they had both been given seats on the aisle ; Palladis behind Balintore. On Balintore's inner side was a tall and burly man of noble aspect — bull-necked ; heavily boned in forehead, nose, and jaw ; tawny eyebrowed, bright blue of eye — who wore conservatively expensive New York clothes.

In the freedom of the upper air they fell into conversation as soon as the stewardess brought them champagne cocktails — which appeared to be obligatory at a certain altitude — and Palladis, who had a good ear, heard much of their conversation. The name of Balintore's stalwart companion was Thorgrim Thorgrimsson, he was a third-generation American citizen, and he nursed a resentment against the government of the United States so bitter that he thought of renouncing his citizenship. He showed Balintore his passport and said, 'When we get to London, I'm going to tear it up and put it down the can.'

This astonished Balintore, who with considerable eloquence began a laudation of the United States, and all its deeds and ideals, from the time of Jefferson onwards. But the more he praised the United States, the more forcefully did Mr. Thorgrimsson denounce his country. He went so far as to compare it unfavourably with Great Britain, and with this comparison Balintore warmly disagreed.

He let a steward give him a slice of truffled pâté of fat liver and a glass of 1953 Léoville Poyferré, and said, 'We all have our faults, but our faults — as a nation — are infinitely worse than yours.'

'That I can't accept,' said Thorgrimsson. 'I admire Britain——'

'I adulate the United States!'

'You in Britain invented all the good games in the world. And the rest of the world took your good games and turned them into bad professions.'

'We lost supremacy in our good games because we're mentally flabby, and idle by habit. Now in the United States——'

'What was invented for pleasure has been perverted into a quest for profit and prestige.'

'Because you take things seriously——'

'Only inessentials.'

'You judge your country too harshly. But that's characteristic of American criticism. And of American humour. I've often said that no hostile country need ever burden itself with schemes or policies to destroy America: it should subsidise American comedians, and they would do the job quicker than anyone else.'

'We've lost our old spirit of independence,' said Thorgrimsson glumly. 'We've thrown away the traditional freedom of the individual. And that's why I'm not going back.'

'Where are you going?'

'To the town where my grandfather was born. That's Akureyri in Iceland.'

'Won't you feel the cold?'

'It's a sun-trap in summer, and in winter no colder than Wisconsin.'

After supper had been served, a steward brought brandy, and Balintore and Mr. Thorgrimsson discussed in some detail the history and state of Iceland. Palladis still listened, but ceased to worry when their talk turned to the incidence of volcanic eruption and the price of fish. They, and he, presently fell asleep and slept till their cabin filled with the intrusive light of a molten sun that appeared to have risen out of Bantry Bay.

A stewardess brought coffee and tea, and Balintore and Mr. Thorgrimsson woke to the realisation that an overnight debate had not been concluded. They washed and shaved in a narrow aluminium stall and then, refreshed, resumed their argument.

'You've maintained your principles — kept them cleaner — than we have,' said Balintore. 'You cherish illusions, that I admit, but you haven't lost sight of principles. Now we in Britain used to have a name for honesty, but what's it worth to-day? Our parliament sanctions retrospective legislation, and that's dishonesty at the very root of things. Our Trade Unions clamour for higher wages, and our workmen scamp their work!'

'You've suffered many casualties,' said Mr. Thorgrimsson. 'Casualties that deserve our deepest sympathy. In two great wars——'

'The first was grotesquely mishandled, the second unnecessary. And in both of them the United States intervened to save us alive.'

'The United States wouldn't exist to-day if it weren't for the United Kingdom! It was your money, in 1914, that made us a world power, and your money in 1939 that pulled us out of slump and depression and made us the richest country on earth. We owe it all to you!'

'That may be so,' said Balintore, 'but it doesn't alter the fact that in both those wars the United States brought victory home to us. By the massive weight of your irresistible power!'

'If it hadn't been for you,' said Mr. Thorgrimsson, 'there

wouldn't have been a war for us to win! Neither in 1918 nor in 1945. It was you kept it going for us.'

'Historically speaking——'

'Historically speaking,' said Mr. Thorgrimsson warmly, 'we've got to thank you for both those wars. Yes, sir.'

'And what did we gain from them?' asked Balintore.

'Nothing,' said Mr. Thorgrimsson. 'Nothing at all.'

'Whose fault was that?'

'Ours. That was our fault. Our strategy was narrow-minded, politically obtuse, and basically wrong.'

'We never presented a clear-cut image of what we were fighting for.'

'And we failed to achieve it because we were too God-damned suspicious of your intentions.'

'And how right you were! We wanted to maintain the power and prestige of the British Empire——'

'And what better cause could you have had? The British Empire,' said Mr. Thorgrimsson with great passion, 'stood for sanity and civilisation!'

'It stood for the maintenance of an archaic and impermissible difference between ourselves and the ancient societies of Africa and the Far East,' said Balintore.

'I revere your Queen,' said Mr. Thorgrimsson.

'I respect your President,' said Balintore.

'I voted against him,' said Mr. Thorgrimsson.

'You were wrong,' said Balintore.

'No, sir.'

'I say you were.'

'Are you trying to teach me my democratic duty — you the representative of an outworn feudal system — do you think you can tell a free-born American citizen how to discriminate between the two great political parties which God created in the United States — one of which is manifestly right and the other demonstrably in error ?'

'I am giving you,' said Balintore, 'an opinion which has been moulded by a thousand years of democratic experience. We in Britain are the senior representatives of government by law and democratic practice——'

'No !' said Mr. Thorgrimsson. 'We in Iceland have the oldest parliament of all.'

'Which does nothing but talk about the price of fish.'

'While your parliament talks in its sleep about dead issues !'

Their argument, which had become confused, was interrupted by the serving of breakfast, but woke again as they went into cloud on their approach to London Airport. Then, resuming his original theme, and praise of Britain, Mr. Thorgrimsson spoke of the sympathy Britain had shown to newly emergent sentiments of nationalism in Africa. 'That,' he declared, 'is a true manifestation of your political genius. You in Britain have always been aware of the changing temper of the world. You led the way to the abolition of slavery——'

'In fact,' said Balintore, 'what happened was that we lost the will to rule, the will to dominate. India's demand for freedom, and the innumerable demands of Africa, all came later than Britain's own renunciation of empire. Do you know the meaning of *aboulia* ?'

'Of what ?'

'Aboulia,' said Balintore.

Further discussion was, for a little while, postponed by a sudden change in the tone of the engines, by a jolting, see-saw movement of the aeroplane, and a glimpse through its windows of a dark gulf in the clouds and beyond it a graver darkness like an apparent cliff. The aeroplane dropped — but its fall was arrested — and Balintore, gripping tightly the narrow arms of his chair, felt his palms grow sticky and a slight constriction of his chest impeded the natural regularity of his breathing. Then through the outer gloom there appeared the roofs and rectangular array of some suburban settlement — the dark elbow of a sullen river — and here and there the shrinking green of diminishing fields. The aeroplane tilted, swung sharply away from its previous course, and the pale brick houses of a larger settlement showed more clearly on the other side.

A few minutes later a broad runway leaned up towards them, pocked with rain, and Balintore felt an irrational anger against the island which covered itself with such unnerving clouds, and gave its visitors — and its returning natives — no better welcome than cold, umbrella-black, shoe-soaking weather.

As they ran slowly towards the airport buildings, and he realised that he was safely home, his anger found a harsh, intemperate voice, and he said, 'The word I used was "aboulia", which means absence of will, lack of guts, the decay and decline of volition. And that's the disease this country is suffering from. We call it tolerance, and pretend it's a virtue, but the truth is that we put up with every sort of iniquity at home, and all manner of insults abroad, because we've lost vitality, we don't care, and we're too near death to feel. We're like bums in the Bowery. Bums in the Bowery of the world !'

At this scurrilous aspersion on Great Britain, Mr. Thorgrimsson's indignation was so profound — and his muscular strength so exceptional — that in his effort to release himself from his seat-belt he tore it from its moorings ; and standing up, hit his head against the sloping luggage-shelf above him. He loomed above Balintore with a menacing fist. 'That is an intolerable and unforgivable libel !' he shouted. 'I admire

Great Britain, I applaud your history, I revere your Queen——'

A stewardess, with the gentleness of assured authority, said, 'Will passengers please keep their seats until the aeroplane comes to a halt before the main airport buildings.' — And Mr. Thorgrimsson immediately obeyed. But when the tall ramp of the gangway was brought to an open hatch, and he and Balintore emerged together into English rain, he spoke with the rumbling fury of a volcano stirring to life. 'I give you a last chance,' he said, 'to withdraw that vicious, abominable, and lying statement——'

'Don't be a fool,' said Balintore, and descended a couple of steps.

'Before you set foot on English soil — the soil of Magna Carta — you're going to apologise for a contemptible slander!'

'Go to hell,' said Balintore, and went a little farther down the steps.

Mr. Thorgrimsson put out a large hand to seize him by the collar, and Balintore, half-turning, struck it away. But he nearly lost his balance, and saved himself from falling only because Mr. Thorgrimsson offered a clumsy, swinging blow, and Balintore was able to grab his wrist. By so doing he pulled the Icelander towards him, and together they fell sprawling down the gangway onto the hard concrete skin that covered the nearer parts of English soil.

There were, unfortunately, photographers present. A young French film-star and a South American diplomat were also aboard the aeroplane and the editors of the more popular newspapers hoped to show their arrival, arm-linked, together. But the photographers immediately recognised Balintore, and took many pictures of his unseemly struggle with Mr. Thorgrimsson. The afternoon papers announced his return to England with manifest pleasure and facetious captions.

Twelve

As Palladis went up the steps at the Piccadilly entrance to Albany, a tall top-hatted porter emerged from his lodge to say, 'Good morning, sir. I'm afraid you're going to be disappointed. Mr. Balintore went out in a great hurry just half an hour ago.'

'Did he say where he was going, or when he would be back?'

'No, sir.'

'Well, that's a little odd. He knew I was coming.'

'Yes, sir. I was rather surprised myself.'

'Did he seem quite normal?'

'He was hatless, sir — though it looks like more rain — and wearing slippers.'

'Oh, dear!'

'On the other hand, it may be a good thing that he's plucked up enough courage to go out.'

'Perhaps.'

'For the last three days, he's been sitting in there, afraid to stir.'

'In a state of siege. But Albany can stand a siege.'

'We don't let undesirables come in. But we've had a lot of trouble with the press: they all wanted to see him.'

'It was a pity that he made so spectacular a return.'

'It's Mr. Balintore's way, to be spectacular, isn't it? But I don't hold that against him. I think highly of Mr. Balintore, and I'm very fond of him too.'

'Though he's given you more trouble than all the other tenants put together.'

'They're pretty quiet nowadays, that's true, but they weren't always so well conducted. And I think it makes a nice change to have someone like Mr. Balintore living here ; it's like a link with the past.'

'Well, I'll go in and wait for him, if you don't mind. I've got my key.'

'Yes, sir, and when he comes back I'll tell him you're here.' Palladis went through the guarded entrance, and slowly along the Rope Walk between the cloistral chambers on either hand. He stood aside to let an elderly, unsteady baronet go by — a baronet who was a Fellow of the Royal Society and a convert to Bahaism — and took off his hat to Dame Ethelinda Rooke ; who smiled charmingly but failed to recognise him. He turned and climbed three shallow stone steps to Balintore's chambers — the outer door stood open — and let himself in.

The sitting-room was furnished, a little too deliberately, in a late Victorian fashion, and on the walls hung large and rather dull paintings by Herkomer, Maclise, and Augustus Egg ; a great disarray of newspapers, scattered over a table, a long sofa and the floor, seemed a very vulgar intrusion on such formality. In a small dining-room breakfast-dishes still stood on the table, and in Balintore's bedroom — that three abstract paintings too assertively decorated — his bed was unmade. In the bathroom a crumpled copy of the *New Statesman* lay half-covered by a damp towel.

Palladis returned to the sitting-room and took a cigarette from an ostentatious silver box. He may be recovering, he thought, or he may — God help him if he is ! — he may be on his way to Reykjavik with Thorgrimsson.

The rough-and-tumble at London Airport had been explained away, more or less convincingly, by a joint declaration from Balintore and Mr. Thorgrimsson, that their fall had been caused by the giddiness consequent on a rough approach; and Palladis, Balintore, and Mr. Thorgrimsson had all driven to Albany where, to Palladis' distress, Balintore and his Icelandic friend had drunk, within three or four hours, three or four bottles of champagne, while Palladis and the porters had resisted the efforts of eighteen or twenty reporters and photographers to gain admission and interview them.

Balintore and Thorgrimsson had easily repaired their quarrel, and found a deeper source of friendship when it transpired that Mr. Thorgrimsson's dissatisfaction with the United States was of recent origin, and easy to understand. It was due solely to the fact that he had lately bought a property in Delaware from owners domiciled in Brazil, and sold it to a company in Caracas at a considerable profit which he had successfully deposited in Switzerland; and was now, quite unreasonably, being dunned by the United States Government for tax amounting to $947,000. Resenting this demand, and while the case was still *sub judice*, he had decided to forfeit his citizenship and retire to live in Akureyri. Balintore, to begin with, had applauded his decision, and almost decided to join him in sub-arctic freedom. But after their fourth bottle of champagne Mr. Thorgrimsson had shown signs of melancholy, and retired to sleep for a few hours in Balintore's spare room.

He had wakened to sadness and remorse, and to comfort him Balintore opened a bottle of brandy: a robust and fortifying Armagnac. Under its influence they recovered faith in each other's country — Balintore in the United States, Mr. Thorgrimsson in the United Kingdom — and before the bottle was empty had affirmed their indissoluble alliance. This discovery of an essential union stiffened Mr. Thorgrimsson's reverence for the Queen, and strengthened Balintore's devotion to the President. He looked with admiration at Thorgrimsson's heroic stature, and decided that he was an asset too valuable for the alliance to lose.

'America needs you !' he said. 'You can't desert America for the sake of a paltry million dollars !'

'I'm beginning to think you're right,' said Mr. Thorgrimsson ; and quietly began to cry.

'Not for all the fish in Reykjavik.'

'You're right, you're God-damned right. But England's always right ! We ought to listen to you, we ought to take your advice !'

'Not always,' said Balintore.

'Well, sometimes.'

'Yes, sometimes. Even if we can't help ourselves, we'd like to help you,' said Balintore ; and moved by some strange emotion, pulled out his handkerchief to wipe tears from his own eyes.

In the early evening they had helped Mr. Throgrimsson along the Rope Walk, and the porter had called a taxi which took their guest to the Dorchester Hotel. Since then they had heard nothing of him, and Balintore had spent the following day in bed, tormented by a catastrophic hangover and fear of the outer world.

Reporters, photographers, emissaries from the B.B.C. and the independent television companies, continued to call, and extravagant offers were made for an interview, for the story of his temporary exile in Jamaica, for an explanation of his quarrel with a fellow passenger in the aeroplane ; and though all were refused, and all attempts at invasion repelled, Balintore in the misery of his hangover was tortured by fears of the beleaguering world that was trying to pierce his defences and stretch him on the rack of intolerable questioning.

He woke, feeling better, on the third day of his return, but still refused to go out. Palladis spent a couple of hours with him, and tried to persuade him to take a walk. The weather had improved and the sun was shining. 'Round St. James's Park and back through the Green Park,' said Palladis. 'No farther than that. It will do you good.'

'No,' said Balintore. 'Wherever I go I attract attention; and my only wish is to avoid attention.'

'You could do that if you behaved more sensibly.'

'It's not as easy as you think. No, it goes deeper than that. They're after me——'

'Who?'

'All the malignancies of the world! I've been a fool, and the ghosts of folly wear black and wait for you like footpads in the dark. Oh, let's have another drink.'

Palladis had a problem of his own that he wanted to talk about, but in Balintore's present mood he realised it was useless to broach it. He wanted to go to Ireland, and his mother had urged him to be selfish. 'A proper degree of selfishness has never done anything but good,' she said. 'You tell me that he has a good daily woman who can cook him a simple meal, and what more does he need? You must be firm and say that you want a month's holiday.' — But the time was not propitious for such a demand.

It was on the following day — the fourth day after their return — that he called again and heard, to his surprise, that Balintore had gone out. He waited in Balintore's sitting-room, and when Balintore's daily woman came in, belatedly, to make his bed and clear his breakfast-table, he listened with a renewal of interest — he had often talked with her before — to her warm expression of admiration for her employer.

'It isn't everyone who'd put up with him, I know that,' she said, 'but I dote on him, I really do ! A man who doesn't give a shake of a bat's tit for anyone — if you'll excuse my language, well, my husband's a sailor, and I'm used to worse than that — a man like him, you take a pleasure in working for, though he's a bloody nuisance often enough — there I go again ! — but think of all the dreary ones, all those with enough money to raise hell twice a week, but just don't want to — they're the sort that I can't stand — but Mr. Balintore, well, you can hear him arguing with the best in the land, and telling them where they're wrong, and the next morning, as like as not, he'll still be in bed at eleven o'clock, with a splitting head and quoting dirty French poetry, and shouting for the alka-seltzer. Well, that's human !

'Oh, I like him ! And then the words he uses ! Mind you, I know a lot of words myself, because I read books, but Mr. Balintore — well, he spills them as if he'd forty thousand more and didn't need to economise. And I like that. I like a man who doesn't give a damn, and speaks like he was tearing up a dictionary that no one ever was going to need any more.

'We have our tiffs, of course — we have our tiffs and rows from time to time — but when he says, "Be damned to you, Mrs. Bint, if you don't want to work for me, go and work for the Archbishop of Canterbury" — well, I just say, "I know my nature, Mr. Balintore, and I'm a woman of your kidney, not his. I'd feel out of my depth in Lambeth Palace" — and that's why I'm still here. And now, Mr. Palladis, what would you like for your lunch ? Mr. Balintore's got an account with those big grocers just across the street, and anything you want, I can nip over and get it for you.'

Her belief in Balintore's splendid indifference to the world had very little substance, thought Palladis ; but it was widely held and accounted for much of his popularity. It would be idle cruelty to tell her the truth about him, and probably a waste of time.

He ate the lunch she brought him, and wrote a few letters. He looked for a book and found Italo Svevo's *As a Man Grows Older*. He was still reading it when, at five o'clock, Balintore came in, his shoulders darkened by rain and his slippers sodden by wet pavements. He kicked them off, and warmed his feet at an electric heater which unsuccessfully imitated a coal fire.

'I couldn't get a taxi,' he said. 'I had to walk.'

'Where from ?'

'Brown's Hotel. I went to see Polly Newton.'

'How is she ?'

'Well enough, so far. But I'm not happy about her.'

'What's been happening ?'

'She rang up this morning to say that her employer had gone off to Newcastle, to look at a house in Northumberland.'

'I like Northumberland. I used to stay with people — very rich then, but not now, alas — in a house called Northern Court.'

'That's where he's going.'

'It's a vast house with a fabulous collection of all manner of things from Chinese pots and porcelain to Italian Primitives. But they have to sell, I hear.'

'Evershrub has gone to see what there is, of the sort he wants, before the sale. The sale's advertised for the week after next. But I wouldn't be surprised if he's preparing a retreat, a hiding-place — Northumberland's discreetly far away — and the next thing on his programme is seduction under the Roman Wall.'

'Is that what Polly's afraid of?'

'No, of course not. She has no notion of the danger she's in. But she doesn't want to stay at Brown's all alone. She's talking of going to a married sister in Islington.'

'I doubt if it's any safer than Northumberland.'

'I told her to wait a day or two — "Don't be in a hurry," I said — because I think this may be my opportunity.'

'Now look here, Ned——'

'I know what you're going to say.'

'You can't afford to get married again.'

'I have no intention of getting married. I've had some experience of marriage — I've made a patient, thorough examination of marriage — and I know that it doesn't suit a man of my sort. I doubt if it suits any man. It helps to keep women off the streets, but apart from that there's not much to be said for it.'

'Then what's in your mind?'

Balintore went to his bedroom to take off his damp coat, and came back wearing a red silk dressing-gown. He took a cigarette from the large silver box and said, 'You're my friend, Guy, and a damned good friend you've been. No one could wish for better, and nothing of what I'm going to say contains any suggestion that our friendship's wearing thin — it will never do that — nor any thought, on my part, that there should be any change in our more formal association. But the fact is that in certain circumstances a man of my sort needs a female secretary.'

'That I can understand,' said Palladis.

'Now don't misjudge me! Or rather, don't pre-judge me. The fact is——'

'Something very different from what you're going to tell me.'

'My intention,' said Balintore with dignity, 'is to write my autobiography. Or, for a start, to explore the possibility of autobiography. I shall call it, I think, *Landscape with a Figure in the Middle Distance*. I mean to be fairly impersonal. I want to show myself in relation to the world I've lived in. I shall try to be objective. But objectivity, however rigorous, can't exclude emotion — that wouldn't serve truth — and I think the presence of a sympathetic girl — a girl like Polly Newton, for example — would help to release emotion. In a minor degree — a very minor degree — she will be my collaborator as well as my secretary.'

'Have you persuaded her to leave poor Mr. Evershrub ?'

'No, not yet. But it may be a week before he sends for her, and in that time——'

'The Figure in the Middle Distance will come into the foreground ?'

'If, in the course of a few days, I make such progress that the value of what I'm doing becomes obvious — and if she's really helpful — then I'll have good reason for asking her to leave Evershrub and work for me.'

'Do you think she will ?'

'I've spent half the day with her,' said Balintore. 'She's living in reasonable comfort, with a private sitting-room. I talked to her, I told her something about myself, and it was she, in fact, who said I ought to write the story of my life. I owe the suggestion to her — though the title is my own — and I feel it won't be impossible to persuade her that it may be her duty to work for me.'

'In which case,' said Palladis, 'you won't need me.'

'I shall always need you ! That's the simple truth, and you must believe it. But it did occur to me that you might like a holiday.'

‘As it happens, I very much want to go to Ireland for a few weeks.’

‘Everything is falling into place ! There’s inevitability in this — I felt it as soon as I went round to see Polly — but why Ireland ? What are you going to do there ?’

‘Help my cousin Honoria, if I can.’

‘Should I know about her ?’

‘I did speak of her. In Jamaica. She’s Honoria O’Turk, and her son, who’s at school, is The Turk of Mayo. From what she says — though she may be exaggerating — his inheritance is in danger.’

‘I remember now. They’re threatened by a mad geologist.’

‘I said an Irish geologist.’

‘And you’re going to lead a counter-attack ?’

‘I really don’t know what she expects me to do.’

‘But you must help her if you can.’

‘That’s what I feel.’

‘Good luck to you,’ said Balintore. ‘But leave your address, in case I want you.’

‘Here it is,’ said Palladis.

Thirteen

BETWEEN Piccadilly and Burlington Gardens — bounded on one side by Sackville Street, on the other by Burlington House — lay the enclosure of silence and decorum where in their day — or their several days — Byron and Gladstone, Monk Lewis and Canning and Macaulay had lived in their several habits of life ; and where now Edward Balintore, nervous and simmering with impatience, stood at his sitting-room window looking at his watch, and then, but without much interest in what he saw, at that small portion of the Rope Walk which his window commanded — he was on the ground floor — and the occasional figures who slowly trod its private pavement.

A youngish publisher, impeccably dressed — bowler-hatted, umbrella neatly rolled — went gravely by, pondering gravely the current state and cost of literature ; an elderly, red-faced man in tweed, with a leather case hanging from his shoulders, was apparently going racing — in April the little two-year-olds were beginning to run five furlongs — and Dame Ethelinda Rooke was going nowhere at all, but walking up and down for exercise.

Balintore looked at his watch again. It was five minutes to eleven, and from his bathroom where Mrs. Bint, again belated, was still swabbing or polishing taps, came a noise at odds with the peace and dignity of her surroundings. She was singing a lugubrious ballad :

> 'She was so innocent and youthful,
> That what I did fills me with shame,
> But I can't lie, I must be truthful,
> Though babes unborn will curse my name. . .'

'Mrs. Bint !' he shouted. 'How much longer are you going to be ? It's nearly eleven o'clock and I want to get to work. I can't work with all that noise going on.'

'Another two minutes,' she answered. 'Two minutes more and I'll have my skates on.' Without pity she continued to sing :

> 'So put me down with a painless killer,
> And tell my mother she'll find me here ;
> Leave me on ice in the deep chiller,
> And she'll still recognise her dear.'

It was ten minutes past eleven before she left, and as soon as she had gone Balintore went to the Piccadilly entrance, where the tall, top-hatted porter greeted him with the cheerful observation, 'No reporters to-day, Mr. Balintore. No reporters, no photographers — life's back to normal.'

'So it seems.'

'Nothing holds their attention very long nowadays, does it ? One day you're famous, the next you're forgotten : that's the way it goes now.'

'I'm waiting,' said Balintore, a little sharply, 'for my new secretary. I thought she might be nervous about coming here for the first time.'

'You haven't parted company with Mr. Palladis, have you, sir ?'

'Oh, no. I wouldn't do that. But he's taking a holiday, he's going to Ireland, and I've been lucky enough to engage a well-trained girl, a very nice girl too, on a temporary basis. — And there she is!'

He ran eagerly down the steps to meet Polly Newton in the courtyard, and taking her by the arm, in a proprietary way, introduced her to the porter.

'Miss Newton will be coming every day,' he said, 'and now that you know who she is, you won't have any hesitation about letting her in, will you?'

'She'll be made welcome, sir, like everybody who comes to see you — except photographers, of course.'

'Made welcome to Albany!' said Balintore impressively. 'And that, I assure you, is a privilege reserved for very few.'

He took her arm again — clasping her left elbow in a firm right hand — and slowly pacing the Rope Walk showed her where Gladstone and Byron had lived, mentioned some more recent celebrities, and bowed to Dame Ethelinda Rooke.

Going up the shallow steps to his own set of chambers he said, 'The spare bedroom's through there, where you can make yourself comfortable — the bathroom's on the left — and when you're quite ready, but don't hurry, I'll be waiting for you in my sitting-room.'

He considered, for a moment, the propriety of welcoming her with a glass of sherry, but on second thoughts decided against it. It would be better to let her grow familiar with her surroundings as a place of business. Strictly as a place of business.

She came into the room with a serious mien, and, as he observed, her professional insignia: a thick note-book and a yellow pencil clasped in her right hand. But how pretty she was! It was very difficult to think primarily of her note-book.

He made a fuss about seating her in proper comfort: the

light must come over her shoulder, and would she prefer to sit at the table — or should he move this small table?

'I'm quite happy here,' she said, and in a large leather chair, with a wing back that cast shadow on her face, neatly crossed her legs and resting her note-book on her knee, held her yellow pencil poised above it.

He turned away, and looking through the window made desperate search in his mind for the proper beginning — or any beginning — of an autobiography. The narrow view did nothing to help him. A clipped and mottled laurel in a tub, and primly drawn white curtains: a conventional view of no assistance. But at last, a little hoarsely, he said, 'Well, I suppose we should make a start, quite formally, with the title. So, for a beginning, write Landscape with a Figure in the Middle Distance, an Essay in Autobiography by Edward Balintore. — And a damned good title it is, though I say it myself! Well, now, they all admit there's nothing so difficult as a beginning, and as we've managed to make a beginning, I think we're due a little reward, don't you? I fancy we're entitled to a glass of sherry now. I certainly need one.'

'We haven't done very much yet.'

'Not quantitatively, perhaps, but qualitatively — well, enough to have earned some sherry.'

Here in his rooms she was more reserved than she had been among the neutral furniture of Brown's Hotel. There she had shown a lively interest in the work he had offered her. She had even preened herself a little at the thought that it was she who had first suggested the writing of a book which might well achieve distinguished and popular success. But now she maintained a professional silence, she waited calmly to record his words, and offered none of her own.

She had, however, dressed with some care, and looked

much smarter than the frightened girl he had comforted in an aeroplane high above the Atlantic. She wore a close-fitting dress of fine wool girdled by a broad leather belt, and admirable shoes and stockings: all, manifestly, bought in New York. Her make-up and manicure were unassertive, her hair was set firmly enough for an advertisement. Despite her silence Balintore grew more cheerful, and poured himself a second glass of sherry.

'I'm afraid you'll have to be very patient with me,' he said. 'The task I've set myself is to project an experience of life — my experience of life — and to do that effectively I have to decide on the pattern, the proper colours, the proper palette to use — or, perhaps more accurately, the appropriate key on which to play my narrative.'

'You should begin at the beginning,' she said.

'That's more difficult than you think —

> *'Ma jeunesse ne fut qu'un ténébreux orage,*
> *Traversé çà et là par de brillants soleils.'*

From the window he looked round to see if she was impressed by his gift of happy quotation, but Polly in a non-committal voice said only, 'I'm afraid I can't take French in short-hand.'

'No, no, I don't expect that, I was only saying — well, that sometimes it isn't easy to find a true beginning. Even a novelist doesn't really devise his own plots; they're forced upon him by what he has to say, and the end he wants to reach. Well, if I'm to write my autobiography, what's to be the end I aim at?'

'I suppose,' she said, 'you'll have to find an explanation.'

'Of what I was, or what I have become?'

'Of both.'

He went to a tall book-case and from a high shelf took a

volume in orange boards in which, after a little while, he found a marked poem that he read :

> 'There is rain in me
> running down, running down, trickling
> away from memory.
>
> There is ocean in me
> swaying, swaying, O so deep
> so fathomlessly black . . .'

'Who wrote that ?'

'D. H. Lawrence.'

'I think,' she said carefully, 'that you'll have to go into more detail if you want anyone to read your autobiography.'

He looked at her suspiciously, but saw she was wholly serious. She was thinking earnestly about a literary problem. 'Ordinary people,' she said, 'and that means most people, like a lot of detail.'

'What I pay for my shirts ?'

'I don't think shirts are important, but the things you've done, and why you did them — everyone would like to know that.'

He put the book back on its shelf, and standing before her, took her by the wrists. In her right hand she still held her yellow pencil. '*Das Ewig-Weibliche*,' he said, '*zieht uns* — no, not *hinan*, but back to earth.'

He stooped and lightly kissed the top of her head.

'No, no !' she said, and thrusting him away, stood up. 'That's not what I came here for — and if you want to write a good book, you shouldn't fill it up with a lot of quotations which most people won't understand.'

'How wise you are ! Much wiser than I was at your age. Perhaps I ought to listen to you, rather than dictate to you ?'

'If you're not going to be serious——'

'I'm perfectly serious. You've discovered, already, one of my weaknesses : I've a good memory, and I fall back on quotations when I haven't a ready-made opinion, or when, for some reason, I'm feeling nervous.'

'You're never nervous !'

'I've learnt how to conceal it. And you have to admit that quotations can be very useful. It was Bertrand Russell who said that the opinions of the average man are less foolish than they would be if he thought for himself.'

'That's another !'

'Because you have unnerved me, and I'm in no state for work to-day.'

'If that's the effect I'm going to have on you, there's no point in my trying to be your secretary.'

'You're going to be of great service to me, of infinite help : I'm sure of that. But not to-day. To-day — oh, let's go for a walk, and then have lunch somewhere.'

They had lunch at the Caprice, where eighteen or twenty people came to their table to congratulate Balintore on his return to health and England ; and Polly Newton was pleased to meet celebrities whom she had previously known only from the great distance of the upper circle or the infinite remoteness of the television-box. She ate a hearty meal, but their conversation, interrupted by so many visitors, was disjointed and added nothing to a solution of the problem of autobiography. Then, when the restaurant began to empty, Balintore called for more brandy and said, 'I depend on you ! Utterly and entirely on you. Come again to-morrow——'

'Of course. So long as Mr. Evershrub doesn't want me, I'll come every day.'

'But not till the afternoon. I'll take you to your hotel, and then I'm going back to Albany to work. What I have to decide — and perhaps this can only be done in solitude — is what I'm going to say, before I think about how I'm going to say it. I'll make a chart and a programme: a chart in time, a programme of events, and then, as I said before, you'll have to be patient. Patient while I improvise and try to find the proper key. I shall probably work all night, so don't come till the afternoon. About three o'clock.'

She was late again — it was a quarter-past three when she arrived — but Balintore was hardly ready for her. Mrs. Bint had wakened him at half-past ten with a cup of tea, but he had fallen asleep again and slept till two. Then he had lain for twenty minutes in a hot bath before shaving, dressing, and eating the lunch which Mrs. Bint had left for him: cold salmon, a salad and cheese, half a bottle of Montrachet in the frigidaire, and magnificent on the sideboard a luscious chocolate cake. Mrs. Bint had a sweet tooth.

Polly Newton came in when Balintore was drinking coffee in his small dining-room, and it became evident that she too was fond of chocolate cake. She sat opposite him and ate a large slice while Balintore spoke of the work he had done — 'It was five o'clock before I went to bed '— and showed her a dozen closely written pages.

'There's my chart and programme,' he said. 'I want you to make a copy of it.'

She read the first paragraph and said with surprise, 'I didn't know you were Scotch.'

'I don't know that I am.'

'But your father was.'

'Look at the next paragraph, and you'll see the circumstances, not of my birth, but of my adoption.'

'You were an orphan ?'

'I don't even know that. I may have been. I may have

been a derelict left by a dead mother, whose male parent was also dead. I may have been the unwanted child of a shiftless couple who were unwilling or unable to support a son who may have been legitimate or illegitimate. I know nothing about my origin. Nothing at all. But I was adopted by Alexander Balintore, of the Chair of Scottish History at Edinburgh University, and Isabella his wife, when I was apparently one year and five months old.'

Moulding in her fingers a little heap of chocolate icing, Polly Newton looked at him with a stricken expression, and said, 'A foundling !'

'Is that how I should start ?'

He wore an exhausted look, and his healthy Caribbean tan was reduced to a yellowish pallor. His eyes were lack-lustre and a little bloodshot ; and the curving lines that forty years had scored on his face, from nostrils to the outer corners of his mouth, were deepened by melancholy. Much of what he had written, during the night, had been extorted from a memory unwilling to release it ; and he had been aware, as he wrote, that his motives for writing were not simple.

He was, by now, obsessed by a physical desire that was still warmly coated with sentiment. Polly Newton, looking lost and tearful at London Airport, had touched his imagination, and he still wanted to cherish and protect her ; but the alchemy that turns pity to sensuality had persuaded him that it was impossible to do any such thing without taking her to bed. He knew, or thought he knew, that material or superficial inducements would fail to serve his purpose ; but he guessed, or intuitively realised, that an appeal for sympathy might open her arms and release a guarded affection. To that end he had sacrificed something of his dignity and set down on paper some fragments of a truth he still felt to be deeply wounding.

But while he wrote — while he wrote and burnt what he had written, and wrote again — another thought entered his mind, and though he recognised its vanity, he did not repel it. He, in the contemporary world, on a contemporary scale of values, had become a figure of recognised importance, and if he confessed the obscurity — indeed the nullity — of his origin, his achievement might well seem the greater.

Such a confession, he realised, would upset an established image. He had posed, successfully, as a person of consequence who had not had to create his authority, but had been born to it. The escapades and transient poverty of his youth were no more than the accidents which would befall any high-spirited boy who chose to flout convention and try his strength against the world. He had never complained of early hardship or identified himself with a majority born to hardship. He had, on the contrary, pretended or let it be assumed that a tone of authority had come to him by right of birth, and his opinions, which were sometimes reactionary — opinions which had involved him in so many public quarrels, and perversely increased his popularity — were the natural issue of a mind accustomed to offend and command.

That was the image he would have to discard, and would the new image built on confession of the truth — or some part of the truth — fill the place of its predecessor, throw a yet longer shadow, and suggest a still larger personality ? In the temper of the time, it was possible, it was even probable. It would be a painful experience, but it might earn rewards. It would surely move Polly Newton to pity and compliance.

'You are the first person,' he said, 'to whom I have ever told my secret story, and I'm still doubtful — very doubtful — if it should be told in public.'

'But you have nothing to be ashamed of! It wasn't your fault——'

'It's my misfortune, and misfortune is often judged more severely than a fault.'

'How long have you known — I mean, how old were you——'

'When I was told the truth?'

'Yes.'

'That's a sore point,' he said, 'and when you read what I've written there, you may be upset by what I've said about my mother: my adoptive mother. I never liked her — I think that's true, though one can't be sure, of course: memory's not honest enough, memory plays politics and tries to please — but I've no recollection of her that isn't coloured by dislike, and dislike certainly changed to hatred when she told me I wasn't her son in fact, but only a waif whom she'd chosen to feed and clothe. That was after my father died: my adoptive father.

'He was a Professor of History — Scotch history — but he made no parade of learning, he wasn't remote or pompous. Perhaps he wasn't a good historian, but he was an excellent father: or pseudo-father. He was serious about golf and fishing and claret, but not much else, and he used to infuriate my mother by saying that history was only a record of crimes committed by the upper classes. There would be no such thing as history, he would say, if the world had had an efficient police force. And when he was in that sort of mood, which was pretty often, I've seen my mother turn white with anger, and get up and leave the table. She thought a professor should be serious — perhaps she was right: I don't know — and every time he made a joke she felt he was undermining his dignity, and threatening hers.'

Balintore poured himself another glass of wine, and Polly refused — but then accepted — another slice of cake.

'And then he died,' he said, 'and I felt as if the house had lost its roof. He was playing golf at Muirfield, on a Sunday in February : a bitterly cold day, and perhaps he had done himself too well at lunch. He collapsed half-way through the second round. But I got it into my head — I was only twelve — that in some mysterious way he had been 'done to death' — that's how I put it — by his partner : a man called Patch, a retired Commander, Royal Navy, who was, as I thought, my mother's paramour.

'There was, of course, no substance — no substance at all — in that notion ; and till a few weeks before I hadn't known the existence of such a word, let alone its meaning. It was a school friend of mine, a rather precocious boy called Ricci — Italian by origin : his grandfather came to Scotland with a pack on his back and made a great deal of money selling ice-cream — well, anyway, Ricci knew how I disliked my mother, and when I told him she had gone to a concert with Commander Patch, whom I disliked almost as much, he had said, "I expect he's her paramour." He explained what it meant, but if he was precocious, I was the opposite, and I don't think it meant very much — except, as I thought, that they had formed some sort of league against my father. And when he died, playing golf with Patch, the inference was obvious : to me, that is, and to Peter Ricci when I told him.

'We had long discussions, I remember, about whether it was our duty to revenge him, and one day we climbed to the top of Arthur's Seat and solemnly pronounced sentence of death on both my mother and her supposed paramour. We went so far as to concoct a plan to murder her——'

'But you didn't——'

'No,' he said. 'At that age, your plans never come to anything. What did happen, however, was that we quarrelled more often, and more violently, and a dreadful evening came when I fell into a passion of tears — why, I can't remember — and told her that I had never had a happy day since my father died.

'And then she told me the truth. Whether it was deliberate, intentional cruelty, or whether I had tormented her past endurance — tormented her till she lost all self-control, and against her will blurted out what she had never meant to say — I don't know. But the cruelty of it was beyond doubt, and what I suffered — no, it's not possible to describe, and I don't want to remember.'

Polly Newton's eyes were full of tears, and when Balintore got up and stooped to kiss her, her lips met his in quick response.

'That's the beginning of the story,' he said, 'and no one but you has ever heard it.'

'I'll never forget it,' she said, and the tears ran down her cheeks.

He kissed her again, and asked, 'Is it a story that everyone should hear, or would it be better to burn those pages — I burnt a good many last night — and give up the whole idea?'

'I want to hear more,' she said.

'Come into the sitting-room, we'll be more comfortable there. And forget your note-book. I've talked enough about myself, I want to listen to you.'

But in the sitting-room he ignored her. He went to the window, and for a long time stood looking out at the Rope Walk; where there was nothing to see.

Deeply moved by his recital, he was not conscious of having lied to her when he said that she was the only person ever to have heard the melancholy story. He had told it to his school-friend Peter Ricci, to a companion of his adventure in Spain, to his first wife, to Guy Palladis, and possibly others ; but in the emotion wakened by yet another revelation he had forgotten those earlier occasions, and to give confession its proper effect — to make it as memorable as it deserved to be — it had seemed necessary to describe it as unique. He had had no wish to deceive her ; he had wanted only to ensure that she listened with a sense of privilege.

In that he had been successful. She too had been deeply moved. He turned and saw her sitting, upright in a large chair, with the look of one who contemplated, far off, a sorrow that she shared.

It would be a mistake, he decided, to take advantage of her sympathy. There was no need for hurry — and it would spoil the picture. He lighted a cigarette and went to a chair on the other side of the fireplace.

'Don't brood,' he said. 'It happened a long time ago, and I didn't tell you the story to make you unhappy.'

'My own life hasn't been so very different,' she said ; and was too busy with her thoughts to see Balintore's look of resentment at this unexpected intrusion into the loneliness of his misfortune. He listened to her with some impatience.

'Like you,' she said, 'I never saw my father. He was a sergeant in the 8th Hussars, and went out to the Western Desert before I was born. He was killed at a place called the Trigh Capuzzo on the 19th of November 1941.'

'You knew who your father was,' said Balintore, 'and that's a consolation denied to me.'

'But I never saw him,' she repeated, 'and when my mother married again, I got a step-father I couldn't stand.'

'Did he ill-treat you ?'

'Oh, no! He's never ill-treated anyone in his life. He wouldn't dare.'

'My poor child!' said Balintore, making an effort to show sympathy. 'We had no luck to begin with — neither of us — but luck may change——'

'I don't complain of bad luck! I've been lucky in lots of ways. I've been to New York——'

'Yes, tell me about New York. What did you do there?'

Her expression changed, and her eyes lighted as if with the glow of radiant memories.

'What didn't I do?' she said, and laughed happily. 'Oh, I could talk for ever about New York!'

She grew animated, and did indeed talk for nearly half an hour, much to Balintore's surprise; for her letters had given no sign of any talent for observation. But now it became evident that as everything had been new to her, so she had looked at everything with a childish fascination that still showed through the enthusiasm of her *reportage*. She had a remarkable memory. She could describe minutely the appearance of a room, or what she had seen in a shop; and repeat with lively exactitude a cab-driver's talk, dialogue from a play, or Mrs. Evershrub's repeated warnings against the dangers that surrounded a young girl in the turbulent great city.

It soon became clear that nothing unusual or of any great moment had happened to Polly during her American visit, but Balintore listened to her with a pleasure that dispelled the gloom of earlier conversation. Her enjoyment was infectious, he laughed aloud, and interrupted her only to say, 'But look at the time! I'm going to give you a cocktail, and then we'll have to decide what we're going to do.'

'I'll have to go and see my sister in Islington.'

'Oh, surely not!'

'She's expecting me — though I didn't actually say I'd go.'

'I thought we might go to a theatre.'

'Oh, I'd like that!'

'What do you want to see?'

'Do you think you can get seats for *Dig the Marquis*?'

'You've chosen the most difficult, haven't you? I know a man who can usually be relied on, but *Dig the Marquis* is booked for months ahead. I'll see what I can do, but you mustn't be disappointed if you've asked for the impossible.'

He went to the telephone in his bedroom and spoke persuasively for several minutes. Then he mixed a dry Martini and said, 'He's going to do his best, but he didn't give me much hope. — What do you know about the Marquis?'

'The scenery's wonderful, I've heard, and so is the music. And Tex Marlowe — I've seen him on films, but never in the theatre.'

'I mean the real Marquis.'

'I didn't know there was one.'

'There was indeed,' said Balintore. 'Before your time, of course, but his resurrection seems to have been welcomed by your generation.'

The telephone rang, and he came back to say, 'Your luck holds good! Two stalls returned within the last few minutes, and I've got them. Now what I suggest is that we have one more drink, then walk down to Wilton's for a dozen oysters — it's almost our last chance till September — and after the play we'll go somewhere for supper.'

'I'll have to go back to my hotel and put on a proper dress first.'

'Oh, nonsense! You're looking very pretty——'

'I'm not going to the theatre dressed like this. Not in the stalls.'

She spoke with the rigour of an ultimatum, and Balintore, not without annoyance, recognised that argument would lead only to his defeat.

'Then you must take a taxi,' he said, 'and hurry.'

'There's plenty of time,' she said, and put down her glass. 'Perhaps you'd like to finish it, it's too strong for me. Now where did you say I was to meet you ?'

'At Wilton's in King Street.'

'I won't be long,' she said ; and as she turned away, desire renewed at the sight of her taught retreat, so slim and rhythmical. And a girl with a character as firm as her figure, he thought.

At Wilton's she kept him waiting for twenty minutes, but her air of gentle dignity in a short black frock did not encourage remonstrance, and she ate a dozen oysters and brown bread and butter with a hearty appetite. Then they went to see *Dig the Marquis*.

The eponymous nobleman was the Marquis de Sade, and the drama, enacted with hilarity to an atonal music, dealt with — though it did not fully explain — the progressive disappearance of nine of his ten pretty little page-boys. Most of the critics, of the better sort, had praised the profundity of human understanding in its daring theme, and for several months enthusiastic audiences had applauded its witty inventions, the agility of an epicene *corps de ballet*, and the close dissonance of the chorus. But neither Balintore nor Polly Newton enjoyed the performance — he because it pleased him to retain some old-fashioned prejudices, and she because she couldn't understand what it was all about — and they left the theatre with no appetite for supper. Polly went home — that is, to Brown's Hotel — in a taxi, and Balintore walked back to Albany.

At eleven o'clock on the following morning Mrs. Bint was in a mood for conversation. She had been reading about travel in outer space, and some of the personal difficulties that astronauts encountered.

'You lose weight,' she said. 'You don't weigh anything, and nothing weighs anything. And very nice too, I thought. I'd go into outer space to get the weight off my feet. But then I turned the page, and what do you think I read next? Why, every time you pull the plug, you sprinkle the ceiling — or words to that effect. Well, there's a topsy-turvy world, I said!'

Balintore listened impatiently. She had finished her work, and nothing prevented her from going but her discovery that he had engaged a new secretary; whom she wanted to see. It was twenty past eleven when Polly Newton arrived, and half-past before Mrs. Bint departed with a meaning wink, whose familiarity Balintore found offensive.

As soon as she had gone, Polly took off her coat with a freedom that suddenly proclaimed her at home in her new surroundings, and said, with a smile of engaging friendliness, 'I never thanked you for taking me to the theatre last night. I didn't enjoy it, — well, not much — but thank you all the same.'

So amicable was her expression that Balintore — moved by her morning prettiness — put two finger-tips under her chin — a slightly avuncular gesture — tilted it, and lightly kissed her.

'And I let you go home without giving you any supper,' he said.

'Oh, I made up for that at breakfast. I had stewed pears, and kedgeree, *and* bacon and eggs. It's a very good hotel, Brown's Hotel, but I'm glad I haven't got to pay the bill.'

'Have you heard from Evershrub?'

'Not a word.'

'Well, there's plenty to do here, if only I could make up my mind how to go about it. To a certain extent, the problems confronting you — if you're going to write an autobiography — are precisely the same as those confronting a novelist.'

'You mean, it isn't going to be true?'

'No, no! But if I'm going to tell the story of my life, truth isn't the only object. I've got to tell it in a way that will interest people.'

'It's bound to do that.'

'Are you sure?'

'Well, you're such an interesting man.'

'Do you really think so?'

'If you knew the number of times you've made us laugh—'

Surprised, and a little hurt, Balintore asked sharply, 'Is that all I've done?'

'It's more than most people can do — in the way I mean. I'm thinking of the way you contradict people when they're talking nonsense — but the rest of us hadn't realised it was nonsense till you said so — and then you tell us the truth of the matter as you see it, and it all seems so easy that you're bound to laugh — especially when someone who thinks himself important is sitting there like a fish out of water, and can't answer you back.'

Gratified by this ingenuous tribute, Balintore went to the window to hide a pleasure which might look foolish. He deepened his voice, and said, 'Well, yes. Yes, in certain circumstances that's what I hope to do — what I try to do — and I think you've put it very well. There's such a phenomenal amount of nonsense spoken nowadays——'

'And you've made us laugh at it. Well, that's a good thing to do.'

She recalled, in detail, several occasions on which his explosive temper, combined with a rational intelligence and a ready memory, had discomfited redoubtable opponents, and Balintore listened to her light-hearted talk with a pleasure that deepened and spread until he seemed to be floating in it, buoyant on admiration. He was not unaccustomed to praise, but the measured praise of a professional critic meant little in comparison with the homage of this tender prattle. Here, in the warmth of pretty Polly's voice, in the dancing light of her eyes — here was his true reward. Though more sensitive, more intelligent than the majority, she was a daughter of the people, and to one who was no demagogue, who had never flattered the rude majority, it was gratifying indeed to find he had served its interests so well. And doubly gratifying to see that his image was stamped so firmly on its charming spokesman. How pretty she was!

It was not until half-past one that he interrupted her to say, 'I think it's time we had some lunch. There's nothing much in the larder — a Melton Mowbray pie and a lettuce, I think — but let's have a picnic meal here instead of going out. I went over to my grocer's this morning and bought a little pot of caviare, so we ought to make some toast and start with that.'

Polly Newton did not much like the caviare — 'It's too fishy,' she said — but she had enjoyed laying the table for their meal, ate with relish Melton Mowbray pie, and drank Vin Rosé in a tall triangular glass. In a moment of childish fun, appropriate to a picnic meal, she laughed aloud when a translucent fragment of jelly from the pie escaped her fork and tumbled to her lap; and Balintore, coming to the rescue with a napkin, took advantage of proximity to kiss the back of her neck, the angle of her jaw, and then her slightly sticky but not unwilling mouth.

She laughed again, and said ingenuously, 'But this is just like a real picnic !'

'There's not much more to eat,' said Balintore, 'except some yellow plums — out of a bottle, I'm afraid — and very thick cream. But with that we're going to share half a bottle of Château Yquem, and if you don't like it, you'll have to go back and work for Mr. Evershrub.'

In these circumstances they found it easy to maintain a conversation which touched peripherally on the subject of autobiography, and about four o'clock in the afternoon their topic was unashamedly the emotion which now united them ; and on the long, broad, comfortable sofa in Balintore's sitting-room they lay in a relatively intimate and overlapping conjunction.

But then he made an untoward movement, and Polly at once withdrew and said in a shocked tone, 'No, no ! Oh, no. Not here. Not in Albany.'

Balintore, releasing her, sat up and said, 'My dear, what delicacy !'

'It wouldn't be right,' she said. 'When I walked past that porter, in his top-hat — oh, I wouldn't know where to look !'

'My dear !' he repeated, and noted, with some surprise, that his voice was a little tremulous when he said, 'I love you.'

Softly, but quite calmly, she replied, 'I love you too.'

'Where shall we go ?' he asked.

'Nowhere to-night,' she said. 'I promised to go and see my sister in Islington.'

'Can't you put her off ?'

'No, not again.'

'Well, to-morrow.'

'Mr. Evershrub may ring up and say he wants me.'

'Write and say your engagement with him is concluded. You're mine now.'

'What does that mean?'

'We'll go somewhere for a long holiday. Have you ever been abroad?'

'I've been to Dieppe. Just for a day.'

'We'll go farther than that. Where would you like to go?'

For half an hour they discussed geography, and Polly cried a little, and said, 'Perhaps I shouldn't go anywhere. Not with you.'

He comforted her and said, 'Come to-morrow and we'll make our plans.'

'Not here,' she said. 'I'd feel a sense of guilt if I came here. Mrs. Bint would look at me as if I was keeping an assignation.'

'Then where shall we meet?'

'That restaurant you took me to——'

'The Caprice?'

'I liked that.'

Their luncheon at the Caprice was again interrupted by many of Balintore's friends who came to enquire after his health and stayed to estimate the attractions of his new companion; but in the intervals between interrogation and idle response they were able to debate the claims of Spain, Madeira, and Tangier; and decide on Italy.

'I can't promise sunshine and warm weather all the way,' said Balintore, 'but if we go, first of all, to Florence, we can see something of Florence and Pisa and Siena, before the tourists come swarming in; and then across to Arezzo, down to Perugia, over to Orvieto, a week or two in Rome——'

'Oh, wonderful !' she said. 'I've always wanted to see Rome.'

'When we've had our coffee,' said Balintore, 'we'll walk down to Charles II Street, I know a very good travel agent there——'

'I'm not going to walk anywhere in this weather,' she said. 'Look at that window ! It's pouring with rain.'

'All the more reason for going to Italy as soon as we can. "April is the cruellest month" — but I apologise. That's another quotation.'

'It doesn't sound like one.'

'No,' he said, beckoning to a waiter. 'Quotations from modern poetry often don't.'

Fourteen

SOME five or six weeks later, in the last days of May, Guy Palladis was fishing a large and viewless lough in the west of Ireland under a vast coverlet of dull, discoloured cloud from which, at intervals, came a wind-slanted drift of rain. A boatman of melancholy aspect rowed him with slow and lackadaisical strokes of the oars: a man with mournful eyes and a long red nose, clad sombrely in a black sou'wester, a ragged black oilskin coat, and cracked Wellington boots.

On their leeward side was a small island, rock-fringed and decorated with thorn trees and tall heather wreathed in mist. Between them and the shore the water lapped in grey, succeeding waves, and suddenly from its depths a trout rose, head and tail, to an unseen fly. Palladis struck on the instant, but touched nothing.

'You nearly had him that time,' said his gillie consolingly.

'It came nowhere near me,' said Palladis, and for another half-hour fished steadily without response.

Then, as if some remote and arbitrary stage-manager had decreed a change of scene, the sky broke and a watery sun glistened on the dull lough and burnished the white blossom of the dripping may trees, while the spreading light steadily exposed a far, romantic shore-line and the silhouette of desolate brown hills. Palladis looked at his watch and said, 'It's time for lunch.'

They rowed into the island, and went ashore on a little

beach. A mallard duck, with her brood pedalling anxiously behind her, fled from a coign in the rocks, and a pair of ringed plover flitted away, piping their complaint. The sun grew warmer, and Palladis took off his short waterproof coat. The gillie brought a satchel from the boat, and Palladis divided a parcel of sandwiches and opened two bottles of beer. The air was sweet with the mingled scents of gorse and may; the melancholy gillie began to sneeze. He sneezed six or seven times in rapid succession, and blew his streaming nose on a dirty handkerchief.

'You've a bad cold,' said Palladis.

'I have that,' said the gillie, 'and I can't get rid of it.'

He looked morosely at his cracked Wellington boots, and said, 'It's the fault of these bloody boots. They've been wet on me all winter.'

There was a jungle of growth on the little island, hawthorn and birch and alder, rank heather and sedges, and bluebells at the edge of the shingle. Palladis walked round the shore and frightened a pair of tufted duck, rose a heron, alarmed a redshank, and listened to a warbler singing behind a screen of dripping may. Black-headed gulls were hawking a hatch of fly, and a moorhen clucked among the reeds.

Now the whole countryside floated in brilliance, and far blue hills rose behind the ramparts of nearer brown. Green fields were emerald-bright beyond the sapphire water of the lough, and whitewashed houses in a blanched innocence shared the idyllic landscape with immaculate neighbours. To the eastward retreating clouds still obscured a segment of the sky and darkened the land, and in the west a little flocculence was creeping up; but the zenith was unflawed cerulean and the water a shimmering calm. Palladis sat on a rock, lighted a cigarette, and waited for the wind's return.

It occurred to him, without hurt to his conscience, that for five weeks — or perhaps it was six — he had lived in contented idleness ; and that, of course, was the benison of Ireland. Great parts of it, especially in the west, were still free from the nagging, protestant sense of opportunity — opportunity to be snatched at, opportunities one dare not miss — which had ruined the temper of the world and turned western civilisation into feverish competition for a place on the treadmill. Here, without reproach or self-reproach, one could do nothing, or next to nothing, for week after week and feel at home with undemanding days.

That he was living on the income of unearned privilege he readily admitted ; and did not let it worry him. — Though, he reminded himself, he must buy Michael Dooley a new pair of boots. — Privilege was a shrinking property, even in Ireland, and to draw a rent from it had become rare indeed. Even Ireland was threatened now by prosperity and industry : the Germans and the Japanese were moving in, and prospectors were piercing its ancient turf in search of oil. If privilege survived, it would be of a different sort and lie in other hands.

It was the erection of an oil derrick, in a field immediately below the north window of his cousin's drawing-room, that had brought Palladis to her country. His cousin Honoria thought it spoiled her view, but the local authorities were unimpressed by so trivial a complaint, and her lawyer in Dublin, after writing 'This is a serious matter and requires the most careful consideration', had gone fishing. In her distress she had written to Palladis, whose acumen and good sense she greatly admired, and soon after his arrival work on the bore-hole had ceased.

This was not due to his intervention. The geologist who occupied the ground had apparently lost interest in his original project, and was now intent on digging in another field, which lay immediately south of the house. To Palladis it seemed probable that his new effort would be as unsuccessful as the first, and in due course Honoria would be left in peace again. He had counselled inactivity and patience, and Honoria seemed willing to accept his advice so long as he stayed to repeat it every few days.

Palladis was fond of his cousin, and her house was not uncomfortable. As week succeeded week he felt increasingly at home, and was unperturbed by the weather ; which had been wet, cold, and windy. The fishing had disappointed him, for the river seemed to be in permanent spate, and there had been no hatch of May-fly to rouse the big trout in the lough ; but he had lived long enough to know that fishing was often disappointing, and a change for the better might come at any moment.

The bright appearance of the lough was altering already. The little clouds in the west had risen higher, a light wind had ploughed blue furrows in the shimmering calm. He called to Michael Dooley and they pushed out the boat.

'We'll go back along the shore,' said Dooley, 'where you rose that trout. You got a bit of encouragement there, and that's what we don't often get.'

His pessimism vanished when, within twenty minutes, Palladis caught a good trout of a pound and a half. 'I told you so,' he exclaimed. 'I knew there'd be one waiting for you here. And there's more to come. Do you go on fishing, and I'll put you over them.'

The wind was freshening again, but Dooley rowed vigorously now — pausing occasionally to blow his nose over the side of the boat with a fine dismissive gesture — and Palladis caught three more fish, the last a two-pounder.

'Didn't I tell you?' said Duffy. 'They're coming bigger all the time, and you'll get a proper one off this next point.'

A point of land ran out to three sharp-edged rocks, as rough as cockscombs, on the farthest of which the water was breaking white; and beyond it there was white lace on the waves. They were beyond the outermost rock before Palladis struck at a rising fish, and a moment later a trout as big as a grilse came arching like a dolphin from the crest of a wave and ran away with twenty yards of line before turning in a wide loop to windward.

'You'll have to follow him,' said Palladis. 'I'm almost down to my backing.'

Dooley turned into the wind — the nose of the boat rose and plunged under a curtain of spray — and rowed with short, hard strokes to keep pace with the fish. Palladis recovered line, but lost it again when the trout turned right-handed and made another run.

'A giant of a fish!' said Dooley, dribbling with excitement. 'I seen it myself. A great warrior too. But we'll get him yet.'

'Pull on your right oar.'

'I can pull all day!'

They were now in deeper water, rolling steeply, and the angle of Palladis' line grew steeper as the fish sounded.

'Steady,' he cried, 'steady! — Oh, for God's sake stop!'

But he spoke too late. Bending and heaving at the oars, Dooley's enthusiasm could not be checked, and his left oar struck the line which, now almost vertical, was taut as a fiddle-string — and like a broken fiddle-string flew suddenly loose above the waves.

'Is he gone?'

'He is,' said Palladis, and controlled his anger when he saw the gaping dismay on Dooley's face.

'He must have turned like a bloody woodcock!'

'He went down to the bottom.'

'It's there I should be myself.'

They sat silent in the rolling boat, and Dooley, catching the wind-tossed line, handed it in till he saw that the cast had been broken at the eye of the fly.

'The biggest trout I ever saw,' he said sorrowfully; and then, with decision, pulled in the oars and motioned to Palladis to come forward while he took the stern-seat.

'It's going to rain again,' said Palladis. 'I think we might go home now.'

'Not till we've had a try for another fish,' said Dooley, 'and I know a good place on the far shore.' He started the outboard motor, and turned the boat to windward again. He opened the throttle and they thudded against the waves, and plunged through them, under a continuous spray that was presently thickened by rain. Palladis sat with his back to the wind, but Dooley faced the storm without flinching, and under his ragged sou'wester his long, melancholy face, glistening wet, looked as resolute as if some noble purpose had made it firm. Palladis resigned himself to discomfort until such time as Dooley might decide that honour had been satisfied.

It was three hours later when they pulled the boat up on a stony beach near the village of Kilcoy. Palladis had caught two more fish — a small one and another two-pounder — and the lough was now so rough as to be dangerous for a less skilful boatman. But Dooley was still morose, and while he was taking down Palladis' rod said gruffly, 'You'll be thankful that this day's past and done with.'

'We've got half a dozen fish, and you'll have a drink before going home,' said Palladis. They climbed into the old Land-rover that his cousin had lent him, and in the village street stopped at O'Hara's Bar. It was dark inside, and almost as damp as under the dropping sky, for a dozen men holding dark glasses of porter stood, still as posts, in wet and sombre clothes that leaked the surplus of the rain they held on the sodden floor. But when Palladis had paid for two glasses of whisky, and two more, the scene grew animated, for Michael Dooley, after sneezing violently for a long time, had begun to tell the story of their misadventure with wild and splendid imagery, and in a voice as fraught with tragedy as the Chorus in a Greek theatre bringing dire news from far Cithaeron. Palladis left before he had finished, and drove to Turk's Court, his cousin's house.

Through tall gates that were never closed — because the hinges had collapsed — he passed a small, empty lodge and drove slowly up a rutted drive that bisected a copse of enormous rhododendrons. The road divided to enclose a circular lawn on which a marble statue of Diana the Huntress, with two leashed greyhounds, stood in the centre of a rose-bed, and by-passed the house to reach a cobbled stableyard.

The house was late Georgian, a large pale building whose architect seemed to have planned it by enlightened guess-work rather than acceptance of established patterns and proportions. It was too tall for its breadth, and the main door, approached by a double flight of steps, led to a stone-paved hall on the first floor. But it had an air of distinction, its dignity was genuine though impromptu, and in comparison with the stables it was not ostentatiously big.

Palladis left the Landrover in what had been the coach-house, and went in by the kitchen door. Two women — Mrs. Moloney who was middle-aged and pink of cheek, Nelly Kate who was young and rosy — welcomed him with exclamations of lively dismay when they saw how wet he was ; helped him take off his outer clothes ; and admired his basket of fish. He went up to his room, and lay for a long while in a hot bath of peat-brown water. He dressed, and went to look for his cousin, whom he found in the small sitting-room that faced south.

She was a tall woman, with a good athletic figure — though she took no exercise — who looked younger than her years despite a sprinkle of grey in her fair, thickly curling hair. She had a round, cheerful face, with a generous mouth — shaped by much laughter — and fine grey eyes. She was taking teasels out of a poodle's ear — a big dog with a lamb's cut — when he went in ; and looking up, said sharply, 'That horrid suit ! I hate green tweed. Why do you wear it ?'

'I must get some use out of it before I give it away. I'm going to give it to Michael Dooley when I go. And he needs a new pair of boots.'

'He's quite well-off, though you wouldn't think so. But he has to support a poor, hard-working bookmaker.'

'He's a good boatman, till he gets excited.'

'You stayed out far too long, in weather like this. Did you get anything ?'

'Half a dozen, and lost a big one.'

'You need a drink. Give me a glass of sherry, and help yourself.'

'What sort of day have you had ?'

'O'Halloran's back. He came to see me, and talked about the Firbolgs.'

'Do you think he's mad ?'

'No, not in comparison with some quite ordinary people I know. He was asking me about the little stream that starts half-way up Slieve Bloom and goes underground. He says it must run under the house.'

'Does it ?'

'I don't know. He thought I might have some old maps.'

'What else have you done ?'

'I went for a walk, while it was fine. I posted your letters — and I was given a telegram for you. Now what did I do with it ? I didn't open it.'

She found it beside a bowl of newly cut and rather rain-beaten roses, and Palladis read : 'In full flight from intolerable situation. Meet me Dublin at Hibernian Hotel to-morrow or soon as possible. Trust you to find secure refuge for me somewhere in civilisation's last stronghold. Now as never before I rely on your help and friendship. — Ned.'

He showed it to Honoria, who read it twice and said, 'Goodness, what does it mean ?'

'Probably less than it says. He's inclined to over-statement. Like Michael Dooley he gets excited, and plunges into bright waves of language as Michael plunges into a head sea.'

'Who does ?'

'Balintore. It's from my old friend, my master and employer, Edward Balintore.'

'I thought you said he was cured.'

'I said he was a lot better.'

'Well, he's had a relapse.'

'That's possible. I wonder what's happened.'

'The last time you saw him was six weeks ago in London, and about a week after you came here you had a postcard from Florence——'

'A conservatively chosen picture of Donatello's St. George.'

'On which he said, "The sun is shining on the Boboli Gardens, you ought to be here with us." — But you've heard nothing since ?'

'Nothing.'

'Who was the other half of "us"?'

'I don't think I should tell you.'

'Oh, come on! You've told me about his breakdown — about Jamaica and New York — about his second wife, and modern art, and the girl who was a secretary — what was her name?'

'Polly Newton.'

'Did he take her to Italy?'

'I suppose it's possible.'

'Then obviously he's in trouble with the police. How old is the girl?'

'Old enough to know her own mind.'

'I've heard the Italian police are very strict about the sort of bathing-suits you can wear.'

'He hasn't been arrested. The telegram was sent from London, this morning, and he expects to be in Dublin by to-morrow.'

'But he's on the run, that's clear enough.'

'I think you're exaggerating——'

'Well, I was only trying to help. I was going to suggest—'

'His coming here?'

'But would it be safe? There's Nelly Kate in the kitchen, she's only seventeen, and if he's in the habit of taking girls to Italy——'

'No, you wouldn't have to worry about that. He's not what your parents might have called a loose liver, so much as an uncured romantic. He's still searching — without much idea where to look — for his ideal woman.'

'Then I might be in danger! Perhaps a young and attractive widow is what he wants.'

'I know you're as young as you feel, but thirty-six isn't what he feels to be young.'

'How offensive can you be? Give me some more sherry.'

'Shall I say he can come here?'

'I know nothing about him, except what you've told me, because television personalities don't register west of Slieve Bloom. But personalities of any sort are rare enough — unless you count fox-hunters — and it might be fun. Tell me more!'

Fifteen

On the following morning, soon after seven o'clock, Palladis was wakened by a knuckled tattoo on his door, and Honoria came in.

'I've ordered breakfast for eight o'clock, which means a quarter past,' she said. 'I'm coming with you.'

'Is that wise ?'

'I woke an hour ago and decided it would be silly to miss the chance of a trip to Dublin. I haven't been out of the house for weeks : well, hardly. But I won't be a nuisance, I'll keep out of your way. You ought to have a long talk with Mr. Balintore, first of all, and find out if he's really in trouble, and if he'd like to come here. So the thing for you to do is to dine with him at the Hibernian, and spend the night there.'

'What will you do ?'

'If we start early we'll get to Dublin in time for lunch, and you can take me to Jammet's. I haven't been there for years, but it's where we used to go. Then I'd like to go to a cinema : almost any cinema. I've friends in Dublin, the Stirlings, and I'll spend the night with them. Anne was at school with me, she's English, and we'll have a giggle about — what did Mr. Balintore call it ?'

'The last stronghold of civilisation.'

'I must tell her : Anne doesn't know how lucky she is. And to-morrow morning I'll do some shopping, and we'll drive comfortably home again after lunch.'

'I like a woman who not only knows what she wants, but makes it clear that she's going to get it.'

'Then you'd better get up. It's a good four-hour drive, counting the time it takes to find a parking-place in Dublin, so we ought to leave at nine.'

It was a grey, clear day, windless and without much colour, and they drove in Honoria's better car: a small, neatly fashioned, black Hillman. Till they reached the little market-town of Claremorris they were on narrow, twisting roads, but then made better speed. Through Roscommon, Longford, and Mullingar Palladis drove in a freedom that motorists in America, England, France, and Germany had long since lost — the freedom from contrary or consorting traffic — for the good road was almost empty except for an occasional grocer's van, or where a monthly cattle-market filled a village street with lowing calves and haltered bullocks. They came into Dublin past Phoenix Park, and promised the Liffey a pair of swans for a near parking-place, but had to go to St. Stephen's Green to find one. They walked back to Jammet's, ate Dublin Bay prawns, and in the afternoon laughed contentedly at Peter Sellers. Then Palladis drove Honoria to her friends' house in Ballsbridge, and returned to the Hibernian Hotel.

He had sent a telegram to let Balintore know when to expect him; whom he found sitting by a window in the lobby. Balintore beckoned to him, held up a finger for silence, and pointed to a group of three people who stood at the reception desk: a small, trimly built, black-haired, bespectacled woman, and two short, sallow-skinned, round-headed men, one of whom wore spectacles and the other had flashingly obtrusive teeth.

'Japanese,' he whispered, 'and an hour ago I saw five of them — a group of five — outside Trinity College.'

'Does it matter ?'

'Downstairs, in the bar, there are three men talking German. The town's full of foreigners !'

'I don't suppose they'll interfere with you.'

'You're taking it too lightly. But we can't talk here, come up to my room.'

He led the way to the lift, and a minute page-boy took them up to the third floor. Balintore unlocked his bedroom door, followed Palladis in, and closed the door firmly behind him.

'From what you told me about Ireland, and about your cousin's house,' he said, 'I thought I could cross St. George's Channel and leave the modern world behind. But what's the truth of it ? Last night I dined, alone, at the Shelbourne : on one side of me were people talking French, on the other side there were Americans. And to-day, wherever I go, I meet Germans and Japanese. Dublin isn't a refuge from the world, it's Babel !'

'Ireland is becoming prosperous. Perhaps very prosperous. And a lot of wideawake foreigners are beginning to see its possibilities and advantages. Germans are buying land to get away, as far as they can, from the Oder-Neisse line, and who's to blame them — while the Japanese, so people say, are coming in to make leprechauns.'

'Leprechauns ?'

'Souvenirs for the tourist trade. They're very good at that.'

'Then it isn't the place for me. I want solitude.'

'There's plenty of that in the west. County Mayo and Connemara are very different from Dublin. But what are you running away from ?'

'I am not running away !'

'Well, let's say you have made a tactical withdrawal — or a strategic retreat. What's your reason?'

'That girl,' said Balintore.

'You were feverish with love's heat-stroke when I saw you last.'

'I was attracted, I admit.'

'What went wrong?'

'She has total recall.'

'Her memory, you mean——'

'Is an endless roll of fly-paper! Everything she has ever seen or done, said or heard, is stuck to it: words and episodes, boy-friends and female cousins as undistinguishable as house-flies, but caught alive and buzzing like mosquitoes! Once you let her begin to talk, she unrolls her catalogue and tells you, item by item, the history, structure, and relations of everything her glutinous mind preserves; and there's nothing it hasn't preserved.'

'I thought she was a shy girl.'

'She was. But she isn't now.'

'So you left her?'

'To preserve my sanity.'

'In Italy?'

'In Rome. But she followed me to London. — Oh, let's go down and have a drink. I can't talk about her without some degree of anaesthesia.'

The bar was crowded, but as they went in two middle-aged men, talking voluble Italian — Balintore winced — left a small table; and as soon as they were seated a plump barman brought them large measures of John Jameson's whisky.

Balintore drank his in melancholy silence, and called for another before he began to speak.

'What still worries me,' he said, 'is that she's a good girl.

A really nice, good girl. And to begin with, I suppose, I encouraged her to talk, because she was so frank and uninhibited — but don't think that implies a looseness of reference, because it doesn't. There was nothing salacious in her conversation. Nothing at all. She was ingenuous, that's what I mean, and because of that I found her amusing. She made me laugh, and for a day or two — yes, I admit it — I egged her on. I wanted her to talk. But then, by God, she wouldn't stop. I had turned on a tap that I couldn't turn off.

'We went to Florence, for a start and I showed her round the proper places. We went to the Uffizi and the Pitti Palace, to San Lorenzo and San Marco. I took her to Fiesole and Pisa, we stayed in Siena for a few days, and had a look at San Gimignano. I showed her enough to give even a girls' school something to think about, and keep it quiet; but everything she saw reminded her of something else. She recognised all Botticelli's models, they had all been at school with her, and she told me anecdotes about every one of them. And yet, you know — you may not believe me, but it's true — I was very fond of her. She has a good appetite, and that was a great blessing, because she didn't talk while she was eating. And I liked to watch her eat, she enjoyed everything so much.'

'And you went as far as Rome with her?'

'Arezzo, Perugia, Orvieto, Rome: I had set my hand to the plough, and I wasn't going to give up without a struggle. But Perugia, because of the view, reminded her of a holiday in Malvern, and Rome started a new stream of memory that ran bigger than the Tiber. She has seen every film that's been made in Italy, she knows the names of all the producers, directors, actors, and actresses. Between the Via Veneto and the Fontana di Trevi I endured a hagiology so crowded, lush, and opulent that I began to think of hermits and Stylites —

sun-dried, filthy, isolated, and remote on their ridiculous pillars — with an overwhelming affection. I left her two days later. Sanity was at stake.'

'You abandoned her? In Rome?'

'I'm not a monster,' said Balintore tetchily. 'I made provision for her.'

'How much?'

'I bought her a first-class ticket to London — by rail, not air — and I left her all the Italian money I had. It would come to about £60.'

'That's not much.'

'I wrote a letter, explaining why I had to leave, and a cheque for £250.'

'You can't afford it.'

'It wasn't a time for petty accountancy.'

'What was the explanation you gave her?'

'Have another drink.'

'Not for me.'

'I think I need one. — Well, we'd spoken of you, of course, and I had told her how dependent on you I am — she was interested in that, and became increasingly interested in you — so I thought a plausible excuse would be to say that I'd had a sudden appeal from you — a telegram, I said — to come to your rescue in a serious domestic difficulty.'

'Like Shakespeare, you saw no need to invent a new story when a very old story would serve your turn.'

'The old stories are best, they've stood the test of time. And, of course, I didn't want her to think I was leaving her because I was tired of her company.'

'Or that you had any selfish motive.'

'I've convinced her of that, unfortunately. I flew back, and the moment I got to Albany I was given a telegram:

"Following you Rome Express tonight. Depend on me to help all I can." At that I had a moment of panic — well, it would have been panic if I hadn't kept my head. As it was, I went in, packed another suit-case, and caught the next plane to Dublin.'

'Did you leave a forwarding address?'

'Of course not.'

'Then you're safe enough.'

'Not here. Not in Dublin. I'm surprised I haven't been recognised already.'

'Honoria wants you to come and stay with us. In the solitude of the west.'

'That's very kind of her. Do you think we'll get on together?'

'I like her. She's English, and she talks a lot; but not as much as Polly Newton. Poor Polly!'

'Poor, poor Polly!' said Balintore lugubriously. 'But it was either Polly or my sanity: I couldn't keep both.'

They went up to the restaurant, and at the entrance Balintore paused to say, in a tragic tone, 'Dido on the desert shore! I feel like Aeneas — as Aeneas must have felt — when he looked back and told himself that he had callously left her, and lost her forever.'

'But your Dido followed her Aeneas.'

'Yes, perhaps that makes a difference. And she'll have no difficulty in finding a new employer, of course: that's another difference. She's a first-rate secretary, and nowadays even fifth-raters can pick up jobs like strawberries in June. And they do!'

He found temporary release from his troubled thoughts of Polly Newton in contemplation of a catholic wine-list. They dined leisurely and well, and presently, having discovered that it was lightly raining, put on waterproofs and went out to walk for a little while.

They looked at Oliver Goldsmith outside Trinity College, and having dutifully remembered Swift and Congreve said, 'That's enough,' and turned back to walk round Merrion Square. The wet black pavements were empty, and the tall houses preternaturally straight-faced. They spoke of Oscar Wilde, and Balintore said sourly, 'If he had been born in our time, he would have put the blame on his parents. They were open to criticism. But he didn't.'

'A paederast and a gentleman.'

'For a different reason, I have never blamed mine.'

'Oh, don't start that again !'

'I might have good reason, if I knew the truth.'

'Look at that doorway. Isn't it fine ?'

'I have never blamed my parents, because I don't know who they were. Or who they are : they may be still alive.'

'If they are, they've forgotten you. And you should forget them.'

'I can't.'

'It was a very good claret we drank at dinner. Why has it made you melancholy ?'

'I told Polly Newton. I regret it now, of course — it was a great mistake — but that's what emotion does to you.'

'If you had told everybody, twenty years ago, you wouldn't give it a thought. You have nothing to be ashamed of——'

'That's what she said.'

'And she was right ! She was absolutely right. But you've chosen to make a secret of the fact that you were an adopted child — I can't think why — and by keeping it secret you've made it a guilty secret.'

'You don't know what it is to feel you have no identity.'

'Most people would say that you have established yours pretty firmly.'

'I have no background, no genetic identity.'

'I suppose one must believe in genes, but I'm sure one shouldn't take them out and look at them. Remember my cousin Weatherby in Jamaica, who's descended from a Regicide and a reformed whore — and from some poor exile out of darkest Africa. He, obviously, is much nicer than his genes.'

'Better a known Regicide than total anonymity.'

'You're wrong, quite wrong. Nothing can be worse than established facts. I once had a friend who was passionately interested in genealogy, and for his birthday I wrote a long poem called *Where my Chromosomes have Rested.* It was all too true, and brought our friendship to an untimely end.'

They stood facing each other on Merrion Street, while the rain fell more heavily. 'I shouldn't have told her,' said Balintore. 'I've given myself away.'

'Tell everyone. Give yourself away completely, and you'll have nothing more to worry about. But I'll carry a knowledge of ancestral crime — and worse than that, ancestral folly — till I die. You're better off, because you're free from blame.'

'That's worth considering,' said Balintore, and took off his hat. The rain fell heavily, and walking perversely slow they went as far as St. Stephen's Green and circumvolved its dark and dripping gardens. Their physical discomfort increased, but Balintore refused to hurry. A rapid change of temper had always characterised him, and now he appeared to have left his melancholy mood behind.

'St. Stephen's Green!' he said. 'It summons a score of thoughts, and at this time of night I can't identify one of them. But I salute them all.'

He waved his hat in the pelting air and said, 'I like your

Irish rain ! It's pure, unsullied, and strangely gentle. I feel, already, that I did the right thing in coming here. Ireland may provide the refuge I'm looking for. We must buy a lot of books before we leave to-morrow : Irish poetry, everything from Tom Moore to Yeats. And Higgins ! I must read Higgins again. Some of his poems have the very rhythm of Irish rain.'

They returned to their hotel — Balintore looking as if he had emerged from a waterfall — and without much more conversation went to their rooms. They breakfasted late, went to several bookshops, and at a quarter to one met Honoria and her friend Anne Stirling, and gave them lunch in the Hibernian Hotel. Balintore was quiet, unassertive, and spoke so discreetly that Mrs. Stirling — who had seen him on several television screens in England — said impulsively, 'I would hardly have recognised you !'

At a quarter-past two they put their luggage into Honoria's small Hillman. Balintore had told Palladis, 'I drink a lot, and sometimes I drink too much. But I never let my thirst drain my host's resources. We'll take with us some gin and some bottles of John Jameson's admirable whisky, and perhaps a little dry sherry.' — With this addition, there was room in the boot of the car for only one suit-case, and Honoria said she would drive. 'And Mr. Balintore will sit in front with me.' Palladis shared the back seat, in some discomfort, with three suit-cases, a dressing-case, a boot-bag, and several parcels.

A dull but dry morning was succeeded by an afternoon in which a changing sky tore skin after skin, as if off an onion, from an ever more shining brightness until the near-by fields, and a glimpse of distant hills, were all lighted with a purity of green and white and gold — of gorse and grass, a straggle of may-trees and a cluster of white houses — and in the exhilaration of the precarious beauty through which they drove Honoria said — this was a mile or two before they came to Mullingar — 'Let us go the long way round, and show Mr. Balintore how lovely Ireland can be when it's wearing its best clothes. Let's go through Galway, and to-morrow, when it's raining again, he'll remember what lies behind the rain.'

Palladis, annoyed by a suit-case, a dressing-case, and a couple of parcels that fell on him whenever they turned to the right, accepted the proposal without enthusiasm ; but Balintore, who, having talked of Italy, had found Honoria to be a willing listener, said loudly, 'Yes, indeed ! Show me all you can. I feel already that never — yes, never ! — can I have too much of Ireland.'

So at Mullingar Honoria bore left to Athlone, and by Ballinasloe and Athenry drove to Galway. There she turned north, on the west side of Lough Corrib, and through the town and the changing countryside beyond it Balintore gratified her by a silence broken only by occasional exclamations of pleasure.

'Words,' he said presently, 'cannot do it justice. We need a recurrence of the gratitude that some sensitive caveman felt when he looked out and saw that spring had come again. Those hills, that glimpse of the sea, these fields — this is beauty as the full but inarticulate mind of the caveman saw it. This is the innocence of beauty, and my country ! I am beginning to believe that this is where I shall live out my life.'

'All my English friends think I'm mad, quite mad, to go on living here,' said Honoria, 'and often I think so too. But every now and then — perhaps once a month — I feel that Ireland is the only place where a sensible person can bear to live. Though you mustn't expect too much of your neighbours, of course.'

Sixteen

'TELL me,' said Balintore, 'what this curious structure is.'

On the previous evening, driving from Dublin to the west, they had dined at a fishing-hotel by Lough Mask, and arriving at Turk's Court after eleven, had gone straight to bed. Now, at ten o'clock in the morning, Palladis and Balintore stood at the south window of the long drawing-room and looked at what appeared to be a stockaded camp or zariba in an open field whose near boundary, barely ten yards from the house, was marked by a broken fence above an overgrown ha-ha.

'That's where O'Halloran is working now,' said Palladis.

'The mad geologist ?'

'You'll meet him, sooner or later. I see him from time to time, and rather like him. But he's a great nuisance to Honoria.'

'Did she give him permission to start mining there ?'

'She's done everything she could to keep him out and get rid of him. She's tried twice to get an injunction against him, she's pleaded loss of amenity as well as actual danger to the house, but her lawyers can do nothing. The law itself is on the other side of the fence. O'Halloran is the legal tenant of two fields, one on each side of the house, and nowadays a tenant's in a stronger position than the landlord. The landlord had a long innings, but he's out of luck to-day.'

They turned and walked to the other end of the long room. It was a handsome room, with a pale golden floor and Persian rugs, eight ancestral portraits of great size and forbidding aspect, a lot of miscellaneous furniture, and dominating all, two vast and glittering chandeliers of Waterford glass. Then from the north window they looked at the derrick which stood less than a hundred yards away. It was some sixty or seventy feet high, sturdily built and firmly bedded on broad wooden sills, and near it was an old-fashioned steam traction-engine.

'He built that when he was prospecting for oil,' said Palladis. 'It's not, I believe, the most modern rig, but very ingenious. There's a heavy bit, a sort of chisel, at the end of the cable, and what's called a rocking-beam bounced it up and down in the hole he was cutting; which gradually got deeper. The traction-engine gave him his power, and used to make a lot of noise.'

'Did he find any oil?'

'Oh, no.'

'Is there any oil-bearing rock in this part of Ireland?'

'O'Halloran thought so. People are drilling in other places, but perhaps only as an experiment.'

'He must have had some reason for sinking a well here. Or starting to sink one.'

'He was using a forked twig, like a water-diviner, and it reacted so strongly here that it brought him to his knees. But more important than that, he's found — or says he has found — a hitherto unknown manuscript of the Annals of Innisfallen in which there's a reference to a hermit who lived somewhere near here in a cell miraculously lighted. Or, as he says, lighted by natural gas.'

'Why has he abandoned his well?'

'I don't think he has. But there's another reference in the Annals — or in his manuscript — to alluvial gold in the little brook that comes out above the village. So he's begun to sink a gold-mine to get enough gold to buy modern equipment to strike oil. Or so I gather.'

They walked back to the south window, and looked at the zariba in the field beyond the ha-ha. From a chimney on the square hut with a corrugated iron roof that stood within the six-foot high wattle fence came little gouts of steam, and they could hear, like an iron pulse, the noise of a small engine.

'There are two things I don't understand,' said Balintore. 'Why, in the first place, is he sinking a mine here if he hopes to find alluvial gold in a brook near the village?'

'I think you should wait till you meet O'Halloran. He can probably give you a more convincing answer than I could.'

'And in the second place, how has it come about that a house of this sort — the great house of the district, a mansion house — lies pinched between two fields whose tenant appears to be mad, and is evidently beyond control?'

'You must ask Honoria about that. It's a thing that worries her very much, and she likes to talk about it.'

'She's an attractive woman,' said Balintore.

'At present,' said Palladis severely, 'I consider myself her guardian.'

'Physically,' said Balintore, 'she doesn't appeal to me. She reminds me of the pineapple you often see at the centre of a dish of fruit on the top table at a banquet. It's agreeably flamboyant, it looks well on a richly appointed table, but it's there for appearance rather than use.'

'I am very fond of her.'

'I admire her. But I don't ask for her any more than I would ask for the pineapple in a pyramid of fruit on a silver platter. What one puts on one's plate is a few grapes.'

'In Ireland you won't even get grapes.'

'I shan't look for them. I've had a surfeit.'

'Let us go for a little drive,' said Palladis, 'and I'll show you something of the country.'

The weather was still warm and bright, and in the Land-rover they drove through the village to the many-islanded lough where Palladis fished with occasional success. The gently coloured scene excited Balintore's lively admiration. Blue hills rose sharply into the mild vacancy of the sky, and rocky islands, turreted or plumed with trees, were lapped by little genial waves. Gorse patched the fields with gold, and faultlessly-white cottages were halted, as it seemed, in an unpremeditated approach to their first communion. A dunlin tip-toed across grey pebbles, and a trout rose in the middle of concentric ripples.

'I haven't fished since I was a boy,' said Balintore. 'My father — my adoptive father — taught me to cast on the little lochs, or reservoirs, in the Pentland Hills. And sometimes we fished a river called the Blackadder in Berwickshire.'

'If you want to,' said Palladis, 'you can fish here every day of the week. And every now and then, if you're persistent, you'll get a good basket.'

'But I haven't a rod. I've got no tackle——'

'You can borrow all you need. There are plenty of rods in the house.'

'When can I start?'

'You'll need a gillie, and if you employ an old fellow called Michael Dooley you'll be doing him a good turn. We'll stop at O'Hara's Bar on the way back, and see if we can find him.'

'I believe,' said Balintore, 'that this is the haven I've been looking for. I thought I had found it in Jamaica, but that was a delusion. The haven wasn't enclosed, it was open to unwelcome visitors and incursions from the past. And talking of Jamaica, have you had any news of Weatherby Scroope?'

'He's married,' said Palladis.

'Married? But he was all against marriage. When he left us he was going to Florida to stop his father getting married.'

'He went to Palm Beach, where he met his father and the woman who was threatening to become his stepmother. They had, I gather, a lively argument. A long and acrimonious argument. Perhaps you could describe it as a row. And the consequence was that the old man had a stroke: a thrombosis, I suppose — that newly devised escape-hatch from the intolerable confinements of modern life. But this wasn't a fatal attack; only disabling. It left the old man partially paralysed and capable only of the infantilities of speech. So Weatherby and the American widow had to nurse him, and in the intimacies of the sick-room Weatherby apparently discovered virtues in her that he hadn't suspected — or, as an alternative, she found in him a livelier surrogate for the comfort she had anticipated from his father — and with the old man's blessing a marriage was arranged, and they have all gone back to the Great House at Fort Appin.'

'Good God!' said Balintore.

'Do you think He is?'

'But that nice black woman with the lovely teeth and the engulfing smile — Mary, who looked after us so well, and was, you said, his mistress — what has happened to her?'

'He didn't speak of her. But black women have always gone into the discard at a certain stage in the game — and I've no doubt that Weatherby has been generous to her.'

'In my opinion,' said Balintore primly, 'that's a shocking and distasteful story.'

'Let us go to O'Hara's Bar,' said Palladis.

He drove the Landrover back to the village, where Balintore

insisted on walking round the little square which was dominated from above by two enormous churches, and consoled on its own level by four public-houses. In the centre of the square stood a time-worn memorial with an inscription long effaced by the weather — but it was generally supposed to commemorate a patriot who had died in 1798 — and east and west from it ran the main street, which was enlivened by a dozen shops with brightly painted fronts, a garage and some petrol pumps, and two more public-houses ; and to the east was ennobled by the ruins of an ancient abbey.

'If, after a few weeks,' said Balintore, 'I become a burden to Honoria, I can, I suppose, find rooms somewhere in the village. — Nowhere in the world have I seen a place that has made so immediate an appeal, that was so instantly attractive, as this. Here's the country I've been looking for, and here, if I can find accommodation, is where I'm going to settle down. Here's where I'll live with contentment as my neighbour.'

'There was a hospice or guest-house in the sixteenth century,' said Palladis, 'but it was burnt by someone trying to pacify Ireland — either for Elizabeth or James I, I can't remember — and it has never been rebuilt. No, you wouldn't find accommodation in the village, but you can stay with Honoria as long as you like. She's always glad of company.'

They went into O'Hara's Bar and found the melancholy Michael Dooley drinking a pint of porter. He was wearing a new pair of Wellington boots, and had almost recovered from his persistent cold. He gladly agreed to look after Mr. Balintore, and promised to put him over rising fish with unfailing regularity. They agreed to meet the following morning, and Dooley accepted another pint of porter.

For a whole week they woke to tall skies and bright, unclouded weather, and Balintore persuaded himself that he had found, not only a delectable refuge in the outermost surviving parts of civilisation, but a hitherto unmapped territory where halcyon days were guaranteed by isobars of incredible benignity. He went fishing every day with Michael Dooley, and though he caught nothing but an occasional six-ounce trout, he would come ashore in the evening and protest his perfect enjoyment. He would repeat the long conversations he had had with Dooley, he would describe inaccurately the wading-birds and ducks he had seen, and usually he produced a bunch of faded flowers, twigs, and rushes — gathered on the island where he had gone ashore for lunch — and asked Honoria to identify them.

At dinner he listened attentively to her gossip of the countryside, and one evening, when she spoke of her late husband, asked her, 'Was it he who gave O'Halloran his lease of those two fields?'

'Oh, no,' she said. 'No, it began earlier than that. It was Charles's father who gave O'Halloran's father a lease, or perhaps confirmed him in a lease that his grandfather had been given: it isn't easy to sort these things out. O'Halloran's father was a sergeant in the Connaught Rangers — they were disbanded, of course: such a pity, don't you think? Those Irish regiments were *so* good, I don't believe we'd have lost our Empire if we'd kept hold of them. But it was all mixed up with politics, of course, and when people get politically interested they lose sight of everything that matters, don't they? — Well, as I was saying, O'Halloran's father was a sergeant in the regiment that Charles's father commanded, and when he was our tenant he was no trouble at all: or so I've always heard. He kept a couple of cows, and did odd jobs about the demesne, and no one could have been nicer. Well, in those old-fashioned regiments everyone was nice, weren't they? But young O'Halloran — our O'Halloran — was a very clever boy, and troublesome from the start; though Charles liked him. Charles encouraged him, and helped him when he decided not to be a priest, as his mother wanted, but to study science. I know Charles lent him money to go to college in Galway, and whether that did him any good or not, who can tell? They teach science in Irish there, and that can't be easy.'

'How old is O'Halloran?'

'He was about the same age as Charles, I think, and Charles was ten years older than me. But haven't you met him yet?'

'No.'

'Oh, you'll have to meet him! Shall we ask him to dinner, Guy?'

'I thought you were bitter enemies,' said Balintore.

'So we are, but that's no reason why he shouldn't come to dinner. He can be very amusing, if he's in a good mood. He's been to Canada and Australia, looking for the sort of things that geologists do look for — minerals, I suppose, though I don't think he ever found any — and in the Hitler war he was in Italy with one of those Irish regiments that we didn't disband, thank goodness. And before that he fought in Spain. For Franco, of course. He was still a Catholic then.'

'He fought in Spain?' said Balintore.

'I don't know for how long, but long enough to get wounded. Charles was very jealous of him, but in spite of that helped him to go to college when he came home from Spain. And you've seen how he rewards us for Charles's kindness!'

'If Charles had lived,' said Palladis——

'It would have made no difference to anyone except me! Charles couldn't have got rid of him, and I can't get rid of him — so let's make the best of a bad business, and ask him to dinner.'

Palladis did not take her suggestion very seriously. From time to time Honoria would say, 'We must have a little dinner-party. I ought to ask the So-and-so's, I'm sure I owe them something. And old Colonel Whatnot, such a bore, but he does enjoy a good meal. Some time next week, do you think ?' — But before she could decide on the appropriate day for her dinner-party her impulse would fade, or she would let a wilful forgetfulness remove from her mind an intention which could not be fulfilled without a great deal of trouble. Her proposal to invite O'Halloran had no substance, thought Palladis. It was a passing whim ; and having passed, it would not recur.

After more than a week of fine weather, the clouds returned and for three or four days the whole countryside retreated from sight. Curtains of rain carried down the darkness of the surcharged sky to hide houses and hills, and dissolve the bright colours of the fields. To the drumming of rain on the windows was added the splash and gurgle of overflowing pipes and gutters, and the complacent chuckle of rivulets that ran ankle-high on either side of the drive.

With some reluctance Balintore discarded his romantic notion that an Irish summer consisted of an unbroken sequence of sunlit days, and showed the resilience of his spirit by finding compensation in the library. This was a dark and unused room in which he had found several hundred novels — many with slightly mildewed boards and a faint smell of damp — by such neglected authors as Charles Lever and Le Fanu and Charles Reade, and Whyte-Melville and Wilkie Collins, and Mrs. Oliphant and George du Maurier and Ouida. The several volumes of Irish poetry that he had bought in Dublin were still wrapped in brown paper, but for several days he read Victorian novels with great avidity, and talked at the dinner-table in praise of their virtues.

'They're so finite and accomplished,' he said. 'They're not afraid of sentiment and not appalled by death. They take sex for granted — they realise it has been in existence for a long time — and give no more thought to its mechanism than Shakespeare gave to Antony's metabolism. I sometimes think that our contemporary authors' preoccupation with sex is merely a symptom of their laziness. They won't bother to put on their boots and go to look for a subject out of doors.'

'In some ways,' said Honoria, 'Ireland is still rather like a Victorian novel. People are more interested in money than in sex — except for stud-grooms and farmers, of course, and that's because it's profitable when it's well managed.'

'You mustn't underrate it,' said Palladis. 'More and more the world becomes a suburban world, and how would the suburbs get on without it ?'

'They do,' said Balintore sourly.

'They read about it.'

'I like to read about it !' said Honoria. 'I think reading takes your mind off it.'

'And consider France,' said Palladis. 'Without its kitchen, its *couture*, and its *connaissance approfondie de la vie*, how would France have survived ?'

'Charles never noticed what I wore or what he ate,' said Honoria.

Conversation relapsed into a gossiping reminiscence of clerical asceticism, the asceticism of maiden ladies, and of eccentric admirals who in retirement chose to live on a diet of ship's biscuit and dry hash. Honoria brought it to an end by saying, as she rose to leave them, 'Charles's great-uncle Kevin lived to the age of eighty and never married. Then, at a party for his eightieth birthday, he fell in love with the granddaughter of one of his oldest friends. But he was a man of great strength of character, so after the ladies had left them he drank half a bottle of port, went down to the beach, and without taking off his clothes — there was a full moon and everyone could see him — he swam out to sea and his body was never recovered.'

Balintore and Palladis went out to look at the weather, and Palladis said, 'You'll have good fishing to-morrow. There'll be a broken sky, wind and sun, and rain from the south-west. Let's go to bed, and make an early start.'

'A little whisky first,' said Balintore. 'I like to prolong this sensation of living on the edge of the world and near forgotten happiness. Let's have a little whisky before we say goodnight to those black clouds and the primrose light of the moon on the fringe of Atlantis. That's Atlantis down there, isn't it ?'

'Nothing but a bucket of rain,' said Palladis.

Seventeen

WEARING sou'wester, oilskin jacket, and waterproof trousers that never quite kept out the wet, Balintore fished the big lough for more than a week in broken weather, and came home day after day with a basket of six or eight or ten trout. Palladis, a better fisherman, seldom did so well ; and with a smug pretence that it was only luck which made the difference between them, Balintore, in O'Hara's Bar, where they usually stopped before returning to Turk's Court, would buy drinks for an increasing audience, and relate every detail of his battle with the fish that Michael Dooley had netted for him.

Within ten or twelve days — for his luck stayed with him — he became something of a local hero ; and that at the cost of no more than several gallons of porter. The children would come out to salute him in the morning, and when he came ashore in the evening he would give them sixpences to buy boiled sweets and ice-cream. He established himself as a figure in the neighbourhood, and two or three times the parish priest took a glass of whisky with him. He began to enquire of Honoria the possibility of buying a small property, and she, with a landowner's interest in dealings of that sort, would speak of little or greater holdings in the district, some of which had been abandoned and others might be in the market if the offered price were sufficient.

Twice she drove him, in the Landrover, over rough and narrow roads to look at lonely cottages and deserted houses, but though he still protested his wish to settle in the neighbourhood — to buy a house with an acre or two of land — he found nothing to please him ; or please him enough to put money down for it.

There came a morning when he and Palladis were driven off the lough by a rising gale, and going into O'Hara's Bar they found ten or a dozen of the villagers gathered about a black-avised man who was loudly complaining, to the proprietor of the local garage, about the failure of a pump he had lately installed.

'It's O'Halloran,' said Palladis. 'You haven't met him, have you? — Mr. O'Halloran, this is a friend of mine, Edward Balintore.'

For a long moment O'Halloran looked at him in silence. 'It's not the name he used to have,' he said ; and turned to put down his glass. The dim light of an angry day illumined, though darkly, his scarred and shadowed face — shadowed by umbrageous eyebrows and a heavily drooping moustache — and Balintore, recognising him, lost half his voice in a gasp of surprise. Thinly he exclaimed, 'It's Dan O'Connell !'

'No longer,' said O'Halloran. 'I took a brave name from the past when I went out to play a brave part in a shabby world — and you, with the same impulse, I suppose, called yourself Alan Breck.'

'A romantic whim,' said Balintore weakly.

'How many years ago would that be ?' said O'Halloran. 'A quarter of a century, maybe more, and here's both of us still alive, by the mercy of God and to the total disqualification of anyone that thinks there's reason in the world. You've brought two old comrades together, Mr. Palladis, and it's a clear case for drinking deep, and drinking again, to celebrate that. — Drink up your porter, boys, and get clean glasses. It's whisky from now on, for I'm greeting a fellow soldier in the Tercio del Alcazar, in the great days in Spain. But I disremember his name, for it used to be Alan Breck when I called myself Dan O'Connell and neither of us had any more right to a noble patronymic than the soaring of our hearts, which were young in those days. What is it you call yourself now?'

'Balintore.'

'Then give me your hand before we drink together!'

Though Balintore was by no means insignificant in appearance — by no means of unimpressive stature — he was dwarfed by the great figure of O'Halloran, dark in rain-soaked dungarees; and the face that had dominated millions from a television-screen looked plain and ordinary in comparison with the wild and extravagant features of the Irish geologist.

'Hurry up with that whisky now,' said O'Halloran, and nervously the small, white-faced, ginger-haired barman filled their glasses. It was his wife who owned the bar — she by birth was O'Hara, but he, who had come down from Ulster as a travelling salesman for sheep-dip, had the less ringing name of Willy Thom — and now his wife, roused by a note of excitement that had reached her in the kitchen, came in to demand, 'What's all the noise about?'

'Give her a glass too,' said O'Halloran, and with a bow to her explained, 'We're about to drink a toast. *Arriba España!*'

'I'm with you, whatever it means,' she said, and with red, impatient fingers combed her thick, untidy hair. She was a tall woman, boldly handsome, with a look of gipsy blood, and she drank her whisky in two gulps, throwing it decisively into a welcoming throat. 'If it's Mr. Balintore you're drinking to, he's been a good friend of ours, and a great fisherman he is too.'

'You know him, then ?'

'Do I know him, you say ? There isn't a soul here doesn't know him except yourself. But you see no one, living like a hermit in the mine, working day and night to find rocks of gold, and God send you'll see the glint of it any day now. But Mr. Balintore's been here these weeks past, and taking more fish out of the lough, and buying more pints of porter, than any visitor we've had in living memory.'

'I think,' said Balintore, 'we must have another round, and it's my turn now. — More whisky, Willy. Whisky for everyone.'

When he first recognised O'Halloran, surprise had winded him as if in a brawl he had been hit on the mark. Indeed, there was something more than surprise in the blow ; but he had been given a chance to recover. O'Halloran appeared to be friendly. Even boisterously friendly. And Balintore had recovered his breath.

He addressed his audience with a semblance of confidence : 'Here among people who, I'm glad to think, I can now call my friends, I'm bound to say that I've not only had a great surprise to-day, but a surprise that's given me uncommon pleasure. For in days gone by Mr. O'Halloran, whom I used to know as Dan O'Connell, was a great hero among those of us who went to Spain to fight for — well, the preservation — yes, the preservation of law and order — and, of course, the Catholic faith.'

From the chorus of villagers there came a warmly approving murmur of applause, and Mrs. Thom loudly exclaimed, 'Isn't Tim O'Halloran the hero of us all ? Isn't it he that's going to bring back riches and prosperity to us all, from spouting wells of petroleum and great hoards of gold nuggets like the kingdom of Tara in its splendour ? And then, be

Jasus, we'll be rid of the landlords for ever, and to hell with them all! — Not that I haven't a great respect for Madame O'Turk, Mr. Palladis, for she's a lady in her own right, as anyone can see, and a friend to the poor as she's proved herself many a time, so there isn't a person here that wouldn't lay down his life for her, and if he hesitated even for a moment it's me would be at his backside to kick him on. — But to hell with the landlords in spite of that, and praise to Tim O'Halloran for opening up the goldfields of old and loosing great floods of petroleum, to bring back to us all the wealth that Ireland knew when Ireland was the sacred crib of civilisation, and the rest of the world no more than a bloody great swamp of darkness!'

'And now,' said Palladis, 'I think it's my turn to pay for a round. Whisky again, Willy.'

'If all the English had been like you,' said Mrs. Thom, 'we'd still be living cheek by jowl on the same pillow, and the nations of the world would be trembling like the tail of an old hen in the wind for fear of what we'd say to them. — Oh, glory be to God for the taste of whisky! — Look at the two of them now: Mr. Balintore the greatest fisherman we've ever seen in Connaught, and Tim O'Halloran the jewel of Spain and Franco's darling! Look at them now, standing in each other's arms like Castor and Pollux who were the patrons of Ireland before the Christians came — may the Mother of God revive that great occasion! — they've the look of champions, haven't they now? Great champions of the sort we need.'

The amount of drink freely provided in a very short time — and the supply continued, for O'Halloran, Balintore, and Palladis still called for rounds in quick succession — had divided the original company into three or four separate groups that, within the damp and murky friendliness of the bar, had each found its own topic of agreement or dissension, and was busily enlarging it. Other villagers, attracted by the warmth that was already emanating from the half-open door, had come in to form a subsidiary group: a lesser group that did not share the dignity and authority of those who had been witnesses of Balintore's meeting with O'Halloran, and were now their beneficiaries.

Balintore and O'Halloran stood apart from the rest, and though they were not — as Mrs. Thom had proclaimed — in each other's arms, they were held together by a noose of reminiscence and a seemingly interminable exchange of question and explanation. Balintore had not seen O'Halloran since the days of their Spanish adventure, and O'Halloran knew nothing of Balintore's ascent to fame or notoriety. It was Palladis, bringing them another drink, who told the geologist that his old comrade-in-arms had become a person of widely recognised importance.

'And here I've been wondering all the time how he could be masquerading as a rich English tourist,' said O'Halloran, 'when I remember him flogging a spare shirt for a bottle of Fundador, and glad to get it!'

'I shared it with you,' said Balintore.

'You did that! And nowadays, if you're all that important, you'll be a rich man too?'

'I'm comfortably off,' said Balintore, 'but not rich.'

'Any man who can call himself comfortable is rich beyond the dreams of avarice! Comfort, be God, is a state I've dreamed about, and lost sight of the moment I woke up. But you — you've got money to spare! — and it's God's own promise of fortune for us both that we've met this day. I'm sinking a goldmine here, in the field by Turk's Court, but with all the water that's been coming in like a flood in the last week or two I've had set-backs and disappointment, and I'm in need of more capital. Well, now, this is your opportunity to rival King Midas in wealth and splendour, for I'll give you a quarter-share in the mine for a down payment of £500 !'

'I should have to think rather carefully about that——'

'Think carefully, you say ! What's £500 to a man like you, that's famous throughout the land and comfortably off as well ? It's me that's offering you great wealth in return for a paltry investment — and it isn't hesitation I look for, but glad acceptance of my offer !'

'Some day, perhaps, I can come and look at your mine——'

'Any day you like !'

'Your glasses are dry,' said Mrs. Thom, brusquely accosting them with her long black hair falling over her face again, 'and a day when two great men meet together for the first time in a quarter of a century isn't a day when anyone should be standing in O'Hara's Bar with an empty glass in the heel of his hand.'

'Another round !' said Balintore. 'Thank you, Mrs. Thom, we must have another round. Where's Willy ? — More whisky, Willy.'

In the outer part of the bar, near the half-open door, stood a burly man of phlegmatic appearance, who until now had swallowed his drink without emotion, and taken no part in either argument or discussion. But now, with a voice of great power and a fine, clear enunciation, he suddenly began to sing :

> 'Some of them came from Kerry,
> And some of them came from Clare,
> From Dublin, Wicklow and Donegal,
> And the boys from old Kildare . . .'

Several of those near him, caught by the rousing melody, joined him and swelled the tune :

> 'Some from the land beyond the sea,
> From Boston and New York . . .'

And then the rollicking air took charge of all, and in a glorious evocation of long-past miseries and triumph their voices rose together :

> 'But the boys that beat the Black and Tans
> Were the boys from the County Cork !'

By this time there was a little crowd of some forty or fifty women and children outside the bar, and Father Aloysius, the parish priest, who happened to be passing, thought it his duty to come in and see what was attracting so much interest.

He was a broad-shouldered, well-fleshed man of genial appearance, with a resounding voice, and the song was cut short when, peering into the smoky gloom of the bar, he entered with the loud enquiry, 'Now, now, then, and what's going on here to disrupt the calm of a decent Tuesday morning ?'

'Come in, Father, come in and take a drink with us,' said O'Halloran. 'You're no friend of mine in the ordinary course of life, but this is a day for tolerance and compassion and great rejoicing. There's a gentleman here that's going to give me £500 to prosecute the great work I'm doing, and enlarge the working of the mine.'

'Is he right in his head ?' asked the priest.

'Sounder than you, with your new latitudinarian notions,' said O'Halloran, and put a glass of whisky into the priest's hand.

'You're a bad influence in the village,' said the priest, 'and here's your very good health.'

'That's more of the lax and libertarian sentiment that's ruining the Church,' said O'Halloran. 'But I'm not quarrelling with you to-day——'

'You'd better not,' said the priest. 'I've been lenient with you for a long time, because you fought for the Faith in Spain and Italy, and were wounded in that cause——'

'It's a cause that you've abandoned!' said O'Halloran. 'The Church I fought for stood for a great intransigent cause, but your Church has come to terms with Moscow and Canterbury and the atheists of the modern world——'

'It's a modern world we live in!'

'It's a damnable and wicked world, and you shouldn't be tolerating it.'

'Who are you to teach me my duty? A sinful man that doesn't come to Mass or Confession——'

'I make my own Confession.'

'You're no better than a black Protestant!'

'Now Father, Father dear,' said Mrs. Thom, 'don't be taking any notice of him, he's up in the air to-day with the promise of £500 from Mr. Balintore——'

'I made no such promise!' said Balintore.

'Hush, hush,' said Mrs. Thom. 'Say nothing to infuriate him, or there'll be no holding him — he's a great champion, and you can do nothing with the like of them but keep out of their way — so come in behind the bar with me, and we'll have a drink in peace. And God's blessing on you, Father, for coming here to-day to lend the honour of your presence to a poor house that's been exalted by the meeting of two great men, and from that meeting there'll be great consequences for the whole village.'

The bar, by now, was full of a splendid, uncoordinated uproar — the confined, dark, smoky air seemed taut as the air in a great drum — and the drum was being beaten by a score of competitive drum-sticks to produce a clamour that made no sense at all, but had a rhythm, a natural tide, an organic pulse of furious assertion and indignant denial.

Palladis, who had a large tolerance for strong waters, was interested in the vagaries of the human mind and its utterance when the censorship of normal disciplines had been relaxed by drink. For some time he went from group to group, listening with lively attention to all that was said ; but when utterance became mere repetition — as presently it did — he looked at his watch, discovered it was long past lunch-time, and decided, for Honoria's sake, that it was time to go home.

With some difficulty he detached Balintore from a sombre but apparently enthralling discussion on the Council of Trent — initiated by Father Aloysius — and guided him through a turbulent throng to the door, and through another crowd on the pavement to the Landrover on the other side of the street. They got in, and Palladis pressed the starter. But the noise of the engine had the effect of a bugle calling obedient soldiers to the parade-ground ; for as soon as it was heard, all those within O'Hara's Bar came hurrying out, and, being joined by the women and children on the pavement, surrounded the car with confused cries, disorderly singing, and a few urgent demands for a speech.

Moving very slowly, Palladis reached the end of the village without accident ; and by then the crowd had diminished. But when he began to drive a little faster, a boy of reckless temper and no great sense tried to run in front of him ; and tripped and fell. To avoid him Palladis swerved abruptly to the right and crossed the road at an angle of sixty degrees. With a violent tug on the wheel he straightened his course, but skidded on a grass verge and slid into a deep ditch.

In a moment the crowd was at full strength again, and now many voices rose in commiseration and as many shouted contrary advice. Willing hands tried to heave and haul the Landrover on to the road, and others, equally willing, laboured to push it deeper into the ditch. With some difficulty Balintore and Palladis got out of the steeply tilted car, and there were loud exclamations of sympathy and horror when it was seen that both were bleeding freely from cuts on forehead or cheekbone. But Palladis quickly took charge, and organised a working party that succeeded, with some difficulty and a good deal of argument, in lifting and pulling the Landrover on to level ground.

The off-side front wheel, however, had suffered a dislocation and was no longer parallel with its neighbour. The car could not be driven, but would have to be pushed or towed. And for this additional labour the villagers were more than willing; they were eager to help and prove their continuing goodwill.

Palladis and Balintore got in again, and as many as could lay a hand on the disabled car shoved and pulled it on a slow, irregular course to Turk's Court. Past the empty lodge and through the dark thicket of rhododendrons they went, and on to a curving arm of the drive. Those who were not pushing or pulling encouraged the others with loud cries and an occasional broken chorus ; and the noise they made brought Honoria out to see what was happening.

She stood at the top of the double flight of steps, before the front door, and waited — not perturbed, exactly, for the voices of the villagers were too lively for a funeral party, or even for the escort of gravely injured men — but with some anxiety, and a frown of manifest displeasure.

The Landrover came to a halt beneath her, and Balintore and Palladis got out. Each had tied a handkerchief about his bleeding cuts, and they wore a bloodstained, piratical look. But the villagers cheered them loudly, and several ran up the steps to explain the accident they had suffered, and protest the great goodwill with which everyone had come to their rescue.

Balintore took it upon himself to apologise for their tardy return. 'I'm afraid we're a little late,' he said.

'It is half-past two,' said Honoria.

'We've been involved in an occasion of some delicacy. We met your tenant, O'Halloran——'

'That man!'

'And I discovered that he's an old friend of mine. Well, to come to the point, I remembered what you said — you said, if you remember, that you would like him to come and dine with us — so I've invited him for Friday.'

'O'Halloran?'

'At half-past seven for eight o'clock. He accepted with pleasure.'

Balintore took a step backwards, and would have fallen but for the presence, close behind, of eight or ten of the villagers who had followed him up the steps to hear what he had to say to Honoria. He smiled, and made a little bow to excuse what might have been an embarrassing mishap.

Breathing heavily, his supporters brought with them the heavy odours of O'Hara's Bar; and Honoria, wrinkling her nose, said coldly, 'You had better come in, Mr. Balintore.'

Eighteen

THEIR misbehaviour bred disorder in the house. Mrs. Moloney said to Nelly Kate, 'They'll not be wanting dinner to-night, that's one mercy.'

'After all the drink they've taken,' said Nelly Kate.

'And them sitting round the table till half after three, and us with all the dishes to wash!'

'Did you hear them roaring and laughing?'

'Not Madame! She sat with them for the sake of good manners, but there was no laughter in her voice, not that I could hear.'

'And the eyes of her as cold as door-knobs on a frosty morning,' said the girl.

'Let them sleep it off,' said Mrs. Moloney, 'and a poached egg will do for Madame, as it does when she's all on her own, poor soul.'

After their late lunch Balintore and Palladis did indeed go to their rooms and sleep for a couple of hours; but they recovered sooner than Mrs. Moloney had expected. By half-past seven — having washed and dressed and resumed a respectable though slightly harassed appearance — they were drinking pink gin in the library, and at a quarter to eight they went to Honoria's small sitting-room, where they were in the habit of meeting her before dinner. Honoria did not come, and when a clock chimed eight they went, a little worried, to the dining-room.

There they found their hostess, solitary at one end of the table, with a copy of the *Spectator* propped against a carafe in front of her, eating slowly a poached egg on toast.

'I'm afraid I hadn't expected you,' she said, 'but I dare say Mrs. Moloney can find something for you, if you don't mind waiting a little while. She's been rather upset because it was her afternoon off, and you kept her here till half-past three.'

They made a scanty and uncomfortable meal off cold mutton and a cold bottle of claret, and Honoria, after watching them with a disapproval as chill as the wine, relaxed when Palladis gave her a glass of port — there was a decanter, half-full, from the previous night — and said, 'Well, you've behaved very badly, and though half the village seems to have been just as bad, or even worse — oh, I've been out! I've heard the whole story! — it's you they'll remember, it's you they'll talk about, and I'll be maligned, because you're living here, as if I kept a disorderly house. But I'm a long-suffering, Christian woman, and in spite of the abominable procession that brought you home——'

'It really wasn't my fault,' said Palladis.

'And, of course,' said Balintore, 'I'll pay for any damage to the Landrover.'

'Indeed, I hope you will,' said Honoria. 'But that's not the point. The point of what I'm telling you, or trying to tell you, is that I'm a very tolerant woman with an unconquerable impulse to forgive or forget injuries and insults — otherwise, of course, I couldn't have lived in Ireland all these years — and while you two were sleeping off the consequences of drinking yourselves silly in O'Hara's Bar——'

'I don't think we did anything very silly,' said Palladis stiffly.

'You looked extremely silly,' said Honoria. 'But, as I was saying, I've forgiven you, and while you were sleeping it off, I've been doing what I could to arrange a dinner-party for you and your friend O'Halloran.'

'I'm not sure that I can call him my friend,' said Balintore. 'I used to know him——'

'According to the story they're telling in the village,' said Honoria, 'you were comrades-in-arms — blood-brothers in the good cause, I heard one woman say — in that tiresome war in Spain. And it was you who asked him to dinner.'

'After you had suggested it,' said Palladis.

'Well, yes, I admit that. I thought he might be good for a giggle, and I still think so. But it's a damned nuisance trying to arrange a dinner-party, and I've gone to a lot of trouble.'

'Who's coming?' asked Palladis.

'I tried to get old Colonel Goode, but his wife's in London and he has to stay at home and look after his invalid daughter. And the Sullivans can't come, because he's got gout, and the Harringtons said no, because she's doing a retreat — she's Anglo-Catholic — and he's off to Monte Carlo. So I had to fall back on local talent, and that means Dr. Brennan and his wife, who's English, and her sister who's staying with them, whom I haven't met.'

'Brennan doesn't believe in professional reticence,' said Palladis, 'so we ought to avoid any reference to accident, disease, or hereditary ailments.'

'And his wife doesn't utter,' said Honoria, 'unless you ask her about the children. You can say anything you like to her, and be sure of a patient, sympathetic hearing — so long as you keep off the subject of little Sean and little Norah, her pigeon pair.'

'We're going to have a pleasant evening,' said Palladis.

'You've brought it on yourselves,' said Honoria complacently.

The following day they fished again, with indifferent success, and when they came home in the evening a serene, untroubled sky promised a return of fair weather.

The morning broke bright and calm as a mediaeval painting. They gave up all thought of the lough, and about eleven o'clock, when they were discussing without enthusiasm a suggestion of Honoria's that they should drive to the seaside and picnic on a beach, they were startled by a muffled explosion and a slight tremor of the ground beneath them.

'O'Halloran,' said Palladis. 'He's blasting again.'

'I suppose he knows what he's doing ?'

'I sometimes wonder.'

'Do you think there's any danger ?'

'He's not very far away.'

'Perhaps we ought to go and have a word with him.'

'He doesn't encourage visitors.'

'We both know him — I've known him for a long time, if it comes to that — and he was quite friendly the other day.'

'If he hopes to get £500 from you, he has a good reason to be friendly.'

'He isn't going to get a penny out of me, but I needn't tell him so. Not yet. And as a prospective shareholder I'm entitled to have a look at the mine.'

'All right, let's go and call on him.'

They crossed the ha-ha and the limply-wired fence, and walked to O'Halloran's zariba. A notice on a door in the high wall of wickerwork read DANGER ! KEEP OUT !, but the door hung loose on its hinges, and beside the wooden hut within the enclosure they saw O'Halloran with the three men who worked for him.

He came towards them and said sourly, 'Can you not read?'

'The other day,' said Balintore, 'you asked me to take an interest in your mine.'

'You promised me £500.'

'I did nothing of the sort. But you asked me for £500, and I want to see the property you expect me to invest in.'

'You've come at the wrong time. We've run into a little bit of difficulty.'

'Well, surely — as a possible investor — I'm entitled to see what your difficulties are ?'

Unshaven and out of humour, O'Halloran looked a formidable obstacle to their curiosity. He frowned, and seemed about to speak — thought better of it — and then said harshly, 'Come on, then. It's nothing to worry about, but I'll be needing more money.'

He led them into the hut. At one end were his living quarters, furnished with a stove, an unmade bed covered by army blankets, a large cupboard, a wash-stand and a bucket, a table and a couple of chairs, and a paraffin lamp ; the other end was an office more tidily arranged, with maps and diagrams on a long table, and a shelf of books against a wall.

'What's your trouble ?' asked Balintore.

'You can see for yourself,' said O'Halloran, and pointed to a coloured diagram. 'There's more rock than I expected.'

The diagram looked like a cutting through a large and very badly made Neapolitan ice-cream, with a diagonal bisection that apparently represented a steep, downhill approach to a dark blue line entitled *The River*.

'I don't quite understand it,' said Balintore.

'That's because you're not a geologist,' said O'Halloran.

'Where does the river come from ?' asked Palladis.

'You can see for yourself, on the hill beyond.'

'The little stream that rises by the wood on Slieve Bloom, and then goes underground and disappears ?'

'It comes into the open again at the top of the village, and that's where they used to wash for gold in the days gone by.'

'But why do you think its underground course takes it this way ?'

'You need to be a geologist to understand that.'

'How do you know,' asked Balintore, 'that they used to wash for gold where the stream comes out at the top of the village ?'

'It's in an old book I found, called the Annals of Innisfallen. The book's well known, but the manuscript I found has never been seen by living eyes, except my own ; and the description is there.'

'Have you got the manuscript here ?'

'I'm showing it to no one !'

'But if they used to find gold at the end of the village, why do you sink a mine here ? Why don't you look there ?'

'They got all there was,' said O'Halloran. 'They got all that was washed through.—It's alluvial gold I'm talking of, you understand that, do you ?—Well, so much was washed through, into the open stream, and all that was taken in the olden days. But what they didn't know then was the course the river took, and the depth of it. It opens into a shallow lake —underneath us here where we stand, and under the big house—and that lake's like a sump or trap to catch all the gold that's been running off the mountain for thousands of years. It's a treasury of gold that lies beneath us !'

'You're quite sure of that ?' asked Balintore.

'I'm telling you what's there ! I'm a geologist, and I know.'

'How much blasting have you got to do ?' asked Palladis.

'There's more rock than I expected.'

'And if part of the lake is beneath the house, won't there be some danger to it, as you tunnel towards it?'

'No danger at all. We shan't go near the house.'

'You're not far from it now.'

'There'll be no danger, I tell you. We're on solid limestone here.'

'I wish I could see that manuscript you say you've found,' said Balintore.

'Come and I'll show you the mine,' said O'Halloran.

He led them to a hole in the ground that had been opened beside an outcrop of rock, and followed a rock wall down into the earth. The roof was supported, a little casually, by timber frames, and the downhill path was steep. Then it levelled, and an old-fashioned stable-lamp showed them a narrow passage with rock on either side. Steps had been cut in a gravelly soil for the next descent, and it became apparent that O'Halloran had found a soft approach, through a fault in the rock, to what might be a series of small caves. Here and there the walls had been revetted, and a doubtful roof shored-up; but the men who worked for him had not had to carry out a great weight of spoil. Where charges had been fired, the raw limestone shone white as cottage-cheese in the lamp-light.

They went down, by more steps, into a cave as big as a billiards-table, but barely high enough to stand upright in; and O'Halloran said, 'After all that rain we had, this place was flooded to the roof, and I hadn't a pump that could deal with it. I was in despair, I didn't know what to do. And then overnight the water found its own way out. It disappeared, and you see what that means, don't you?'

'There's a crack in the floor, presumably,' said Balintore.

'A crack that goes all the way down to the river! It's proof positive that the river's below us.'

'That's a possibility, but——'

He was interrupted by the loud, reverberating chatter of a pneumatic drill, that filled the cave with an intolerable din. O'Halloran put his mouth to Balintore's ear and shouted, 'They're drilling holes for the next shot,' and led them forward, by another sloping corridor, to a little chamber like a crypt. This was brightly lighted by pressure lamps, and rough debris from the last explosion still lay pale and bright on the floor. The man with the drill appeared to be boring into solid rock with little more hope of penetrating it than if he had been using a dentist's drill ; and two others stood watching him in attitudes of tireless patience. When O'Halloran spoke to them they turned and replied with what looked like a meaningless, gibbering ferocity ; for, in the appalling clamour of the drill, neither Palladis nor Balintore could hear a word.

Presently O'Halloran led them back to the surface, and said to Balintore, 'Are you satisfied now ?'

'It's all very interesting.'

'I'm needing the money, I tell you.'

'But £500 is a lot of money, and there's no evidence — none at all — that I'll get any return for my investment.'

'There's the evidence of that old manuscript, and the evidence of geology.'

'I haven't seen the manuscript.'

'And you're not going to ! But I tell you this : you'd better make up your mind quickly.'

'Surely there's no immediate hurry,' said Palladis soothingly. 'We can talk it over to-morrow night — you're coming to dinner, you remember ?'

'I remember,' said O'Halloran sullenly.

They left him at the door in the wicker fence, and Palladis said, 'I hope he remembers to shave.'

'He threatened me,' said Balintore. 'That was certainly a threat.'

'Was there anything behind it?'

'Bad temper, I suppose.'

'No guilty secret?'

'Of course not.'

'Then you've nothing to be afraid of.'

'I'm not afraid. But it's annoying to be threatened by a man like that. A man who's coming to dinner.'

With Honoria they discussed at length O'Halloran's mine, and late that evening, and again in the morning, they heard the dull sounds of subterranean explosion. In the library Balintore found a set of shabby volumes that contained ancient chronicles of Ireland: four volumes of the Annals of Ulster; the Book of Leinster; and a Calendar of Irish Saints. But in none could he discover any description of gold-mining.

On Friday evening Dr. and Mrs. Brennan, and her sister Miss Prynne, arrived punctually at half-past seven; and were followed by O'Halloran only a few minutes later. He wore a well-cut suit of Donegal tweed, he had shaved with care and clipped his moustache, and appeared to be in a mood of dignified reticence.

He was at once engaged in conversation by Miss Prynne, a tall lady of massive build who wore a dress of bright brown silk and what seemed a superfluity of bracelets, necklaces, brooches, and ear-rings. She was a librarian by profession, and an ardent lover, as she quickly told him, of all things old and Irish. She had heard of his discovery of an ancient manuscript, and she thought she could guess what it was.

'Is it,' she asked, 'the Annals of Clonmacnoise?'

'It is not,' said O'Halloran.

Dr. Brennan was a short, round man with a dark, close-cropped, round head, and weather-beaten complexion. He drank his sherry at a gulp, and said to Balintore, 'Have you had good fishing ?'

Balintore refilled his glass, and told him at some length of his fortune on the lough. He spoke of Michael Dooley, his gillie, and Dr. Brennan said, 'It's a great family for tubercle. I've signed death certificates for seven of them, young and old.'

Honoria said to Mrs. Brennan, 'I hope the children are well ?' and left Palladis to listen to her reply while she went down to the kitchen to make sure that Mrs. Moloney was keeping an eye on the clock, and the girl Nelly Kate wasn't giving way to excitement.

They sat down to dinner at a quarter-past eight, and Palladis, who had looked after the wine, was assiduous in refilling glasses. It was a burly Chambertin they drank, and when Honoria said to O'Halloran, who sat at her right hand, 'Will you be dining off gold plate next year, Mr. O'Halloran?' he answered generously, 'It's a cup of gold will be the first thing that's shaped, and that for your own hands.'

'Well, what could be nicer than that !' said Honoria. 'I've always wanted a gold cup.'

'In the old days,' said Miss Prynne, 'Ireland was famous for the purest gold in the world.'

'And kept none of it,' said Dr. Brennan.

'From the beginning of time,' said O'Halloran, 'we've been robbed of our birthright.'

'I wish we knew more about the Firbolgs,' said Miss Prynne.

'Why ?' asked Honoria.

'Well, they were very early inhabitants, and it's said they came from Greece. But I think it's much more likely that they came from Bulgaria. Fir-*bulgs* may have been an earlier form of their name.'

'That's nonsense,' said O'Halloran. 'We've all heard stories of great waves of people coming out of the Mediterranean and settling down here on the Atlantic shore, and there's not a word of truth in any one of them. The truth is that civilisation began here in Ireland, and when it was ripe for the move we put out to sea and founded Greece.'

'How interesting,' said Miss Prynne. 'How very interesting !'

'I can prove it,' said O'Halloran, 'and you can see the proof with your own eyes. You know Dun Aengus, the great round fort on Inishmore ?'

'Where is Inishmore ?' asked Balintore.

'The Aran Islands. And that great fort is a wonder of the world. But it's not unique, there's masonry of that sort in other places. You'll know where Stonehenge is ?'

'I have seen it,' said Balintore.

'And Maeshowe in the Orkney islands ? That's the finest megalithic tomb in Europe. Well, think of those three together, and where else can you find architecture of a like sort ?'

Palladis refilled his glass, and O'Halloran, looking round the table, waited for an answer.

No one ventured to reply, and O'Halloran said quietly, 'In Mycenae. The Lion Gate of the Treasury of Atreus. There and nowhere else ! And Mycenae was built by the sons of the builders of Dun Aengus, who did their work here, and then went to Greece as teachers and the bringers of civilisation.'

'Well, I do think that's a good idea !' said Honoria. 'I've never been able to understand why people should leave the

Mediterranean to come and live here ; but to leave Ireland and go to Greece — well, that makes sense, doesn't it ?'

A somewhat confused debate on the movements of antiquity occupied their attention till the ladies left the table ; and when O'Halloran and Dr. Brennan, and Palladis and Balintore sat down again, O'Halloran said to Balintore, 'Have you made up your mind yet ?'

'Yes,' said Balintore. 'I'm not going to invest money in your mine till you can show me that I'm likely to get some return for it.'

'So that's the line you're taking ? Well, now, and there's something I might be telling these gentlemen that they'd find very interesting. Have you ever told Mr. Palladis, for instance, how you happened to get wounded when you and I were in Spain together ?'

'That was too long ago,' said Balintore, 'to be of any interest now.'

'I'm not so sure of that.'

'Were you badly wounded ?' asked Dr. Brennan.

'No.'

'I want to know,' said Palladis, 'why you fought for Franco.'

'I was a good Catholic then. Not now, you understand. I gave up the Church when it got too lax and liberal. If the Pope had done his duty — that's the old Pope I'm talking of — he'd have excommunicated the Russians, one and all, when they betrayed the Poles in Warsaw. But he gave way to expediency, and look what that's led to ! To tolerance and broad-mindedness and plain indifference, so that nowadays the Pope — the new one, I mean — will sit down to tea with Anglicans and the riff-raff of the world. It was different in 1936.'

'It was your ardent Catholicism, and nothing else, that took you to Spain?'

'I wouldn't say nothing else. I went out in the Irish Brigade, under General O'Scruffy, as we called him, and when they went home again, not having done much for the good name of Ireland, I stayed on and joined the Requetés. I was in the Tercio del Alcazar for two years, a commissioned officer at that, with a silver badge on my good red beret. And that's where I met Mr. Balintore. I was with him when he got wounded.'

'I was wounded at the Casa del Campo,' said Balintore.

'It's another time I'm thinking of.'

'It's a trivial story of no interest,' said Balintore.

'I think the gentlemen would like to hear it,' said O'Halloran.

'Not now,' said Palladis. 'We've been sitting here long enough, and we ought to join the ladies.'

'It wouldn't take more than three minutes——'

'You can tell me later on,' said Palladis; and got up, and opened the door.

In the long drawing-room Miss Prynne immediately advanced on Balintore and said, with a sort of luxury of self-reproach, 'You will hardly believe it, but I have only just discovered that you are *the* Mr. Balintore! Though I live in England, I am one of that small minority — perhaps I might say that exclusive minority — which doesn't own a television-set. So I didn't recognise you, and though your name was familiar I certainly hadn't expected to meet *the* Mr. Balintore in such unlikely surroundings as the wild west of Ireland. It must be a strange experience for you to find yourself in a country where you're not instantly recognised.'

'It's a great relief,' said Balintore.

'You don't feel an alarming sense of isolation ?'

'In a world like this, isolation is an enviable condition.'

'How true !' said Miss Prynne with warmth in her voice. 'I myself often long for solitude.'

Honoria was speaking to O'Halloran ; though he wore a surly expression that seemed not to encourage conversation. 'Before I drew the curtains,' she said, 'I saw lights at your mine ; or rather, in the little wooden house on top of it. Do you always make your men work so late ?'

'We're in a hurry,' he said, 'and I've promised them a bonus if we get through within the month.'

'But is it safe to leave them there alone ? Without supervision ?'

'There's two of them with good experience : Tom Devlin and Patsy Ryan. Devlin was a miner at Noranda in Quebec, till he got homesick for the old country, and Ryan was a quarryman. He's worked all over, and might be a manager to-day if he could keep off the drink. Dan Clancy's just a labourer, but the others will see to it that he does no harm.'

'Do you really think you can find a way, or open a way, down to the river ?'

'No fear of that ?'

'And quite soon ?'

'I've got the materials. I've enough gelignite to blow the front off the Four Courts, I'm not worrying about that. It's shortage of capital and the thinness of my purse that's a plague and perplexity, as it has always been — and if you'll excuse me I'll just go and have a word with Mr. Balintore, who's promised to help me if he can.'

His intention was interrupted by the appearance of Palladis who, still playing the butler, came in carrying a silver tray on whose burden of glasses and a decanter of whisky the light of the two great Waterford chandeliers found genial reflexions. It was too early for whisky, but Palladis had pleaded his duty to escape a harrowing tale, which the Brennans told as a duet, of their younger child whose fingers had been trapped between the chain and driving-wheel of a bicycle.

He put the tray on a small table, and turned to see O'Halloran beside him.

'Would you like to hear that story now ?' asked O'Halloran.

'What story ?'

'About the way Balintore got wounded.'

'Why do you want to tell it ?'

'I'd like to have your opinion on it.'

'Is it a discreditable story ?'

'To the like of you or me it would make no difference at all. But for him——'

'Are you going to tell me that he wasn't wounded in battle ? That he never fought in Spain ?'

'Ah, he fought all right ! We were together in the Tercio del Alcazar : didn't I tell you that ? And we'd fighting enough, at the Casa del Campo in the siege of Madrid, and then at Bilbao, and down on the Guadalajara front. We'd a bellyfull of fighting.'

'Then whatever you say can't discredit him very seriously. Unless you murdered your prisoners or set fire to a house full of women and children ?'

'We did not ! We left that to the Republicans !'

O'Halloran looked earnestly at the decanter, and said, 'It's a shame to see good whisky sitting there ignored by all, and no one making use of it.'

Palladis poured him a stiff tot, which O'Halloran drank neat. Not greedily, not in a single gulp, but slowly and thoughtfully. Palladis waited for him to speak again, but he remained silent till he had finished his drink ; when he held out his glass and said, with simple gravity, 'A bird never flew on one wing.'

Palladis gave him another tot, and O'Halloran walked to the far end of the room where Balintore, though restless now, was still held in conversation by Miss Prynne.

'You'll forgive me for intruding,' said O'Halloran in a truculent tone, 'but there's a matter of some urgency that Mr. Balintore and I have been waiting all evening for a chance to discuss.'

'That isn't quite true,' said Balintore.

'It'll be true enough when you've heard what I'm going to tell you now !'

Miss Prynne, in some alarm, looked from one to another, and retreated in a discomfiture made evident by the shimmer and tinkle of her abundant jewellery. O'Halloran pushed Balintore into a corner, and began to speak in a low, menacing voice.

In the middle of the room Mrs. Brennan was beginning to say that it was time they were going home, but Dr. Brennan, talking to Honoria with a tumbler of whisky and water in his hand, paid no attention ; and Miss Prynne, to repair her shaken nerves, let Palladis pour a little whisky for her, while assuring him that to drink spirits was quite contrary to her habit.

Gradually they became aware that the discussion at the far end of the room was growing unfriendly. A mutter of storm — as if waves were breaking on a distant beach and a far-off gale was harassing the clouds — came from the corner where Balintore and O'Halloran still argued.

Then O'Halloran said loudly, 'All right, if that's your

decision you'll have to take the consequences, but don't say I didn't warn you !'

They both advanced on Honoria and her startled guests, and Balintore said, 'I beg you to disregard what this man is going to tell you. It's an idle tale of no importance——'

'Let them judge for themselves,' said O'Halloran.

'I can't stop him telling it, without using force——'

'Nobody's going to use force on me ! And it's a story that, in my opinion, you'll enjoy. It's a story with a fine setting, for one thing : the beautiful town of Seville, no less. We were there together, on leave from the front, where we'd had a hard time of it, and we were in a mood to enjoy ourselves, as we deserved to. Yes, I'll grant him that. But Mr. Balintore went too far——'

'I was very young,' said Balintore.

'He disgraced the regiment, the Tercio del Alcazar, and the uniform we wore ! We were at the bullring, you understand, and he was as pissed as a newt.'

'He was *what* ?' asked Honoria.

'He was drunk,' said O'Halloran. 'And what do you think happened to him ?'

Before he could tell them, the house was shaken, as if by earthquake, by a deafening explosion that was repeated before the first blast had spent its energy. The double shock split, with a rending crash, the tall south window and lifted the heavy curtains as if a gale of wind were filling them. Pictures fell from the wall, and rugs blew across the floor. The ceiling shook, the floor trembled, and the two great chandeliers of Waterford glass began to swing in a wild and agitated movement with an incessant, high-pitched chatter and tinkle.

'My chandeliers !' cried Honoria, who had fallen backwards on to a sofa.

'Stand away !' shouted Palladis.

His warning came too late. After a violent and convulsive lurch, the chandelier nearer to the south window broke from its anchor in the ceiling and fell — exploding like shrapnel — in a brilliant hail of glittering, sharp-edged pieces. O'Halloran and Mrs. Brennan were both hit and slightly wounded, but Balintore was knocked unconscious. At the centre of the chandelier had been a huge, many faceted pineapple of solid crystal, and this, breaking free with great velocity, had struck him with a shattering impact on the left temple. He lay motionless on the floor, and his larger need for sympathy helped the others to recover from their fright.

Nineteen

It was not till late the following afternoon that Balintore recovered consciousness. He had stirred and wakened — or appeared to waken — a little before noon, but paid no attention to what was said to him. After about ten minutes his eyes had closed, and he relapsed into coma or deep sleep. At five o'clock Palladis, who was sitting with him, heard him sigh, or lightly groan, and saw that his eyes were open and intelligent again.

Palladis asked gently if he was comfortable. There was a long silence before Balintore replied.

'Who am I?' he asked.

'You're still rather mixed up, aren't you? The question you ought to ask is *Where am I?*'

'Don't be a bloody fool! I know perfectly well where I am. But who am I? Who, who?'

'At this moment you're an invalid suffering from a slight concussion.'

'A damned ponderous concussion! What time is it?'

'Five o'clock on Saturday afternoon.'

'Was O'Halloran hurt?'

'A cut on the cheek, not deep.'

'That's a pity.'

'Would you like a drink?'

'Soda water.'

He drank thirstily and said, 'Now I'm going to sleep again.'

He woke at ten to say he felt well, and was hungry. He insisted on getting up to wash, and then, sitting up in bed, ate toast and scrambled eggs, and drank several cups of tea.

'What hit me ?' he asked.

'A piece of Waterford glass about the size of a pineapple.'

'There was an explosion at the mine ?'

'It seems they had drilled holes for two sets of charges, loaded them, and by some mistake fired both together. A man called Ryan was more or less responsible, and he was drunk.'

'Was he hurt ?'

'The roof fell in, and he and another man called Clancy were trapped. O'Halloran and the Doctor organised a rescue party, and got them out alive. But Ryan has a broken leg and Clancy a broken arm.'

'And this house ?'

'The drawing-room looks as if a small shell had burst in it.'

'It wasn't my fault,' said Balintore.

'No one has suggested that.'

'Even if I had submitted to blackmail and promised him £500, it wouldn't have prevented an explosion.'

'What was the story he was going to tell ?'

'A damned silly story. We'd been in the line for weeks on end — more than a month — and when we came out we got a few days' leave. We went to Seville, just the two of us, and got drunk. I was very drunk. I was only — how old was I ? Twenty, I suppose.'

'What happened ?'

'We went to a bullfight. We were standing at the barrera, and I had a flag that we'd taken from a battalion of F.A.I.'

'What does that mean ?'

'*Federación Anarquista Ibérica.* It was a red and black flag, and I thought it would be amusing to wave it. But a couple of peons on the other side of the barrera thought different, so I jumped over to argue with them. I knocked one of them down, and ran out into the middle of the ring. Then I saw the bull, and waved the flag at him. He didn't seem to like Anarchists any more than I did, and charged. I turned and ran like hell, but not fast enough, and the next thing I knew I was on his horns. He threw me, and tried to steam-roller me. But they got him away, and I was invalided out of the army with a cornada in my left cheek.'

'You've led an even fuller life than I had supposed,' said Palladis.

'Now O'Halloran has got it into his head that I can't afford to let that story be made public, and I ought to pay £500 for his silence.'

'But you refused.'

'I refused. And I shan't see him again, if I can help it. I'm not going to be blackmailed, and I don't want to be persecuted!'

'Don't get excited. You're quite safe from him here — and I think you ought to go to sleep again.'

The following morning Balintore ate a large breakfast, but was in a melancholy mood. He had slept poorly, he said, tormented by bad dreams.

'That damned fellow was after me,' he said, 'and I seemed to spend half the night running away from him in the senseless, agonised panic of nightmare. At one time my feet were stuck in a bog and I couldn't move, and the next moment I'd be swimming in dark water or floating through the clouds. I was like Rimbaud's drunken boat, "*perdu sous les cheveux des anses, jeté par l'ouragan dans l'éther sans oiseau*". And when I woke up, dog-tired, I began asking myself again, Who am I ?'

'Without reply ?'

'It's a question that will never be answered.'

A few minutes later he asked, 'Have you any strong feelings about incest ?'

'I can understand the Church's objection to it, and I suppose the biological arguments against it are sound enough, if it's carried to excess. But it must have been fairly common in northern countries in the winter ; and in the slums of the industrial revolution. I suppose it's only in primitive or tribal society, governed by unbreakable tabu, that it has never occurred.'

'I,' said Balintore, 'have always had an intense desire to commit incest with my sister.'

'But you haven't a sister.'

'I may have a dozen sisters, or half-sisters. And whenever I'm strongly attracted to a woman, I always hope it's a guilty, incestuous attraction. But it never has been, and perhaps it never will be.'

'How do you know ?'

'Sooner or later something happens, or she says something, that makes it quite impossible to suppose we're blood-relations. I can't believe a sister of mine would be so stupid as they always are.'

Dr. Brennan came in about midday and assured Balintore that he had suffered no serious or incapacitating injury. 'No fracture, not even a chip. Oh, there's nothing like a good thick head,' he said cheerfully, and put a thermometer into his patient's mouth.

'A bit over 100,' he said. '100·4, if I can see it properly. You'd better stay in bed for another day or two. Eat what you like, and if you want to drink, put plenty of water in it.'

He went down to inspect the damage in the drawing-room, where he found Honoria, Palladis, and two men from the village who were re-glazing the south window. Two massive portraits, their heavy frames split and showing plaster under the gilt, stood against a wall, and on a table were heaped, in a glittering pile, the many dismembered parts of the fallen chandelier. There was a gaping hole in the ceiling.

'It might have been worse,' said Dr. Brennan. 'Oh, it might have been much worse. You'll be insured?'

Honoria was not so easily comforted. Being English, she set a higher value on material possessions than did Dr. Brennan, and stood with a woebegone expression as she tried to arrange bright pendants and rosettes of scintillant glass in the patterns they had once adorned.

'The story that Dan Clancy's telling now,' said the Doctor, 'is that they drilled two sets of holes, one for a charge to be fired that night, and one the next morning. But Ryan, he says, was drunk, and that's like enough, and out of excessive zeal and devotion to duty loaded them with twice the proper dose of gelignite, and by a mistake that he can't understand fired all together. But Ryan says it was all Clancy's fault, and God knows what the truth is.'

'What is O'Halloran doing?' asked Palladis.

'You'd be heart-sorry for the man to see him now,' said the Doctor. 'This drawing-room looks like the picture of an Ideal Home Exhibition in comparison with the mine, and he and Tom Devlin are working like heroes, trying to clear up the mess, and taking no heed at all of danger to themselves.'

'You needn't expect me to sympathise with him,' said Honoria.

Palladis went out with the Doctor, and at the south-eastern corner of the house they looked at a pile of broken slates.

'But it's an old roof,' said the Doctor. 'A lot of those slates would have been lying loose, just waiting the excuse of a good westerly gale to come down. It's the foundations and walls of an old house that are made to last : if this was a new house, it wouldn't be a house at all to-day.'

In the afternoon Palladis took Honoria for a walk, and tried, with what skill and ingenuity he could muster, to find consolation for her. But she was deeply upset by what had happened, and the ruin of her drawing-room seemed to her like a mockery of the lonely years she had spent in Ireland since her husband's death. It was not for her own pleasure she had chosen to live there, but to keep and preserve — for her son who was at school in England — the house and remaining acres of the estate that his father had loved and mismanaged. But what hope of conservation was there in a land where drunkards were left in charge of gelignite ?

'There's a quality of destruction in the country, and in the people too,' she said, 'and sometimes I hate them for it, but sometimes I think they're right. For nothing lasts, and we shouldn't set our hearts on what can break or be lost. But oh, I loved those chandeliers !'

They turned and walked home in silence ; and were the more surprised, when Palladis opened the front door, to hear a furious din of angry voices. It came from the drawing-room, where they found Balintore, bare-footed and wearing only pyjamas, brandishing a poker at an equally irate O'Halloran who, dirty and unshaven, had obviously come straight from the mine.

'You maladroit, evil-minded, blackmailing bog-trotter !' shouted Balintore. 'Get out of here, or I'll beat your head in !'

'Put down that bloody poker,' said O'Halloran, 'and for God's sake listen to the voice of reason ! If I tell that story you'll be the laughing-stock of the world, and I'm offering you a fair bargain. I need that money——'

'What you need is a strait-waistcoat and a gag in your mouth! You've a demented mind, and no one can blame you for that who didn't know your parents. It may be the only inheritance they were able to leave you——'

'Don't you say a word against my saintly mother!'

'— but your manners are what you've made for your own use, and what were the models you chose? A wart-hog for stark insensitivity, a wolverine for greed, and for impudence a Cairene belly-dancer!'

'Now keep your tongue clean, Balintore! Can you not see there's a lady in the room?'

Still in the doorway, Honoria and Palladis had been listening to this exchange with some displeasure at so vulgar a debate; but with sufficient interest in what was being said to keep their displeasure silent. Now, however, Honoria came into the room and said coldly, 'I once invited you to dinner, Mr. O'Halloran, but I didn't give you the freedom of the house. If you have come to apologise for the damage you did, please do so, and then go.'

'It wasn't me that did the damage. You can't blame me for that!'

'It was entirely your fault.'

'I've suffered more than you. The mine's a ruin, and there's the only man rich enough to help me, and he'll do nothing for me, though we fought side by side in the bloody trenches of the Casa del Campo!'

'I think you had better go,' said Palladis.

'Not till I tell Madame O'Turke the story of the last time I saw him——'

'I don't want to hear it.'

'There he was, sitting on the horns of a great black bull that took him three times round the ring at Seville — him in the uniform of the Tercio del Alcazar — and twenty thousand people on their feet to see him, all jeering and throwing cushions at him !'

Honoria had gone to speak to Balintore, who, after his show of defiance, appeared to be exhausted, and sat listlessly in a chair still holding his defensive poker. She persuaded him to go back to bed, and promised to bring him a drink.

The fight had gone out of O'Halloran too, and he let Palladis lead him to the door. He stood at the top of the steps and said sourly, 'Throwing cushions at him. Cushions and bottles and anything they could lay their hands on. That's what they thought of him in Seville — and tell him from me that he hasn't seen the last of me yet !'

Balintore, in bed again, was querulous and looked a little fevered. He spoke at great length, and with self-pity, about O'Halloran's invasion, and said that he must not be left alone. 'He'll watch the house, and if he sees you and Honoria going out, he'll come again, he'll come and pester me again, and though I'm not frightened, it takes too much out of me to have to deal with him !'

'There's nothing in his threat of blackmail. Nothing to alarm you.'

'I know that as well as you. But he's a maniac, and now he has the idea that I'm refusing to give him money that he's entitled to. The fact that he's wrong makes no difference to a maniac.'

At midnight Balintore came into Palladis' room and woke him. 'I can't stay here any longer,' he said. 'We're leaving tomorrow.'

'Why ?'

'He's been walking round the house for the last hour. I've been listening to him.'

'Have you seen him?'

'It's too dark. But every now and then I've heard his footsteps.'

'You've been dreaming.'

'No.'

'Well, if he wants to walk about, let him. He can't do any harm.'

'With gelignite in his possession?'

'Stay here,' said Palladis, 'and I'll go and find some whisky.'

He returned in a few minutes with a bottle, two glasses, and a carafe of water. 'Now let's talk this over,' he said.

Balintore drank deeply and said, 'I have made up my mind. I thought, to begin with, that I had found refuge here. The sort of refuge I was looking for. But that man has made life intolerable. I'm not going to give him the money he wants, and a thwarted maniac — well, how far's a thwarted maniac from murder? Round the corner from murder: no farther than that.'

'Now you're talking nonsense.'

'Your life isn't in danger, mine is.'

Balintore, walking to and fro in a yellow dressing-gown, looked gaunt and feverish. 'You ought to go back to bed,' said Palladis.

'I shall, as soon as I've persuaded you that we must leave to-morrow.'

'Where do you want to go?'

'Give me another drink.'

'Will that be good for you?'

'Give me a drink — and try to remember some of the conversation at that damned dinner-party. There was a ridiculous discussion about prehistoric migrations, and O'Halloran, the fool, said civilisation began here, and went east to the Mediterranean. Then Honoria said, "Well, that makes sense. I can't imagine anyone leaving Greece to come to Ireland, but to leave Ireland and go to Greece——"'

'I remember.'

'That's where we're going.'

'But it's impossible ! Nowadays you can't travel spontaneously, you have to make arrangements three or four months ahead. Hotels are booked up, aeroplanes full——'

'You're very good at making arrangements. You always know someone useful, someone with influence.'

'I still say it's impossible ! You know what a state Honoria's in — I've never seen her so upset — and we can't go off at a moment's notice, and leave her all alone.'

'Ask her to come too. I daresay she would like a holiday in Greece.'

'She can't afford it. She's not a rich woman.'

'She will come as my guest, of course.'

'Oh, go to bed,' said Palladis.

'Certainly,' said Balintore, 'now that has been settled.' He filled his glass again, and taking it with him, returned to his room.

Palladis spent a restless night, and at breakfast told Honoria that he thought Balintore was in danger of a relapse into the nervous condition that had made him leave London early in the year. He repeated some of their midnight conversation, and to his surprise Honoria exclaimed, 'But oh, how right he is ! I feel exactly the same. I would give anything to go away for a month or two.'

'He suggested that you should come with us. As his guest.'

'Where ?'

'To Greece.'

'Oh, no !'

'You don't want to go there ?'

'I mean it's too good to be true !'

'You would like to come ?'

'But of course I'm coming !'

'He wants to leave to-day.'

Honoria grew thoughtful. 'No, I can't do that. I'd have to make *some* arrangements. But to-morrow — ask him to wait till to-morrow !'

But on the following evening, in Dublin, Honoria came down in tears to the bar of the Hibernian Hotel and told them, 'It's all off, and I can't come. Oh, I'm so miserable !'

'What has happened ?'

'I rang up Kevin at school, and discovered they've been trying to telephone to me all afternoon. Kevin fell downstairs this morning and broke his leg, badly. You can't blame him, they're horrible stairs — he's in one of those old, dark houses — but I wish he hadn't been in such a hurry. But there it is, and now, instead of going to Greece——'

She sniffed, and blew her nose. 'But I've no right to be sorry for myself, I ought to feel sorry for Kevin. Poor boy, he does love the summer half, and now he won't be able to play cricket, so it will all be wasted.'

'Where will you stay ?' asked Palladis.

'His tutor has asked me to stay with them — so kind, and he's got a very nice wife, I don't know how she puts up with him — oh, I'll be all right. But it won't be like going to Greece, will it ?'

They dined sadly and without appetite. Balintore, who had complained of a headache while driving to Dublin, ordered champagne to comfort Honoria ; who talked with a shallow gaiety except when she fell into melancholy silence. After dinner Balintore tried to cure his headache with brandy.

In the morning they flew to London ; where, regretfully, they said good-bye to Honoria, and in his chambers in Albany Balintore went to bed. Palladis telephoned to the doctor who had previously attended him.

Twenty

BETWEEN the classical assurance of a blue Hellenic sky and the ruined nobility of Pentelic marble — warm to the touch under a noonday sun — the modern world, like flies on a cracked but enduring sweetness, moved in restless enquiry, pious or bewildered, bored and dutiful and loudly ecstatic, and took photographs of each other and the Erechtheum with equal enthusiasm.

Balintore stepped out of the line of sight of a camera held in the firm red hands of a corpulent tourist from Bremen, and was angrily reproved for getting in the way of a crop-headed young man from Minneapolis who was pointing his at a Caryatid. A blonde and bony lady from Zurich, in a summer frock of starched aggressive cleanliness, politely asked him to move away and let her take a picture of the Caryatides *en échelon* ; and a student from Ghana, his sable skin gleaming in the sun, protested volubly when Balintore cast his shadow on the base of a broken column. Nervously he looked this way and that for a lane of escape, and felt like a condemned prisoner whose firing party, numbering several hundred, stood round him on every side. Whichever way he faced, he was confronted by the black, accusing muzzle of a camera.

He had lost Palladis. Together they had climbed the steps of the Propylaea, and together stood and looked with awe at the eroded grace of the Parthenon. But then a chattering procession of school-children had separated them, and when he turned to say 'A forest of marble under a frozen canopy', he found himself speaking to an indignant lady from Clermont-Ferrand who said her light-meter wasn't working properly.

He looked for Palladis on both sides of the Temple of Athene, and on its terrace thought the great view over the Saronic Gulf would be the better if there were fewer people to share it; but all the Acropolis was as crowded as the approaches to Wembley on Cup Final day — and a group of burly young men, who might well be a football team on holiday, jostled him to make room for themselves in a solidly smiling group: they had come to be photographed.

Dodging accusing cameras — wincing at their threat — he continued his search, and found Palladis at last smoking a cigarette on a convenient plinth near the Museum.

He spoke angrily and said, 'I've been looking for you for half an hour.'

'A little while ago I was talking to a young German who had lost his wife. They have only been married for forty-eight hours, and she has, he told me, no sense of time or direction. He was very agitated.'

'My God, I'm tired!'

'Sit down and have a cigarette.'

Balintore's hands were trembling, and he wore a look of pain or mental stress that Palladis thought exaggerated. It was nearly three weeks since they had left Ireland — even Palladis' wide acquaintance with people of influence had failed to get them accommodation in any shorter time — and Balintore's doctor had told him he was physically fit to travel anywhere. His recurrent fever had subsided, and he had had no more headaches. But he still complained, sometimes absurdly, of bad dreams.

On their return to Albany he had heard, with consternation,

that Polly Newton had repeatedly called to ask if he was in residence, or if she could be given his address. 'But that,' said the porter, 'we couldn't do, because we didn't know it ourselves — and even if we could, we wouldn't, of course, not without your instructions — but in consequence of not knowing where you were, I'm afraid, sir, that you're going to get a shock when you see your letters. There must be hundreds.'

'When did Miss Newton last come here ?'

'About a fortnight ago, sir, as far as I can recollect.'

'I'm still not feeling very well——'

'I'm sorry to hear that, sir.'

'— and I'll be going away again as soon as possible. So while I'm here — it will only be a few days, I hope — I don't want any visitors. No visitors at all : you understand ?'

In a great accumulation of letters there were three addressed in Polly's handwriting. These Balintore burnt, unopened. Palladis dealt with the rest, tearing most of them into a large laundry-basket but paying a couple of dozen bills.

'Strangely enough,' he said, 'your financial position is sound. You're not quite as well off as you were last year, but the re-investments I suggested have all done well, and you've no need to worry. You spent a lot of money in Jamaica and New York, but very little in Ireland, and you've saved a few pounds on postage. If we had been living here I would have had to reply to all these letters, and what a waste of time and money that would have been. Nowadays most people only write letters to give their secretaries something to do.'

But though Balintore had no financial anxiety, he worried about Miss Newton's pertinacity, and refused to go out until Palladis had reconnoitred and made sure that she was not lying in wait for him.

In Ireland, feeling with some reason that he had treated her not ungenerously, he had been able — or nearly able — to dismiss her from his mind. But now, made suddenly aware that she had not forgotten him, he began to reproach himself for his abrupt desertion, and said to Palladis, with shame and horror in his voice, 'She may be in love with me ! You never know with a woman, do you ? Well, about other women — those women I married — I had no compunction at all, because I was quite sure, long before we separated, that they were as glad to get rid of me as I was to be rid of them. But Polly — well, I was tired of her, because of that damned memory of hers, but perhaps I didn't give her a fair chance to tire of me. And I blame myself for that. I should have been more patient.'

'Do you think she fell deeply, genuinely in love with you?'

'She talked so much, it's very hard to tell.'

'You should have read her letters.'

'No, I don't like women's letters. They're too self-indulgent — and damned ungrammatical when they're not damned untrue.'

'Well, try to forget her.'

'I wish I could !'

But the bad dreams which the explosion at Turk's Court had started, were now complicated by another pursuer ; and Balintore's sleep was harassed alternately by a roaring Irishman who demanded money, and a weeping girl who cried for love. Palladis sympathised, but found it difficult to show a continued interest in the content of the dreams ; which Balintore insisted on telling him. His distress was obvious, and after a good night's sleep his relief was unconcealed, sometimes even exuberant ; but to Palladis it seemed that he encouraged his unhappiness by memorising and elaborating it. He would turn his recollection of a dream into a formal narrative, and sometimes decorate description of a nightmare's landscape with an apt — or too apt — quotation.

One morning, at the breakfast-table, he was relating, in some detail, a visionary flight — the morass that held him, the snow-slope that betrayed him, the forest that bewildered him — then, after noisily drinking his coffee — 'and so on, "down the labyrinthine slopes of my own mind".'

'Francis Thomson,' said Palladis, 'wasn't running away from an Irish geologist.'

'No,' said Balintore. 'No, he wasn't.'

He put down his cup, and went to his room without finishing either his story or his breakfast.

That was three days before they left for Athens, where an agent had found them rooms at the Athenee Palace. They arrived in the early evening, dined late at a rowdy tavern in the Plaka, and the following morning Balintore said, 'I've had the best night's sleep since we left Ireland.'

'Foreign travel or a long voyage is still good medicine,' said Palladis.

'On the other hand,' said Balintore, 'it may be that God has turned his back on me.'

'Apollo rules here,' said Palladis — and then both were distracted by a loud English voice from the table behind them, where a family of four were breakfasting. It was a ringing female voice, and decisively it announced, 'The Parthenon can wait ! The first thing Moira and I are going to do is to look for a good hairdresser.'

Soon after that Balintore began to show signs of a new phobia. They hired a motor-car and drove to Port Sounion where, debouching from several large buses, they encountered a crowd of two or three hundred people who presently mingled with the larger throng who were already admiring the gaunt ruin of Poseidon's temple, and taking photographs of it and each other. The sun was hot, the sea was blue, and the stark surviving columns stood majestically above the waves that the angry god had ruled; and amateur photographers from Birmingham and Hamburg, from Stockholm and Geneva, from Scranton and Kansas City and St. Louis trained their lenses on the scene to shoot a view and take its carcass home.

Again and again Balintore and Palladis got into the line of fire — were warned, with anger or reproach — and hastily removed themselves; and at dinner that night Balintore said fretfully, 'I still see those black muzzles. You can't escape them, can you?'

Now on the soaring Acropolis, sitting on a convenient plinth near the Museum in the luminous air of Greece — and sweating slightly in the heat of the Hellenic sun — he said to Palladis, 'It's too much for me. It's too much!'

'The crowd? It's a good-humoured, harmless crowd.'

'And armed to the teeth! Every one of them — quick on the draw, or cuddling his weapon like marksmen at Bisley — pointing his camera at you!'

'They don't hurt you.'

'They get on my nerves.'

'We'll go, then. Perhaps the sun's too hot for you. We'll go and find somewhere cool, and drink ouzo.'

At night — they dined in their hotel — Palladis spoke seriously and said, 'I'm thinking of giving you notice. Or, to put it more politely, of offering my resignation.— No, don't interrupt me. Wait till I've finished.— I have been your secretary for about four years now, and you have treated me very generously. I, on my part, have worked with you, and for you, and done all I could to help you.— Wait, wait!

I'm not asking for overtime or claiming a bonus.— But since January, since we went to Jamaica, I've been saddled with a responsibility that I hadn't anticipated. I was prepared for eccentricity, I welcomed the chance of working with a distinguished eccentric. For characters — I mean "characters" — are almost as rare in the world as the white rhinoceros. But I wasn't, and I'm not, prepared to nurse indefinitely a neurotic who is letting his neurosis take charge of him ; and that's what happening to you.'

'Wait ! I haven't nearly finished. Take some more of that retsina, we'll get another bottle.— I'm going to remind you of your initial collapse, when you said on the television screen, with half England watching you, that what you were really afraid of was being "found out." And I'll admit, for a start, that I had sometimes thought your stories, of what you had seen and done, were probably more fiction than fact. Your stories of fighting in Spain, for example. But O'Halloran — though you can blame him for trying to blackmail you — has disproved that. You have nothing to be afraid of in that respect.— Well, what else is there ? You're a foundling, and possibly a bastard — I'm using the word in a legal, not a pejorative sense — and public discovery of that would do you no harm at all. In the present temper of the world it would, more probably, do you good. Well, then, what is there to be frightened of ? What false claim have you made, what false feathers are you wearing, that make you afraid of the truth coming up like the morning sun to expose their falsity ? — And forgive me for talking like that. It's the way O'Halloran might talk. I must have drunk too much Irish whisky at Turk's Court.'

'Everything I've told you,' said Balintore, 'is true. And no one can deny it.'

'Why are you afraid of cameras?'

'They seem to look through and through you.'

'And what do they see?'

Balintore filled his glass from another bottle of retsina, belched, and with solemn sentimentality replied, 'That I've got the best friend in the world, and I've never told him a lie.'

'You still haven't told me what you're afraid of.'

'So long as you stay with me, I'm afraid of nothing.'

'Not even of dreams?'

'I think I've stopped dreaming.'

'I nearly said good-bye to you at Turk's Court,' said Palladis. 'When you told me you were determined to leave the following day, and wanted to go to Greece — your only reason being Honoria's discovery that pre-history had moved that way — I was on the point of writing our separation order. But then I thought you might be moved by something I don't believe in, and that's a homing instinct. Geese have got it — grey lag and pink-foot navigate by instinct — but we've long lost the gift. Or have we? For suddenly I remembered, or the thought occurred, that if Greece is anything in the history of the world, it's the home of sanity. And sanity, God knows, is the home that you and I, and all of us, ought to be looking for.'

'You,' said Balintore, 'are as drunk as I am.'

'It may be so,' said Palladis. 'It may well be so. You've been keeping company with an unacknowledged fear, and get bad dreams. I've been keeping company with you, and get drunk.— Not as a habit, though! I haven't been drunk for a long time. A very long time. I can't remember being drunk.— But to walk on the Acropolis with a man who's frightened of cameras is enough to drive any man into the refuge of alcohol. And this I tell you, once again: I'm going to leave your employment unless you discard and forget your neurosis — and I think you could do it. I think you're cossetting and encouraging it, because in a perverted way you're enjoying it. Well, that's one alternative — you can go on doing that — and the other is that you bring your neurosis out into the daylight, and we'll see if we can deal with it.'

'Otherwise,' said Balintore, 'you're going to abandon me?'

'Yes.'

'But the trouble is that I don't know the answer. You say to me, "You're afraid of being found out"——'

'It was you who said it.'

'All right. But now you're saying it. And I'm asking myself, what is there to be found out? And I don't know.'

'You've done something you're ashamed of——'

'Hundreds of things! Who hasn't?'

'What's the worst?'

'I think,' said Balintore slowly, 'that it was accepting the present of a stamp-album. I was only a boy — I was sixteen, I think — and I hated the man who gave it to me. It was a valuable collection, but he thought I needed it. He thought I needed something to comfort me. Though, as a matter of fact, I didn't. So he offered me his stamp-album, which he valued very highly, and I took it. And that, I think, was a shameful thing to do.'

'It isn't the sort of thing to ruin a man's reputation.'

'I can't think of anything worse.'

'In Jamaica, you remember, we met those people called Bulfin.'

'And they said I had stolen a novel written by Tom Bulfin. But that isn't true. I told you the truth.'

'You ought to see an analyst, of course.'

'That I shall never do.'

'Then we'll have to wait for a catalyst.'

'Another explosion?'

'I'd prefer something quieter.'

'Let's have some brandy.'

'No, it's bed-time. We've an early start to-morrow. We're going to Delphi — in a bus.'

Twenty-one

BARE and vast, Parnassus rose in forbidding grandeur on their right-hand side, and the voice of an American woman in the seat behind them complained, 'I thought Italy was a fert'le country.' She was reproved by her daughter who said tartly, 'We left Italy Tuesday.'

In the seat in front sat an old Englishman and his wife: he, of time-engraved, proconsular appearance, wore a panama girt with an Old Etonian ribbon, and she — who was plump and looked kind, but with the kindliness of innate authority — a hat like a small blue bee-hive of plaited straw ornamented with a fragment of fish-net and some cockle shells.

'How appropriate!' said Palladis. 'A cockle shell is the pilgrim's emblem, and all good travellers are pilgrims at heart.'

'Pilgrims or fugitives,' said Balintore in a voice that discouraged conversation.

The day was fine, and the growing warmth of the sun lulled the tourists into a drowsy silence as the long bus climbed the hillside road. Their guide — an attractive and well-informed young woman — who had spoken with nice discrimination about Eleusis and Boeotian Thebes, was now engrossed in private conversation with the driver, and only the voices of two young men — tall, broad-shouldered, with close-clipped hair — broke the mechanic undertones of their journey.

'Xenophilia,' said one of them. 'I thought it was a disease, but you say it means that Greeks like foreigners.'

'So they say, and I guess it's true enough. But I wish they'd learn to spell. If you want a drink, it doesn't help you to find what you're looking for when they spell it *Mpar.*'

'They haven't taught their dogs about xenophilia. You ever been attacked by a Greek shepherd dog?'

'You got to sit down and keep still. Then the dog comes right up and licks your face. There's this girl I know——'

'Maybe it's different for a girl.'

'— she and a college friend of hers were hiking through the mountains, and two dogs came running up as if they were going to tear 'em apart. Well, they sat down, right there, and the next thing they knew, the dogs were nuzzling behind their ears. And that wasn't all. About two minutes later a couple of big, rangy shepherds came round the shoulder of the hill, and these two girls — well, they didn't know much about life except what they'd learnt back home in Illinois, and the least thing they expected was instant rape. But no, sir. These shepherds made the dogs lie down and the girls get up and go with them, all the way down hill to a kind of cabin in a draw of the hill, and there they said, in their own language, "Meet the old lady!" And their mother — she was right there waiting for them — she set them down to a dish of fried eggs and goat's milk cheese. Well, they didn't get the big story they might have had to take home, but they did learn about xenophilia.'

As they approached Delphi their guide broke off her conversation with the driver to tell them about the Castalian spring, whose escaping rivulet they crossed at walking pace, and presently, having peered up at the radiance of the great cliffs above the Theatre, the tourists stiffly emerged when their bus stopped beside the Museum.

Balintore and Palladis let the old proconsular Englishman and his wife go out before them ; and heard him say, in a high, crackling, but decisive voice, 'To-morrow morning — quite early, before there's a crowd — I want to go down to that spring and drink the water.'

'For poetic inspiration ? You're much too old.'

'You made me get Jordan water when the children were baptised——'

'That's quite different.'

'Mind the step, dear.'

'I see it.'

'I don't want to write poetry, but I'd like to have a moment of inspiration, or clear sight, before I die,' he said ; and chuckled happily as he helped her down. 'But it isn't likely, is it ?'.

Shepherded by their guide, they slowly climbed the Sacred Way, silenced by toil and simple awe beneath the majesty of the cliffs ; and most of them were much confused by what they were told about Apollo and the Pythian oracle.

Crowded with broken monuments of the past, the huge amphitheatre was more densely packed with the present. There were tourists everywhere, brightly clad in summer clothes, and the murmuration of a thousand voices re-echoed from ancient walls. In the Theatre, high on the hillside, there was a more purposive noise, and it became apparent that a rehearsal of some sort was going on, though in great disorder.

Leaving their fellow tourists, Balintore and Palladis climbed to the top row of curving, white stone seats — that commanded a view, not only of the ancient stage, but of an enormous valley enclosed by golden hill and flamboyant cliffs — and watched a director or *régisseur* attempting to drill opposing choruses that were impeded by numerous spectators intent on taking photographs.

In the row below them were the two young men, with hair clipped short and brightly patterned shirts, who had sat near them in the bus; one of whom said, 'It's some college outfit. They're going to play Oedipus.'

'Iphigeneia in Tauris,' said his companion.

'One or the other, I couldn't tell 'em apart.'

'That's Iphigeneia over there — the big blonde in toreador pants — that's how I know.'

'She's well stacked.'

'I'll say.'

'And who's this?'

From one of the choruses a girl in faded blue denims stepped forward and in a clear, slightly nasal voice recited carefully:

'Tisiphone donned the head of a dog,
Alecto flew on bat's wings,
Megara's serpents she combed like hair,
And this is the song she sings:
"Respectable women, such as we,
Have a duty that none of us shirks,
So Alecto squeaks a curse in his ear,
And Tisiphone waits till it works. . . ."'

The director silenced her with an agitated hand, and Palladis said, 'They appear to have found a new translation.'

'I'm out of my depth,' said Balintore. 'Who is Tisiphone?'

'She and the others — Alecto and Megara — were the Furies who haunted Orestes, and drove him mad, after he had killed Clytaemnestra.'

'His mother.'

'Who had murdered Agamemnon his father.'

One of the young men in front of them, who had turned to listen, said gravely, 'That must have been a very traumatic experience for Orestes.'

'I guess there's no drama without trauma,' said the other.

'She's going to say her piece again.'

The girl in blue denims repeated her lines, with more animation in her voice, and Balintore and Palladis left the Theatre to walk westward a little way and inspect the narrow Stadium.

'The only explanation of Greek tragedy,' said Balintore, 'is that everyone in it was mad from the beginning.'

'But logical,' said Palladis.

They walked the length of the Stadium, and back again.

'I dislike this place,' said Balintore.

'The Stadium ?'

'Delphi.'

'It's usually considered——'

'One of the most beautiful sites in Greece, combining mystery, majesty, and primal awe : I read that in the guide-book. But I don't like it.'

'Wait till the morning. We'll go down and drink at the Castalian spring.'

'Where do we sleep ?'

'The hotel's a little west of the village.'

They walked downhill, and came on to a path that suddenly gave them a cerulean glimpse, between grey and golden hills, of the Gulf of Corinth. White-walled beneath them was a small hotel.

Neither was pleased by the discovery that they would have to share a room, but after dinner — the night was clear and star-lit — Palladis insisted on their walking five or six miles in the hope that Balintore, after drinking another bottle of retsina, would sleep soundly.

He slept, indeed, till after three, when he woke shouting wordlessly ; and when Palladis turned on the light he saw

Balintore, with horror on his face, at the open door, looking up the narrow corridor that led to their room.

'They're after me!' he said.

'You've had a nightmare?'

'Who are they? They're called the Solemn Ones.'

'Those young Americans?'

'I think they're women — not the Americans, but the people I couldn't see, though I know what they're called.'

'Were you dreaming about Polly Newton? Polly and her sister?'

'Not them. I was frightened out of my wits.'

'It's the usual effect of a nightmare.'

'If it was only that——'

'You'd better have some brandy.'

Palladis got up and took a flask from his suit-case. He poured a judiciously measured dose into a tooth-glass, and Balintore, now sitting on the edge of his bed, said with a look of bewilderment, 'But who are the Solemn Ones?'

'I don't know. It must be a name you've invented.'

'I heard it. There was someone speaking through my dream. A sort of commentary, as if on a race. But it wasn't a race, it was flight — flight and pursuit — and they were gaining on me.'

'Drink your brandy and go to sleep again.'

Obediently — with the obedience of a man still dazed by shock — Balintore lay down, and Palladis put out the light. They woke when dawn brightened the window of their room, and dressed without much conversation. 'A walk before breakfast will do you good,' said Palladis.

They went through the village and down the road to the Castalian spring. There they surprised the old proconsular Englishman and his wife. He, who was kneeling to fill a thermos flask, appeared to be slightly embarrassed, but she, with a comfortable assurance, explained, 'It's for our grandchildren.'

Balintore and Palladis splashed their faces with the bright water; cupped their hands and drank. The sun was already warm when they turned to climb a rough path, through litter of ancient marble, to the steep hillside above the Theatre. Now they could feel the enormous view was their own — or almost theirs — for only a dozen tourists, a scattering of early risers, were to be seen meditative in the Temple of Apollo or respectful in the Treasury of the Athenians.

For perhaps half an hour they sat in the topmost row of white stone seats — the vast amphitheatre under its bright impending cliffs seemed charged with drama, though no one walked on its tremendous stage — and suddenly Palladis remembered who the Solemn Ones were. It was another name for Tisiphone and Megara and Alecto: the Furies or the Kindly Ones, the Mad Goddesses or the Solemn Ones — so they had been called, according to time and circumstance. This knowledge, of no great worth, he owed to some forgotten schoolmaster, and Balintore's memory, awaking in the middle of a dream, had presumably a like origin. The theme of his recurrent nightmares had always been flight and pursuit, and now something had happened to make him identify his pursuers with the Furies who had hounded Orestes.

Delphi itself: that was what had happened. Orestes in despair had fled to Delphi, and Balintore, dreaming in Delphi, had heard a schoolmaster's voice rise from the deep-sea depths of memory to worry the surface of his sleeping mind. That, surely, was what had wakened him to fear.

'You did learn Greek, didn't you?' he asked. 'At school I mean.'

Balintore, in a tired and hollow voice, said, 'I went to a good Scotch school. An Edinburgh day-school. And thirty years ago all good Scotch schools taught Greek. Though we only learnt enough to pass examinations, of course.'

He stood up, with a sudden shiver in the hot sun, and said, 'This may be the most magnificent view in Greece, but too much has happened here, and I don't like it.'

'We go back to Athens this afternoon.'

'And then ?'

'Either Rhodes or Paros.'

'Paros where the marble came from ? It sounds too bleak. We'll go to Rhodes.'

Two days later they flew to Rhodes, and the next morning, at the Hotel des Roses, Palladis was shocked to see Balintore come down to breakfast, unshaven, in a shirt that had obviously been worn, in hot weather, for several days.

'I haven't unpacked,' he said. 'It hardly seemed worth while.'

'We're staying for a week. Perhaps longer.'

'I doubt it. There are too many people here.'

He drank a cup of coffee but ate nothing, and Palladis had some difficulty in persuading him to go out and look at the town. Under a sapphire sky, in streets bright with flowers and pottery and silversmiths' work, or splendid with the architecture of a stubborn chivalry — in gardens of oriental brilliance under the blown petals of innumerable butterflies, or on ramparts of knightly grandeur that frowned upon a radiant sea — he walked disconsolate and resentful of his fellow tourists ; of whom, indeed, there were too many. A cruising ship had just unloaded some twelve or fourteen hundred for a day's sightseeing, and most of them carried cameras.

The sea offered release. Their hotel had a private beach,

and when Palladis first suggested swimming they found it, by chance, almost empty. For a couple of hours Balintore swam or floated on an inflated mattress, and thereafter spent much of each day in the water; turning an angry face to anyone who came too near his floating island.

But Palladis watched him with increasing anxiety. Balintore was still careless about his appearance. He ate little and drank too much. There was a local wine of which he grew fond, and whisky was cheap. But wine did not make him high-spirited and loquacious — whisky did not release a torrent of outrageous talk — as they had done in the past. He was moody and taciturn; and exposure to the sun, together with a recurrent forgetfulness to shave, gave him the look of a sullen beachcomber. He lost weight, and under his dark sunburn his face was gaunt and bony.

When Palladis asked if he still slept badly he said, 'I've learnt how to deal with a nightmare. I put a squib under its tail.'

'How do you do that?'

'I've taught myself to wake as soon as it starts running — or almost as soon — and I take a bottle of whisky to bed with me. After four fingers of whisky the nightmare usually bolts — and if it starts again, I can bolt it again.'

While Balintore swam, or floated on his rubber mattress, Palladis went sightseeing. He enjoyed the Museum and the Street of the Knights, he bought a crateful of decorated pottery and sent it to Honoria. He drove one day, with a couple of casual acquaintances, to Lindos; and the thought occurred to him that Balintore might find the refuge he had sought elsewhere in one of the little houses of the tightly packed village that clustered under the Acropolis.

The next morning he hired a car and persuaded Balintore

to go with him. They made an early start, and found Lindos in its native quiet. They climbed the steep slope to the ruined castle, and Balintore showed a little animation, a little interest in the scene. To the north rose a tall foreland, boldly and fantastically shaped, and the blue sea was trapped in a bay of paler blue. Below them the town was like a honeycomb of white houses. 'I like the look of it,' said Balintore.

They went down again, and walked through twisted lanes in the dazzle of the sun. 'This is where we should have come,' said Balintore.

On a seat beside the small enclosed harbour he looked at the white terraces and the quavering reflexion of boats in the water: 'It's ridiculously attractive, isn't it?'

Silence was broken by the blare of a motor-horn, and the first of a fleet of buses arrived, that disgorged several hundred tourists. Balintore fell into a sudden rage, then shrugged his shoulders and said they had better return to Rhodes.

At dinner that night he said, 'You're not going to abandon me, are you?'

'I don't think I can.'

'I want to make another effort — I shan't give in till I have to — and that marble island you spoke of, that sounded so bleak — it might suit me.'

'You mean Paros?'

'Can you arrange it?'

'I'll see if it's possible. I can send a telegram to-morrow. We'd have to fly to Athens again, and take ship from Piraeus.'

'Do your best,' said Balintore, and beckoned to the head waiter. 'I want a bottle of whisky in my room.'

Three days later they flew to Athens, slept again at the Athenee Palace, and in the morning drove to Piraeus, where they boarded a small, rather slovenly steamer. Within the next hour or two it filled with a noisy and cheerful horde of passengers, all but a few of whom were native Greeks, and many of whom were accompanied not only by a great deal of luggage, but by domestic animals. Sheep and goats came aboard, as well as several mules.

They left the dirt and clamour of the port for the cleanness of the sea, but off Cape Sounion met a movement of the sea that reduced many passengers to inert and jaundiced misery. The decks were like a battlefield on which few survived to carry off the wounded and the dead, and the small saloon looked and stank like a casualty clearing station.

The brilliance of afternoon left the dancing sea, which under the cliffs of an approaching island took on a lavender hue. Presently the ship was no longer tumbling, but gliding slowly into the harbour of Syros. Sailors and longshoremen unloaded passengers, cargo, and animals with great speed and dexterity, and the ship put out to sea again.

It was pitch-dark when she arrived at Paros, in the midst of the Cyclades, and Balintore and Palladis went ashore, to a shore invisible under midnight, in a genial but impatient throng of islanders, sheep, and goats.

Twenty-two

UNDER the brilliance of the morning sun — that dazzled a windy sea — the small town was a sinuous white lane of houses that threw triangles of black shadow on blanched walls and in unexpected corners grew flowering trees. At intervals a lesser lane disclosed a church or, on the sea-road, an elderly fisherman patiently thrashing an octopus. Here the marble remnants of a fallen temple had been used to build a wall, and there a view opened of a brick-red hill. The main street, or principal lane, led to an open market-place and a foreshore where fishermen mended their nets, and a dozen caiques, with their bluff bows and round bottoms, lay at anchor or alongside a short pier. At a table in front of a tavern, under a red and white awning, Balintore and Palladis sat drinking ouzo.

They had been a week in Paros, and Balintore had a relaxed and healthier look. Their hotel was small but comfortable, and there seemed to be no more than a score of foreigners in the town, most of whom were quiet and unobtrusive. There was very little to do except walk, or swim from a beach on the other side of the bay, or sit outside a tavern and drink ouzo. But this simplicity had suited Balintore, and Palladis had begun to put away the anxiety he had felt in Rhodes. That morning Balintore had made discreet enquiry about the price of property in the island : a little house with a fig-tree at its door had taken his fancy.

The stiff breeze which pointed the water of the bay, and

raised a line of white about the rocky islets that guarded the entrance, had dissuaded them from swimming, and in weather cooler than it had been they were discussing the possibility of walking to the marble quarries which had once made Paros famous. They could not learn exactly how far away they were, but thought it probable that the distance was no more than three or four miles.

They had another glass of ouzo, to prolong discussion and postpone the walk, and their attention was taken by the appearance of a boat at the entrance to the bay. It was rolling steeply in rough water, and every now and then threw up a curtain of spray that hid it from sight. When it came nearer they could see that it was a caique, of native build, but larger than the local fishermen's boats and much more smartly painted. It had a deck-house and a cabin-top which had been added to its original design.

'We're going to have rich visitors,' said Palladis. 'That boat has been converted and furnished for the sort of people who can afford to pay £350 a week for it.'

'It might be a good idea,' said Balintore, 'to buy a boat instead of a house. I imagine you could get an old one fairly cheap, and when you got tired of Paros you could run over to Naxos, and from Naxos to Delos and Mykinos. Even as far as Chios, perhaps. I'd like to go to Chios.'

'And if you were surprised by a northerly gale, which isn't uncommon, you might not have to worry about your next anchorage.'

'They're very seaworthy.'

'When properly handled.'

The boat they were watching turned into the wind, stopped, and dropped anchor. There were two seamen in the bows, and from below came a tall, trousered woman and a short, broadly built man, both in white, who stood talking on the after-deck with the blue-jerseyed skipper.

'A boat,' said Balintore, 'gives you mobility, and you can't say that of a house.'

'Which, however, has a stability that often seems desirable in a boat.'

They had another glass of ouzo, and agreed that it was now too late to walk to the quarries; but decided to go there on the following day, and start soon after breakfast.

In the morning they borrowed a knapsack, and burdened with a loaf of bread, a large piece of cheese, and a bottle of retsina, set off on an uphill walk that gave them wide views of a reddish, almost treeless landscape, criss-crossed by low drystone walls — a bare but curiously friendly land, beatified by light and bordered by the sea — and after going farther than they had expected, came to a scarred, an excavated, hillside, where a rough road ended at a level space carpeted with a white and brilliant gravel.

At the end of the road stood an elderly American motor-car, and thirty yards farther on, conferring with the driver, were a tall, trousered woman and a short, broad-shouldered man whose voice could be clearly heard.

'I don't give a damn what it costs,' he was saying. 'I'm going to get a ship-load of this stuff out to Australia, and we're going to have the finest approach-road — with a big circle in front of the front door — the best and most expensive carriage-drive in Queensland. A carriage-drive of pure white marble chips. Ay, that'll set them talking!'

He spoke loudly, with a strong Scotch intonation, and Balintore and Palladis, a little embarrassed, stopped and felt disinclined to go on, lest they intrude on a scene of domestic privacy; for the tall, trousered woman, though her voice was too quiet to be heard, was manifestly objecting to her husband's extravagant proposal.

The broad-shouldered man stooped and gathered a double handful of the shining gravel. 'Look at it!' he said. 'Isn't that just beautiful? Beautiful! And I'll need about three thousand tons.'

He tossed the marble chips into the air, brushed his hands, and saw Balintore and Palladis. He hesitated a moment before saying, 'You're English, by the look of you?'

'No more English — no more English than you,' said Balintore in a voice that quavered, but recovered its strength.

The broad-shouldered man came towards them, staring suspiciously at Balintore, and then exclaimed, with deep emotion, 'It canna be? After a' these years — oh, it canna be!'

'Peter Ricci,' said Balintore.

'Ned Balintore!'

He took Balintore's hands in his — his hands were large and muscular — and shook them violently, while down his weather-tanned cheeks tears streamed from his eyes unchecked, and strong teeth showed in a mouth that opened widely, as if for speech, but could find no sound nearer to speech than uncontrollable, delighted laughter.

Then, with an effort at self-control — wiping with his coat-sleeve his weeping eyes — he took Balintore by the elbow and pulled him towards the tall woman who stood self-consciously aloof, perhaps bewildered, perhaps coldly disapproving — and loudly declared, 'Here's my oldest friend in the world! The friend o' my schooldays in Auld Reekie! In Edinburgh, the bonniest toon in all the world — and I meet him after near thirty years on a bloody, barren Greek island, and him a famous man! You've heard of Ned Balintore?'

She offered a seemingly reluctant hand. 'The wife,' said

Ricci, and Balintore, as if apologising for his unexpected appearance, said, 'It's true, you know. We were — we are — old friends.'

He was manifestly nervous: breathing too quickly, with a light and shallow rhythm, but also pleased, and obviously pleased, by an encounter, so wildly improbable, with the closest friend of his boyhood. He put his arm, a little shyly, round Ricci's broad shoulders and said, 'Peter! Oh, God, there's no end to surprise!'

Peter Ricci, unashamed of emotion, said with a louder warmth, 'This is a great and memorable day! I havena been so happy since — ah weel, there'll be time enough to tell you about that. But who's your friend?'

Palladis was introduced, and got a crippling handshake from Ricci, a cooler welcome from his wife — 'Call her Myrtle,' said Ricci — and for the next ten minutes there was a confused and often interrupted explication of two simple occurrences. The Riccis had to be told how Balintore and Palladis had come to Paros, and they were informed that Ricci, in a chartered yacht, had run in for shelter when the weather worsened. After considerable repetition, and some unnecessary detail, these facts were established, and there fell upon them the sort of silence that often occurs when old friends meet, and having spent the exuberance of first enquiry, are temporarily at a loss for new topics of conversation.

The uneasy pause was broken by Palladis, who asked, 'How much would it cost to take three thousand tons of marble chips to Australia?'

'I'm going to make serious enquiry about that,' said Ricci. 'There's a lot of idle shipping in Piraeus — ships laid up and doing nothing to earn their keep — and I might make a good bargain.'

'But to charter even an old tramp——'

'Ay, it would cost money, I'm no denying that. But I'm building a new house, and this stuff would give me the bonniest carriage-drive in the Antipodes. And when you've set your heart on something, you canna let money come between you.'

'Only a rich man can talk like that,' said Balintore.

'I've done well for myself, I canna complain.'

'Where is your new house ?' asked Palladis.

'Have you heard of a place called Townsville ?'

'No, I'm afraid I haven't.'

'Ah, we're just wasting our time here. I've got so much to tell you, Ned ! Biography to begin with, and geography too, it seems. We'll go back to the harbour, and you'll come aboard my boat, where we can sit in comfort and talk in peace, and have a dram forbye.'

They returned to the car he had hired, and Ricci said, 'I'm broader in the beam than either of you, I'll sit in front with the driver. You'll have plenty of room in the back, for Myrtle's all length and no girth.'

Palladis, who sat in the middle, tried to make conversation with her, but found it difficult. She was quite young, a pale blonde with an oval face and big blue eyes : a girl of striking and memorable appearance, but curiously subdued. When she spoke her words conveyed nothing but gentle agreement with what Palladis had said, and her soft voice held only the whisper of an Australian accent. When Palladis asked her about the house for which Ricci envisaged a marble carriage-drive, she took from her handbag several photographs of a large though unfinished bungalow, designed apparently after a Spanish style of architecture, and said proudly, 'It was Peter who planned it all. He's very, very clever.'

At the harbour a fisherman rowed them out to the anchored

caique, where they sat comfortably under an awning that covered the after-deck. The crew were ashore, and Myrtle asked what they would like to drink.

'I canna drink Greek beer,' said Ricci, 'and there's none aboard. You'd better bring whisky : you canna go far wrong with whisky.'

She went below, and he said to Palladis, 'You didn't get much change out of her, did you ? No, I didna think you would. And twelve months ago there was no livelier, more talkative girl in Queensland. The life and soul of Lennon's Hotel — Lennon's in Brisbane : you'll have heard of it ? A fine hotel — and then she met that damned American. A smooth-talking Californian engineer with half a dozen college degrees——'

He stopped abruptly as Myrtle came on deck with whisky and soda water, glasses and a bowl of ice. She carried the heavy tray easily, and set it on a small table. She appeared to have gained in confidence since coming aboard, and poured their drinks with quick dexterity.

'I'm going to leave you here,' she said softly, 'while I get a lunch ready — if you can make do with a cold lunch ?'

Balintore and Palladis protested against her going to so much trouble, but Ricci assured them that Myrtle enjoyed all housekeeping tasks, and said to her, as she was about to go below again, 'While you're on the move, hen, you might bring up the big atlas, will you ?'

Obediently she returned with a large volume, and Ricci opened it to show a map of Queensland. With a blunt forefinger he traced the coast north from Brisbane till he came to Townsville, and said, 'It's there I'm building my new house, and there' — his finger moved some five or six hundred miles inland — 'there's where the money came from ! You see a place called Cloncurry ? Well, about a hundred miles north and west of there, the old geiger counter started clicking, and I went to sleep in the firm conviction that I'd wake up a millionaire.'

'Are you a millionaire ?' asked Balintore.

'As near as makes no difference,' said Ricci complacently.

'Uranium ?' asked Palladis.

'It's desolate country,' said Ricci, 'and dangerous country to get lost in. All red rock and spinifex. But a few years ago they found uranium down there, just east of Mount Isa, and I remembered a place very like the valley where now there's a big mine called Mary Kathleen. I was working at Mount Isa myself, and every now and then I'd take a dander up north, looking for that place I remembered from the days when I was riding-up cattle——'

'You've been a cattleman as well as a miner ?'

'I've done all manner of things, from shooting kangaroos to pearling off Thursday Island and washing dishes in Sydney. Ay, Sydney. And it's you that took me there, Ned. If it hadna been for you I might never have seen Australia — and never heard a geiger counter clicking over a million pounds.'

'What happened then ? What did you have to do to turn uranium under red rock into money in the bank ?'

'Well may you ask !' said Ricci. 'Finding it was only the beginning, the real work came later on. I staked my claim, of course, and registered my claim, and then I had to raise money to prove what the claim was worth. And that brought in all the sharks and the wide boys, the lawyers and the city slickers, and at times I thought I was going out of my mind ! There, you see, was a million pounds under the red rock — as you yourself said. Ay, and better than a million, for I'll be drawing royalties till the day of my death — but before I could lay hands on it I had to do battle with the lawyers and the wide boys, and it was then I met Myrtle, and she saved my sanity.

'I was staying at Lennon's Hotel in Brisbane, arguing with three different groups that all wanted to buy Auld Reekie — that's what I called it: the claim I'd staked — and Myrtle was a barmaid there, the life and soul of the place, though you wouldn't think so now. And she married me before the worth of the claim had been proved. It wasna for money she married. For all she knew, and for all I knew, the claim might not have been worth a docken.

'But from the day we married all went well. As things turned out, I'd put myself into good hands, and a month later I knew beyond all doubt that the first million wouldna be long in reaching my pocket. But then we met that damned American, him that called himself an expert, and had college degrees to prove it. He was looking for a job, and he thought the best way of getting it would be to make himself pleasant and useful to Myrtle. But he went the wrong way about it. He told her one day — with the best of motives, I've no doubt — he told her, in these very words, "You're a swell looker, honey, but if you're going to travel in Europe, and live in millionaire circles, you'll sure have to catch up on your culture".

'And Myrtle took that to heart! You see, she wasn't a girl that had ever read books — she didn't need to! — but suddenly it came into her mind that she wasna fitted to play her proper part in the new world that great wealth was opening before her. Well, I did what I could to reassure her, but damn the difference it made. She lost all her confidence. She said she couldn't even speak like a millionaire's wife, so off she went to a teacher of elocution to get rid of her accent. And what good did that do ? She's got no accent now, none at all — and she's got nothing to say ! But before she met that damned American — when she spoke with an Australian accent as rough as the Tasman Sea — she never stopped talking, and every man within hearing would be doting on every word she said.'

Ricci looked glumly at the sparkling sea, and was about to pour himself another drink when Myrtle came on deck to say, 'Your lunch is ready, so don't drink any more whisky.'

'We've had a great deal to talk about,' said Ricci.

'Well, come downstairs, you can go on talking there.'

They followed her into an elaborately furnished saloon — 'Too fancy for my taste, but comfortable,' said Ricci — and sat down to a substantial meal of smoked salmon, veal-and-ham pie, a Stilton cheese.

'The bread and butter are Greek, and there's retsina if you want it, but the rest comes out of a good cold store I put in before we left Piraeus,' said Ricci. 'I've earned my comfort, and I enjoy my comfort.'

He leaned across the table and said to Myrtle, with a renewal of emotion, 'He's my oldest friend — him that's sitting beside you — and if it hadna been for him I might never have gone to Australia, I might never have met you, hen ! We went to the school together — and bad, bad boys we were! — and together we ran away from school and went to sea in a great sailing-ship the like of which no longer's to be seen. We made voyage after voyage — how many voyages, Ned ?'

'Five or six. I made one more than you.'

'That's a true story, is it ?' asked Palladis.

'Did you doubt it ?' asked Balintore.

Palladis looked at him in surprise. There was a ring of

authority in his voice, and his face wore again its once familiar look of innocence and truth and arrogance. 'I thought,' he said carefully, 'that you might have embroidered it — exaggerated here and there——'

'Frequently,' said Balintore, 'I have been guilty of understatement — about myself, that is — but I have never exaggerated. I have never felt the need to.'

He had recovered, or seemed to have recovered — if only for a little while — his old temper of assurance. Perhaps it floated insecurely on whisky — perhaps more safely on the warmth of Ricci's manifest affection — but it was buoyant; and that was a change indeed.

'She was a great ship, the *Herzogin Cecilie*,' said Ricci. 'We joined her in Copenhagen. We sailed from Leith to Copenhagen, and Ned paid our passage. You remember, Ned? We were tired of school, we had made up our minds to go to sea, and then we read in the paper that the *Cecilie* was likely to be held up in Copenhagen, short of her proper crew, and God knows her proper crew was small enough.'

Palladis and Myrtle, eating veal-and-ham pie and Stilton cheese, listened for a long time to burly reminiscence of their life under sail. Their first voyage was to Lourenço Marques, then on to Australia to load with grain, and home round Cape Horn in a roaring gale that shredded sails and carried away one of the lifeboats. There was a day, on a later voyage, when they made 340 miles, and a day when they lost a score of sails off the Lizard. There were shipmates they remembered, sometimes with admiration and respect, sometimes with mockery. There were the Old Man and the Cook, there were Cape pigeons, and corposants burning blue at the yard-arm. There was the last voyage when the old barque came home in 86 days, and ran ashore on the coast of Devon.

'I wasna with you that time,' said Ricci. 'I jumped ship in Port Lincoln, and went to Sydney.'

'But you were aboard when she was wrecked?' asked Palladis. 'Why have you never told me?'

'It's something I've never spoken about,' said Balintore. 'It was a thing I tried to forget. She was a great ship, as Peter says, one of the last of the old sort, and I'd sailed in for her, three years, in every sort of weather. Damnable weather, and days of pure serenity. She was a match for every season, and nothing daunted her. But what could she do in a blind fog? She was blind when she ran aground on Bolt Head, and — oh, let's talk of something else! She fell away from the rock when she struck, and nothing could hold her. She was done for, and a thing of beauty went out of the world. God knows why.'

'I remember the day when the news reached Sydney,' said Ricci, 'and I sat down and wept. Then I got up and drank ten pints of beer — I was working in the kitchen of a cheap and dirty restaurant — and I hit the boss over the head with a soup-ladle till he fell to the floor crying for his mother. We were both greetin' — I was greetin' fou — and we were both Italian by blood, though not according to the passport. So he understood how I was feeling. He'd been a sailor himself at one time, though only on a steamer.'

He helped himself to more whisky, and Balintore said, 'It was after that I went to Spain.'

'Ay, Spain!' said Ricci. 'You'll need to tell me about Spain.'

He drank his whisky, leaned back on the cushioned settee, and began to breathe more deeply. His eyes remained open, but no longer looked at Balintore; no longer looked at anyone. His features retained their composure, and to casual inspection he seemed a man in excellent health and still tolerably alert: a good-looking, burly man with a square, weather-hued face, brown eyes, short nose, square chin, and curling black hair brushed back from his forehead and distinguished by a white mèche. But his breathing was deep and slow, and his eyes were unfocussed.

'He's fallen asleep,' said Myrtle softly.

'With his eyes open ?'

'It's one of his peculiarities. He's a very remarkable man, and when he gets excited he sometimes drinks too much ; and then, quite suddenly, he'll fall asleep. But as long as it's daylight he doesn't close his eyes.'

'We'll have to go,' said Palladis.

'You're welcome to stay. He won't sleep for more than an hour or two.'

'No, no,' said Balintore. 'We've stayed too long as it is, and given you far too much trouble.'

'I've enjoyed having you ; and we'll see you to-morrow, won't we ? You've given Peter so much pleasure.'

She went on deck with them, and to their surprise put two fingers in her mouth and emitted a piercing whistle. She resumed immediately her demure appearance, and on the beach the fisherman she had summoned pushed out his boat.

Balintore and Palladis were rowed ashore, and walked to their hotel.

'I haven't drunk whisky at midday since we had a party in O'Hara's Bar,' said Palladis. 'And, like Ricci, I'm going to sleep it off.'

'My oldest friend,' said Balintore solemnly, 'and we meet after twenty-seven or twenty-eight — after nearly thirty years, in the middle of the Cyclades !'

'You must tell me more about him at dinner,' said Palladis. 'But I may be late for dinner.'

It was half-past nine when they met again, and Balintore,

who had wakened earlier, had already drunk several glasses of ouzo. He was eager to talk, and began his tale of the Riccis over a plate of fish-soup.

'His grandfather came into Scotland with a pack on his back, and a couple of years later was selling ice-cream from a barrow in Leith Walk. We're xenophiles in Scotland, like the Greeks: we've domesticated Irish and Lithuanians, Italians and Poles — ay, and English too!'

'You needn't imitate Ricci's accent,' said Palladis.

'I wish I'd kept it. I used to speak as he does, and it did me no good to anglify my voice.'

'Tell me about his grandfather.'

'I never knew him, but Peter used to speak of him. He wasn't ashamed of him. Old Pietro Ricci bought a shop in Leith, and did well for himself. There's hardly an Italian in Scotland who hasn't done well, and most of them started with ice-cream. In a social history of Scotland the ice-cream barrow shouldn't be ignored — and those who pushed them were fine people!'

'You're slipping into that accent again.'

'And what's the harm in that?'

'None at all. But you don't sound like yourself. And I want to hear about Pietro Ricci.'

'He prospered. But he and his wife had only the one child, who was Peter's father. He was given a good education, trained as a chemist, and in due course the old man set him up in business in his own shop. A shop in Queensferry Street, not far from where we lived. I can see it still, with the name *Antony Ricci, M.P.S.* in a label of great gold letters over the window; but it's no longer there. And we lived in Eton Terrace: over the Dean Bridge and turn right. It's not half a mile away. And Peter and I were friends from the start.

And better friends than ever when I learnt what I was: not the legitimate son of Professor Balintore of the Chair of Scottish History, but a foundling and a bastard. A bastard in all probability. And Peter being a foreigner — well, that seemed to bring us nearer together.'

'According to him, you were both bad boys.'

'We were too damned clever to put up with the majority: that's what he meant. It was a good school we went to — all those Edinburgh day-schools are good: Watson's and Heriot's, the Academy and the Royal High — and ours was probably the best of them, but too prosaic, too sensible, too addicted to the middle of the road for our liking, and we rebelled. From the schoolmaster's point of view we may have been bad — — but now Peter's a millionaire, and I, before I cracked, before I tripped and tumbled off the pavement of common sanity, with eight million people watching me — I was a person of some consequence wasn't I?'

'You enjoyed a great reputation, and had earned it,' said Palladis gently.

'No! I'd won it like a cheap-jack taking money from yokels at a country fair.'

'There's a persistent majority of yokels in the world.'

'That doesn't justify the cheap-jack and his tricks.'

'If he amuses the yokels——'

'He damns himself.'

'You've had a good day,' said Palladis. 'Don't spoil it by bitterness.'

'No, by God, I'll say no more. To meet Peter Ricci again, and remember the days aboard that old lurching barque, roaring round Cape Horn under the cliffs of the sea — there's no bitterness there, and it leaves no room for bitterness. Let's have some brandy.'

By the following morning the wind had gone down, and while they were still at breakfast a messenger arrived with a note from Ricci that read : 'Come down as soon as you're ready, and bring pyjamas and tooth-brush. We're going for a little cruise round to Andiparos where, I'm told, there's good bathing. No hurry, but the sooner we start the sooner we get there. Back to-morrow night.'

'I never thought I'd go to sea again with Peter Ricci,' said Balintore.

'We must cultivate Myrtle,' said Palladis. 'I'm very sorry for that poor girl.'

'She's very rich.'

'She has been impoverished by Ricci's wealth.'

'There are compensations in that sort of pauperdom,' said Balintore.

An hour later the caique's anchor was aboard and her deck was responding, like a muffled drum, to the beat of a powerful diesel engine. She was heading at half-speed for the rocky islets that guarded the entrance to the bay. Balintore and Palladis met the skipper, who wore a gold ear-ring and looked like an ill-made copy of an ancient Greek ; for his features were grimly classical but his legs short and bandy. There was an engineer, who was also the steward, and the two seamen were young and cheerful. The caique had ample room for visitors : she was broad in the beam though shallow of draught, and about fifty feet over all. As well as the owner's cabin aft of the saloon, there were two good cabins forward.

They turned south, round the southern foreland of the bay, and presently went more slowly as the sea, shoaling quickly, turned from pale blue to apple green ; and a boy in the bow shouted incomprehensibly to the skipper in the deck-house. The russet land of Paros, cut into trapezoid shapes by low stone dykes, shone like a tarnished cameo, of onyx or agate, to the left ; and the modest slopes of Andiparos emerged gradually from the sea on their right. Peter Ricci, bare-headed, walked to and fro with Balintore, and Palladis, with a troubled sympathy, talked to Myrtle. For several weeks past, he discovered, she had been trying to read a book called *The Living World of Literature, from Lao-Tsze to Henry James.*

'Oh no !' he exclaimed. 'Read books, by all means ; but avoid literature at all costs.'

'It's for Peter's sake,' she said gravely.

'He won't thank you if he finds Lao-Tsze on your pillow. Or Henry James either.'

They dropped anchor off a rocky point, and went ashore to a small sandy bay where Balintore and Palladis and Ricci swam conservatively in the shallows, while Myrtle in a black suit went, swift as a dolphin, into greater depths and traced the crystal line of her movement on blue water half a mile from shore. They watched her with admiration, and greeted her with respect when she came back to the beach with water-drops pearling her arms.

She smiled happily and said, 'It's nice to be able to swim without looking over your shoulder for sharks.'

The voracity of sharks off the coasts of New South Wales and Queensland emerged as a topic for conversation, and that, and other of the more vivid or astonishing aspects of Australian life held their attention till a little while after noon ; when they rowed out to the yacht again. There they found the after-deck sheltered by its awning, and in its shade a table well furnished with assorted drink. Within a little while conversation reverted to Edinburgh and the boyhood of their host.

Peter Ricci recalled the fine house in Eton Terrace where Balintore had lived : it had roused his envy, in youth, because across the road from it were hanging gardens, to which householders held keys, that reached down to the Water of Leith. A pleasanter place to live, he had thought, could hardly be imagined. Balintore's father, the Professor, he also remembered with affection, and spoke of his early death with what appeared to be genuine regret.

'A man of consequence,' he said, 'and a fine-looking man forbye. My own father held him in high regard. "A scholar and a gentleman, an asset to the whole city," is what he used to say. Ay, many's the time I've watched the three of you on your way to the Kirk. Up Queensferry Street, on the opposite side to us — we lived above the shop. You remember that? — You'd be going to St. John's, at the corner of Princes Street? Just so! And your father in his top-hat glinting in the sun. We must have had fine weather in those days, for that's the way I remember it: always a glimmer of sun on his black silk-hat. And never a silk-hat have I seen since then, for they're not much worn in Queensland.'

Balintore, muttering under his breath, helped himself to another drink.

'What did you say?' asked Ricci.

'I was trying to think of a poem I read somewhere; but I can only remember two lines of it:

> 'The Cuckoos in my Family Tree
> Calculate Heredity.'

'And what's the meaning of that?'

'He wasn't my father, he was only my adoptive father. You know that as well as I do.'

'I remember the day you told me, and that was a right surprise! It was almost as big a shock to me as it had been to you. You swore me to secrecy, and I kept it a secret. I never spoke of it from that day to this.'

'I was only twelve when he died,' said Balintore. 'I still thought he was my real father, my natural father — and he might well have been, the way I missed him. I used to dream of him. Dream that he was opening my bedroom door and saying, "Hullo, Ned ! Sorry I've been away so long." '

'I never saw my father again after we left Edinburgh,' said Ricci. 'He died in 1941 when I was in the army. I was in Tobruk when he died.'

He got up and refilled their glasses. 'What the hell !' he said. 'It's all ancient history, there's no need to go into mourning now.'

'Is anyone beginning to feel hungry ?' asked Myrtle.

'There's no hurry,' said Ricci.

'If you want lunch within the next hour, I'd better go and see to it myself.'

She went below, and Ricci said, 'It's funny that neither of us ever liked your mother.'

'She wasn't my mother.'

'If we'd been fond of her — if you had been fond of her — you might never have discovered that.'

'She would have had to tell me some time.'

'Ay, maybe. But as things turned out, we forced her hand, so to speak.'

'What did you do ?'

'We made up our minds to murder her,' said Ricci.

'To murder his mother ?'

'It was boyish nonsense,' said Balintore with a loud and sudden irritation in his voice. 'Adolescent nonsense — not vicious, not really wicked — but romantic. Romantic after a fashion.'

'The inspiration,' said Ricci, 'being Paymaster Commander Wilfred Patch, late of the Royal Navy. "The Commander," your mother always called him. He became a friend of your family — of your father as well as your mother — after he retired from the navy and got a job with the Country Gentlemen's Association, selling cultivators and lawn-mowers and grass-seed mixtures at a discount to landed proprietors in East Lothian.'

'I disliked him from my first sight of him,' said Balintore, 'and he tried to make friends with me. He used to slip me half a crown — and I, God forgive me, used to take it.'

'He gave me half a crown once,' said Ricci, 'and told me the best steward they'd ever had aboard some bloody cruiser he was serving in, in the Mediterranean, was a man called Ricci. A Maltese. He wondered if he was a relation of mine.'

'And after my father died — the man I'd been taught to call my father——'

'He went to your house, and was seen at your house, more and more.'

'And she told me one night, after I'd come home from school, she told me that he'd asked her to marry him — and because she was lonely, after my father's death——'

'She hoped it would make you happier too ! That's what she said, didn't she ?'

'She said it would bring happiness to both of us.'

'And the next day you told me the whole story——'

'And we decided,' said Balintore, 'to kill her.'

'Because what she suggested was an insult to your father,' said Ricci.

'That's what we felt.'

'But what did you do ?' asked Palladis.

'For about three weeks,' said Ricci, 'we did nothing but talk. We talked and borrowed books from the Public Library: books on crime. And finally we decided that the best way to do her in was a way that had been used by a man called Smith, who used to murder his brides in the bath. Because Ned's mother——'

'Call her Mrs. Balintore — or Mrs. Patch.'

'— because she used to take her bath every day at half-past six in the evening, regular. And she'd lie in it for a full half-hour. So that was our opportunity. And the only obstacle, so far as we could see, was the bathroom door, which was closed by a wee bolt. And then Ned had a good idea.'

'I thought it was yours?'

'No, it was you who thought of chewing-gum. And it worked fine. I went home with you, about five o'clock, or maybe a bit later, and one or other of us chewed a stick of gum till it was soft, and filled the slot with it so that when it hardened the bolt couldn't go in. And then we waited. We waited till your mother went into the bathroom, and we heard her running the bath, and we waited another ten minutes, watching the time by the big grandfather's clock that stood in the hall.—You remember the grandfather's clock? — And by that time we were so excited we might have been running the Junior School Hundred Yards. We were both of us just about thirteen: the same age. But you said "It's our duty," and I said "Out of respect for your father," and we shook hands, down there in the hall, and ran up the stair, and with one shove on the bathroom door it flew wide open. And your mother sat up with a howl of wrath — the room was full of steam and smelling of some fancy scent — and we made a dive for her feet, for that was the plan we'd concocted.'

Palladis looked from one to the other with a slightly gaping incredulity, with an expression of close but strained attention; and Balintore, sipping his drink, stared over the rim of his glass with the glum indifference of an ill-made mask. But Ricci spoke with serious and lively recollection of an unforgettable scene.

'But to drown a woman in her bath is more difficult than you might think,' he said. 'Oh, much more difficult ! Maybe it's easy enough if she's lying half asleep, and before she gets a guess at what you're up to, you snap up her ankles and pull her towards you till her head's under water ; which is what we'd hoped and planned to do. But Mrs. Balintore — she was a big woman, mind you ! — she was sitting up in her bath, and when Ned and I made a dive for her feet, she kicked out like a breaking scrum with a loose ball in front of it, and Ned got a jolt on the chin that sent him flying, and I was near drowned with the water she threw up.

'And the next we knew — she was a big woman, I said — there she was, striding across the floor, naked as the dawn and screaming like fury in that room full of steam, and Ned and me, half-soaked and half-stunned, running out and running down the stair like a couple of wee mice with a tom-cat at their tails. And Ned slept in our house that night, above the shop in Queensferry Street, being feared to go home.'

'I'm not surprised,' said Palladis.

'It was my father who went and made peace between them,' said Ricci. 'Or what could be regarded as peace, giving a liberal interpretation to the word. He'd a certain advantage, you see, being Italian. He'd a good command of the English language, for one thing, and he could talk about jealousy with less restraint, and a deeper knowledge than a typical, well brought-up Edinburgh man would have considered decent. He persuaded Mrs. Balintore that Ned's behaviour, bad as it was, was no more than could be expected from a boy so consumed by love of his mother that he couldna bear to see her bestow affection on anyone else: meaning, that is, Paymaster-Commander Patch. So she agreed to let Ned come home again, and promised not to punish him. But you could hardly say she kept her promise, could you?'

'She took a fiendish revenge on me,' said Balintore. 'She told me the truth. The truth about myself.'

'Till then,' said Palladis, 'you had never suspected——'

'Till then,' said Balintore, 'I had been brought up as the son of Professor and Mrs. Balintore, with no suspicion that I had not been begotten in their legal bed; though I had always found it difficult to accept, still more to understand, my presumptive father's apparent affection for my presumptive mother. But now she told me I was an adopted child, a foundling taken in because they, being unable to beget or bear — I don't know which — had felt that a house without a child was almost as unnatural as a house without a cat and a dog. — They had a white Persian, perpetually moulting, and an ill-tempered Border terrier to which she was devoted.— So I had been acquired, as another household pet, and she had, she said, no intention of repudiating her responsibility for me. But what had become obvious, she told me, was that I had been born of low, debased, and probably criminal stock — otherwise my behaviour was incomprehensible — and I could no longer expect to be trusted or shown affection. A roof above my head, a sufficiency of clothes, and food on the table — that was all I could look forward to. And six months later she married "the Commander", who made things worse by being sorry for me, and kind to me.'

'There's no telling who a woman will marry if she gets the chance,' said Ricci, 'but even she could surely have found something more attractive than him.'

Myrtle came up from the saloon to say, 'Lunch is ready at last, and I hope you like fish. It's red mullet.'

There was little conversation over the luncheon table, and thereafter they retired to their cabins to sleep for an hour or two. At about half-past four Myrtle and Palladis swam from the anchored yacht, and after they had climbed aboard again, the engine was started, and they cruised slowly south ; returning to their good anchorage before dusk quite obscured the shore-line.

When the engineer, who was also the steward, again brought drinks up to the after-deck, Palladis said, 'I wish you would tell me how you provision your ship — on what scale you provision her — when you're setting out on a cruise.'

'We don't always drink as much as this,' said Myrtle, 'but Peter likes to have plenty on board, just in case of visitors.'

'At present,' said Ricci, 'I'm only experimenting. As yet, you see, I havena had much experience in being a millionaire, and I'm just going about it cautiously, trying to make the best of it. I'm building a house in Townsville, as I told you — a house that's going to have the finest carriage-drive in the Antipodes — and a friend of mine, a naval architect in Sydney, is designing a boat for me. A boat about the size of this, but a different hull altogether, that we can use for cruising about the Barrier Reef, and up to the Islands : to New Guinea, and maybe as far as the Solomons, if we want to.

'Well, that will keep us busy for part of the year. But I was born in Scotland, and I'm not forsaking Europe altogether. Oh, no ! So we came here, for a cruise among the Greek islands, to see what sort of a boat would be suitable for these parts. And when we've decided I'll build another here in Greece, and keep her in Greece, and we'll spend part of the year in the Mediterranean, and Myrtle can do some shopping in Rome. If you've time to spare it's easy enough to combine good sailing with a few weeks ashore to look at the shops. It's a small auxiliary schooner I think I'll build here, and man her with a Greek crew. They're good sailors, the Greeks.'

Balintore and Palladis listened with admiration to Ricci's projected policy for life-with-a-million-pounds : 'And royalties coming forbye : don't forget that,' he said. They offered suggestions, as to where he should go ; and how, to best advantage, he should spend his money. They had found a subject that held them enthralled in argument — in project and counter-project, in extravagance and ultra extravagance — for three or four hours. They went down to dinner, and had finished dinner, before they had exhausted their ideas for deploying wealth in a campaign for enduring pleasure ; and with invention worn out, but their brandy glasses generously filled, they sat for some time in comparative silence, their minds still occupied with elusive or vicarious enjoyment.

It was Ricci who brought them back to reality — or the realities of ordinary life — by leaning across the table and saying to Balintore, 'And thirty years ago, ay, thirty years ago and more, if we had a shilling or two to spend, how did we spend it ? As like as not we'd go down to the Portobello Baths, and a swim there would give us more pleasure than swimming nowadays on the finest beaches of the Mediterranean Sea or the Pacific Ocean !'

This observation provoked no response but the acquiescence of bored agreement, and Ricci, with a little more assertiveness in his voice, said, 'You settled down fairly weel after your mother married the Commander. You canna say your life was one long, stark chapter of unrelieved misery.'

'I endured it,' said Balintore. 'I was thirteen when she married him. What else could I do ?'

Myrtle yawned and said, 'I think I'll go to bed.' But Ricci said, 'No, hen, don't leave us ! I like to have you here, where I can look at you.'

'So do I,' said Palladis.

Myrtle sat down again, and Ricci said, 'There's one thing that's always puzzled me. After your mother died — and that was two or three years after she married the Commander : it was just before we ran away and went to sea — well, what I'm thinking of is this : the Commander gave you his stamp-album. Now that collection of his, they were all British Colonials, was a valuable collection. I remember him showing it to us and saying, "Many of these stamps are worth a lot of money." And he set great store by them, there's no doubt of that. But when your mother died, he gave them to you. Well, why ?'

'He was sorry for me,' said Balintore.

'That's a poor reason. That's no explanation at all.'

'I fell ill——'

'You took to your bed and stayed away from school — you stayed away for a week — because you were due a thrashing from the Rector.'

'I was ill.'

'I don't believe it. No, what I believe is this : your mother had diabetes——'

'What has that got to do with it ?'

'My father was a chemist, and I know this : that if someone has diabetes, it's easy enough to kill him — or her, as the case may be — by depriving him, or her, of their proper dose of insulin. Now the Commander was away from home when your mother died——'

'She wasn't my mother.'

'I know, I know that. There's no point in harping on that. The point is that the Commander had gone to Loch Leven for a week's fishing, and two or three days later his wife died in coma. And when the Commander came home he gave you a collection of British Colonial stamps. A valuable collection.'

'And you've reason to be grateful to him.'

'I'm aware of that. When you and me decided that we'd had enough of school, and enough of Edinburgh, and wanted to go to Copenhagen to join the *Herzogin Cecilie*, we sold his album to a junk shop in the High Street for £40. They gave us £40 without question, and that means the album was worth £400 at the very least. Well, why did he give it to you?'

'I've already told you——'

'No, no. There's a stiffer reason than that. And my belief — it's always been my belief — is that the Commander murdered her, and bribed you to keep your mouth shut, if you suspected anything.'

'Why should he want to murder her?'

'She left £22,000 and that fine house in Eton Terrace. And he got it all.'

'But how,' asked Palladis, 'could he murder her when she was in Edinburgh and he was fishing on Loch Leven?'

'She was a diabetic,' said Ricci, 'and had to take a big dose of insulin every day. I know, because the insulin came from our shop, and my father was a friend of old Dr. Ogilvie — he must have been near eighty — who was her doctor. Well, then, what happened was this: Mrs. Balintore, or Mrs. Patch as she had become, had her proper supply of insulin when the Commander went away. You get insulin, if you need it, in wee bottles with a thin rubber top, and when you want to give yourself a dose you poke a syringe through the rubber, suck up the dose, and shoot it into your arm. It's easy enough, anyone can do it.'

'I still don't see——'

'Just a minute,' said Ricci. 'Now another thing that's easy to do is to take a syringe, and empty three or four of those wee bottles, and then — still using the syringe — refill them with water from the tap. Then you go off to Loch Leven, and your wife gives herself a dose, not of insulin, but plain water. What happens then? She begins to feel ill. Miserable and drowsy and ill. So she gives herself another dose, and that does no good either. She tries again, with a bigger dose, and maybe the following day, when she's really ill, and worse than she thinks, she rings old Dr. Ogilvie, and tells him she can't understand what's wrong with her, for she's taken twice or three times her ordinary doses, and it's done her no good at all.

'Well, by the time Dr. Ogilvie goes round to see her, she's in a coma, and from what she's told him he concludes she's in insulin coma, due to over-dosing. So what does he do? He injects a solution of sugar, and the poor lady — who's had no insulin at all — dies in diabetic coma. And no one has any reason to suspect foul play.'

'So it was the doctor who killed her,' said Balintore.

'Put it that way if you like. But the man to blame was him who emptied the wee bottles and filled them with plain water.'

'But did that happen?' asked Palladis. 'You don't know, do you? You're only guessing.'

'The day before he went to Loch Leven the Commander came into the shop and bought a new syringe. And when he came home and found his wife dead, he gave Ned a valuable stamp-collection. Well, why? To keep his mouth shut.'

'No,' said Balintore. 'I didn't like the man, but he wasn't

a murderer, and you mustn't blacken his name. All that you've said is true, but it wasn't Commander Patch who filled the bottles with water.'

'How do you know that?'

'Because that's what I did. — And now I'm going on deck for a breath of fresh air. It's very stuffy down here.'

Twenty-three

WHEN they followed him, perhaps ten minutes later, he had gone. Somewhere down below the crew were sound asleep, and the deck was empty.

'I heard a splash,' said Myrtle. 'I'm sure I did !'

'I heard nothing.'

'The dinghy's alongside,' said Palladis. 'We can look for him.'

'There !' cried Myrtle. 'There !'

She pointed to something which she alone could see in the darkness, and kicked off her slippers. She stood on the low rail and went overboard in a long, shallow dive. She was wearing only a shirt and narrow trousers, and her long legs thrashed the dark sea, that now a fresh breeze ruffled, to a diamond of dancing phosphorescence.

Ricci and Palladis got into the dinghy and rowed after her. They found her, some forty yards away, supporting Balintore, who was unconscious.

'He was on his face,' she said, 'but he's still alive.'

They pulled him in over the stern of the dinghy, and went back to the caique ; whose skipper and engineer were now awake and on deck. Balintore was lifted on board. They laid him down with a folded coat under his chest, and Ricci, kneeling astride of him, pushed against his lower ribs and rocked to and fro. Balintore vomited sea-water, and within a few minutes regained consciousness. He muttered something which could not be heard. Then, more loudly, repeated, 'I fell. I fell and hit my head.' There was, indeed, a bruise on his right temple.

They took him down to his cabin, undressed him, and put him to bed. He said again, 'I fell. When I went on deck the cooler air made me dizzy. Perhaps I had drunk too much. It wasn't suicide.'

'Are you all right now ?' asked Palladis.

'Give me some brandy and I shall be.'

Myrtle had taken off her wet clothes and put on a dressing-gown. 'I'll sit with him till he goes to sleep,' she said.

Ricci and Palladis went on deck again, and Ricci asked, 'Do you think he was telling the truth ?'

'It's hard to say.'

'If it was suicide, or attempted suicide, then I'm to blame.'

'That's going too far. Much too far.'

'It was me that made him tell the truth about his mother's death. — Though she wasn't his mother ; it's bad enough, but no so bad as that.'

'Had it never occurred to you that he might have killed her ?'

'Never ! As I saw it, the guilty man was the Commander, and proof of that was the stamp-album.'

'But surely you spoke about it ? When you were boys together in that ship ?'

'Never,' said Ricci again. 'At the age of sixteen, which was our age, there's a sort of reluctance — or is a sort of delicacy ? — that disappears as we get older. A delicacy about our parents, or the older members of the family. We don't think too much about what goes on in their minds ; or in their bedrooms either. Would you call that delicacy, or tact ? Or maybe a natural prudence ?'

'A mixture of all three.'

'Well, whatever it is, it kept me from asking questions, and after we'd flogged the album Ned never spoke of it again. Nor of the Commander. Never a word till now. And what made him tell the truth after all these years?'

'Honesty,' said Palladis. 'At the very root of his mind there's a respect for honesty. He couldn't sit quiet and let you blacken the Commander's name: those were his own words. Well, give him credit for that.'

'I'm not blaming him! To my mind she deserved what she got. But I blame myself, for what I've done — though I did it in all innocence — has finally exposed him. To you and me, and Myrtle too.'

'And to himself,' said Palladis.

'Do you mean that he'd put it out of his mind?'

'Out of his conscious mind, certainly. I've known him intimately for over four years, and he had a remarkable faculty for putting everything out of his mind that he didn't want to keep in it. But this, of course, was a more absolute expulsion — a much more serious and deliberate expulsion — than forgetting small, unpleasant things. In the ordinary way his memory worked like a healthy metabolism: it got rid of what it couldn't assimilate.'

'As a boy,' said Ricci, 'he was damned clever. The cleverest boy at school. But he wouldna work, and he didna take kindly to discipline. He used to say, "I know what I want, and some day I'll get it. And get it on my own terms. I believe in my destiny." And when I began to read stories in the newspapers about the appearance of a new personality in Britain — a man called Balintore — I just said to myself, "You were the first to hear of him. Long years ago in Edinburgh he told you this would happen."'

'From the beginning of this year,' said Palladis, 'he hasn't been following his destiny, but running away from it. He's been looking for sanctuary.'

Myrtle came on deck to say that Balintore was sleeping soundly, and she thought it safe to leave him.

Ricci said, 'An hour ago I was beginning to feel sleepy, but now I'm wide awake again.'

'So am I,' said Palladis.

'We'll give ourselves a small drink, and you'll tell me what's been happening these last six months.'

He went down with Myrtle, kissed her good-night, and came on deck again with glasses, a bottle of whisky, and a siphon of soda water.

For an hour they walked to and fro in the starlit darkness — the breeze freshening, falling away, and freshening again — and Palladis told the tale of their wanderings, from London to Jamaica, to New York and London again, to Ireland and at last to Greece. 'And from the beginning,' he said, 'though in the beginning it wasn't quite explicit — or perhaps I didn't recognise it as quickly as I should have done — his motive, his purpose, was to find sanctuary. I knew he was running away from something, but I thought the mere act of flight would exhaust the impulse. I thought he was running from some temporary fear — he had made a fool of himself in public, with gross publicity : perhaps he was in flight from that image of collapse — or some haphazard memory that had prompted it : a trivial, passing fear. But after a few weeks, after the healthy exercise of flight, I thought he would go back to London and back to work, like any ordinary convalescent after a month in Switzerland. It's only lately that I've begun to realise his fear is permanent, and his flight will be permanent unless he finds sanctuary.'

'And where will he find that?' asked Ricci.

'Not in himself.'

They decided it was time to go to bed, and slept late into the morning. When they went to see Balintore they found him apparently calm, and none the worse for his accident. With some formality he thanked Myrtle for having saved his life.

'I only turned you over,' she said. 'You were floating face down, and I turned you over: that's all I did.'

'But for you, I shouldn't be alive to-day,' said Balintore.

Myrtle flushed, very prettily, and looked shyly at her husband as if to assure herself that he had heard. 'Well,' she said, 'well, in that case I'd better go and see about your breakfast.'

'Are you going to get up?' asked Palladis.

'No,' said Balintore. 'I think I'll stay in bed. I'm very comfortable here.'

Later in the morning Palladis and the Riccis rowed to the beach, and swam or idled for an hour. When they returned to the caique Balintore was still in bed, and wanted something to read. There were few books on board, other than Myrtle's *Living World of Literature*, and a couple of Admiralty Pilot books. Balintore was given the larger volume, and Ricci came on deck with the Mediterranean *Pilot*.

He said to Palladis, 'Do you know anything about Mount Athos?'

'Not very much,' said Palladis, 'but I have an uncle who lives there. My mother's younger brother.'

'What had he done?'

'Nothing criminal, so far as I know. He lived a rather fashionable life in the 1930's. He was what used to be called, in simpler times, "a man about town." Then he went into the Army in 1939, and by all accounts fought a very good war. He was in Greece, in the latter part of it, and became very fond of the country and the people. About 1948, or '49, after his wife had left him — I don't blame her, he can't have been easy to live with — he decided to go back. And when my mother next heard of him he was living in a monastery on Mount Athos, where he has been ever since. And apparently quite contented.'

'Was he a religious man ?'

'I should have thought not. But he used to fast, often for a week at a time — that was after the war : the war changed him quite a lot — and I remember my mother saying, with some disgust, "Harry now pretends that he has acquired a personal relationship with God by the simple process of giving his bowels a rest." She herself approaches God with the help of a very elaborate ritual.'

'Do they insist on fasting in Mount Athos ?' asked Ricci.

'I'm not quite sure. What I do know is that their monasteries are of two different sorts. There are those that are called coenobitic, where the monks live very plainly and simply, and are subject to a pretty severe discipline : they probably go in for fasting, and never eat very much. But in the other sort of monastery — they're called idiorrhythmic — the monks have their own quarters, and within limits — I imagine they're fairly narrow limits — live as they feel inclined. No women are allowed, nor anything female : they can't keep hens, they're not even allowed milk. But I'm told they produce some very good wine.'

'This uncle of yours——'

'He's an idiorrhythmic, of course.'

'He lives quite comfortably, does he ?'

'He has his own books and his own furniture ; but his

notion of what's comfortable is probably more restricted than yours.'

'I wasn't thinking of going to live there myself,' said Ricci.

The dawn of understanding lighted Palladis' face. 'But for Ned——'

'It just crossed my mind. I was looking at the *Pilot*, and the port of entry is called Daphne.'

'I believe,' said Palladis slowly, 'that you've hit on the very place.'

'As a boy,' said Ricci, 'he was brought up in the Scotch way to go to church, and Sunday school too. There's a difference, of course, between the Kirk of Scotland and what they call Greek Orthodox, but how big a difference it is I just don't know.'

'"I fled Him down the nights and down the days."'

'Who's that you're talking of?'

'Ned. Ned quoting poetry. He's fond of quoting poetry. And once — I can't remember where or when — he was talking to me, about himself, and he quoted that line. I think you've solved the problem.'

'Well,' said Ricci modestly, 'it just occurred to me, looking at the *Pilot*, that Mount Athos might come in useful.'

'Can you take us there? In this boat?'

'I was planning to go as far as Salonika. And Mount Athos isn't very far from there.'

'I'll go and talk to him. He may need some persuasion——'

'Ay, it's a big step to take. And if I were you I'd let him lie quiet for a day or two before suggesting anything of the sort. He's had a shock, poor Ned — ay, a double shock! The shock of exposure, and the shock of near drowning; however that came about. And it wouldna be a kindly thing to let him think we were taking advantage of him, when he's in a state of weakness, and forcing him to a decision. If he goes to Mount Athos it must be of his own free will.'

'You're right, of course,' said Palladis. 'I was tempted, for a moment, into rushing things. I've been under something of a strain myself——'

'That I can well believe. But him and me are old friends — and here's Myrtle to say it's time for lunch.'

In the afternoon they returned to Paros, where Palladis went to the hotel, paid their bill and packed their clothes. They lay at anchor that night, and in the morning, in fine weather, sailed to the neighbouring island of Naxos. Palladis and the Riccis went ashore, did some sightseeing in the little town under the hill, and idly said, 'We must come back some day and spend more time here.' Balintore stayed in bed, reading *The Living World of Literature*, and in the evening Palladis sat with him for a long time, and gently and tactfully began to speak of Mount Athos, of his uncle who lived there, and of the possibility that Balintore might find in one of its monasteries a refuge from the world, of men and memories, that had become intolerable to him.

Balintore listened quietly, without apparent surprise, and said, 'It sounds a very good idea. Give me time to think about it, will you ? I'd like some whisky before I go to sleep.'

'To-morrow,' said Palladis, 'we're going over to Delos. To Delos and Mykonos. There's a promise of good weather, but the skipper says the sea may be a little rough.'

'It won't worry me. I'm an old sailor.'

'You'll come ashore with us, won't you ?'

'On Delos ? There's nothing there but a ruined town and a row of old marble lions. And Mykonos — that's where the tourists go. No, I think I'll stay where I am. It's very comfortable here.'

At ten o'clock in the morning they anchored off Delos, and Palladis and the Riccis went ashore to look at the roofless town and the marble lions. In the afternoon they crossed over to Mykonos, where they dined at a tavern on the quay. But Balintore lay in bed, eating well, reading *The Living World of Literature*, and drinking a good deal of whisky.

They stayed another day in Mykonos, and then, while a north-easterly wind blew with increasing force, ran up under the lee of Tinos and Andros to a sheltered bay near the southern end of the long island of Euboea.

They lay at anchor, safe and snug under the lee of the land, and before dinner, under a moving sky that seemed reluctant to let go the radiance that had coloured their voyage — a radiance of gold and sapphire, dwindling to amethyst and violet — Ricci said, with an edge of irritation on his voice, 'I wish you could give me a plain answer. Is he willing to go, or isn't he?'

'He says it's a good idea.'

'We need something more definite than that.'

'He hasn't shaved since we left Paros.'

'What's that got to do with it?'

'No beardless man can live on Mount Athos. Women and bare faces are barred.'

'So you think he has made up his mind?'

'Let's assume that he has. When we get to Chalcis I'll tell him I have to go to Athens, to make the necessary arrangements — he'll need money, and permission from the Ministry of Foreign Affairs — and that will give him a chance to say no. Let him say no if he wants to, but don't force him to say yes.'

'Is that fair?'

'It's easier to say no.'

They spent two days in the long gulf between the southern

half of Euboea and the mainland, and the next morning, with the fast north-going current beneath them, ran through the very narrow gap at Chalcis and tied up to a wharf in the northern part of the town.

Balintore still spent most of the day in bed, and preferred to have his meals served in his cabin. When Palladis said he was going to Athens, and told him why, he remained silent for a little while, and then, as easily as if they were planning a move of no great consequence, said, 'That's very kind of you. Will you buy me some good, heavy underwear? I'll need it for the winter, won't I? Heavy underwear, and books. I'll have a lot of time on my hands, and I'm going to read. Novels of the nineteenth century to begin with: Dostoievski, the Brontës, Stendhal — get me all you can. And don't worry about money. Cable to my bank to send what you need——'

'There are still restrictions on sending money abroad.'

'You'll find someone in Athens who can arrange that sort of thing. I'll want a couple of hundred pounds or so, to give a present to whichever monastery decides to take me in, and then, of course, a certain sum will have to be remitted every month, or every quarter, to pay for my board and lodging. I remember reading somewhere that all the monasteries are hard-up nowadays, and can't afford indiscriminate charity. Well, I shan't ask for that, but I rely on you to make arrangements. And don't forget my underwear.'

'I shall probably be away for four or five days,' said Palladis.

'Don't worry about that. The Riccis will look after me.'

Balintore yawned, and lay back on his pillow. 'I haven't dreamt since we left Paros,' he said. 'I think we have out-distanced the Solemn Ones.'

Palladis reported his conversation to Ricci, and caught a bus to Athens. The Military Attaché at the British Embassy was a distant cousin who invited him to stay. 'Every hotel is full to the transoms,' he said, 'but we have a spare bedroom to which you're very welcome.'

With some assistance from the Embassy Palladis quickly got permission from the Ministry of Foreign Affairs for Balintore to visit Mount Athos, and an introduction from the Archbishop of Athens to the Holy Synod. Without reference to the Embassy he found a dealer in antiques who, in addition to his classical knowledge, had an up-to-date acquaintance with the modern world and its financial systems ; and with his help Palladis was able to open an account at the Bank of Greece.

He remained six days in Athens, and returned to Chalcis with a suit-case full of underclothing, and a large parcel of books.

The Riccis said they had enjoyed their chance to explore the gracious, nobly-forested hills and fertile valleys of Euboea, but they were worried and puzzled by Balintore's behaviour.

'He's been acting,' said Ricci, 'like a well-mannered stranger. Like the sort of man you find aboard a big passenger-ship. You're introduced to a man sitting next to you at the Purser's table, or the Doctor's table. You talk to him, and he talks to you, about nothing in particular, but always in a decent, civil fashion. And that's the way Ned has been talking to us : to me, that's his oldest friend, and to Myrtle who saved his life.'

'Except once,' said Myrtle.

'When he was drunk.'

'We went to say good-night to him, and he told me I might have done more than save his life. He said, "You've given me a chance to save my soul."'

'Has he been drinking much ?'

'Very little, except that day. We were ashore — it's a bonny island, Euboea ! I'd like to come back here — and while we were ashore he got up and found a bottle of whisky.'

'Did he never go ashore with you ?'

'Only once. We went north, up the gulf, and over to the other side : to Thermopylae. And he did come ashore there. He said he'd always wanted to see Thermopylae.'

'There's a remnant of good sense in him,' said Palladis.

'No more than that ?'

'In his present state of withdrawal he doesn't let you see much more, does he ?'

'I still don't see why he wants to act like a stranger.'

'In preparation for what he's going to be.'

'A stranger for the rest of his life ?'

'A stranger to us, I'm afraid.'

In his cabin Balintore examined with care the store of winter underclothes that Palladis had bought, and said, 'Yes, this is just what I wanted. You've done very well : very well indeed. But I didn't want all these Trollopes.'

'There wasn't very much choice.'

'I'll have to give you a list of what I want before you go back to London. You'll be going straight home, won't you?'

'If you want me to put your affairs in order——'

'I expect you to do that, of course. I'd better give you a power of attorney, hadn't I ?'

'It would help.'

'I do like these vests,' said Balintore.

On deck again, Palladis said to Ricci, 'He may treat you like a stranger, but he treats me like a valet under notice of dismissal.'

'I once had a girl friend,' said Myrtle softly, 'who had to

go to prison for stabbing her boy friend. I used to go and see her on visiting days, and that's how she treated me. I think it was to stop me feeling sorry for her.'

'Well,' said Ricci, 'we may as well set a course for Mount Athos. There's nothing to hinder us now.'

'I hope the weather stays fair. We've a long passage in open sea.'

'The engine's all right. I had it overhauled while you were in Athens, and it's running sweetly.'

They sailed at dawn, and anchored for the night a little north of Thermopylae. The next day, again leaving at dawn, they reached Skiathos, and lay there for a day, buying fruit and crayfish and red mullet. There was a full moon and they made a night passage to Cape Ambelos over a calm sea, but off the Cape ran into a sudden gale, and for two or three hours plunged uncomfortably in quick-rising waves. Then the weather moderated, the morning sun shone hotly, and they approached the wooded, mountainous peninsula of Mount Athos over dancing blue water.

Balintore dressed and came on deck to look with lively interest at his destination. He became a little more cheerful, and spoke almost easily — almost in his old manner — to Palladis and the Riccis. He took Palladis by the arm, and leading him apart, said, 'The last few weeks must have been almost as difficult for you as they have been for me. I'm well aware of that, and don't think I'm not grateful. I shall never cease to be grateful. Never. But there's one thing I want to know, and that is who it was — which of the two of you — who first thought of bringing me here?'

'Ricci.'

'I guessed as much. When we were boys together he often had good ideas — and let me put them into practice.'

He went back to the bows, and stood snuffing the land-breeze. The lower part of his face was now completely covered by a short but thickly growing beard.

Ahead of them lay a little harbour and a line of small houses. Apparently they were approaching a fishing village, but in the wooded slopes of the long mountain range above it the sun lighted, here and there between tall trees and sudden glens, brown roofs and high stone walls and small blunt towers; and about the harbour black-draped figures slowly moved.

When they were less than a mile from the shore Myrtle fell into a panic and exclaimed, 'Perhaps I shouldn't be looking at them!'

'You won't be allowed to land.'

'I know. And if you dress up as a man, they poke you in the chest, just to make sure——'

'They wouldna need to do that, hen.'

'All right, I'm not going ashore. But perhaps I shouldn even look at them.'

'Maybe you'd better go down to your cabin, and stay there till we leave.'

'I must say good-bye to Ned.'

'I think he's left us already.'

In the bow of the boat Balintore stood intent on the approaching land. He said good-bye to Myrtle without emotion; and she, in sudden tears, turned and ran down to her cabin.

To Palladis he said, 'Do you think your uncle will come to meet me?'

'I wrote to him when I was in Athens, and sent a telegram just before we left Chalcis. But I know nothing about postal deliveries to a monastery.'

When they were within a hundred yards of the harbour,

a tall monk, blackly habited, under a black cylindrical hat and a black umbrella that he used as a sunshade, came with long strides out to the end of the little pier, and waved to them. 'If that is Uncle Harry,' said Palladis, 'how glad I am that my mother isn't here. That beard!'

It was indeed a remarkable beard, a crisply-curling, bright-ginger beard, that jutted fiercely forward, and above it were a broad-winged moustache, a great aquiline nose with sunburnt skin peeling from its scarlet ridge, and, under thick sandy brows, pale-blue eyes of a startling brilliance.

'Yes,' said Palladis, 'it's Uncle Harry.'

A clear, high-pitched voice — a voice that carried into the bright Greek air the echoes of a cavalry mess — hailed them across the narrowing water: 'How are you, my boy? How nice to see you after all these years. My word, how you've grown!'

They drew alongside, and Palladis stepped ashore.

'How's your mother?' asked Brother Henry. 'I've fallen out of the habit of writing letters, you know, and when you don't write to people, they don't answer you, do they? But tell me — yes, tell me how she is? She's all right, is she?'

'Very well indeed,' said Palladis. 'Let me introduce Edward Balintore, about whom I wrote to you, and Peter Ricci.'

'I'm delighted to see you all. Welcome to Mount Athos! Now let's go ashore, there aren't many formalities, but we may as well get them over and done with. All these dear people are good friends of mine. Very good friends indeed.'

He spoke in fluent Greek to a customs official, an indifferent policeman, and a functionary whose duties were obscure; and led them to a small tavern before whose white walls stood some warped benches and sun-cracked wooden tables.

He shouted an order through an open window, and said, 'We'll have some wine, don't you think? — My word, Guy, how you've grown! — Some of these monasteries make excellent wine. Better wine than you get in the rest of Greece. Oh, much better! And we need it, especially in winter. After prayers at midnight, prayers at four o'clock in the morning — we do a lot of praying, you know. There's great need for it. Oh, great need, with the world getting worse and worse all the time — and after praying really hard on a cold winter morning, well, a glass of good wine is very welcome, I assure you.'

'I've come here as a visitor,' said Balintore, 'but it's my hope to remain. To remain——'

'As one of us, you mean? How splendid, how perfectly splendid! We need recruits, you know, we're getting rather thin on the ground, and I hope you're going to set a trend. I hope your example will encourage more Englishmen to come here. Only the other day I was saying to our librarian — I'm on very good terms with the librarian — I was saying "What we really need is a dozen or two good, hearty, healthy young Englishmen" — and bless my soul, Guy's letter about you came two days later. I said to the librarian, "God's got long ears, hasn't he?" — and the old boy laughed like anything. He's got very long ears himself.'

He swigged off his wine, clapped the brown table-top, and laughed full-mouthed, above his jutting beard. His light-blue, blazing eyes flashed from one to another, and then, jumping up, he shouted incomprehensibly to two elderly monks — clad like himself, but, with black beards, all of one colour — who, under their umbrellas, were walking slowly on the white dusty road.

'I've been staying with them for the last couple of days,'

he said, 'at their monastery, which is called Xeropotamou. It isn't far from here. That's where our new recruit and I will sleep to-night. And to-morrow we'll set off for Great Lavra, right down at the tip of the peninsula ; or not far from it. And how jolly it will be to have someone to talk to who can talk English ! — Though you'll have to learn Greek as quick as you can, of course.'

An hour later, Palladis and Ricci went back to the boat. Balintore had said good-bye to them with a courteous acknowledgment of their help and kindness to him, but without visible emotion ; and when they looked back they saw him, already forgetful of them, deep in animated conversation with Brother Henry.

'Have you got a feeling,' said Ricci, 'that all we've done is just what we had to do ?'

'I'm not superstitious,' said Palladis, 'but sometimes, I admit, it does seem that a pattern of events finds its own conclusion.'

'What does that mean ?'

'Now that you ask me, I'm not very sure.'

'I'll be thankful when we get to sea again,' said Ricci. 'No disrespect to your uncle, but those monks send shivers down my back.'

They went aboard, and as the caique drew away from the pier, fishermen on the shore, mending their nets, looked up with brief curiosity about an unknown boat. From his seat under the white tavern wall Brother Henry stood up and waved good-bye, but Balintore, his elbows on the table, did not move.

Twenty-four

UNDER the bright canopy of spring London looked gay and charming when, towards the end of May in the following year, Palladis left his mother's house in Mount Street and walked towards Piccadilly. He looked at his watch, and saw that he was going to be much too early for his appointment with Charles Mulligan in Albany. He was annoyed with himself for this betrayal of his feelings. A lot depended on what Mulligan had to say, but it was undignified — it was humiliating — to be anxious about his reception : to be eager for Mulligan's approval. He tried to banish from his mind all thought of the approaching interview, and walking briskly through the Green Park crossed over into St. James's Park. For several minutes he stood on the bridge and looked gravely, but without much interest, at the ducks.

He turned north again, and as he passed St. James's Palace it seemed to him that the sentries were smaller and less formidable than they used to be. The windows of the clubs in St. James's Street shone cheerfully in the sun, but no longer looked interesting nor woke — as they had when he was younger — a curiosity about what men talked of, in those guarded rooms, and how the patterns of conversation differed between this side of the street and that. To-day there was no difference at all, and all looked dull.

But this is absurd, this state of mind, he thought. I know what is wrong with me — I am depressed by anxiety — and I can do nothing about it. Nothing is of any interest to me except my interview with Mulligan, and what he's going to say. What a harrowing existence one is condemned to, for writing a book!

He looked at his watch again, and saw that he was still too early. He turned west and went into the Ritz, where he drank a large brandy and ginger ale. It had no flavour that he could discern, and as he crossed to the north side of Piccadilly he was aware of a gathering sense of gloom. The fatal gift of drink, he thought, is that it prepares one for the worst.

He passed Burlington House with a shudder. Another of those exhibitions! Art should be a private thing, the exposure of heart and mind to the sympathy of heart and mind: an act of devotion and passionate response to a passionate need. This flaunting display was a symbol of the modern world and its vulgarity: everything that was made was made to be sold, and man's aspiring mind aspired only to salesmanship.

And books — why, books were worse than pictures: even pictures in Burlington House. For books demanded ten thousand readers, while a picture looked only for a single lover. Oh, how depraved and damnable a thing it was to write a book, and expect a publisher's approval, and hope for general favour! The lowness, the squalor of such a hope. . . .

He turned into the courtyard of Albany with the decision in his mind to say to Mulligan, 'Give me back my manuscript. I've changed my mind, and I don't want you — neither you nor anyone — to publish it.'

The top-hatted porter greeted him and said, 'It's a long time since we've seen you, Mr. Palladis. And how's Mr. Balintore getting on?'

'He's well,' said Palladis. 'He's very well indeed. But he won't be coming here again.'

'No,' said the porter, 'I gathered as much when I heard he was selling his lease. And we were very sorry to hear he'd sold it.'

'Yes,' said Palladis, 'it's a break — you could call it a painful fracture — in an old association.'

'I wouldn't say a word against Albany or the gentlemen who live here,' said the porter, 'but we do miss a gentleman like Mr. Balintore, who brought a spice of variety to the place — well, sir, you know what I mean, and you know where Mr. Mulligan lives, don't you?'

While working for Balintore he had often met Mulligan: met him on the Rope Walk, stopped to speak to him, and occasionally, in Mulligan's chambers or Balintore's, had drunk a glass of sherry with him. But they had never been on terms of friendship, for Mulligan, though an admirable publisher — a publisher respected by authors and enriched by success — was a dry, unapproachable man who seemed to exhibit and emphasise an impersonal quality by dressing always in the formality of short black coat, black Homburg hat, and striped trousers. No one had ever seen him clad otherwise, and it was rumoured that his pyjamas were tailored with equal severity. He came from the north of England, where his father had made a fortune during the war; and with money behind him, and intellect and ambition to use it, he had become within a dozen years a person of considerable importance in the literary world.

Palladis turned left off the Rope Walk, past a tub of clipped laurel, and climbed the shallow steps to Mulligan's chambers.

Mulligan opened the door, and with a dry smile parting his thin lips, extended a dry, bony hand in greeting. Formality continued with the offer of a glass of dry sherry, and Mulligan said, 'Well, let us not waste time. I asked you to come here, rather than to my office, because private walls are more appropriate for what we have to discuss.

'I have read your manuscript, and I have no hesitation in saying that you have written a remarkable story with grace and skill, with enviable humour and a steadily increasing sense — increasing sense and a gathering momentum — of its inherent drama. But I see no possibility of publishing it.'

Palladis' reluctance to face the vulgarity of authorship — his decision to withdraw his manuscript — vanished, or was rescinded, immediately. Now he was prepared to fight for his work, and warmly he said, 'If it's as good as you say it is — and I'm entirely of your opinion — then it must be published. There may be some difficulties, more apparent than real——'

'To me,' said Mulligan, 'they are both apparent and real. You have written what purports to be a biography of Edward Balintore——'

'A biography that is uncommonly true to fact.'

'Which makes it the more dangerous. Balintore was known to millions of people — he was one of the best-known men in the country — and to accuse such a man of murder——'

'He admitted it.'

'From a legal point of view, that's of no importance. He could take me to court, sue me for publishing a libel, and be awarded enormous damages.'

'But he won't.'

'What makes you so sure?'

'He has become a monk in a monastery on Mount Athos. He has taken vows——'

'Vows can be broken, monks can run away from their monastery.'

'He won't,' said Palladis again.

'What guarantee can you offer?'

'He could be charged with murder.'

'On no evidence but his own alleged confession, which he could deny?'

'You haven't read the book carefully enough. When Balintore admitted that he had murdered the woman who was his adoptive mother, he was releasing a fact which he had buried in the hinterland of his mind; where — because it was buried alive — it was slowly driving him mad. He couldn't deny the murder without reburying the truth, and losing his sanity.'

'I'm not sure that I agree with you. Your argument——'

'You haven't heard it all. What you don't understand is that on Mount Athos Balintore found what he was looking for. He was looking for sanctuary, and having found it, he's happy. And that's what will keep him in his monastery. He won't leave it.'

'He doesn't seem to have been a religious man. Certainly not in any conventional way.'

'He was brought up in a church-going Scotch household, and in his ordinary conversation you could hear, again and again, the vestiges of that training. He stopped going to church after he left home — he never went while I knew him — but he couldn't get God out of his mind.'

'And now——'

'They have a great deal of freedom in an idiorrhythmic monastery, but they spend a lot of time in prayer, so he's able to let an old, shadowy, but persistent faith come out into the open.'

'Forgive me if I'm being impertinent,' said Mulligan, 'but you yourself — do you accept, or respect, a religious faith?'

'I have a quality,' said Palladis, 'about which I've been

very complacent since I discovered, on Keats's authority, that I share it with him and Shakespeare. He called it Negative Capability, and explained it as a capacity to be "in uncertainties, mysteries, doubts, without any irritable reaching after fact and reason." I have always gladly acknowledged the mystery of life, and never teased myself by looking for explanations which can't be found.'

'Very interesting,' said Mulligan ; but without any show of interest. 'And now, to come back to the matter of this manuscript——'

'You have changed your mind ?'

'Not at all. When I first read it — and I have read it twice — I knew it was a book I should like to publish. A book I should be proud to publish. It tells an astonishing story about a man who was widely known, it's uncommonly well written — if you'll allow me to say so — and it would, if it were published, be immensely popular. It would make a great deal of money, and every publisher needs books which will give him a profit. You call it *A Man of our Time*——'

'He is, isn't he ? Not only because of the peculiar profession he chose, but because — and this comes out clearly in the story — because in our times the impostor or fraud isn't a man who claims to have done extraordinary things when in reality he's done little or nothing ; but a man who has done extraordinary things, and pretends to have done less. We have lived in a time when experience has become too lavish for belief ; and therefore too lavish to be talked about.'

'That may be so,' said Mulligan, 'I, however, am still thinking of the risk involved in publishing your book — the legal risk — and it has occurred to me that if you are so sure that Balintore will take no exception to what you have written about him — to many things which to me seem actionable, quite apart from the charge of murder — if, as I say, you are so confident, then you can have no objection to signing a clause, additional to that in our normal contract, in which you specifically accept full responsibility should Balintore raise an action against us.'

'Oh, I'll do that,' said Palladis. 'Willingly.'

'You're quite sure that you know what I mean?'

'You mean that if Balintore calls for a dirty tune, I'll have to pay the piper.'

'That, I suppose, is what I have in mind.'

'I agree to that without hesitation. And you, for your part, will do your utmost to see that the book has the success — the commercial success — which, as we're both agreed, it deserves?'

'I do that for all the books I publish.'

'But not all your books are likely to sell — shall we say, 50,000 copies?'

'I wish they would.'

'But mine will, won't it?'

'A large number, certainly.'

'So you'll pay me a large advance?'

'Are you in need of money?'

'You may remember — as you've read the book twice — that a year ago Balintore offered to take my cousin Honoria to Greece; but she had to refuse, and naturally was very disappointed. Well, I've been living in Ireland, at Turk's Court, since I came back from Mount Athos — I wrote the book in Ireland — and Honoria's in London now, at my mother's. This morning I got a letter from Peter Ricci, who's in Rhodes. He's built a boat of his own — I mean, he's had it built there — and he says it's a very good boat, and he's proposing to cruise from Rhodes through the Dodecanese and the Aegean islands to Istanbul.'

'A very pleasant prospect.'

'Isn't it? And he and his wife — that good Australian girl, Myrtle — want Honoria and me to join them.'

'Are you going?'

'It costs a lot of money to fly to Rhodes. And there are two of us.'

'Will £500 be enough?'

'You had better make it £1,000.'

'It won't cost as much as that——'

'I've had other expenses. That unfortunate geologist, O'Halloran, got into grave difficulties after his mine collapsed, and I bought his lease from him — his lease of those two fields — for £300, and gave it to Honoria, who was very pleased to get it. And then Polly Newton turned up again. She went on writing to Ned, and when I came home I found her letters, and told her to come and see me. — That was before I went to Ireland, of course: it took me a couple of months to settle Ned's affairs. — Well, that was embarrassing, but not so bad as I had expected. She's a sensible girl, in fact, and she's gone back to New York, to Mr. Evershrub, who was delighted to get her again: he says she's the only secretary he's ever had who can remember things. But he refused to pay her fare a second time, so I did that——'

'You were still settling Balintore's affairs?'

'That was my own decision, and I paid for it. I drew my salary for the two months I was working for him, and then discharged myself with a month's notice.'

'Did you handle all Balintore's business?'

'For more than four years, yes. And since his — his retirement, shall we say? — I have had to persuade his several ex-wives to accept a final settlement, and still leave enough to assure him a reasonable income — an income, that is, that's sufficient for him so long as he remains in his monastery.'

'And he has accepted your terms ?'

'He says he is very pleased with them.'

'In that case,' said Mulligan, 'I think we can go ahead. I have, as it happens, a form of contract here——'

'I'm sure it will be satisfactory. But before I read it, may I use your telephone ?'

'Of course.'

'I want to speak to Honoria, and tell her to send a cable to the Riccis. And she'll have to buy some clothes. She has hardly anything, poor girl, except Irish tweeds and oilskins ; and they won't do for the Aegean.'

'What sort of clothes is Balintore wearing ?'

'Black,' said Palladis. 'But if I hadn't looked after him, he'd be wearing a coffin.'

THE END

PRINTED BY R. & R. CLARK, LTD., EDINBURGH

By Eric Linklater

NOVELS

White Maa's Saga
Poet's Pub
Juan in America
The Men of Ness
Magnus Merriman
Ripeness is All
Juan in China
The Sailor's Holiday
The Impregnable Women
Judas
Private Angelo
A Spell for Old Bones
Mr. Byculla
Laxdale Hall
The House of Gair
The Faithful Ally
The Dark of Summer
Position at Noon
The Merry Muse
Roll of Honour
Husband of Delilah

FOR CHILDREN

The Wind on the Moon
The Pirates in the Deep Green Sea
Karina with Love

SHORT STORIES

God Likes Them Plain
Sealskin Trousers
A Sociable Plover

AUTOBIOGRAPHY

The Man on My Back
A Year of Space

BIOGRAPHY

Ben Jonson and King James
Mary Queen of Scots
Robert the Bruce

ESSAYS

The Lion and the Unicorn
The Art of Adventure
The Ultimate Viking
Edinburgh

HISTORY

The Campaign in Italy

VERSE

A Dragon Laughed

PLAYS

The Devilsi e News
Crisis in Heaven
To Meet the Macgregors
Love in Albania
The Mortimer Touch
Breakspear in Gascony

CONVERSATIONS

The Cornerstones
The Raft *and* Socrates Asks Why
The Great Ship *and* Rabelais Replies

PAMPHLETS

The Northern Garrisons
The Defence of Calais
The Highland Division
Our Men in Korea